ARCHMAGE

THE LEGEND OF DRIZZT

Follow Drizzt and his companions on all of their adventures
(in chronological order)

FORGOTTEN REALMS®

HOMECOMING

BOOK I

ARCHMAGE

R.A. SALVATORE

ARCHMAGE
Homecoming, Book I
©2015 Wizards of the Coast LLC.

Published by Wizards of the Coast LLC. Manufactured by: Hasbro SA, Rue Emile-Boéchat 31, 2800 Delémont, CH. Represented by Hasbro Europe, 2 Roundwood Ave, Stockley Park, Uxbridge, Middlesex, UB11 1AZ, UK.

Cover art by: Aleksi Briclot
First Printing: February 2017

9 8 7 6 5 4 3 2 1

ISBN: 978-0-7869-6613-4
ISBN: 978-0-7869-6585-4 (ebook)
620C3054000001 EN

The Hardcover edition cataloging-in-Publication data
is on file with the Library of Congress

Contact Us at Wizards.com/CustomerService
Wizards of the Coast LLC, PO Box 707, Renton, WA 98057-0707, USA
USA & Canada: (800) 324-6496 or (425) 204-8069
Europe: +32(0) 70 233 277

Visit our web site at **www.DungeonsandDragons.com**

Prelude

THE HULKING DEMON SNORTED FIRE WITH EVERY GREAT breath, clawed hands twitching, eager to grab at the great flaming whip set in a loop on his hip. This was Balor, the mightiest of his kind, massive and powerful, with great leathery wings, a whip of fire, a sword of lightning, and a keen understanding of battle. The demons that took his name and form were known as the generals of the Abyss, used by the demon lords to guide their armies in the never-ending wars that scarred the smoky and dismal plane.

Balor was itchy now, wanting his weapons but not daring to reach for them. The creature in front of him, half spider, half beautiful drow, had not come here to request his service as a general.

Far from it, it seemed.

"You wish to strike out at me?" the Spider Queen remarked, her eight arachnid legs clattering on the stones as she moved around the beast. Behind her lay a wake of lesser demons—shredded manes, balguras pummeled into piles of mush, shadow demons robbed of their life energy that lay there as smoking clouds of insentient darkness.

"Why have you come to me, Lolth?" Balor asked. "Why have you destroyed my minions? I am not at war, with you or any, and am not now in service to any."

The Spider Queen twisted her drow torso to regard the carnage she had inflicted. "Perhaps I was bored," she answered casually. "No matter."

Balor issued a little growl, but kept his composure. He knew that it—that all of this—was something more, something more dangerous. Lolth had been in the company of the balor Errtu extensively of late, and Errtu was Balor's greatest rival.

"You have not answered my question," Lolth remarked. "Do you wish to strike out at me?"

Balor couldn't deny the eager twitching of his clawed hands. He had served all of the demon lords over the centuries, of course, but Lolth was his least favorite. She was something more than the other Abyssal lords, a goddess relying on the prayers and fealty of some puny mortal race on the Prime Material Plane, beings Balor would use as . . . food. Her eyes, spider or drow—or whatever other form she chose to take—were not focused here in the Abyss, but were ever elsewhere. Like her ambitions.

"Do it," Lolth teased.

Another growl escaped Balor's lips, and how he wanted to comply.

"Ah, but you cannot," Lolth went on. "Because I can unmake you with a word, or make of you something else, something less."

Balor's nostrils flared, fires coming forth. She was not bluffing, of course. She was a demon queen and on this plane, the Abyss, her power over creatures such as Balor was absolute. On another plane of existence, perhaps Balor would strike out at her—and how delicious that would be!—but in the Abyss, he could not.

"I will not unmake you," Lolth promised. "I will not obliterate you. I am curious, beast of fire. Long have I wondered about the sting of your whip. How sharp the flames? They can melt the skin from a manes, but how would they fare against the hide of a goddess? I do not fear your fire, Balor."

The demon did not make a move.

"I will not unmake you," Lolth stated flatly. "You are the favored of Baphomet and Kostchtchie, and as much as I might enjoy the spectacle of mighty Balor reduced to inglorious irrelevance, you are not worth the bother to which such an act would give rise."

The words spun in Balor's thoughts. Baphomet had indeed used him, and recently, to command his legions, and Kostchtchie, the Prince of Wrath, had always called upon Balor first and foremost. But what was this about? Why would Lolth even be here, in Balor's castle?

"I played no role in the failure of Tiamat's rise," the demon told her, wondering if that might be the reason for her visit. There were rumors that Lolth was trying to help the minions of the great catastrophe, Tiamat, in resurrecting her castle and body in the Prime Material Plane, a tremendous effort by the dragons of that plane that had, so said the rumors, spectacularly failed. "I would be glad to be rid of the witch."

"I have made no accusation," Lolth said slyly.

"Then why?" a frustrated Balor roared, fire flying like spittle from his great maw. "Why are you here, Demon Queen of Spiders? Why do you taunt me?"

"When has Balor considered a challenge to be a taunt?"

"A challenge? Or a goading—a prelude to an excuse!"

"Strike me!"

"No!"

"Then I shall unmake you!" Lolth's eyes flared with sinister promise.

Before he could even consider the movement, Balor had his sword in hand, lightning spraying from its tip, and his whip in his other hand, the length of it becoming a living flame.

Lolth reared up, her four front legs coming off the stone to wave in the air, her arms up high, her face a mask of ferocity, mouth opening impossibly wide in a great hiss.

Balor raised his whip arm, the fiery line rolling up high above his shoulder. It felt as if he had dunked that arm under water. Something grabbed at it and slowed it.

A new smell joined in the sulfuric haze of the Abyss, a sharp, burning hiss, and Balor did not have to turn to know that a great conflagration blazed behind him. With a defiant roar, the beast yanked his arm free and sent his whip cracking out in front of him, snapping out at Lolth.

Her legs blocked, the fiery instrument scored her hide with an angry tear and blister. But the Spider Queen's cry was more of joy than pain, or, more likely, it was both.

On she came, lightning flashing from every drow fingertip, four spider legs kicking out to batter at Balor.

And more, the demon realized. The air around him filled with floating webs, Lolth's webbing, and every filament, it seemed, carried a spider, ravenous and biting.

The whip cracked again. Balor thrust forth his sword, the blade extending with a great blast of lightning, one that had Lolth backstepping from the sheer weight of it.

But on she came again, bolt after sharp bolt lashing out from her fingertips, stabbing at Balor. Her eyes flared with fire and she vomited acid and poison, spraying it all over Balor.

His whip arm went back again. This time, the webbing grabbed at it more fully, like a smoking wall moving at Lolth's command, rolling forward to enwrap him. He opened wide his wings, trying to burst free, but he couldn't. The wall closed nearly around him, and millions of spiders leaped upon him, biting at his flesh.

He thrust forth his sword and felt it bite into Lolth's flesh, but she screamed again as if in ecstasy. And when Balor went to retract the blade, he could not.

He glanced down to see the Spider Queen holding the blade in her grasping hand.

Holding the blade!

In desperation, he threw forth another blast of lightning through the blade, perhaps the greatest he had ever evoked, and he saw it enter Lolth's hand, saw it fly from the blade to the gaping wound the blade had gashed. And Lolth took it, accepted it fully into her great frame, and from her free hand came a shock of lightning that seemed her own and Balor's combined, slamming into Balor and driving him back.

He wrenched free his sword, and now he did hear pain in Lolth's cry as her hand came with the sword. But any joy that realization might garner proved short-lived as he felt the pillow-like softness behind him. The wall of webbing grabbed at him. His thrashing only brought it closer around him.

Hatefully, Balor looked at Lolth, at her smile, even though she was holding up her arm, spraying blood, ending in a torn and fingerless stump.

She vomited onto him again, her poisonous spittle covering him, burning at him. She bade her webbing to complete its roll around Balor. Her million spiders eagerly released their filaments, redoubling their efforts to bite at him.

Balor's whip flashed out and connected with nothing, the swing smothered by the too-thick blanket of webbing and spiders.

All sense of balance left him. He could not move, could feel nothing but the poison of Lolth and the tiny bites of her unrelenting minions.

And he knew of the most insidious part of that poison. In her venom Lolth carried confusion, an unrelenting dizziness that defeated any attempt at magical defense or escape as surely as a globe of invulnerability.

Balor was caught, fully enwrapped, hanging upside down, displayed like a trophy.

And still Lolth's spiders bit at him, and they would, he heard her promise, for a decade.

◆ ◆ ◆

MATRON MOTHER QUENTHEL Baenre's red eyes flared, belying her otherwise outwardly calm demeanor. Gromph marveled at her control, given the image he had just presented to her in the scrying bowl. Her great achievement on the surface in the Silver Marches, the Darkening, was no more. The sun was shining across the Silver Marches and the orcs were running for their holes in the mountains.

"Bregan D'aerthe's spies indicate that Drizzt Do'Urden facilitated the dissolution of Tsabrak's dweomer," Gromph remarked, just to twist the blade a little bit. Gromph knew very well what had happened to the magical Darkening, for he had been there when the spell had been defeated. For he, using an unwitting Drizzt as the conduit, had been the one to dissolve the magic. "Drizzt's human wife, another Chosen of Mielikki by all accounts, looked on with tears of joy. Lady Lolth has lost the battle for the Weave, and now, too, she has been bested in the Silver Marches."

"Beware your tongue, brother," Matron Mother Baenre warned in a very deadly tone. Her eyes narrowed, accentuating their sharp edges to give her angular features a harsh attitude.

"True, and well advised, Matron Mother," Gromph said, and he gave a polite bow. "I should have said that Lady Lolth's proxies were defeated by those of Mielikki. The failure is—"

"Not ours," the matron mother interrupted sharply. "We left. We had accomplished all that we had set out to accomplish. Our time there was done, our gains left to the idiot orcs, whom we knew would lose them in short order. That is not our concern, and never was."

"Surely it is Matron Mother Zeerith's concern, and the concern of her fledgling city," said the archmage. "Tsabrak Xorlarrin's channeling of Lady Lolth's power was bested by a heretic rogue who is not even skilled in the Art. And her family and city has suffered greatly in this campaign. By my count, near to a hundred and twenty dark elves were killed in the Silver Marches War, and more than four out of five of those were drow of Q'Xorlarrin."

"She will request our help, of course," Matron Mother Baenre said, as if that was a good thing.

But Gromph wasn't letting Quenthel off the hook that easily. "Your own position is compromised."

The matron mother sat up straight at that, her red eyes flaring dangerously yet again.

"Lady Lolth will not blame you," Gromph was quick to explain. "But the other matron mothers . . . you have tightened your noose around their necks. Tos'un Armgo is dead, his *iblith* daughter missing. Matron Mother Mez'Barris has lost her one fingerhold to the Eighth House of Menzoberranzan, and so she will view the reconstituted House Do'Urden with great suspicion and dismay."

"I will allow her to appoint another noble of Barrison Del'Armgo to serve in the hierarchy of House Do'Urden."

"She will refuse."

The matron mother clearly wanted to argue the point, and just as clearly had no valid argument with which to do so.

"House Hunzrin hates House Xorlarrin," Gromph reminded. "And more important, hates the concept of Q'Xorlarrin, a city that threatens their trade dominance. And House Melarn hates . . . well, everything. If those fanatical Melarni priestesses come to believe that Tsabrak Xorlarrin's failure and House Xorlarrin's losses indicate the displeasure of Lady Lolth, they will surely join in with House Hunzrin to . . ." He let his voice trail off and heaved a great sigh. "Well, will they perhaps, shall we say, conclude the experiment of a sister city so near the surface in no uncertain terms?"

His coyness didn't seem to impress his sister, but he didn't want it to. He just wanted to anger Quenthel, to stick verbal pins into her, to force her hand.

To force a mistake.

"Do you think I am unaware of these threats, Archmage?" the matron mother said coolly, back in complete control. "Or do you believe me incapable of properly seeing to them? Your lack of confidence is both touching and insulting. Perhaps you would be wise to consider that dueling truth."

Gromph bowed again and bid farewell. He had almost reached the room's exit when he glanced back over his shoulder and said, "And do not forget the loss of a dragon. Or that Tiamat's disciples were defeated in their quest to return their dragon mother to the Prime Material Plane."

Matron Mother Baenre twitched, despite her resolve. The chromatic dragons—reds, blues, whites, greens, and blacks—had plotted to horde such a treasure that they would bring their goddess Tiamat and her grand castle back to the Prime Material Plane, to unleash unspeakable devastation across the lands.

But they had failed, and in the attempt, Matron Mother Baenre's own actions had brought about the downfall of a white dragon, Aurbangras, son of the great Arauthator—who had been chased back to his mountain home.

Lady Lolth had apparently approved of the chromatic dragons and their plans for Tiamat. Through the matron mother, she had called for the enlistment of the white dragons, and had insisted that Arauthator and his son be given huge amounts of treasure in return for their services.

And now that, too, had failed.

Gromph nodded and did well to hide his satisfaction at Quenthel's clear discomfort. He left her chamber then, but did not depart House Baenre, for there was another matter needing his full and urgent attention.

He moved for his own private quarters, a suite of rooms where he rarely resided, but one that served as home to House Baenre's newest high priestess, Minolin Fey Baenre, who was Gromph Baenre's wife and the mother of his all-important baby daughter.

◆　◆　◆

THE MOMENT GROMPH was out of the room, Matron Mother Quenthel Baenre checked her magical wards and guards against scrying, then unleashed a tirade of invective and magical power that left two of her servants writhing on the floor in agony and a third one dead.

Matron Mother Zeerith had already contacted her, begging help and information, for she feared exactly the alliance—Hunzrin and Melarn—of which Gromph had just warned. Her House and city of Q'Xorlarrin were truly depleted. The list of the compromised and the dead was impressive, with two nobles, the wizard Ravel and High Priestess Saribel, serving in House

Do'Urden; her daughter, High Priestess Berellip, murdered very recently by Drizzt and his friends; her house weapons master, the great Jaerthe, slain on some ridiculous venture to the frozen wilderness known as Icewind Dale; and a hundred of her warriors and wizards killed in the Silver Marches.

The troubles of Matron Mother Zeerith were not, in and of themselves, a bad thing for Matron Mother Baenre. She had never intended Q'Xorlarrin to be anything more than a satellite of House Baenre, after all, despite the pronouncements of it as a "sister city" to Menzoberranzan. Q'Xorlarrin, combined with Bregan D'aerthe, would serve as House Baenre's way of competing with House Hunzrin for trade with the surface dwellers. That was the only seam in Baenre's armor, the only advantage the other Houses could use against the mighty First House of Menzoberranzan.

Nor was Quenthel overly concerned over the reported death of Tos'un Armgo, a deserter rogue who was never much in Matron Mother Mez'Barris Armgo's favor anyway, and never anything more than a minor noble in House Barrison Del'Armgo.

The combination of those things, though, along with the death of a white dragon and the destruction of Lady Lolth's Darkening, could lead to all sorts of trouble. She worried that Matron Mother Mez'Barris would throw in with Houses Hunzrin and Melarn, and so House Baenre would face all three in defending Q'Xorlarrin. If so, then surely the Seventh House of Menzoberranzan, House Vandree, would side with the conspirators.

Matron Mother Baenre believed that the rest of the Ruling Council was on her side, but would they pledge allegiance to her openly, with warriors, priests, and wizards?

And these were drow Houses, after all, known for reliability only in the fact that they could not be considered reliable. These bonds were not alliances as much as they were compacts of convenience, and Quenthel had turned the thumbscrews down hard on the other matron mothers, both in her actions in the Silver

Marches and in the reestablishment of House Do'Urden—and, of course, in appointing a *darthiir*, a surface elf, as the matron mother of that Eighth House.

Matron Mother Baenre had pushed them all to the edge, had slapped them all in the face, to demonstrate her superiority and thus put them in line. And it had worked thus far, but now, in the aftermath of the fall of the Silver Marches to the previous powers there, would be the critical time.

"But it was always to be like this," she told herself, pushing aside the defeat of the Darkening and the death of a white dragon—and the defeat of Tiamat's ultimate plan.

Quenthel nodded and closed her eyes. She was Matron Mother Baenre. Lolth was still with her, she believed. And she felt it then, warmly.

She had tugged the whole of Menzoberranzan into her iron grip, as Lolth had demanded of her.

But how to keep them there in this dangerous and uncertain time?

Quenthel closed her eyes and fell deep into meditation, deep into the memories she now held that were not her own. The memories of her mother, Yvonnel the Eternal, that had been telepathically imparted to her by the squirming tentacles of the mind flayer who had served as her mother's closest advisor, those were the memories she considered now.

She saw Menzoberranzan, then, in a light as never before. The great cavern housing the city appeared more natural, far less shaped by drow craftsmen, far less highlighted by drow illumination, like the faerie fire outlining the great houses or the glow of Narbondel, the heat-clock.

She knew that she was seeing the earliest days of the city, tumultuous, yet only built and settled in pockets.

In this atmosphere had House Baenre become ascendant. In this time of potential had House Baenre realized it most of all.

She saw the drow.

She saw the demons.

So many demons! Scores of them, from the worthless manes, the fodder of the Abyss, to the great glabrezu, marilith, nalfeshnee, and even mighty balors. They wandered the streets, rampaging, feasting, engaging in orgies with the drow, engaging in battles with the drow, engaging in whatever impulse crossed their chaotic and destructive desires.

There was chaos, truly!

But it was superficial, Matron Mother Baenre realized, like a series of bar fights in a city full of overlords and armies.

And that superficial chaos was enough. The demons caused enough grief, enough trouble, enough chaos, to keep the lesser Houses fully occupied. They could not align and plot against ascendant House Baenre with demons literally knocking on their doors.

Matron Mother Baenre watched in amusement as her borrowed memories revealed a balor in battle with a band of insectoid chasme.

The demons were no threat to the greater Houses of the city, even then, in Menzoberranzan's fledgling days. Never could they coordinate enough within their own ranks to pose any significant threat to the order of Menzoberranzan, an order being imposed by House Baenre and House Fey-Branche.

But the demons, so thick about the city, had surely kept the lesser matron mothers busy with thoughts of self-preservation. Those lesser Houses were too busy securing their own fences and structures to contemplate invading others.

Matron Mother Baenre blinked open her red eyes and considered the glorious revelations.

"Chaos begets order," she whispered.

Yvonnel the Eternal's memories had shown Quenthel the way.

"No, she said more loudly, shaking her head, for surely this diabolical possibility had been divinely inspired. "Lady Lolth has shown me the way."

◆ ◆ ◆

HIS SLY TAUNTING of his sister did little to improve Gromph's bitter mood. Even if he toppled her, even if he destroyed every matron mother and high priestess in the city, what would he accomplish?

He was a male, nothing more, and even when Lady Lolth had turned to the Weave, to a domain he had come to dominate more than any dark elf in centuries—in millennia, in perhaps the entire history of the race—Lolth's gratitude had not reached to him, nor his fellow male wizards.

Sorcere, the drow school of arcane magic, the academy under the control of Gromph, had counted among its students almost exclusively male drow, with only a few notable exceptions of priestesses looking to enhance their magical repertoire by adding arcane spells to their divinely inspired magic. Yet as soon as the Weave had become a web, as soon as it appeared that Lady Lolth would steal the domain of the goddess Mystra, the noble Houses had flooded Sorcere with their daughters as students.

The matron mothers, with Lolth's blessing, would not suffer the males of Menzoberranzan their position atop the ranks of Lolth's arcane disciples.

Would Gromph's ultimate title of archmage have proven secure?

But Lolth had lost her bid for the Weave, so Gromph had learned, though the details were not yet known to him. The Weave was no longer in her spidery claws and the city and school would return to normal, perhaps. Gromph would remain the archmage, and, he now even more poignantly understood, would remain a "mere male" in Menzoberranzan.

Or perhaps not, he mused as he pushed through the door of his private chambers, to see Minolin Fey seated on the great-backed chair, their tiny child Yvonnel suckling at the high priestess's breast.

"Your presence is long overdue," the infant said in a gurgling, watery voice. Baby Yvonnel turned her head to stare hard at the archmage, her threatening visage only slightly diminished by the spit and mother's milk dribbling out the side of her tiny mouth.

Her eyes! Those eyes!

Gromph remembered that look so well. With that one petulant expression, Yvonnel his child had thrown him back a thousand years and more, to the court of Yvonnel his mother.

"Where is Methil?" the infant demanded, referring to the ugly illithid who had imparted the memories and knowledge of Yvonnel the Eternal, Gromph's mother, the longest-serving matron mother Menzoberranzan had ever known, into the malleable mind of this tiny creature before she had even been birthed. "I told you to bring Methil."

"Methil will soon arrive," Gromph assured her. "I was with the matron mother."

That brought a bit of a growl from the child, one that sounded almost feral.

Gromph courteously bowed before his baby.

The side door to the chamber banged open then and in slid a handmaiden, an ugly yochlol, resembling a huge, half-melted gray candle with waving tentacles.

"The illithid has arrived for your lesson, Yvonnel," the demon creature said in a bubbly, muddy voice that still somehow managed to hold the sharp edge of a shriek. The handmaiden slid over to the child, leaving a trail of muddy goo, its tentacles reaching for the babe though it was still several feet from Minolin Fey—who was all too happy, even eager, to surrender the baby.

Out of the room glided the yochlol, one tentacle dragging back to clasp the door and slam it shut.

Minolin Fey slumped back in the high-backed great chair, not even bothering to straighten her gown to cover her exposed, leaking breast. Her breathing was quite raspy, Gromph noted, and more than once she glanced at the closed door with an expression that seemed to be clearly approaching panic.

"She is beautiful, is she not?" Gromph asked, and when the high priestess snapped a surprised glare at him, he added, "Our child."

Minolin Fey swallowed hard, and Gromph laughed at her. Whatever her feelings, Minolin would not dare harm Yvonnel.

She would do as she was told, as Lolth's avatar had instructed, because in her heart, Minolin Fey was truly a coward. Even in their previous plotting to overthrow Matron Mother Quenthel—before the end of the Spellplague, before the Darkening, before Methil had imbued Quenthel with the memories of Yvonnel much as the illithid had done with the child in Minolin's womb—Minolin had slithered in the shadows. She had remained in the background, prodding others into the forefront to hunt for K'yorl Oblodra in the Abyss, and whispering to those other Houses that would bear the brunt of Matron Mother Baenre's wrath if the plot unfolded badly.

"You do not understand!" Minolin Fey snapped at him in a voice as shrill as any she had ever dared use with Gromph Baenre.

"I?"

"To have your body so invaded . . ." the high priestess said, lowering her gaze and looking thoroughly, pathetically broken. "Those illithid tentacles, invading my flesh, probing me," she said, her tone hinting that she was barely able to speak the words. "You cannot know, husband."

She dared look up, to find Gromph glaring at her.

"You know nothing of what I know or do not know, Minolin of House Fey-Branche." His reference to her lesser House, instead of naming her as a Baenre, was a clear and sharp reminder.

"You are not a woman," Minolin Fey said quietly. "There is nothing more . . . personal."

"I am not a woman," Gromph echoed. "A fact of which I am reminded every day of my life."

"The child . . ." Minolin Fey said with a disgusted shake of her head.

"Will become Matron Mother of Menzoberranzan," Gromph stated.

"In fifty years? A century?"

"We shall see." Gromph turned on his heel and started for the door.

"There remains K'yorl," Minolin Fey dared remark before he reached the exit, referring to their previous plans to be rid of Quenthel.

Gromph stopped and stood staring at the door for a few heartbeats. Then he snapped about, eyes and nostrils flaring. "This is not Quenthel any longer, who serves as Matron Mother of Menzoberranzan," he warned. "Not simply Quenthel, at least. She knows as Yvonnel knew, and as our child Yvonnel is coming to know."

"Knows . . . ?"

"The history of our people, the living truth of the ways of the Spider Queen, the myriad plots and contortions of the many, many Houses that have come before. You would do well to remember that, Minolin Fey. Our union has served me well." He glanced at the door where the yochlol and the baby Yvonnel had gone. "But if you conspire and connive, and so invoke the wrath of Quenthel—of Matron Mother Baenre—then know that I will not protect you. Indeed, know that I will destroy you, in service to my beloved sister."

Minolin Fey could not match his gaze and lowered her face.

"Treat our child well, my wife," Gromph warned. "As if your very life depended on doing so."

"She demeans me," Minolin Fey muttered under her breath as Gromph turned once more to leave. And again the archmage spun on his heel.

"What?"

"The child," the high priestess explained.

"The child demeans you?"

The high priestess nodded, and Gromph chuckled once more. "You understand who that child has become?" Gromph asked rhetorically. "Beside her, you deserve to be demeaned, and mocked.

"But fear not," Gromph added. "Perhaps if you treat her well, and feed her well with your breasts, she will not utterly obliterate you with a Lolth-given spell."

Still chuckling, though not really feeling any better than when he had entered the room, the archmage departed.

Sometime later that day, Gromph became aware of a major demon, a gigantic canine-faced four-armed glabrezu, wandering the ways of Menzoberranzan near House Baenre. After that, a courier from the matron mother arrived and informed him that more demons would follow, and he was not to destroy or banish them except in defense of his very life.

The archmage's expression grew sourer still.

◆　◆　◆

SEATED AT THE right foreleg of the spider-shaped council table, Matron Mother Mez'Barris Armgo trembled visibly after High Priestess Sos'Umptu Baenre announced that their scouts had located a very-much-alive Tiago Do'Urden, thus finishing the full recounting of the results of the Silver Marches War—full, except for the not-so-minor detail that the sun had returned to that region of the World Above, the Darkening spell dismissed, and the fact that her words about Tiago were untrue, issued only to annoy Matron Mother Mez'Barris Armgo of the Second House.

"Issues, Matron Mother Mez'Barris?" the matron mother asked when Sos'Umptu moved back around to the far side of the table and took her seat, the Ruling Council's new Ninth Seat, between the matron mothers of House Vandree and House Do'Urden.

"Too many to recount in the hours we have, perhaps," the matron mother of House Barrison Del'Armgo retorted.

"Then the most recent, if you please."

"Did you not hear your own sister's words?"

Matron Mother Baenre shrugged dismissively.

"Drow nobles were killed," Mez'Barris said.

"Drow nobles are often killed," Matron Miz'ri Mizzrym of the Fourth House obediently pointed out. Miz'ri had become little more than an echo for the whispers Matron Mother Baenre did not wish to speak aloud. As she looked from Miz'ri to the matron mothers Vadalma Tlabbar and Byrtyn Fey, she was reminded of the tightening and dangerous alliance between House Baenre and the Third, Fourth, and Fifth Houses of Menzoberranzan.

Mez'Barris had to unwind that alliance if she was ever to be out from under the squirming shadow of the wretched Quenthel Baenre. She turned her stare over Miz'ri once more and added a sly and knowing grin, pointedly letting her gaze drop to the ornate necklace of gemstones Miz'ri had worn to council this day. Rumors about the city claimed that House Mizzrym was dealing with enemies of Menzoberranzan, including the deep gnomes of Blingdenstone, and that, of course, would explain the precious gemstones around Miz'ri's neck.

Perhaps that was Baenre's hold over Matron Mother Miz'ri, Mez'Barris mused. It was no secret that House Mizzrym was trying to build a trade market beyond Menzoberranzan to rival that of the ever-dangerous House Hunzrin, and perhaps the matron mother was granting Miz'ri dispensation to bargain with enemies, even the hated deep gnomes, with impunity.

It was just a hunch, but one worth investigating and perhaps exploiting.

"It is curious, though, that with the discovery of a living Tiago, of the Do'Urden nobles who went to war, only two were killed," Mez'Barris remarked. "And those two of the same family line."

"Are we to believe now that you ever truly claimed the *darthiir* half-breed daughter of Tos'un as a true member of House Barrison Del'Armgo?" asked Dahlia—Matron Darthiir Do'Urden—and the whole of the Ruling Council, with the exception of the two Baenres, gasped in unison, not so much at the bluntness of the remark but that the wretched elf who all, even the allies of House Baenre, knew to be no more than a second echo for Matron Mother Baenre's votes, had spoken the open accusation.

Seated beside Dahlia, High Priestess Sos'Umptu Baenre smiled unabashedly, as if she cared not at all that the puppet master's strings were visible to the audience.

"Tos'un Armgo died honorably," Matron Mother Baenre boldly pronounced, abruptly deflecting the conversation before it could be reduced to an open show of sides. "He rode Aurbangras, son of Arauthator, into battle even as Tiago flew Arauthator beside him. There, above the battlefield, they met the enemies of the white dragons, a pair of copper wyrms, in great combat. If there are any implications to your remark, Matron Mother Mez'Barris, perhaps you should first consider that neither I nor any others of Menzoberranzan hold sway over dragons, particularly not those of the metallic persuasion."

"And Doum'wielle?" Matron Mother Mez'Barris retorted, and she was sorry she had blurted that from the moment it had left her mouth, particularly given the words of Matron Darthiir Do'Urden.

Seven of the nine members of the Ruling Council openly laughed at Mez'Barris's remark. Only Zhindia Melarn of the Sixth House sat grim-faced, suspecting, no doubt, the same thing as Matron Mother Mez'Barris: It was no accident or simple matter of fate that neither Tos'un Armgo or his daughter Doum'wielle had returned from the surface campaign, or that now, apparently, all of the others—Tiago of House Baenre, Ravel of House Xorlarrin, and Saribel of both those Houses—would once more serve as nobles of the reconstituted House Do'Urden in Menzoberranzan.

Any thoughts Mez'Barris might have entertained of holding any influence in the Do'Urden compound were now clearly dashed.

The city was Matron Mother Baenre's.

For now.

Mez'Barris glanced at Zhindia Melarn. She had never held any love for the fanatical Melarni priestesses, but it seemed to her that they were destined to ally now, given the unabashed and continuing power grab by Matron Mother Baenre.

She turned her gaze to Miz'ri Mizzrym, whose alliance with House Baenre was surely tentative. Miz'ri walked the fine line between rival merchant groups and House Baenre, who were reaching out for surface trade through both the rogue band Bregan D'aerthe and the new city of Q'Xorlarrin, which was fast becoming little more than an outpost of House Baenre.

But House Hunzrin, far more powerful than their rank on the Ruling Council might suggest, would not be pleased—and indeed were outraged that the matron mother had reestablished House Do'Urden from thin air, thus blocking the logical ascension of the other Houses with House Xorlarrin's departure from the city—and Bregan D'aerthe was less controllable and predictable than any of the matron mothers ever dared openly admit.

Yes, there were cracks in Matron Mother Baenre's designs, particularly now that the Spider Queen had failed in her bid for the Weave. And by all accounts Q'Xorlarrin had suffered greatly in the war. While this would surely send the sniveling Matron Mother Zeerith closer to Matron Mother Baenre's side, would House Baenre be able to afford to send Zeerith the soldiers she might need to defend a concentrated assault by several drow Houses?

That suspicion was somewhat confirmed a moment later, when Matron Mother Byrtyn Fey, at best a very recent convert to Matron Mother Baenre's circle of allies, unexpectedly changed the subject.

"Why did we not foresee the coming of the metallic wyrms?" she asked the matron mother, her tone not sounding critical, but her question surely biting. "The enlistment of Arauthator and Aurbangras to our cause, the joining of our cause to that of the goddess Tiamat, was a blessed thing. The execution of that alliance and the fall of Aurbangras, however, was not."

"Matron Mother, surely you understand that the will and actions of dragons . . ." Matron Mother Baenre started to reply.

"Yes, of course," Byrtyn Fey interrupted—interrupted!—and with impunity she kept going. "But our own forces were in full recall to Menzoberranzan when Aurbangras was killed by the copper wyrms. Surely that fact will not serve Lolth well in her dealings with the goddess Tiamat."

"The grandson of Dantrag Baenre was astride one of those white dragons in the last battle," a clearly perturbed Matron Mother Baenre replied with an open sneer.

"One of only a handful of our people remaining in the Silver Marches," Byrtyn argued. "Had our army been on the field below—"

"The outcome of the dragon fight would not have changed," Matron Mother Baenre snapped.

"But the Spider Queen's position before Tiamat would have been strengthened. Do not run from errors, Matron Mother. Let us perhaps examine together how we might have better served Lady Lolth."

And there it was, Mez'Barris knew. She could barely contain her giggle. The words "examine together" when uttered by any matron mother to another matron mother, particularly at the table of the Ruling Council, were an accusation of failure far more than they were an offer of coordination. Those words stood among the oldest of drow verbal daggers. Drow matron mothers never "examined together" anything, other than the corpse of a third matron mother they had temporarily allied against and deposed.

The whole of the Council Chamber moved on edge, then, Mez'Barris noted to her delight, and even the wretched Quenthel seemed shaken, more like the old, ridiculous, and weak Quenthel Baenre whom Mez'Barris had known before this recent and inexplicable transformation had come over her.

Quenthel's nervousness lasted only a heartbeat, though, and she settled back comfortably and managed an amused look at Byrtyn Fey, like a silky cat looking into a rat hole with a promise that the occupant would not avoid the dinner table for long.

The room's door banged open then and a pair of towering creatures, humanoid and massively muscular but with a dog's face and a goat's horns, and an extra set of arms sporting giant pincers that could scissor a drow in half, stormed into the chamber.

Behind them came a slithering, naga-like creature, its lower body that of a serpent and upper body that of a shapely, naked woman, except with six arms all sporting axes or swords of various cruel design.

The matron mothers all started, some even rising, some beginning spells—except for the matron mother and Sos'Umptu, and of course, the impotent puppet, Darthiir Do'Urden.

Mez'Barris quickly calmed at the sight of the demons, the two glabrezu and the greater female, whom she recognized as either Marilith or Aishapra—this type of powerful demon looked too much alike for her to be certain.

"They are here with the blessings of Lolth," Sos'Umptu explained.

"Forgive my intrusion," said the female demon, and Mez'Barris knew from the voice that it was indeed Marilith, the greatest of her kind. Mez'Barris recalled then, as well, that yes, it was Marilith whose left breast was considerably larger than her right for some symbolic reason that no drow had ever discerned. Demons of this power could easily rectify such physical deformities if they so chose. Mez'Barris knew, too, from the female demon's tone and personality, that the vile and dangerous creature cared nothing for forgiveness, nor would ever offer any.

"I learned of your council and wanted to see how many of the ruling matron mothers were still known to me," Marilith went on. "It has been more than a century . . . a fleeting time, no doubt, but I care so little for drow that my memories of you are not forefront in my thoughts."

Screeches, like those of great birds, echoed out in the hall behind her and her glabrezu guards, and strange creatures that seemed half-human and half-vulture—vrocks, they were called, hulking and vicious, and standing nearly as tall as the ten-foot glabrezu—stalked into view along with a couple of clearly and understandably nervous dark elf sentries.

"Still, it's good to be back," Marilith said. She slithered around in a wide arc and departed, her hulking glabrezu guards close behind.

As the door shut, the matron mothers heard the agonized, horrified scream of a drow, and all suspected that one fewer sentry now guarded the sacred Council Chamber.

Demons were like that.

PART 1

The Quality of Vengeance

NEVER HAVE I SO CLEARLY COME TO KNOW THAT THAT WHICH I DO not know, I do not know.

I did not expect to rise into the air in the middle of that field, in the middle of the dwarf army. When beams of light burst from my fingertips, from my feet, from my chest, from my eyes, they came without conscious thought—I was nothing more than a conduit. And I watched as surprised as any around as those light beams shot into the sky and melted the roiling blackness that had darkened the land.

When I sank back down from the unexpected levitation, back to the ground amongst my friends, I saw tears of joy all about me. Dwarves and humans, halflings and elves alike, fell to the ground on their knees, paying homage to Mielikki, thanking her for destroying the darkness that had engulfed the Silver Marches, their land, their home.

No one shed more tears of joy than Catti-brie, Chosen of Mielikki, returned to my side by the grace of the goddess, and now, clearly, finding some resolution to the trials for which she and my other friends were returned to the realm of the living.

Catti-brie had oft speculated that her battle with Dahlia in the primordial chamber of Gauntlgrym had been no more than a proxy fight between Mielikki and Lolth, but of course, she could not be certain. But now this spectacle of my body being used in so dramatic a manner to defeat the darkness, the Darkening, of the Spider Queen, could not be questioned, so she believed. So they all believed.

But yet, I do not know.

I remain unconvinced!

I was the conduit of Mielikki, so they say, so it would seem, for I am no magic-user and surely know of no such dweomer as the one that escaped my mortal coil. Surely something, some power, found its way through me, and surely it seems logical to ascribe that power to Mielikki.

And so, following that logic, I was touched by the hand of a goddess.

Is it my own intrinsic skepticism then, my continual need to follow evidence, which prevents me from simply accepting this as true? For it simply did not seem to me to be that which they claim, but then, what might being so touched by a goddess actually feel like, I wonder?

This is my continuing dilemma, surely, my nagging agnosticism, my willingness to accept that I do not know and perhaps cannot know, coupled with my determination that such knowledge or lack thereof has no bearing—has to have no bearing—on how I conduct myself. I found Mielikki as a name to fit that which was already in my heart. When I learned of the goddess, of her tenets and ways, I found a melody consistent with the song of my own ethical beliefs and my own sense of community, with people and with nature about me.

It seemed a comfortable fit.

But never had I been able to truly separate the two, that which is in my heart and some extra-natural or supernatural other, whether ascribing that name to some higher level of existence or to, yes, a god indeed.

To me, Mielikki became a name to best describe that conscience within, and the code of existence that fits most smoothly. I did not find the need to search further, for the truth of Mielikki's existence or her place in the pantheon, or even the relationship of the one true god—or gods and goddesses, as the case may be—to the mortal beings roaming Faerûn, or more pointedly, to my own life. Ever has my chosen way come from within, not without, and truly, that is how I prefer it!

I did not know of the existence of, or the rumor of the existence of, some being named Mielikki when I walked out of Menzoberranzan. I knew only of Lolth, the Demon Queen of Spiders, and knew, too, that that which was in my heart could never reconcile to the demands of that evil creature. Often have I feared that had I remained in Menzoberranzan, I might have become akin to Artemis Entreri, and there is truth in that fear in regards to the hopelessness and apathy I see, or once saw, in the man. But long ago, I dismissed the possibility that I would have become like him in action, whatever my despair.

Even in the domain of the Demon Queen of Spiders, even surrounded by the vile acts and unacceptable nurture of my kin, I could not have gone against that which was in my heart. My internal god of conscience would not have allowed it. I would have been left a broken man, I do not doubt, but not, but never, a callous destroyer of others.

No, I say.

And so I came to the surface world and I found a name for my conscience, Mielikki, and I found others who shared my mores and tenets, and I was at spiritual peace.

Catti-brie's declaration regarding the irredeemable nature of evil of goblinkin and giantkind shook that tranquility, as surely as her tone—and that of Bruenor—shook my more earthly sensibilities. I knew in that moment that I was likely at odds with a pronouncement my beloved wife claimed had come straight from the goddess. I have tried to rationalize it and tried to accept it, and yet . . .

Discordance remains.

And now this. I was lifted into the air, my body used as a conduit, the result presenting light where there was once only darkness. It was good. Good—there is no other way to describe the change that Mielikki, if it was Mielikki—but how could it not have been Mielikki?—created through our magical communion.

Does not this godlike presence, then, command me to subjugate that which I believe to be just and right within my heart to the supposed command Mielikki relayed to me through Catti-brie? Am I not now, in the face of such powerful evidence, bound to dismiss my belief and accept the truth of the goddess's claim? When next I happen upon a nest of goblins, even if they are acting peaceably and bothering no one, am I therefore bound to battle within their home and slaughter them, every one, including children, including babies?

No, I say.

Because I cannot. I cannot dismiss that which is in my heart and conscience. I am a creature of intelligence and reason. I know what actions please me and put me at ease, and which pain me. I will kill a goblin in battle without regret, but I am no murderer, and will not be.

And that is my pain, and my burden. For if I am to accept Mielikki as my goddess, the circle cannot square, the yawning gulf of disagreement cannot be bridged.

Who are these gods we serve, this pantheon of the Realms, so rich and powerful and varied? If there is a universal truth, how then are there so many realizations of that truth, many similar, but each with rituals or specific demands to separate one from the other, sometimes by minute degree, sometimes by diametric opposition?

How can this be?

Yet there is universal truth, I believe—perhaps this is my one core belief!—and if that is so, then are not the majority of the pantheon claiming themselves as gods and goddesses truly frauds?

Or are they, as Bruenor had come to believe in the early years of his second life, cruel puppeteers and we their playthings?

It is all so confusing and all so tantalizingly close, but ever beyond the reach of mortal comprehension, I fear.

And so I am left again with that which is in my heart, and if Mielikki cannot accept that of me, then she chose the wrong conduit, and I named the wrong god.

Because despite what Catti-brie insisted, and what Bruenor came to declare with eager fire, I will continue to judge on the content of character and not the shape or color of a mortal coil. My heart demands no less of me, my spiritual peace must be held as the utmost goal.

With confidence do I declare that the edge of my scimitar will sooner find my own neck before it will cut the throat of a goblin child, or any child.

—Drizzt Do'Urden

CHAPTER 1 ◈

Of Orcs and Dwarves

UNDREDS OF DWARVEN CROSSBOWS WERE LEVELED ATOP the fallen logs of what used to be Dark Arrow Keep. A monstrous band approached: a score of the ugly orcs, a handful of goblins, and a frost giant.

And a dark elf named Drizzt Do'Urden.

"Lorgru," Sinnafein explained to the dwarf kings. "Lorgru, who would have become the next King Obould had not Warlord Hartusk usurped the throne."

"The retreating orcs flocked to him in the mountains, so said Drizzt," Catti-brie put in, and Sinnafein, whose scouts had told her the same thing, nodded her agreement.

"Lorgru ain't for shieldin' the dogs from me boys," King Harnoth proclaimed. "If he's looking to take up the fight, Adbar'll finish it for him!"

"Aye, but I'd like his ugly head on a pike outside our western gate," Oretheo Spikes added, and other nearby dwarves nodded at that.

King Emerus and Bruenor exchanged concerned glances. They had known this wasn't going to be easy from the first reports that the orcs were congregating around the deposed Lorgru in the Spine of the World.

Bruenor moved up to the central barricade and climbed atop the log. "Put up yer bows, boys," he called down the line after a cursory scan of the incoming forces. "No threat to be found. Durned elf'd kill 'em all afore ye let yer first bolt fly, if it came to fightin'."

The dwarves around him relaxed somewhat, but grumbled, too, more than a little disappointed that the meeting would most likely go off as planned.

Bruenor turned and held his hand up high. Drizzt responded in kind, and walked his unicorn mount, Andahar, around in front of the leading orcs, halting their progress.

"Ye with me?" Bruenor asked, turning around. The other three dwarf kings, Catti-brie, and Sinnafein of the elves moved to join him. Aleina Brightlance, who had been given the title and role as Emissary of Silverymoon and Everlund, rode forth as well.

Out from the other ranks rode Drizzt upon Andahar, along with an orc upon a snarling worg, a goblin shuffling fast along behind them, and the frost giant pacing them with its long strides.

"Who will speak for the Alliance of Luruar?" Drizzt asked, purposefully and pointedly evoking the alliance that had crumbled with the march of the Kingdom of Many-Arrows.

All turned to Bruenor.

"King Bruenor," said Emerus Warcrown. He turned a sly eye upon his opponents, particularly upon Lorgru. "Aye, that Bruenor," he explained to the visibly startled orc. "The one what signed the Treaty of Garumn's Gorge with Obould the First them years and years ago."

"I had thought King Bruenor long dead," the orc leader replied.

"Well, ye thought wrong, I'm guessing," Bruenor answered and stepped forward. "Is yerself speaking for them goblins and giants, too?"

"You are Bruenor?" Lorgru asked, incredulous, for surely the dwarf standing in front of him was very young.

"Don't matter who I be," the dwarf answered. "I'm speaking for 'em, and they're agreeing, eh?" Behind him, the others all nodded.

That seemed to satisfy the orc, who nodded, though still wore a confused expression. "I speak for Many-Arrows," he said.

"There ain't no Many-Arrows," King Harnoth said from behind, drawing winces from several of the others, Drizzt included.

"The orcs fleeing the field have returned to me," Lorgru explained to Bruenor. "Never would I have sanctioned such a march against your people, or such a war. It is not the way of Obould!"

"And where's yerself been this last year o' fightin'?" Bruenor asked, suspicious.

"In the mountains, in exile," Lorgru answered.

Drizzt looked at his red-bearded friend and nodded solemnly.

"My kingdom was stolen from me," Lorgru continued, "by factions determined to return to the warlike ways of the orcs. I reject those ways! She"—he pointed to Sinnafein—"is alive and free by my choice, though I could have ordered her killed, legally, even by your own laws, for intruding upon my kingdom."

All eyes went to Sinnafein.

"King Lorgru speaks truly," Sinnafein confirmed. "He would have been within his rights to execute me, but he did not."

"Are ye expectin' cheers?" King Harnoth said with a growl, looking from Sinnafein to Lorgru.

"I expect nothing," Lorgru replied. "I ask for a truce."

"A truce? Now that we got yer dogs runnin'?" Harnoth argued. "A truce so that ye can put 'em all back together and come hunting dwarfs once more?"

"Bruenor speaks for us, King Harnoth," Emerus Warcrown said, an edge of anger coming into his tone. Harnoth returned his angry stare, but Connerad Brawnanvil was quick to back up King Emerus, as was Aleina Brightlance.

"Bah, but I'm not needin' ye," Harnoth grumbled at length. "The boys o' Adbar alone can finish the job."

"Aye, but ye won't," Bruenor said in a tone that brooked no debate. The red-bearded dwarf spun on Lorgru. "A truce, ye're wanting?"

The orc nodded.

"Ye want us to leave yerself and yer boys alone in the mountains, do ye?"

Another nod.

"Well ye hear me good, then, King Lorgru, or Obould, or whate'er name ye mean to put on yer ugly face. Yerself and yers ain't welcome in the Silver Marches anymore. There's no Kingdom of Many-Arrows, and any o' yer boys that come out o' the mountains south of this ruined keep's north wall, or in the Lands Against The Wall, or anywhere else in the Silver Marches'll be counted as raiders and treated as such. We'll be watching ye, don't ye doubt, and first fight's last fight, for don't ye doubt that we'll be coming in to find ye."

King Lorgru glanced around like a caged animal, a look that changed to unmistakably crestfallen, as if only then did he realize that the dreams of his ancestors were lost to him. There would be no resurrection of Dark Arrow Keep, no return to the relationships and treaties the orcs had known before the rise of Warlord Hartusk.

He wanted to argue, they could all see, and even started to rebut. But he bit back his argument and accepted Bruenor's terms with a nod.

"Perhaps one day we will prove ourselves worthy of your trust," he said.

"I trust an orc corpse," said King Harnoth. "So there's a start to an understanding."

"Ye stay in yer holes," Bruenor warned. "Ye stay clear o' the Silver Marches. Or don't ye doubt that we'll hunt ye down, every one, and kill ye to death. Every one."

King Lorgru nodded and held forth his hand, but Bruenor didn't take it, and indeed, it seemed to all looking on that it took every ounce of control the fiery dwarf could manage to stop him from leaping out and murdering Lorgru then and there.

"What o' yerself?" Bruenor demanded of the goblin.

The diminutive creature glanced around nervously. "We are done the war!" it shrieked, and cowered.

Bruenor's gaze shifted to the frost giant, tall and proud, and clearly unbended by the weight of guilt or defeat.

"I am Hengredda of Starshine," he said in his beautiful and resonant voice. He gave a little chuckle. "It seems that I am all that is left of Starshine."

He shrugged, as if that was simply the accepted way of war, which to frost giants it surely was.

"I wish to go to Shining White and Jarl Fimmel Orelson," the giant explained. "I wish to tell him that the war is ended."

"And why would ye wish to do such a thing as that?" a skeptical Bruenor asked.

"So that Jarl Orelson ends his preparations to continue the war," Hengredda said with surprising candor.

"Are ye sayin' he's meaning to come back with his boys?" Emerus Warcrown demanded.

The frost giant shrugged. "If there is war, Jarl Orelson will fight. If there is war no more, he will not."

Bruenor turned back to regard the other dwarf kings before he responded, mostly seeking the approval of King Emerus, who was old and wise and had been through this many times before. When Emerus nodded, the red-bearded dwarf turned back to the frost giant.

"Ye go and tell Jarl Orelson what I told Lorgru here," Bruenor instructed. "He stays away and we'll leave him—we'll leave ye all—be. But if a dwarf o' the Silver Marches falls to the blade of a frost giant, then tell your Jarl Orelson that we'll be melting Shining White to a puddle, aye, and one red with giant blood, don't ye doubt."

"You boast loudly for such a little creature," Hengredda remarked.

Drizzt, Catti-brie, and all the dwarves around gasped at that, expecting Bruenor to spring upon the giant and throttle him. King Harnoth even started forward threateningly, but Bruenor swung out an arm and held him back.

Bruenor just stood there and smiled, staring at Hengredda for a long, long while.

"Nothin' worth sayin' to the like o' yerself," said Bruenor. "I told ye what was what, so do what ye want with it. But take yerself a good look at the field behind us, giant. At the big holes we're filling with dead enemies. Ye might want to tell yer Jarl Orelson about that."

The frost giant snorted derisively.

"And if yer sense of honor, or whatever stupid thing's driving ye makes ye think ye're wantin' to fight me, then go and deliver the message to Shining White and come back," Bruenor offered. "We'll fight it out, me and yerself—just me and yerself. And when we're done, me boys'll dig a hole and put ye in it."

"Brave words, dwarf," the giant replied.

"Not just any dwarf," King Emerus said, stepping forward. "King Bruenor Battlehammer, Eighth King of Mithral Hall, Tenth King of Mithral Hall, who slew Hartusk. So go and run yer errands, boy, and ye come back and play. Ye'll get the chance to kill a legend, or think ye'll get the chance, because we're knowin', and yerself should be too, that Bruenor'll cut ye down bit by bit and spit in yer eye afore he finishes ye."

Through it all, Bruenor never blinked, never changed his expression, never seemed anything but calm.

Hengredda, though, did blink. "Aye, I will! I will come back and kill a legend!" he said, but no one, not even Lorgru and the goblin standing beside him, believed him.

"Ye don't come back," Bruenor warned Lorgru. "And ye don't get too many o' yer dogs all in one place, or we'll find ye and break ye. Now get on. Go to yer holes and stay there."

Lorgru, looking thoroughly defeated, nodded his agreement and led the others away.

"We'll watch for the giant," Connerad assured Bruenor.

"He won't be back," Bruenor told him. He noted then the scowl of King Harnoth, off to the side and standing beside Emerus, so he moved over to the pair, with Connerad in tow.

"Ah, but we erred in lettin' that dog go," Harnoth insisted. "He's an orc king and they'll swarm about him, and so we're to be knowin' war soon enough."

"No," said Sinnafein, off to the side, and she, too, moved over to join the impromptu meeting. "Lorgru is not like Hartusk or the other war chiefs. He is the son of Obould, and traces his bloodline to the first Obould. He believes in that vision."

"Then he shouldn't've let his dogs come huntin'," was all that Bruenor would say.

❖ ❖ ❖

"KING HARNOTH WANTS to push into the mountains to hunt down the orcs," Catti-brie explained to Drizzt, the two off to the side and watching the small gathering. "Bruenor won't let him, and Emerus and Connerad back Bruenor. Harnoth may still go. He is outraged about the death of his brother and will never rest easy knowing the orcs are so close."

Drizzt spent a long while staring at her, measuring her tone and the tenseness within her strong frame. "You agree with Harnoth," he said.

Catti-brie matched his stare but didn't respond.

"Because of the goddess," Drizzt reasoned. "You think it our . . . *your* duty to hunt down and kill the orcs, one and all."

"We did not start this war."

"But we ended it," Drizzt replied. "Lorgru won't come back."

"What of his son?" Catti-brie asked. "Or his grandson? Or the next warlord who usurps the throne with visions of glory in his eyes?"

"Do you mean to kill every orc in all the world?"

Catti-brie just stared at him again, and Drizzt knew then that he and his wife would spend many hours on this topic in the coming days and months. Many unpleasant hours.

Drizzt turned back to the dwarves and nodded at Bruenor. "Do you think he's told them yet?"

Even as he asked the question, King Harnoth cried out in dismay.

"He has now," Catti-brie dryly replied.

Bruenor had confided his plans to the couple. He was going west with as many soldiers as the three dwarven citadels of the Silver Marches would afford him. Bruenor meant to reclaim Gauntlgrym from the drow and any other inhabitants who might have made the place a home.

Across the way, Harnoth had become quite animated, waving his arms and stomping in circles. Drizzt and Catti-brie went over to lend support to their dwarf friend.

"Why don't ye just empty all the durned citadels and let the durned orcs come walking in?" Harnoth roared.

"Never said I'd empty any," Bruenor calmly replied.

"Four thousand, he said," King Emerus added solemnly, his demeanor cutting at Harnoth as much as his words. "We've twice that number and half again right here on the field. And we've all left worthy garrisons back behind us."

"Four thousand!" said Harnoth. "That orc swine ye just sent walking's got ten times that number! *Twenty* times that number!"

"And you've got Silverymoon and Everlund," Aleina Brightlance remarked, all the dwarves turning to regard her with surprise—and in the case of all but fiery Harnoth, with gratitude.

"We'll not be abandoning you," Aleina vowed. "And we will rebuild Sundabar, do not doubt. The alliance will be stronger than ever, if the three dwarven citadels and the Moonwood elves so desire it."

"Aye," Bruenor, Emerus, and Connerad all said together, while Sinnafein nodded.

"My people will serve as your eyes in the north," Sinnafein added. "If the orcs begin to stir, we will know, and you will know, and any march they might make will be hampered by the sting of elven arrows, do not doubt."

"The dogs almost won this time," King Harnoth warned. "And now we'd be down four thousand dwarves, and with Sundabar a shell o' what she was, and with so many others dead—all o' Nesmé dead! Who'll stop 'em this time if they come calling?"

"They didn't get into the halls afore, and they won't next time, if there's e'er to be a next time," Bruenor insisted. "And now we're knowin' the threat and there are ways we can better prepare."

"Some of us always knew, King Bruenor," Harnoth said, and it was clearly meant as a jab at the dwarf who had signed the Treaty of Garumn's Gorge.

"Are ye thinkin' to drive us apart, King o' Adbar?" King Emerus was quick to retort. "Cause aye, that's what yer words're doing now. And don't ye doubt that Felbarr'll be standin' with Mithral Hall if ye keep on with it."

"As will the cities of Silverymoon and Everlund," Aleina added with an equally grim tone.

King Harnoth, young and full of pride, started to respond in an animated and angry fashion, but Oretheo Spikes put a hand on his shoulder to calm him, and when the young king snapped his head about to regard the Wilddwarf, Oretheo nodded and led him off to the side.

"He's a stubborn one," Catti-brie remarked.

"He lost his father not long ago, and his brother was slain in the war," Drizzt reminded. "As were many of his most important advisers. He sits atop a throne now, alone and unsure. He knows that he erred many times in the last year, and that we saved him from certain doom."

"Then he might be offerin' some gratitude and a dose o' well-earned humility, eh?" asked Bruenor.

Drizzt shrugged. "He will, but on his terms."

"If Adbar refuses our plan, then yerself and meself'll raise the army we're needin' to get yer quest done, me friend," King Emerus promised.

"We'll not be raising that number without Adbar," Bruenor said.

"So we'll go to Mirabar and find more allies—should be thinkin' that anyway," said Emerus. "Them boys are Delzoun, and so're yer boys in Icewind Dale. We'll get back Gauntlgrym, don't ye doubt!"

" 'We'll'?" Drizzt asked, catching on to Emerus's hint.

"Much to talk about," was all the King of Citadel Felbarr would say on that subject at that time.

Harnoth and Oretheo Spikes came back over then, the King of Adbar seeming much less animated.

"Me friend here thinks Adbar's holding strong with two thousand less," Harnoth explained. "So half yer force'll be marchin' under the banner o' Citadel Adbar, King Bruenor."

"No," Bruenor immediately replied, even as the others began to smile and even cheer. All eyes turned sharply on the red-bearded dwarf with his surprising answer.

"No banners for Adbar, Felbarr, or Mithral Hall," Bruenor explained. "As in the war we just won, we're walkin' under the flag o' our Delzoun blood, the flag o' Gauntlgrym!"

"Ain't no flag o' Gauntlgrym!" Harnoth protested.

"Then let's make one," Emerus Warcrown said with a wide grin. He held up his hand to Harnoth, and after only a slight hesitation, the young King of Adbar took that hand firmly in his own.

Bruenor, meanwhile, began producing flagons of ale from behind his magical shield, one for each of the four dwarf kings assembled on the field.

And so they toasted, "To Gauntlgrym!"

◆ ◆ ◆

THE WORK AT the ruins of Dark Arrow Keep continued for several tendays, with the massive orc fortress being stripped down to a watch-post with only a couple of towers left standing. There had been a small debate about whether to dismantle the place or perhaps refit it more to accommodate dwarven sensibilities, but Bruenor had pointed out, rightly so, that leaving any semblance of Dark Arrow Keep intact might entice the orcs to try to reclaim it.

Reclaiming it, after all, would be a lot easier than rebuilding it from rubble.

So they ripped the rest of it down, except the meager watch-towers, and they carried the great logs to the river and floated them downstream where they could be caught at Mithral Hall and used as fuel for the hearths and forges.

The docks, too, were dismantled, as were the surrounding orc villages, now abandoned, erasing all remnants of the Kingdom of Many-Arrows from the Silver Marches. As summer turned to fall, the dwarves and their allies marched for their respective homes, with the three citadels pledged to meet throughout the winter months to plan the spring march to the west.

"What's troubling you?" Catti-brie asked Regis on that journey to Mithral Hall. Regis had joined in the cheers and drinks and "huzzahs," of course, but every passing day, Catti-brie had watched him, and had noted a cloud that often passed over his cherubic face.

"I'm weary, that's all," he said, and she knew he was lying. "It's been a long and difficult year."

"For all of us," Catti-brie said. "But a year of victory, yes?"

Regis looked over at her, his seat on his pony far below the tall shoulders of Catti-brie's spectral unicorn. His smile was genuine, though, as he quietly offered, "Huzzah for King Bruenor."

But there was the cloud again, behind his eyes, and as he turned back to the road in front of them, Catti-brie figured it out.

"You're not coming to Gauntlgrym with us," she stated. In the shadows of his eyes, she didn't have to ask.

"I have said no such thing," Regis replied, but he didn't look at her when he spoke.

"Nor did you deny it, even now."

She watched the halfling's face tighten, though he still would not look over and up at her.

"How long have you known?" Catti-brie asked a short while later, when it became apparent to her that Regis was simply not going to lead this conversation.

"If Bruenor was marching to war in Gauntlgrym, and Drizzt was in Cormyr, or the Bloodstone Lands perhaps, what would you do?" Regis asked.

"What do you mean?"

"Would you accompany Bruenor on his quest, this latest quest in a perhaps unending line of quests, or would you desire to find Drizzt once more and resume your life beside him?"

"Donnola Topolino," Catti-brie realized then.

"My love for her is no less than yours for Drizzt," Regis explained. "I left her to fulfill my vow, and because I knew my friend Drizzt needed me. And so I traveled from Aglarond halfway across Faerûn to Icewind Dale, and stood with you and the others as we found our friend near death."

The woman nodded, her open, sympathetic, and inviting expression prompting him forward.

"And this war we have just won," Regis explained. "It was important, and in truth a continuation of that which we had started those decades ago. I served as Steward of Mithral Hall in the days of the first Obould."

"I remember well, and you served with great honor."

"And so I came back to finish what we started, to complete the circle," the halfling explained. "In both of these duties, I nearly died—I'm not afraid to die. I never was, and certainly am not after my time in the enchanted forest of Mielikki."

"But you are afraid that you will never see your beloved Donnola again," the woman reasoned.

"This is a dwarf war, the quest of the Delzoun brotherhood," Regis tried to explain. "I'm not a dwarf. Drizzt has said that taking Gauntlgrym from the drow could take years, and then holding it will likely prove to be a task that will stretch for decades. At what point . . . ?" His voice trailed off, the question unasked.

"Have you finished your service?" Catti-brie finished for him, and Regis finally did look up at her, plaintively. Her smile was warm and disarming. "You have done more than any could ask, my friend. None will judge you for leaving now, though surely we all will miss you."

"Brother Afafrenfere is only passing through Mithral Hall," Regis explained, "then going south to Silverymoon and Everlund, and to the south road to Waterdeep."

"He has explained as much, that his time here is at its end," Catti-brie agreed. "All are grateful for his actions here, for indeed he is credited in no small part in killing the white dragon on the slopes of Fourthpeak. A great ally is Brother Afafrenfere."

"From Waterdeep, he'll find the Trade Way, which I rode with the Grinning Ponies before I found you on the banks of Maer Dualdon. I will go with him, all the way to the port of Suzail, and I'll sail home east to Aglarond while he sails northeast to the city of Procampur and the Bloodstone Lands."

"I wish I could dissuade you."

"You know that you cannot."

"You are in love, Reg . . . Spider Parrafin," Catti-brie said. "I only hope that one day I will meet this halfling woman, Donnola Topolino, who has so stolen your heart."

"You will," Regis vowed. "I will lead her to the road of adventure beside me, or so I hope. And that road will lead to Gauntlgrym."

"It is a wider world than you imagine, I fear. When Wulfgar left us for Icewind Dale, did we not proclaim that we would all meet again."

"I did—with Wulfgar, I mean. As did Drizzt."

"And?"

The halfling swallowed hard at that poignant question, for that meeting with Wulfgar in Icewind Dale had been friendly enough, but strangely unfulfilling to all three of them.

"Are you saying that I should not return? Or that I should not go?"

"I surely do not want you to go!" the woman replied. "But no, you have no choice, my dear friend. I have seen you looking east in your quiet moments—we all have. You cannot spend your days wondering about your beloved Donnola. You'll always have the Companions of the Hall, Spider of Aglarond. Always will you remain one of us, and so, always welcomed wherever we are, with open arms and wide smiles, and kisses from me— so many kisses!"

"I tried to be worthy of the Companions of the . . ." Regis started to say, but his voice trailed away.

It was becoming very real to him, then, Catti-brie knew. He was leaving them, and the weight of that was only now truly descending on his small shoulders.

"Worthy? You are a hero, in every sense of the word. You saved Wulfgar's life in the tunnels south of Mithral Hall. Twice!"

"After he came for me."

"It is what we do for each other," said Catti-brie. "I only wish I could accompany you to Aglarond."

Regis nodded and swallowed hard, and forced Catti-brie to look him in the eye, his expression very serious, which confused the woman.

"Wulfgar has agreed to come with me," Regis explained.

For a moment, Catti-brie seemed unbalanced, as if she would simply fall off the side of her magically summoned mount. She steadied herself quickly, though, and managed a nod.

"He has agreed to stand beside me in my journeys," Regis explained. "Perhaps he feels as if our trials together in the Underdark . . ."

"He owes you a life debt."

"One for which I would never demand payment."

"He is happy to repay you. Likely, he is happy to find the open road and more conquests . . . of various natures."

"Say nothing, I beg you," Regis was quick to reply, as if Catti-brie's remarks had reminded him of something. "Well, we will go to Drizzt and Bruenor together, but for now, it is our secret. Agreed?"

"Why?"

Regis motioned forward with his chin, leading Catti-brie's gaze to Wulfgar, and to the Knight-Commander of Silverymoon.

"Aleina Brightlance is quite smitten with him," Regis explained.

"Perhaps she will go with you."

Regis was shaking his head before Catti-brie finished the thought. "Her duty is to Silverymoon. There are rumors that she will be given command of Sundabar when it is rebuilt."

"You have chosen love," the woman reminded. "Perhaps she..."

"I do not think Wulfgar would want her to come," Regis explained. "He's ... different now. I don't believe he desires a family—he already had one, in his previous life. Children, grandchildren, great-grandchildren—he knew them all. He outlived many of them. He had already mentioned to me that his biggest regret in the road I have chosen is that he'll not travel with you back through Longsaddle."

"Penelope Harpell," Catti-brie said with a laugh.

Regis shrugged. "Our secret?"

"One we have to share soon with Drizzt and Bruenor, that we can all properly prepare to say good-bye."

The halfling nodded and turned his focus once more on the road ahead. He had to do that, Catti-brie knew, to make sure she didn't see the tears that were welling in his eyes.

◆ ◆ ◆

LATER THAT DAY, the great marching force split, with the elves turning east to the River Surbrin, where their boats waited to ferry them and the thousands from Citadel Adbar across to the Glimmerwood.

King Emerus and his charges of Citadel Felbarr could have gone that way as well, but he opted to march farther south, to the Surbrin Bridge, beside his friend Bruenor so they could further discuss this great adventure that awaited the dwarves in the most ancient Delzoun home of all.

That very night, Catti-brie and Regis found Bruenor, Wulfgar, and Drizzt alone by a fire. They took their seats beside their friends, with food and drink all about.

"Call in Guenhwyvar," Regis bade Drizzt.

The drow looked at him curiously, for it seemed a strange request.

"Ain't none in the world to attack the army about us," Bruenor said.

But Regis looked to Drizzt and nodded, and Catti-brie did, too, and so the drow pulled out his onyx figurine and brought in the sixth member of the Companions of the Hall.

All gathered then, Regis and Wulfgar announced their plans, and Bruenor's cry of dismay split the night and turned many nearby eyes their way.

"It's me greatest quest!" the dwarf protested, on the edge of desperation. "I can'no be doin' it without ye!"

"Yes you can," Catti-brie answered. "*We* can. Drizzt and I will be beside you, and thousands of your sturdy kin as well."

Bruenor looked at her sharply, clearly feeling he had been deceived, or as if he was the last to know.

"They have to go," Catti-brie insisted. "Their business—Regis's business in particular—is no less urgent than your own. More urgent than your own, I say, for Gauntlgrym has been there for thousands of years, and will be there for thousands more, no doubt, but Donnola . . ."

She looked at Regis, who nodded his gratitude.

"Yer girl?" Bruenor asked incredulously, as if the thought of chasing a woman when such a grand adventure lay in front of them was perfectly ludicrous.

"The woman I will make my wife," said Regis. "Perhaps we will name our first child Bruenor, though I fear his beard will disappoint you."

Bruenor started to argue, but the halfling's words turned that into a sputter, then a laugh.

And so they ate and so they drank, and many cheers and flagons of ale were lifted into the night air, and many promises that they would see each other again, in Gauntlgrym likely. This was no good-bye, they all declared, but merely a temporary parting of the ways.

How many have made those often futile promises?

"Are we disturbing your private gathering?" came an unexpected voice. Jarlaxle walked into the firelight, flanked by the sisters Tazmikella and Ilnezhara.

"We've room for more," Drizzt said quickly, before Bruenor could protest. He slid along the log he had taken as a bench, making room for the newcomers.

"A drink?" Drizzt asked, looking to Bruenor, who scowled for a heartbeat, but produced another flagon.

Ilnezhara handed the first flagon along to Jarlaxle and explained, "I prefer blood," as Bruenor reached behind his shield once more. The dwarf stopped and stared at her.

"You walk openly among the dwarves and others," Drizzt said quietly to Jarlaxle.

"The war is over and so I have come to try to mend relations between the races, ostensibly," the drow mercenary replied and took a sip of the ale. "Though, of course, I am here as a spy for Matron Mother Baenre, to whom I will, of course, provide a complete accounting."

Wulfgar bristled and Bruenor hopped up at that declaration.

To which Jarlaxle merely shrugged and smiled, and looked to Drizzt. "My use of 'of course' two times in one sentence did not properly relay my sarcasm?"

"It's been a long year," Drizzt replied.

"Ah," Jarlaxle agreed. "Well, good dwarf and man-giant, do be at ease," he said. "I will tell Menzoberranzan nothing more than that which they already know. The dwarves won, the orcs fled, the human kingdom will be built anew, and for all of our—of *their*—efforts, this war Menzoberranzan prodded onto the Silver Marches has done little more than strengthen the bonds of the alliance of Luruar."

"That's what ye're meaning to tell 'em, eh?" asked Bruenor.

"Aye," Jarlaxle answered. "In exchange for a small favor."

Bruenor straightened at that, and cast a sour look Drizzt's way, but Drizzt held up his hand, begging the dwarf for patience.

"I have two associates, both known to you, who are intrigued at the prospect of your intended reclamation of Gauntlgrym," the drow explained.

"Them two?" Bruenor asked, pointing to the sisters.

"Try not to be so foolish," Tazmikella said.

"Good dwarf, we are already long bored," Ilnezhara agreed.

"Not them," Jarlaxle explained, "but dwarves, including the newest member of Bregan D'aerthe. Both have asked for a leave, that they might march beside you to your homeland, and given all that they have done, I would be a terrible leader and a worse friend to refuse them." He lifted his hand and motioned, and into the firelight hopped Ambergris and Athrogate, holding hands and grinning hopefully.

"Ye want me to take these two?" Bruenor asked.

"Powerful allies," Jarlaxle said.

Bruenor seemed at a loss. He looked from the drow to the dwarves to Drizzt, then back and forth again. "Aye, I can'no deny the truth o' that."

"I been granted back me old home o' Felbarr," said Athrogate.

"And meself can return to Adbar and all's forgiven," added Amber Gristle O'Maul, of the Adbar O'Mauls. "And we're owing ye all for that."

"Aye, and we'd rather be takin' the road aside ye," Athrogate said. "Fore'er more."

"And what of yourself?" Drizzt asked Jarlaxle.

The mercenary shrugged. "I've to report to the matron mother, of course, and then I have another road before me."

"He's off to find Effron, don't ye know?" Ambergris interjected. "Aye, to find the poor boy and give him a hug for meself."

"Do we have an agreement?" Jarlaxle asked.

"And if I'm sayin' no?" Bruenor asked.

"Then I will report the same tale to the matron mother, but you will have lost a pair of fine and powerful companions."

Bruenor looked to Drizzt. "What says yerself, elf?"

"In a fight, those are two dwarves I would want on my side."

"Good enough, then, and glad to have ye," Bruenor said to the pair, who grinned all the wider, bowed, and moved back out into the darkness between the campfires.

"And now I must be off," Jarlaxle said, draining his flagon, tipping his cap, and rising. "Farewell and not good-bye, for I've no doubt that our roads will cross again, my friends." He started to bow, but Tazmikella grabbed him by the sleeve and with frightening ease pulled him back down to sit beside her. She began whispering in his ear, and pointed across the firelight to Wulfgar.

Jarlaxle laughed.

The big man scowled.

"My friend here is wondering if you are in need of a fine bed this night," Jarlaxle said.

The stunned Wulfgar seemed at a loss, muttering "umm" repeatedly.

"She's a dragon, boy," Bruenor said to him.

"Why does everyone keep saying that as if it is a bad thing?" Jarlaxle asked. He looked to Wulfgar and grinned slyly. "Enticing, yes?"

But Regis answered before Wulfgar could. "Aleina is not far, and she is expecting you," he reminded, and the growing smirk disappeared from the big man's face.

"I . . . with sincere gratitude . . ." Wulfgar stammered, but the sisters laughed at him and stood up, hoisting Jarlaxle between them and tugging him away.

"I will have to suffer greater trials for your absence," Jarlaxle said with feigned regret. He tried to bow again, but was off the ground, lifted over the log, and easily slung over Ilnezhara's shoulder.

"Alas," he said with great lament, and he awkwardly managed to tip his outrageous hat.

"Dragons . . ." Catti-brie said incredulously, and she looked to Wulfgar and shook her head with disgust.

"It does present an intriguing . . ." Drizzt kidded, and he ducked fast from Catti-brie's good-natured slap.

To Wulfgar, though, there remained a look of clear interest as he watched the trio depart. He considered the beautiful sisters and what he, surprisingly, found to be an intriguing offer. And he looked, too, at Jarlaxle, envying the carefree, self-serving drow.

Had Jarlaxle found what Wulfgar sought?

◆ ◆ ◆

HORNS BLEW AND the cadence of a drumbeat was matched perfectly by the thousand dwarves of Citadel Felbarr, stomping across the Surbrin Bridge, escorted away by the cheering of their Battlehammer kin.

"He's supporting you with everything he can," Drizzt remarked to Bruenor as they watched Emerus Warcrown depart.

"He's a good man, is me friend Emerus," Bruenor replied solemnly. "He'll be generous when we meet at the year's turn. Many who're marchin' beside us, elf, will be from Citadel Felbarr, don't ye doubt."

"I don't," Drizzt agreed.

Another horn blew, this one to the south, and Drizzt noted that Bruenor swallowed hard at this one, the muster call from the Knights in Silver. Drizzt, too, breathed a long sigh.

"Me girl's with 'em," Bruenor remarked. "Let's go and say our good-byes . . ." His voice trailed off and the sturdy dwarf bit back a chortle. He looked up at Drizzt and nodded, and the two started off.

They found Catti-brie with Wulfgar and Regis a few moments later, Aleina and Brother Afafrenfere standing off to the side, waiting patiently.

Bruenor began pulling flagons of ale out from behind his shield the moment he arrived, handing them around to the other four, then lifting his own up high.

"To the Companions of the Hall," the dwarf said in a strong and loud voice—loud enough so that many nearby turned to regard the gathering of the five friends. "If ne'er we're to meet again, then know in yer hearts that few've knowed a friendship as deep."

Regis winced at that, and it seemed to Drizzt as if he was on the verge of breaking, perhaps renouncing his intended journey to Aglarond.

"We'll meet again," Drizzt said to assure them all, particularly the halfling, though in truth, he doubted his own words.

"Aye, in this world or the next," Catti-brie confidently added.

Drizzt noted that this time both Wulfgar and Regis winced. He understood.

They toasted and drank, toasted some more and drank some more, though the horns to muster were growing more frequent and more urgent in the south. Finally Aleina Brightlance walked over. "We are off," she told Wulfgar and Regis.

Hugs and kisses, and the five left, all with tears in their eyes. When he hugged Drizzt, Regis whispered, "I have to go" into the drow's ear, as if asking permission.

"I know," the drow said.

And so they did, moving down the riverbank to the south with the soldiers of Silverymoon and Everlund, leaving Drizzt and Catti-brie and Bruenor to contemplate their long road ahead without the pair.

CHAPTER 2 ◈

Walking the
Nether Planes

ATRON MOTHER ZEERITH XORLARRIN JOINED HANDS
with her mighty nephew, the wizard Tsabrak, and began
her spellcasting. Similarly, the wizard launched into his
own casting, the two twining their magical energies into
a unique spell, both arcane and divine.

Across the altar in the primordial chamber of
Q'Xorlarrin, High Priestess Kiriy, Zeerith's oldest daughter,
held her breath in anticipation. She had never seen this ritual
performed before, though she was well versed in necromancy.

"Dwardermey," Tsabrak whispered a long while later, evoking
the name of one of the fallen drow in the Silver Marches.

"Dwardermey," Matron Mother Zeerith echoed, and they
both repeated the call many times.

The body came from inside the stone block altar itself, facial
features forming within the stone, and growing, rising. Then it
was separate from the altar, the body of a slain dark elf, torn by
swords and axes.

"Kiriy!" Matron Mother Zeerith said sharply, and the high
priestess realized that she was taking too long. She put aside her
astonishment and launched into a simple spell to animate the dead.

A few moments later, the corpse of Dwardermey Xorlarrin
sat up on the altar, then stiffly shifted to the side, legs hanging
over the altar slab.

High Priestess Kiriy looked to Matron Mother Zeerith, who
nodded, and so Kiriy commanded the zombie to stand and

walk. The unthinking zombie did walk, directly away from the high priestess, as ordered. It did not pause when it reached the lip of the primordial's pit. It made not a sound when it pitched over the edge, tumbling through the swirl of the trapped water elementals to land on the lava skin of the godlike beast.

The primordial drew Dwardermey in.

Tsabrak blew a great sigh. "This will take us tendays," he said. "I am exhausted already, as are you."

"We must," Matron Mother Zeerith replied. "In this duty, we will salvage the goodwill of the Spider Queen."

High Priestess Kiriy held her tongue, unsure that the exercise of summoning the corpses from the distant battlefield and properly disposing of them would do any such thing. But they had to try, she knew, for she understood as her mother understood: Lady Lolth was not pleased with their failures in the Silver Marches.

Perhaps that was why the dark elves killed in that war were so disproportionately Xorlarrin warriors.

So now they would perform their tedious duty, in the hopes that they would garner some measure of forgiveness or clemency from the merciless Spider Queen. Such a task would consume them for hours each day, and was no inexpensive feat. Tsabrak had to destroy a valuable gemstone for each summoning.

Perhaps it would be easier, Kiriy thought—but surely did not say—if Matron Mother Zeerith simply sent Tsabrak to the Silver Marches to physically reclaim the fallen dark elves of Q'Xorlarrin.

But of course, her mother would never do such a thing.

Tsabrak was Zeerith's lover now, her partner, and she had secretly elevated him to a position of power nearly equal to her own.

And that, Kiriy feared—but again dared not speak aloud—might be the truth behind Lady Lolth's disapproval.

◆ ◆ ◆

A FIREBALL STOLE the darkness in a far corner of the great cavern that housed Menzoberranzan. It was something more than a wizard's blast, Gromph knew, as he watched from his window at the drow academy of Sorcere.

Cries drifted across the cavern, echoing. A battle raged, drow against demon, likely, or just as likely, demon against demon.

The Abyssal beasts were thick about Menzoberranzan now, these ugly creatures of destruction and chaos, wandering freely, untended, uncontrolled. Gromph had lost two students caught in a skirmish with a glabrezu over in the district called the Stenchstreets—the body of one apprentice wizard had been sent to him in two equal-sized boxes.

The gates of every house in the city were closed, sealed, every sentry on a nervous edge, every matron mother plotting and fretting in turn, wondering if she might turn a demon to her advantage or fearing that a horde of the beasts would descend upon her House and obliterate it. They could find no pattern to alleviate their fears. These were demons, changing direction at a whim, destroying simply for the joy of destroying.

A low growl escaped the archmage's lips. What idiocy was this? What demons, literal and figurative, was his arrogant sister unleashing upon the city of Menzoberranzan?

He heard a knock on his door but ignored it. More bad news, likely: another student torn apart by a glabrezu's giant pincers, a lesser House invaded, perhaps.

Another knock sounded, this one more insistent, and when Gromph didn't respond, he heard, to his absolute astonishment, the door creaking open.

"You are fortunate that I did not enable my wards," he said dryly, never turning. "Else you would be a red puddle from which a wounded frog would hop."

"Truly, husband?" came the surprising reply, the voice of Minolin Fey. "Perhaps in that event you would find me more attractive."

"What are you doing here?" Gromph demanded, and still he did not bother to turn to face the priestess.

"The matron mother is quite pleased with herself," Minolin Fey replied. "The other matron mothers are too busy securing their gates to think about colluding against her."

"Perhaps if she just burned down House Baenre, she would have even less to worry about," Gromph sardonically replied.

He took a deep breath and finally turned a serious expression upon the high priestess. "How many has she summoned?"

"Who can know?" Minolin Fey replied. "Now the demons are summoning each other. The matron mother might as well have thrown fifty scurvy rats into a nest, the beasts reproduce so efficiently. Except that even scurvy rats have a few tendays of helpless infancy. The summoned demons are quite mature and capable of havoc from the moment they emerge through the dimensional gate."

"Why are you here?" Gromph asked again.

"The true matron mother does not sit on the throne of House Baenre," Minolin Fey dared to whisper.

"What are you suggesting?"

Minolin Fey swallowed hard and struggled for a reply.

Gromph knew well. Not so long before, Minolin Fey and some others, including Gromph on the periphery of their treachery, had conspired to bring down Quenthel's reign. They had found a weakness, a seam in the matron mother's armor, and one dating back to the Time of Troubles. In that chaos, as the gods returned to prominence in Faerûn and the divine powers were restored, Matron Mother Yvonnel the Eternal, Gromph's mother and the ruler of Menzoberranzan for longer than the memories of the oldest drow, had channeled the unbridled power of the Spider Queen. Lolth's magnificence had flowed through her as she utterly destroyed House Oblodra—the compound and almost all of the noble family. The Oblodrans had sought the quietness of the gods, of Lolth in particular, to seek great advantage, for they were an order of psionicists, whose magic was not dependent upon such divine beings.

A very few Oblodrans escaped the wrath of Matron Mother Yvonnel, the wrath of Lady Lolth—only Kimmuriel was now known to Gromph—but all of the other notables had been slaughtered in the catastrophe, except for one. Death would have been too easy for K'yorl Odran, the Matron of House Oblodra. No, Yvonnel had not killed that one, but had spared her and sent her to the Abyss, to the eternal torment of a great balor named Errtu. When Minolin Fey and her fellow conspirators had learned of this, they had hatched a plan to rescue the vicious and strangely powerful K'yorl, with her illithid-like psionic abilities. They would turn her upon the then-weakened House Baenre and the pitiful Matron Mother Quenthel, who would never survive such an unexpected onslaught.

"Surely the Spider Queen cannot be pleased by these actions," Minolin Fey pleaded. "And surely, Lady Lolth knows that the better choice, the better matron mother . . ."

"Bite back your words or I will remove your tongue," Gromph warned her.

Minolin Fey blanched and fell back against the door, knowing well from his tone that he was not speaking idly. The archmage's eyes flared with frustration and rage, and he sneered and growled again.

But then he sighed, the moment passing.

"She is not merely Quenthel any longer," Gromph calmly explained. "She is not weak, nor is House Baenre."

"We can do it through proxies," Minolin Fey started to add, but Gromph cut her short with a glare that froze the blood in her veins.

"Never speak of K'yorl again," Gromph warned. "Are you so foolish to miss the small matter that the matron mother now has an illithid at her disposal? Methil El-Viddenvelp serves my sister as he once served my mother."

"As he has served your child," Minolin Fey reminded him.

"Do not presume to understand anything about Methil. And I say again, for the last time, never speak of K'yorl again."

"As you demand, Archmage," the high priestess said, deferentially—and wisely—lowering her gaze to the floor.

"Get back to House Baenre and our child," Gromph ordered. "You dare leave her unprotected in this time when demons haunt the ways of Menzoberranzan?"

Minolin Fey didn't look up and didn't answer, other than to slowly retreat back out the door, never turning her back to the archmage.

Gromph took little satisfaction in hearing her footsteps and the rustle of her robes rushing down the hall. Despite his outward anger, Gromph knew that her fear of Quenthel's growing power was correct.

The old archmage looked back out the window, shaking his head. Quenthel had been brilliant in so locking down the city—perhaps that was what galled him most of all.

And Gromph had erred, he knew. He had come to hope that Yvonnel, his child, possessed of his mother's memories and soon enough to be crowned as Matron Mother of Menzoberranzan, would serve as his ladder to ascension against the dark realities of Lolth's failure to secure the Weave, and the Spider Queen's apparent indifference to him even had she succeeded.

Soon enough, Quenthel would have Matron Mother Zeerith begging her to keep the city of Q'Xorlarrin as a Baenre satellite, and now, with the constant demonic threat lurking in every shadow, any movement by House Barrison Del'Armgo, House Melarn, House Hunzrin, or any others, had surely been halted.

"Brilliant," he admitted, staring out at the city as another demonic fireball erupted.

He glanced back at the door, at where Minolin Fey had been. Perhaps it was time for him to go and speak with the Matron of House Fey-Branche, Minolin's mother Byrtyn.

One of the former conspirators.

The one who had found K'yorl Odran.

◆ ◆ ◆

A GRAY AND ugly fog blew in, sometimes thin and blurring the giant mushroom stalks into ghostly figures, other times so thick as to block Kimmuriel's vision for more than a few feet in every direction. A great stench was carried on that steaming wind and fog, the aroma of rot and death, of burning flesh and hearty vomit.

Kimmuriel was too disciplined to let that bother him. So many who came here to this wretched plane of existence grew distracted by the grotesque sights and smells, and that distraction often led to violent ends.

The drow walked steadily, his eyes and his mind's eye probing all around him. He would not be caught off guard.

He could hear her now, calling to him as she had done when he was a child—not with her physical voice, but psionically.

Kimmuriel Oblodra tried to hold his calm. He came in sight of her, of K'yorl, his mother, then, as she leaned against a mushroom stalk, looking every bit the same as she had on that awful day more than a century before, when Matron Mother Baenre had wrenched the whole of House Oblodra up by its stony roots and dropped it into the Clawrift, the great chasm that split the cavern that housed Menzoberranzan.

K'yorl had gone over with that tumbling stalagmite house, and Kimmuriel had thought her dead.

That notion hadn't bothered him too greatly, though. He had already all but left House Oblodra to join Jarlaxle's mercenary band, and he was not one to be bothered too greatly by such destructive and useless emotions as grief.

Or elation, he pointedly told himself as he once again looked upon his mother.

Gromph had sent him to Byrtyn Fey and she had directed him here, to the Abyss, to the throne of the great balor Errtu.

To K'yorl Odran, Errtu's slave.

"My son, you are all that remains," K'yorl greeted.

"It would seem that you, too—"

"No," K'yorl interrupted. "I am dead in every way that matters. The Prime Material Plane is beyond me now, my mortal coil no more than an illusion, a manifestation here to keep Errtu amused." She paused and shot him the slyest of looks as she added, "For now."

Kimmuriel couldn't miss the seething anger in her voice and behind her fiery eyes—orbs that had not lost a bit of their luster in the century and more of her imprisonment. After all these decades, the fiery and vicious K'yorl had not cooled.

"Matron Mother Yvonnel Baenre is long dead," he said, to try to calm her.

"Cursed House Baenre just replaces her, one after another, but House Oblodra, our House, all that we had built, is no more!"

"You erred in the Time of Troubles," Kimmuriel bluntly replied. "You reached too high and when the divine powers returned, you were punished for your hubris. We all were."

"But you survived."

Kimmuriel shrugged, as if it hardly mattered.

"And what have you done to repay Baenre?" K'yorl demanded sharply.

"I?" Kimmuriel replied incredulously. "I have served myself, as I please, when I please, how I please."

"With Jarlaxle."

"Yes."

"Jarlaxle *Baenre*," K'yorl said pointedly, for she was one of the few who knew the truth of that strange, Houseless mercenary.

"It is not a name he uses."

"He serves House Baenre."

"Hardly. Jarlaxle serves Jarlaxle."

K'yorl nodded, digesting it all.

"It is time to pay them back," she said at length. "Quenthel is a weakling, and she is vulnerable."

"She has tightened her noose on the city."

"And when it loosens? A dragon is dead, the Darkening has been defeated, and the fledgling city of Matron Mother Zeerith hangs by a single strand of a spider's web."

"I am surprised that you are so informed of the—"

"I have nothing but time," K'yorl interrupted. "And Errtu torments me by showing me the turning of Menzoberranzan without me."

"Then you know that Matron Mother Baenre will see to Matron Mother Zeerith's troubles as well."

"With demons."

"You know much for a slave in the Abyss," Kimmuriel said again, even allowing a bit of sarcasm into his normally impassive tone.

"I know much because I *am* in the Abyss! Errtu does not fear me, surely, and so he does not fear letting me know of Menzoberranzan."

"Demons, yes," said Kimmuriel.

K'yorl gave a little laugh, a wicked one indeed. "You must be my conduit, Kimmuriel. You must exact the punishment House Baenre rightly deserves."

Kimmuriel dismissed that foolish notion even as the matron mother spoke it. He wasn't about to go against Matron Mother Baenre and her vast array of powerful friends. Still, he heard and sympathized with every word. He hated Quenthel Baenre. Despite any logical protestations to the contrary, a simmering rage burned within Kimmuriel Oblodra for all that he had lost, for all that House Baenre had taken from him. He watched again in his memories the tumbling structure of House Oblodra, pitching over the side of the Clawrift, so many dark elves, his family, tumbling into oblivion.

For a long while, for many years, Kimmuriel had hated House Baenre. When first he had learned of Jarlaxle's heritage, he had even considered murdering the mercenary.

That was a long time ago, of course, but now, hearing K'yorl, Kimmuriel realized that he hadn't dismissed those feelings of rage quite as thoroughly as he had believed.

"I do not expect you to expose yourself to suspicion," K'yorl said, as if reading his thoughts—and she probably was, he reminded himself, throwing up more mental guards.

"You ask me to serve as your instrument, your assassin against House Baenre, but do so without wishing me to expose myself to their wrath?" he asked skeptically.

"Not my instrument, but my conduit to my instrument," K'yorl said with a crooked and knowing little smile, one that took Kimmuriel back across the centuries, one that he had known well in his youth.

"A mighty Baenre studies under you, I am told," K'yorl said.

It was beginning to bother Kimmuriel more than a little just how much K'yorl was being told.

"The archmage, no less," she said.

Kimmuriel remained impassive—there was no need to confirm anything, apparently.

"And how does Gromph Baenre feel about his sister the matron mother filling the streets of Menzoberranzan with demons?"

"He thinks it a brilliant ploy to insulate the matron mother from the wrath of the Ruling Council over her . . . choices."

"But how does he *feel*? Is he pleased by his sister Quenthel's dangerous ploy?"

"You clearly know the answer."

"He hates her. They all do," K'yorl said. "She imposes order on a city of chaos. It will not stand."

"I will not stop it."

"Not directly."

"I do not enjoy cryptic conversations, Matron Mother," Kimmuriel said, and what he really didn't enjoy—and he knew that this drow in front of him understood it well—was not being able to read her thoughts. Kimmuriel was used to holding a huge advantage in such conversations, with all but the mind flayers and Jarlaxle, for he could read the meaning behind every word with a simple glance into the flittering thoughts as the words were spoken.

"Fan the flames in the archmage's humors," K'yorl explained. "Subtly suggest a way for him to strike back at his sister. Let him battle demon with demon."

"You ask me to implant a suggestion into the mind of the arch-mage to summon demons of his own? Into the mind of Gromph Baenre?" Kimmuriel didn't try to hide his doubts. Those dark elves expecting and hoping for a long life simply didn't do such things.

"It will be no difficult task. Gromph's thoughts already flow in that direction."

Movement to the side caught Kimmuriel's attention, and he noted a massive, leather-winged beast moving toward them, one he knew to be the mighty balor Errtu. The creature moved close enough to tower over Kimmuriel, and sniffed the air a few times before plopping down in a mushroom fashioned into a throne just off to the side, one Kimmuriel hadn't even noticed before—had Errtu brought it with him?

"To have Gromph call in a balor, perhaps?" Kimmuriel asked K'yorl, but he was looking at Errtu.

"Think bigger," K'yorl replied. "Perhaps Gromph will think he is calling forth a peer of Errtu, but let his spell draw a bigger prize, a prize beyond his control?"

"You?" Kimmuriel asked dryly.

Both K'yorl and Errtu laughed at that.

"You cannot return to the Prime Material Plane at this time," Kimmuriel said to Errtu.

The balor growled, but nodded. Errtu had been defeated on the Prime Material Plane, and so banished, a penalty of a century of exile.

"Banished by a Baenre," K'yorl said. "Tiago Baenre."

"Who is now Tiago Do'Urden, if he is even still alive," said Kimmuriel.

"All the more reason to hate him," said Errtu. The demon stared hard at Kimmuriel and focused his thoughts at the drow psionicist, who was overwhelmed by the sheer wall of demonic hate emanating from the creature.

"What do you know of the Faerzress?" K'yorl asked.

"What every drow of Menzoberranzan is taught at the Academy," said Kimmuriel. The Faerzress was a region of the

Underdark teeming with magical energy—the very stones of the region glowed with the power of magic, both the Weave and the extraplanar energies of the lower planes. Through the emanations of the Faerzress, the drow gained their innate magical abilities, and their innate resistance to magic. With the permeating glow of the Faerzress, drow smiths fashioned their fabulous weapons and armor. As the sun nurtured the surface world with its warmth and life energy, so the Faerzress fed the darkness of the Underdark.

"I will give you a spell," K'yorl said, and closed her eyes. "Open your mind."

Kimmuriel similarly closed his eyes and focused on receiving—and studying—K'yorl's psionic impartation. He didn't know all the words, for it was an arcane chant and not a psionic pattern.

"Give that to Gromph during your sessions," she bade him. "Bit by bit, inflection by inflection. Let him find the strength to battle his sister and foil her plans, and so we will pay back House Baenre."

Kimmuriel opened his eyes to stare at her intently.

"Would it so pain you to see House Baenre punished and Menzoberranzan thrust back into chaos?" she asked. "Would not Bregan D'aerthe profit from such . . . tribulations?"

"And you would find a deep sense of sweet revenge?"

"Do you expect me to deny it?" K'yorl asked.

"No."

"And would you not share in your mother's satisfaction?"

Kimmuriel said nothing.

"Then we are agreed?" K'yorl asked.

"When next Methil summons me to Gromph's chamber to continue our work, I will offer him a view of what he might do to counter the matron mother. And, too, I will begin showing him a more powerful gate to the Abyss."

"He will light the Faerzress with the power of that spell, and oh, but his surprise will delight you, my noble son."

Despite himself, Kimmuriel grinned. He nodded and bowed deferentially to the mighty Errtu, then bent time and space and was once more back in Faerûn, in a tavern called One-Eyed Jax, in the port city of Luskan.

◆ ◆ ◆

"WHAT IS WRONG?" Matron Mother Zeerith asked when Tsabrak walked into her private chamber—unannounced and without knocking. She could see the look on her most powerful ally's face, though, and so she knew he had not shown the disrespect out of anything more than abject misery.

"Tsabrak?" she demanded as he moved over and numbly sat down on a chair across from her.

"I looked in on the Silver Marches," he said, his voice a defeated monotone. "I went to see if I could confirm the areas where our other warriors likely fell. It would make the corpse summoning easier, of course, if we knew . . ." His voice trailed off.

"What do you know?" Matron Mother Zeerith asked, moving forward, sliding from her chair and across the floor to kneel before the seated mage, one hand on his knee, the other holding him by the chin, forcing him to look into her eyes.

"It's gone," he said.

Matron Mother Zeerith's face screwed up with confusion as she tried to decipher that. " 'It's'? What is gone?"

"The dweomer."

"The dweomer?" she echoed, but suddenly it hit her and her eyes widened.

"The gift Lady Lolth imparted through my physical form," Tsabrak confirmed. "The Darkening, Matron, it is gone."

"Gone? The sky over the Silver Marches is cleared?"

"The sun shines brightly," the despondent wizard replied.

"How can this be?" Matron Mother Zeerith looked all around. She rolled away from Tsabrak and up to her feet to begin pacing, muttering to herself. The implications were staggering. The Darkening had been channeled through Tsabrak, through a representative of House Xorlarrin, who had become the archmage of Q'Xorlarrin. Tsabrak was a powerful wizard—none would doubt that—but Zeerith wanted him spoken of in the same hushed tones normally reserved for Gromph Baenre alone.

The Darkening was the achievement that afforded him that possibility. The Darkening had elevated him in the eyes of all the drow. Few in Menzoberranzan would utter the name of Tsabrak Xorlarrin without the title of archmage attached.

But now it was gone.

Would the others see this as a sign that Tsabrak had lost the favor of Lolth, Matron Mother Zeerith wondered? Would they extend that criticism to House Xorlarrin, to Q'Xorlarrin?

"I felt the power," she heard Tsabrak muttering to himself, and she turned back to regard him. He sat in the chair, eyes downcast, shaking his head slowly.

"True power," he said. "The goddess flowed through me in beauteous power. She would take the Weave and make of it the Web. The new age would be heralded in, and I, Tsabrak, would lead that new age."

"You alone?" Matron Mother Zeerith asked sharply, and Tsabrak looked up at her.

"House Xorlarrin," he quickly corrected himself. "Who better? We have the most wizards. We—you!—have ever exalted in them, in us, in me, and have given to the males of your family hope unknown among the others of Menzoberranzan. I was positioned—"

"*We* were positioned!" Matron Mother Zeerith interrupted.

Tsabrak nodded. "But it is gone, Matron Mother. The skies are bright once more. And there were whispers . . ."

He lowered his gaze once more and looked as if he might break down.

"What did you hear, Tsabrak?" Matron Mother Zeerith demanded. "When you walked among the folk of the Silver Marches, what did you hear?"

"Mielikki, the goddess," he whispered. "It is said that she countered my magic, and did so through the body of the heretic Drizzt Do'Urden." He looked up as Matron Mother Zeerith gasped.

"I have failed the Spider Queen," Tsabrak said. "You should give me to the primordial."

Matron Mother Zeerith dismissed that with a snort, and waved away Tsabrak's words. "If you truly failed the Spider Queen, we would make of you a drider, fool."

"Then do so!"

"Shut up!" she ordered. She rushed back at Tsabrak and skidded down to put her face right near his. "You did not fail. The magic failed, expired, or was defeated. We cannot know which. How draining was it for the Spider Queen to hold back the light of the sun on the World Above? Perhaps she intended the Darkening for only a certain period of time, and when our people withdrew, what was to be gained by holding strong to it?"

"It pains me to think that our beloved goddess has suffered yet another defeat . . ."

"Enough of such foolishness," Matron Mother Zeerith warned.

"And one with which I was so intimately involved," the wizard said.

"We do not even know that it was a defeat," Matron Mother Zeerith reminded him. "We will continue our work in bringing home our fallen and properly disposing of them. We will give due thanks to the Spider Queen with our every action. We cannot know her thoughts, and so we act with only good intentions to her, our Lady of Chaos."

Tsabrak stared for a long time, but gradually began to nod. "Thank you," he said. "My shock—"

"Say no more about it," Matron Mother Zeerith interrupted. She pulled his head close against her and stroked his short, thick mop of white hair, comforting him, cooing softly in his ear, reassuring him.

But inside, Matron Mother Zeerith was anything but calm or reassured. Tsabrak's dismay was clear, and surely a straight line from it to the now-failed Darkening gave him reason to worry.

For Matron Mother Zeerith, though, that fear was multiplied a hundredfold. She was until recently the Matron Mother of the Third House of Menzoberranzan, Lolth's own city. She was a high priestess of Lolth, but she was not much like her peers, not the Baenres or the fanatical Melarni. Matron Mother Zeerith did not adhere to the hierarchy so common in Menzoberranzan. House Xorlarrin's power came from the men of the House, not the women, from the wizards and not the priestesses.

It had been Matron Mother Zeerith's hunch that this would be the new paradigm, and she thought her instincts correct when Lolth made a try for the goddess Mystra's Weave. She thought her efforts well rewarded when Tsabrak, not Gromph Baenre, had been chosen to enact the Darkening.

In the new paradigm, would any House hold higher favor with Lady Lolth than House Xorlarrin? Would not her new city become the glorious enclave of Lolth, and so Menzoberranzan would be the satellite?

But now the Darkening was no more.

And Q'Xorlarrin was burying scores of dead.

Zeerith had suffered great losses in her entourage, in her family.

Lolth was angry, Zeerith believed. Would she focus that anger on Q'Xorlarrin, on Tsabrak, on Zeerith herself?

She continued to stroke Tsabrak's hair for a long while, drawing as much comfort as she was giving, for what that was worth.

Matron Mother Zeerith, who understood well the wrath of the Spider Queen, feared that it wasn't worth much.

◆ ◆ ◆

ERRTU CHUCKLED, a wet and throaty noise that sounded as if it was soon to be accompanied by fountaining gouts of vomit.

"You are a beautiful one," he said to the small figure standing in front of him.

Off to the side, out of the swirling, fetid mists, came a hulking, vulture-like vrock, a battered drow form writhing in one of its powerful clawed hands. On a nod from the other drow female, a doppelganger to this very captive, the vrock dropped its battered prisoner and bird-hopped away into the shadows.

That drow, prone in the muck, managed to turn her filthy head to regard the other, the one that looked exactly like her.

But looked like her for only for a moment longer, as the imposter K'yorl burst free of that restrictive drow form to become once more a creature with the lower torso and legs of a gigantic spider, and the shapely upper body and painfully beautiful face of the most exquisite drow of all.

She held up her right hand, nodding contentedly at the small digits that had already regrown to replace the ones Balor's lightning sword had taken from her.

K'yorl whined and buried her face in the muck before the deadly brilliance of Lady Lolth.

"Your physical beauty is exceeded only by the beauty of your cunning, Goddess," Errtu said, grinning widely.

"When Gromph weakens the barrier, Menzoberranzan will know chaos as never before," Lolth replied.

"And you will rid yourself of the pesky demon lords, and when they have abandoned the Abyss to play in the Underdark of Toril, you will build your army," said Errtu.

"Beware your tongue, Errtu," Lolth warned. "Your betters lurk in the fog."

The mighty balor grunted, but nodded.

"We had all thought you defeated, Spider Queen," Errtu said. "When you lost the Weave, and then watched as Tiamat's plans, too, were foiled, we wondered, truly, if perhaps you would recede."

"In reminding me, do you gain pleasure, Errtu?" Lolth asked. "For I should remind you that were I to destroy you here in this place, your home, you would truly be obliterated, never to return."

"But it is a great compliment that I offer," said the balor. "For you have not receded, skulking into the shadows, and truly, great Lady of Spiders, great Goddess of Chaos, this ambition and plan are your greatest scheme of all."

"And you stand to gain," she reminded him. He nodded, growled wickedly, and smiled hopefully. "Did I not promise you that Balor would be removed? That you could thrive in his absence?"

"Unending ambition, great Lady of Chaos," said Errtu, who was clearly elated by the developments. "It is how we survive the boredom of passing millennia, is it not?"

"And yet, if you climb to the highest point you will ever know, it will leave you merely at the lowest point I have ever known," Lolth said, a most vicious reminder of their relative stations.

Errtu scowled.

"Do not kill this one," Lolth instructed. She waved her hand and a powerful roll of energy lifted K'yorl from the floor and sent her flipping and spinning through the air. "I might need her again."

"Kill her?" Errtu asked as if the very thought was preposterous. "Torturing her brings me great pleasure, Lady of Pleasure and Pain!"

"I feel the same way about balors," Lolth remarked, and she was simply gone in a puff of acrid black smoke. "And do take care that she cannot use her psionic trumpets to warn Demogorgon or Graz'zt, or any of the other demon lords."

Errtu sat on his throne and tapped his clawed fingernails together in front of his flame-filled eyes.

So much to hate.

That was his nourishment.

CHAPTER 3 ◈

Unusual Ascension

M E THINKING'S NOT CHANGED. FOUR THOUSAND'RE needed," Bruenor explained late that year of 1485 DR. Outside, winter was on in full, but in Mithral Hall, all seemed cozier than it had in many a year. The tunnels to Felbarr and Adbar were secured, and couriers moved between the three dwarven fortresses on a regular basis, with every new dispatch bringing news of growing excitement for the march to Gauntlgrym. The threat of the orcs felt far removed now.

"Might be more than that," King Connerad remarked. "Harnoth's had his griping, but Oretheo Spikes's been there, every hour, whisperin' in his ear. Now the young king's thinking that Adbar's best served by bringing the biggest force to Gauntlgrym."

"Might be that he's got his eyes on the throne," General Dagnabbet chimed in.

"That ain't for happenin'," said Bruenor. "But let the hungry young one think what he's thinkin' if it's getting me the warriors I need."

"If Gauntlgrym's all ye say, then might be harder to keep the three citadels o' the Silver Marches open and manned," King Connerad said, with something in his tone that gave Bruenor pause—and not for the first time over these tendays of anticipation. Bruenor looked to Drizzt, who nodded, obviously catching the other king's demeanor as well.

"So when're ye meanin' to speak it clear, me friend?" Bruenor asked pointedly.

Connerad looked at him with puzzlement.

"I'm knowin' yer heart, young Brawnanvil," said Bruenor. "As I knowed yer Da's, as I'm knowing me own."

By that point, all eyes were squarely focused on the young King Connerad.

"Ye ain't gettin' Gauntlgrym's throne," said Bruenor.

"Not wantin' it," Connerad replied.

"But . . ." Drizzt prompted.

Connerad sighed, snorted, and said nothing.

"But ye're wantin' to go," said Bruenor.

Connerad snorted again, as if the mere suggestion was preposterous. But Bruenor never blinked, and his probing expression would not let go of Connerad.

"Aye," the young king finally admitted.

"Ye got Mithral Hall," Bruenor replied. "We been through it, lad. I ain't for taking that from ye."

"Been all me life here in the Hall," said Connerad, and with that, Bruenor nodded his agreement.

"With half that life havin' yer arse on the throne," said Bruenor. "Weighin' on ye, is it? Aye, I know, lad."

"Weighed on yer own arse when ye left," said Dagnabbet, and there was an unmistakable edge in her voice that gave Bruenor, and some others, pause.

"Suren that ye're not for thinking that King Bruenor owed the hall more," Connerad scolded the general.

"Never said that," she replied.

"Then what?"

"Aye," Bruenor agreed. "What?"

General Dagnabbet swallowed hard, her deep breaths showing that she was at a crossroads and trying to find her heart. "Was me grandfather that chased the gray dwarfs from Mithral Hall," she said. "Was me grandfather and me Da that readied the throne for King Bruenor's return from Calimport, and was them that served well aside ye."

"Aye, as was me own Da," Connerad Brawnanvil said. "Served King Bruenor and the king afore him."

"Aye, and yer legacy's no greater than me own," General Dagnabbet blurted, drawing gasps from everyone else.

"Careful lass, he's yer king," Bungalow Thump warned.

"Me king who's wantin' to leave, he just said," Dagnabbet pressed. "As yerself's leaving to serve as Bruenor's shield."

Off to the side, Catti-brie chuckled, and when Bruenor looked from Dagnabbet to his adopted daughter, he noted Catti-brie nodding in approval to Dagnabbet.

"What're ye sayin', girl?" Bruenor demanded of the young but capable general. "Just speak it!"

"Me own claim on Mithral Hall's throne's no less than Connerad's, except that ye gived the throne to his Da, Banak," she said bluntly. Bungalow Thump wailed, but Connerad calmed him with an upraised hand. "And I'm not doubtin' yer pick o' Banak, as me own Da and Grandda were dead under the stones."

"But?" Drizzt prompted again.

"But me friend's not thinkin' Mithral Hall's needing a steward on her throne when I'm aside ye on the road to Gauntlgrym, King Bruenor," Connerad explained. "She's thinkin' Mithral Hall's needin' a *queen*."

Bruenor stared hard at General Dagnabbet, who matched his look without blinking, not backing away a finger's breadth from the accusation.

"Throne's not me own to give," he said at length, and both turned to Connerad.

"Queen Dagnabbet?" the young Brawnanvil mused aloud, and he chuckled and nodded. He and Dagnabbet had been dear friends for all their lives, military nobility in Mithral Hall's proud ranks. He turned to Bruenor. "She's speakin' truly," he admitted. "None're more distinguished, none more deservin'. If me own father'd had been killed to death in the Obould war, who'd Bruenor've chosen, meself or Dagnabbet?"

Bruenor shrugged, not willing to go there.

"If ye'd choosed meself, then me friend Dagnabbet would serve ye well, as she's served me well," said Connerad. "And if ye'd choosed to make a Queen Dagnabbet, then know she'd've had no more loyal friend and general than meself."

"And now ye're leavin'," said Bruenor. He turned to Dagnabbet. "And yerself's stayin'."

"Then Queen Dagnabbet," Connerad said to Bruenor, and he wasn't asking, for in truth, it wasn't Bruenor's—or anyone else's—place to offer an opinion. Succession was the choice of the king of Mithral Hall, and Connerad was the king of Mithral Hall.

"Are ye askin' or tellin'?" Bruenor did reply.

"Both."

"Then aye, and aye!" said Bruenor.

"Queen Dagnabbet!" Bungalow Thump shouted, and the huzzahs and heigh-ho's filled the audience chamber and exploded out to echo down the corridors of Mithral Hall.

Dagnabbet bowed respectfully, then stood up straight, seeming hardly shaken and looking every bit the ferocious leader of Mithral Hall. "Me first request's an easy one," she said to both Connerad and Bruenor. She smiled and turned to Bungalow Thump. "Once ye get done chasin' the drow from Gauntlgrym, ye give me back me Bungalow Thump. Mithral Hall's not to be without him."

"Honored, me king!" Bungalow said, punching his fists together. It took him a while to realize why everyone in the room was staring at him then, and with expressions full of amusement.

"Honored, me queen!" the embarrassed Gutbuster corrected, and Dagnabbet led the ensuing laughter.

◆ ◆ ◆

WHEN THE COUNCIL of the three dwarven citadels convened in Citadel Felbarr in the second month of 1486, Queen Dagnabbet was announced formally as the ruler of Mithral Hall, and King

Connerad, now shield general of Bruenor's impending march, did not even make the trip to Felbarr, busy as he was organizing the warriors Mithral Hall would send to the west.

King Harnoth seemed stupefied by the action, incredulous that any dwarf would surrender a throne, perhaps. He was young, Bruenor knew, and still a novice in the ways of being a king. The burdens would weigh on him in another century, likely, if he managed to stay alive that long—something of which Bruenor could not be certain, given Harnoth's recklessness in the war, and his stubbornness subsequently.

King Emerus, though, not only seemed less than surprised, his nod was one of approval.

A few moments later, when Emerus announced that he, too, would be abdicating his throne to join with his old friend Bruenor in the march to Gauntlgrym, the chorus of gasps were not enhanced by Bruenor.

"What am I hearin'?" Harnoth cried, in disbelief and clear dismay.

"That you are now the longest-serving dwarf king of the Silver Marches," said Drizzt.

"Madness!" Harnoth fumed, and he slammed his fist down on the table. "All me life, me Da spoke o' King Bruenor and King Emerus, and now ye're both for leavin'? We won the war and all the land's scarred, and now ye're leavin'?"

"Scars'll heal," Emerus said solemnly, his resonant voice showing that he wasn't taking this lightly. "With or without meself and Bruenor and Connerad. Felbarr's got her succession as Mithral Hall's got hers." He leaned forward and looked down the length of the long table, and Parson Glaive nodded, showing his king, who was now his subject, great deference.

"Citadel Felbarr is mine," the high cleric announced.

"Huzzah to King Parson Glaive o' Felbarr!" Emerus toasted, rising up and lifting his flagon.

"Huzzah!" all replied.

"And huzzah to Queen Dagnabbet o' Mithral Hall!" Bruenor cheered, and the boisterous shouts filled the hall once more.

Bruenor looked to Emerus and nodded, sincerely thrilled and grateful that his old and respected friend would be accompanying him on the journey to reclaim the most ancient Delzoun homeland.

"Mithral Hall on the first day of spring!" Ragged Dain added. "And let the ground shake under the fall o' four thousand dwarf boots!"

"Eight thousand, ye dolt," Bruenor corrected, hoisting his flagon so forcefully that half of the contents splashed out. "Most've got two legs!"

"Huzzah!" they cheered.

◆ ◆ ◆

"I SHOULD DESTROY you for coming here," the great white wyrm roared.

"You should reconsider your dangerous impulses," came a calm reply, and it was a sincere response from an archmage who had lived closer to two centuries than one, and who had come to the lair of Arauthator, the Old White Death, fully prepared to survive a dragon's onslaught.

"The attempts to bring Tiamat to the Prime Material Plane have failed, and so I understand your frustrations, great wyrm," Gromph added. "But so, too, has Lolth failed in her quest for the domain of magic. These are the provinces of the gods and we can do that which we may and little more. The world goes on, as does Arauthator, as do I."

"The philosophy of a weakling," the dragon replied. "To so dismiss failure."

"To so dwell upon it, when time moves forward," said Gromph, with a "tsk, tsk" and a shake of his head.

"You mock me?"

"I only mock those I consider pathetic," the archmage answered. "I have never thought that of you, surely."

"The world goes on without my son," said the dragon.

"Do you pretend to care? I know enough of your kind, and of you, to believe that such a claim is one of false appeal."

The dragon chuckled, a low and rumbling sound that sounded as if a prelude to an earthquake, and, Gromph knew, often was.

"You were rewarded well for your efforts in the war," Gromph reminded the wyrm. "The treasures from Sundabar alone . . ." He let the thought hang in the air, and shook his head.

"Then let us put that which is past behind us," the wyrm agreed. "So why are you here, in this, my home?"

"You were not alone in your last battle of the war," Gromph explained. "Nor was your son. We have found the body of the noble drow killed with Aurbangras."

"But not that of your impetuous and impudent nephew," the dragon commented.

"Tiago, yes," Gromph agreed. "A favored noble of the Matron Mother Baenre, though one who has grown tiresome to me."

"He is not."

"Digested?" Gromph asked dryly.

The dragon paused and spent a moment letting the quip register before offering an amused, rumbling chuckle in response.

"It is an honest question," the archmage said.

"He is not here, nor has he been in my presence since the battle above the Surbrin Bridge," the dragon replied.

"A battle in which he rode astride you?"

"Yes."

"A battle from which you flew directly home?"

"Yes."

"Must I follow all the possibilities?"

"Tiago was shot from my back in the fight, by a drow no less, with a bow that spat arrows of lightning."

Gromph took a deep breath. Drizzt again.

"Drizzt slayed him in the midst of an aerial battle?"

"I did not say that."

"You said . . ." Gromph stopped and silently recounted the dragon's exact words.

"The clever archer shot the cinch from the saddle, and so Tiago fell from his seat," the dragon explained. "We were up by the roiling blackness of Lolth's inspired spell, and so miles above the ground. You might search the lower ground north of the dwarven stronghold to see if you can locate a drow-shaped splatter upon the ground."

Gromph nodded, though he was hardly listening, playing it all out in his thoughts. He, of course, knew of the magical House Baenre emblems, which could impart near weightlessness with but a touch. So perhaps Tiago was not dead, and was down there still—and, likely, still hunting Drizzt.

"He is such a fool," the archmage muttered under his breath, but not enough so to keep the words from the keen hearing of an ancient white dragon.

"Which?" Arauthator asked. "The archer or your nephew? Or are you, perhaps, speaking of me, in which case I find that I am suddenly hungry."

"Dragon, you bore me," Gromph said, and waved his hand. With that movement, mighty Arauthator sprang to the attack, the great wyrm's serpentine neck sweeping forward, the toothy maw snapping over Gromph.

Or the projected image of Gromph, for the archmage was far from that place, and farther still when the dragon's killing jaws snapped, teleporting away almost instantly and leaving Arauthator defensively crouched and growling.

◆ ◆ ◆

"THEY WILL LEAVE on the first day of spring," Doum'wielle told Tiago.

"You are certain?"

Doum'wielle answered him with a stare. She wiped the mud and makeup from her face and began to unbraid her hair. She couldn't travel about the region without some minor disguise. Some might well recognize her as the daughter of Sinnafein.

"The dwarves are all chattering about it," she explained. "They're thick about the wall they have constructed near to where Dark Arrow Keep once stood, convinced that Lorgru will return."

"And will he?"

Doum'wielle shrugged.

"You should be more thorough in your scouting, *iblith*," Tiago scolded.

And I should kill you while you sleep, Doum'wielle wanted to reply, but did not.

"There has been no sign of the orcs since Bruenor sent them running," she answered. "Even those dwarves skeptical about this march to the west have come to believe that it will be a good thing."

"And what is in the west that is so enticing them?" Tiago remarked, walking out to the northeastern edge of the encampment, looking out at the campfires dotting the distant hills.

"Does it matter?"

Tiago spun around, his expression sharp.

"How long do you intend to play this game, Tiago?"

The drow inhaled, nostrils flaring, Doum'wielle thought, as if he meant to leap upon her and throttle her.

"*Duke* Tiago," she obediently corrected, and she lowered her gaze.

"Drizzt will be with them," Doum'wielle said. "And the woman, Catti-brie. Do not underestimate her. They whisper that she is a Chosen of Mielikki, and her magical powers, both arcane and divine, are considerable."

"Then she can properly consecrate Drizzt's grave," Tiago said, turning back to the campfires. "Even without his head."

Indeed, Khazid'hea said in Doum'wielle's mind, and the woman chuckled.

Tiago spun back again.

"You doubt me?" he said with a growl.

"The thought of a headless Drizzt amuses me," Doum'wielle said, and she wasn't lying.

"And you will amuse me," Tiago said and started for her. "Now."

Doum'wielle lowered her gaze once more, and when Tiago pushed her down to the bedroll, she did not resist.

Patience, her magical sword told her repeatedly throughout her ordeal, the long-plotting sentient weapon assuring her over and over again that she would get her revenge, but in a more profound and satisfying way.

A short while later, it was Doum'wielle's turn to linger at the northeastern edge of the firelight, looking out over the rolling hills to the campfires of the distant dwarven encampments. Despite her resolve to suppress her wistful nature, her thoughts drifted farther to the east, and inevitably out across the river. She loved the Glimmerwood in the winter, when the pine branches bent low under the weight of new-fallen snow. She thought of sleigh rides she had taken along the paths between those trees, the heavy canopy creating an enchanting roof of bending branches and multiple skylights, the stars shining through to evoke wispy sparkles all about the snowpack.

She heard the elfsong in her mind, the many voices lifting to the starlit sky, past the natural canopy, calling to the patterns of twinkling lights they had named for this creature or that. The Rushing Crayfish had ever been Doum'wielle's favorite, with a cluster of bright stars outlining one huge claw, dimmer stars showing the second as a smaller outline, as if the astral creature was reaching forward with that one claw, beckoning.

And it was a call Doum'wielle wanted to answer, then and now. Her eyes drifted up to the heavens, to a million million stars twinkling in the cold night.

There were no stars in the Underdark, in Menzoberranzan. It had its own beauty, surely, with the faerie fire limning the stalactites and stalagmites.

But it didn't have stars.

And the elves of Menzoberranzan didn't lift their voices as one to the heavens.

Patience, Little Doe, the woman heard in her mind. Images of great glory and greater power filled her thoughts, and she lost sight of the stars above as surely as if a heavy cloud front had swept in and stolen the eternal mystery.

Two tendays later, Tiago and Doum'wielle were awakened one bright morning by the sound of drums. Remembering the significance of this day, the pair rushed to a high vantage point on a steep-sided hillock, and peered against the glare of the rising sun to the southeast.

There marched the dwarves, under a banner of a living fire in humanoid form, its arms uplifted and holding a great anvil and throne.

The leading troupe crossed to the south of Tiago and Doum'wielle's position, their line stretching far back, with many pack mules, heavily laden.

And with a drow on a white unicorn trotting easily beside an auburn-haired woman astride a similar mount, but one that seemed made of the essence of light itself, spectral and sparkling.

Doum'wielle looked at Tiago, the drow fixated on the vision. His every dream marched in front of him.

◆ ◆ ◆

"WELL, THAT WAS unnecessary," Jarlaxle quipped when Gromph warped into the room where he and Kimmuriel waited.

"You think me frivolous?" There was a decidedly deadpan tone to Gromph's voice, as if the words were simply a prelude to a storm.

"Or foolish," Jarlaxle replied. "Why would you taunt an ancient wyrm?"

"You think me weak?" Gromph asked, with that most sinister edge to his voice that he had perfected over the centuries. And the storm clouds seemed closer to Jarlaxle. And darker.

"I think a dragon mighty, and fear you underestimate—"

"So now I am a fool?"

Jarlaxle sighed.

"He knew that he could escape instantly," Kimmuriel interjected, as he psionically imparted to Gromph, *Jarlaxle thinks it was truly you standing before the wyrm, and not merely a clever image. In that regard, you must admit that his concerns are valid. A dragon is, after all, a dragon.*

Gromph let his amusement flow back to the drow psionicist.

"With the psionic teleport you have taught him," said Jarlaxle.

"Taught?" Kimmuriel replied. "That is not the correct word. I have opened possibilities. The archmage has learned how to walk through those less-than-tangible doors."

"It is not the first time I have used this new ability," Gromph reminded them. "I find it . . . interesting."

"That you were able to concentrate so fully as to succeed speaks well of your discipline, Archmage," Kimmuriel said with a bow. "I am impressed that one of your meager training has come so far."

"I wanted to see if I could perform the teleport under extreme duress," Gromph said, his gaze darting back and forth at both of his companions, gauging their reactions.

"Well played, then," said Jarlaxle.

"You heard my conversation with the wyrm?"

Jarlaxle nodded.

"Tiago is almost certainly alive. Find him."

"I would hope to find his body. For that task, I would actually . . . well, search," said Jarlaxle.

"It was not a request," Gromph said. "Find Tiago. Put out your scouts, all of them. Tiago is alive and in the North. Find him."

"So that you can retrieve him for Quenthel and all will be forgiven?" Jarlaxle dared to reply. "And will you then betray my actions to our sister, brother, to better your own prospects in her court?"

He expected a tirade, of course, but surprisingly, Gromph did not react angrily.

"I'm not going to betray you for your role in bringing the copper wyrms to the fight," he said. "Not yet. But I warn you, do not give me reason to do so. I know what you did, *brother*. Never forget that."

Gromph paused and sighed, then said, "I go!" And he did, instantly disappearing from the room.

"A strange encounter," Jarlaxle remarked.

"Both of the archmage's encounters this day, I agree," said Kimmuriel.

"There is a sadness to Gromph," said Jarlaxle.

"Lolth lost her quest for the domain of magic."

"Worse, had she won, Gromph now understands that the benefit would have been reserved for the matron mothers and their female protégés. He stands at the pillar of his power, and knows that is not so high a tower in the City of Spiders."

Kimmuriel shrugged as if it did not matter, and Jarlaxle smiled knowingly. Kimmuriel, after all, didn't seem to measure his worth by such metrics. His reward was knowledge alone, as far as Jarlaxle could decipher.

"The archmage will find his way," was all Kimmuriel said, and he started for the exit from the cavern Bregan D'aerthe had taken as a base in the Silver Marches.

"It wasn't him," Jarlaxle said, stopping Kimmuriel cold just a couple of strides from the corridor. The psionicist slowly turned to regard the grinning mercenary.

"Standing before the dragon," Jarlaxle explained. "Do you think so little of me as to believe that I would be fooled by a magical illusion, a projected image?"

Kimmuriel started to respond, but bit it back, and Jarlaxle smiled knowingly, quite pleased that his psionicist friend was clearly realizing the context of his remarks. After all, Kimmuriel had only made the demeaning quip concerning Jarlaxle telepathically to Gromph.

And Kimmuriel had no reason at all to believe the Jarlaxle could so eavesdrop on a psionic communication.

Which of course, Jarlaxle could not. He had merely guessed regarding Kimmuriel's silent interactions with the archmage. But now, of course, given Kimmuriel's reaction, Jarlaxle knew that his guess had hit the mark.

"How many of our scouts will you need to find Tiago?" a shaken Kimmuriel asked, trying to change the subject.

"Just you," Jarlaxle replied, and the psionicist cocked an eyebrow suspiciously.

"If Tiago is alive, then he's after Drizzt, and so will not be far afield of Bruenor's march," Jarlaxle explained. "I have Athrogate and Amber already in place among Bruenor's entourage. Use your psionic energies to see through the eyes of those the dwarves march past and we will find Tiago, and so you can deliver to Gromph that which he desires."

Kimmuriel nodded and left, and Jarlaxle leaned back against the wall, considering the whole of that encounter. Something was going on that was beyond his understanding. Something with Kimmuriel, probably perpetrated by Kimmuriel, and likely involving Gromph. He wasn't afraid that Kimmuriel was trying to be rid of him to claim sole leadership of Bregan D'aerthe. Quite the contrary—Kimmuriel wanted Jarlaxle around so he did not have to assume the mundane burdens of such a role.

No, it was something else, Jarlaxle figured, something extraneous to him, something beyond the scope of, and purview of, Bregan D'aerthe even.

❖ ❖ ❖

SEVEN DWARVES LED the vast procession of the Silver Marches army from the Surbrin Bridge, marching in ranks of two, three, and two. King Bruenor Battlehammer centered the leading formation in the second rank, flanked by Bungalow Thump and Connerad Brawnanvil, with Amber Gristle O'Maul and Athrogate close behind as his personal bodyguards.

Two other bodyguards had joined Bruenor's personal entourage at the beginning of the march, gifts given to him by King Emerus Warcrown in his last declaration as leader of Citadel Felbarr. And to be sure, the dwarf lasses Fist and Fury—Mallabritches and Tannabritches Fellhammer—could not have been more thrilled at their permanent assignment, especially when their old friend Bruenor positioned them right in front of him.

Right in front of all of them, leading the march!

CHAPTER 4 ◈

The Physical Manifestation of Chaos

ATRON MOTHER MEZ'BARRIS ARMGO OF THE SECOND House of Menzoberranzan tried not to look shocked when, yet again, major demons entered the chamber of the Ruling Council.

"Is this to be the new normal, Matron Mother?" she dared to ask a very smug Quenthel Baenre when Nalfeshnee—a most horrid beast with a great rounded belly and leathery wings too small to support its great girth—wobbled out of the room, mercifully taking its stench with it. The ridiculousness of the bulky creature's appearance somehow added to the menace of the beast, as if Nalfeshnee and other demons of his type were intentionally mocking conventions of beauty. "Are we to be entertained by the antics of demons with each meeting, instead of discussing the very real problems we now face in the wake of the disaster in the Silver Marches?" Mez'Barris continued.

"Disaster?" the matron mother replied incredulously. "We scarred the land, sacked a great human city, and left the kingdoms of Luruar in disarray. And all for the cost of a few drow lives. Disaster? Do you think Lady Lolth would agree with, or appreciate, your description, Matron Mother Mez'Barris?"

"I think we gained nothing, nor did the dragons."

"That is your opinion. To my eyes, our journey to the World Above was well worth the effort and the cost of a few warriors, mostly males." She paused there and smiled wickedly at Matron Mother Mez'Barris. "And only a very few noble drow."

Only two, actually, they both knew, and both those fallen from House Barrison Del'Armgo, if the rumors of Tiago's survival proved true.

"Do the demons trouble you?" Matron Mother Baenre asked. "They are servants of the Spider Queen, are they not? The physical manifestation of chaos itself. We should consider ourselves blessed that so many have chosen to haunt our city."

Even Matron Mother Baenre's allies on the Ruling Council bristled a bit at that—except for Sos'Umptu, of course, who sat with the same smug expression as her sister the matron mother, and Matron Darthiir Do'Urden, the surface elf named Dahlia, who sat with the same blank stare that she always brought to council. The demons were growing unmanageably thick about the city, and bringing havoc to every House, even those of the Ruling Council.

Even House Baenre.

In that light, the others all understood that the only one benefitting from the presence of so many demons was probably Quenthel Baenre herself, her position growing more secure with the ever-present troubles distracting any who might plot against her.

But since they were all coming to understand this new reality . . .

"They are glorious creatures, gifts of the Spider Queen to us, the priestesses who have the knowledge and power to summon them," Matron Mother Baenre declared.

"They are summoning their own now," Matron Miz'ri remarked.

"Minor minions," said the matron mother.

"A pack of glabrezu marched past my gate this very day," Matron Mother Byrtyn Fey argued. "A pack! A score of the brutes. They alone could likely topple some of the lesser Houses."

"They are too undisciplined to so organize," Sos'Umptu Baenre said from the back of the room. "You need not fear."

"I do not fear!" Matron Mother Byrtyn Fey retorted angrily, standing and pounding her small fist on the spider-shaped council chamber in a most unexpected and very out-of-character display. She turned to stare hard at the matron mother. "My priestesses ask Lolth for the permission to begin banishing the demons, and the moment the Spider Queen gives her assent, I will make it my duty to cleanse Menzoberranzan of any Abyssal creatures who are not willing to submit to the will of the Ruling Council. Enough, Matron Mother, I beg!"

Quenthel stared impassively at Matron Mother Byrtyn Fey. She leaned forward in her chair, just a bit, and brought her hands up onto the table in front of her, interlocking the fingers. She didn't lash out, and she didn't blink, her posture and poise screaming at Byrtyn Fey to continue—and at the same time, warning the diminutive fool that she probably would be much better off doing no such thing.

Byrtyn Fey, who had witnessed the incarnation of Lolth's avatar at her Feast of the Founding, who had lost her House's high priestess, her daughter Minolin, to the favored Quenthel and House Baenre, was wise enough not to continue. She quietly slipped back down to her chair.

The matron mother was pleased at that. Quenthel had tightened her grip on the city and the council once again. Even her allies were none too happy. But they were paralyzed, all of them, by the threat of so many demons wandering Menzoberranzan. They were all, even Mez'Barris Armgo, so consumed by trying to keep their compounds secure and their nobles and other notables alive, that they had no opportunity to organize against House Baenre.

Because they knew.

The demons were Quenthel's doing, mostly, though now the creatures had indeed taken to gating in other creatures from the Abyss on their own.

And if they were Quenthel's doing, then she had done so with the blessing of Lady Lolth.

They knew.

Quenthel couldn't suppress her wicked smile.

◆ ◆ ◆

MALAGDORL DEL'ARMGO, WEAPONS master of Barrison Del'Armgo, cut a striking figure among the downtrodden of the Braeryn, the poorest and most crowded district of Menzoberranzan, a place so full of offal, living and not, that it was commonly referred to as *Quis'kenblum*, the Stenchstreets.

"Uthegental!" one sickly drow male said from a decrepit doorway, and when the weapons master spun on him, he fell away with a cry and gasp.

But in truth, the weapons master of Barrison Del'Armgo smiled upon hearing the name, the name of his great uncle, who, by Malagdorl's estimation, was the greatest weapons master to ever serve in Menzoberranzan. That very morning, under the guidance of Matron Mother Mez'Barris, Malagdorl had shaved the sides of his head and spiked the short top hair in a thick row, like a line of white teeth running from his forehead over his crown and to the base of his skull.

Matron Mother Mez'Barris herself had cooked the rothé udders to fashion the thick hair gel, and had added a bit of enchantment to it, Malagdorl believed, for she had chanted quietly when she had thickly applied it. Subsequently, he knew that it was more than pride that had swelled his already considerable muscles as the unguent had settled on his dark skin.

So, too, had enchantments been placed upon the other baubles given the weapons master of House Barrison Del'Armgo this day, the mithral ring piercing his nose and the gold pins stuck through his cheeks. These were not the same ones that had decorated the face of Uthegental, as those had been lost in the war with the dwarves in Mithral Hall, but Malagdorl didn't doubt the powers imbued in these replacements. One pin would close his wounds, while the other afforded great biting power to his square jaw, and magical volume to his battle cries.

Matron Mother Mez'Barris had been cryptic about the powers of the nose ring, but Malagdorl held faith that they were considerable indeed. She had promised him that it would prove the most valuable item of all if ever he found himself in dire trouble.

No replacement pieces were needed for the black plate armor and great trident Malagdorl carried this day, for these were the very armor and weapons wielded by Uthegental. How shocked had the young weapons master been the previous night when his matron mother had revealed to him the great prizes. How she had obtained them, how they had ever been recovered after a century or more, he could not begin to guess.

Nor did he much care. He was Malagdorl Del'Armgo now, not merely Malagdorl Armgo, granted the full surname by the matron mother of the House, in accordance with the honors given to Uthegental. Outfitted now with powerful items, he would carry on the tradition and live up to the savage reputation of Barrison Del'Armgo weapons masters.

He reached over the side of his subterranean lizard mount, his great trident held upright, and tapped the butt of the weapon on the floor, signaling for the others to halt.

The six elite guards did, dismounting efficiently and drawing their weapons as they fanned out wide about the weapons master.

Malagdorl commanded a garrison of a thousand well trained and magnificently armed and armored warriors, and among that regiment, these six were among the finest, all handpicked by Malagdorl himself.

He slipped off the side of his disciplined lizard mount and motioned to the drow warrior nearest the door where the sickly male had been.

That Armgo warrior rushed into the hovel, returning just a few heartbeats later with a terrified male, and with another couple of drow, male and female, as well. He herded them over to stand in front of the imposing figure of Malagdorl.

And it was an imposing figure. Uthegental's armor had not needed alteration to fit this huge and powerful dark elf. Malagdorl stood above six feet tall, and though not quite as thick as Uthegental—yet—he was near to two hundred pounds, almost all of it muscle.

"There are demons about, I am told," he said to the sickly looking drow who had named him as Uthegental from the doorway.

The poor fellow seemed confused, as did his companions, and he wagged his head about, scanning, then pointing to a chasme demon, like a huge and ugly rot fly, buzzing the rooftops along a nearby lane.

"Something bigger and more formidable!" Malagdorl scolded, and the drow shrank away from him.

Malagdorl started to reach out, thinking to throttle the Houseless fool, but a shriek from nearby stayed his hand and saved the sickly drow weakling. All seven of Malagdorl's troupe turned as one to regard a large structure in the midst of the rundown region.

The door banged open and out staggered another Houseless drow rogue, stumbling to the hitching post set in front of the inn, tumbling over it to lie twitching on the stone boulevard, thrashing from some internal agony, likely poison.

The sounds of swordplay rolled out of the open door, and more dark elves appeared, stumbling and scrambling to get away.

Malagdorl grinned and nodded at the door, and his troupe set off as one, ready to make their mark, for the glory of House Barrison Del'Armgo.

"A marilith," Malagdorl whispered as they neared the door and noted the demon wreaking havoc inside, with six arms swinging deadly weapons and that serpentine body slithering about.

Malagdorl reached his left hand into his belt pouch and brought forth fingers dripping with red dye, which he streaked across the left side of his face. He flipped his magnificent trident to the other hand and similarly dipped his right hand into a second pouch, this time bringing it forth dripping with yellow dye.

To the drow around him, all older veterans, he looked even more like the reincarnation of Uthegental. And so they followed him into the inn, into the waiting embrace of the six-armed demon.

◆ ◆ ◆

QUENTHEL BAENRE GLIDED through the corridors of House Baenre with her chin up and shoulders back, feeling no weight whatsoever from the myriad complaints rolling in at her and about her from the other noble Houses. They could only complain with a modicum of volume, for they all knew that Matron Mother Baenre acted in accordance with the demands of the Spider Queen.

Still, for all her resolve, the matron mother couldn't begin to manage a smile as she passed the servants and minor nobles. All bowed before her, many even prostrating themselves on the floor as she passed. Her dour mood, though, was not due to the demons but rather the child she now sought.

She moved into Gromph's private quarters, fearing no wards or glyphs, for he had given her permission to enter at her convenience—she was the matron mother, after all, and if one of Gromph's wards injured her, the retribution upon the archmage would be swift and deadly. Lolth had demanded no less from him, and as troublesome as Gromph Baenre could be, he would not, Quenthel knew, go directly against the Demon Queen of Spiders, particularly not in this place, House Baenre, where any transgressions would be fast relayed to Lolth's ears.

Inside the room, she found High Priestess Minolin Fey Baenre, standing at the ready, a spider-shaped dagger in her hand, a look of anguish on her pretty face.

She wasn't moving. She didn't even seem to be breathing. She just stood there, the knife held at the ready in an overhand grip, her legs anchored as if she had been moving with speed and intent, but had then been simply locked in place.

A spell of holding, the matron mother surmised.

And there was the child, Yvonnel, sitting on the floor and playing casually nearby, as if nothing were amiss. The sight disturbed Quenthel profoundly, for she knew the true identity of this child. This was Yvonnel, her niece, but so, too, was it Yvonnel, her mother. The illithid had gone to the child in the womb and had imparted the memories and insights of Yvonnel the Eternal, much as Methil had given the same to Quenthel.

Quenthel suspected that Methil's work with the baby had been more comprehensive than that which the illithid had given to her.

She stared at the baby playing casually on the floor while a high priestess with clear murderous intent stood frozen in place, helpless against the power the child could wield.

A high priestess!

But no, Quenthel soon realized, Minolin Fey's enchanted state was not the handiwork of the toddler, for within an antechamber, the matron mother noted some movement, and recognized, too, the source of that movement: a handmaiden of Lolth.

"Well met, daughter of Gromph," Quenthel greeted the child, who slowly turned to regard her.

"We have met many times, Quenthel," the child said, and Quenthel had to remind herself to suppress her anger at the lack of respect and the familiarity shown her. This was no ordinary child, no mere niece to the latest Matron Mother Baenre.

"Both in this life, and in mine past," the child said, and she went back to playing with the rothé bones.

"Your guardian?" Quenthel asked, motioning to the antechamber.

"Minolin Fey's, more likely," said the child, never looking up from her game. "Had the priestess continued her stalking of me,

I would have obliterated her. Still, I feel for the poor, confused Minolin Fey. I can hardly blame her for her frustration, even her murderous intent. Alas, but I have robbed her of her attempt at motherhood, so it would seem."

Quenthel's jaw hung open as she tried futilely to digest that ridiculous speech—especially ridiculous when she considered that this was the virtual reincarnation of Yvonnel sitting on the floor in front of her.

Sympathy? Mercy?

It was all for her, Quenthel realized, all to let her know how comfortably in control this matron mother in toddler's clothing truly was. Allowing Minolin Fey to live, given her clear treachery, was simply a reminder from this seemingly helpless baby that she was in complete control—at least in her own room. If not for Quenthel's approach, Yvonnel or her pet yochlol would have very likely destroyed Minolin Fey for her treachery.

Minolin Fey was alive now only because she served as a reminder.

Quenthel stared at the child, who didn't bother to look back.

But the matron mother continued to stare at her, hating her, wanting nothing more than to throttle the little creature. But she could not, of course, not with a yochlol in the other room, watching carefully.

And where did Gromph fit in to all of this subterfuge? He had once, not long ago, hated Quenthel profoundly, and had even conspired against her. She knew that, and it had been confirmed to her when the avatar of Lolth had shown up at House Fey-Branche in the Festival of the Founding.

But Gromph had been the one to bring Quenthel to Methil. In obedience to Lolth, Gromph had granted her such insight and power—would he have done any such thing if he was still plotting against her?

Now this, though, this little creature sitting on the floor . . . Gromph's child, and one the archmage no doubt hoped would supplant Quenthel as Matron Mother of Menzoberranzan sooner rather than later.

Would the archmage help facilitate that usurpation? No doubt, she realized, if the Spider Queen desired it, and no doubt even if the Spider Queen was not actively opposed to it.

Doubts began to swim in Quenthel's thoughts. This plan, this infant daughter imbued from the womb with the memories of Matron Mother Yvonnel the Eternal, seemed suddenly far beyond her, and far above her.

Was there any precedent for her abdicating the throne of Menzoberranzan to one more worthy? Of doing so without being murdered, or turned into a drider? Could she become again a high priestess of House Baenre under the leadership of this newest Yvonnel?

Do not entertain such thoughts! she silently scolded herself. She was the matron mother. She had found the wisdom of Yvonnel and the memories of the early days of Menzoberranzan, when demons, even great and powerful major demons, openly roamed the dark avenues. She had recreated this embodiment of chaos, and that after forcing unity in the city, sublimating Mez'Barris Armgo and stonewalling the plotting of several other Houses. She, Quenthel, had taken control.

"I hold her memories as closely as you," she dared to say to the child.

The little girl slowly turned her head and stared up at Quenthel with a smile so serene as to mock the matron mother's claim.

And the child could not be harmed.

But neither would Quenthel fear her. She decided that then and there.

"I am the Matron Mother of Menzoberranzan," she said, and before the child could reply or react, Quenthel turned and left the chamber.

She wondered what punishment little Yvonnel would inflict upon Minolin Fey when she came out of the magical hold spell.

Perhaps Yvonnel and her yochlol would murder . . .

"No," Quenthel said aloud, and with certainty. She looked into the memories of Yvonnel within her to understand the motivations of the Yvonnel in the chamber behind her. Little Yvonnel wouldn't kill Minolin Fey. Not yet. She wouldn't even punish the priestess in any serious way.

But Minolin Fey would know hopelessness, a dark pit from which she could never hope to escape. And from this point forward, the cowed priestess would no doubt prove to be a wonderful and attentive mother.

Because she now understood the consequences of failure.

◆ ◆ ◆

THE GREAT DEMON towered over Malagdorl and the other drow, even from across the open floor of the common room. Like everyone else in the room, the demon had turned at the remarkable entourage crashing through the doorway of the inn, noticing most obviously the startling warrior centering the newcomers, who seemed a reincarnation of mighty Uthegental, in his black plate mail and with that huge trident in hand.

Beside the demon, held off the floor in the squeezing embrace of her serpentine lower torso, a drow commoner grimaced in pain.

The demon took careful measure of the newcomers, saw Malagdorl, and her eyes sparkled with anticipation. In her flush, she squeezed tighter with her tail.

The captured dark elf's eyes bulged, and he let out a little wheezing sound.

"Have you come to play?" the demon purred. "Such big weapons. Such power and strength. I am overwhelmed."

"Are you done playing with the rabble?" Malagdorl said.

"Rabble?" the demon echoed. "You fancy yourself above them? What say you?" she asked the others in the room, all shying as much from the drow newcomers as from the demon.

"Oh, so you are a drow of importance," the demon said, when no reply came.

"I am Malagdorl Del'Armgo, weapons master of the Second House of Menzoberranzan," the drow proclaimed. "You will soon come to know my name as that of the dark elf who banished you from this plane for a hundred years."

"Do tell," she said, her voice taking on a gratingly sharp edge. Her snake tail unwound, spinning and launching the poor captive across the room to crash into the wall, where he slumped and melted to the floor, gasping for air. Each breath brought a soft cry, his broken ribs aching with the simple movement.

The demon's six arms went to her sides and back, and with the sharp hiss of metal on metal, six weapons came forth: swords and scimitars, a fat khopesh blade and a slender rapier. The weight of each weapon seemed to matter not at all to the huge and mighty demon, possessed of supernatural strength. She spun them about with practiced ease.

"And do you know who I am, Malagdorl Del'Armgo?" the demon purred.

"You are a marilith."

"No, fool, I am not merely *a* marilith. I am *Marilith*!"

Malagdorl puffed out his chest.

"Come, Weapons Master," Marilith teased. "Come and witness the glory of a true master of weapons."

The six blades in her hands moved in a mesmerizing dance. Malagdorl's entourage fanned out around him, three on either side. To a drow, they understood the formidability of this fiend they faced, but these were Barrison Del'Armgo's elite warriors.

They knew no fear.

With a nod from Malagdorl to left and right, the weapons master led the way. The noble drow warriors stalked in slowly, the commoners in the room all backing to the farthest corners, and Marilith smiling, her snake tail twitching, eager for the fight.

Too eager, Malagdorl thought. He and his entourage were elite warriors, veterans, and they had fought side by side for decades. Surely the demon in front of them knew this. Surely the beast was aware of the reputation of House Barrison Del'Armgo. The weapons master glanced around, expecting other demons—minions of Marilith—to leap from the shadows or crash through the walls.

When he noted nothing, Malagdorl leaped into the fray, stabbing his great trident ahead with a powerful thrust.

In from the sides came his entourage, six drow, twelve swords, rushing and circling, skipping ahead to strike, falling back with great agility.

Marilith's arms were a blur of motion, her weapons ringing against drow blades, parrying almost every strike. The khopesh swept three swords aside with a single parry, and the rapier darted in behind to drive the nearest foe back. Almost every strike was parried, and those few that got through did little damage against the demonic creature. From the waist up, Marilith appeared as a naked human woman, though gigantic. But her skin was surely that of a major fiend, and even the fine edges of masterfully crafted drow blades could barely dig in.

Her center arms on each side came together in a crossing motion, turning aside Malagdorl's powerful stab. Back out they went, nearly tearing the trident from the mighty drow's grasp. He staggered backward a few steps to regroup and secure his grip on the weapon.

And to let his lesser companions bear the brunt of the demon's initial surge.

Both lines of three became a weave, the drow leaping to and fro, swerving around each other, constantly changing positions and attack angles.

Marilith's blades worked furiously to keep up, and the ring of weapon-against-weapon became a continuous metallic screech.

Her tail swept out around her left flank, and the three dark elves leaped straight up and tucked their legs—one, two, three—dodging perfectly, and then again as the serpent tail rushed back and swept all the way around to the right.

The three dark elves on that side similarly began their evasion, but Marilith stopped and swung around, bringing all six of her blades to bear on the three now slightly off-balance on her right side, six swords meeting six, though with the strength of a major demon behind the attacking blades.

Her tail snapped the other way, whipping across, and up went the drow again. This time, though, the demon lashed out at them with a spell. She grabbed a huge table from across the room with magical telekinesis and hurled it at the agile trio.

Normally, they would have easily dodged, but now they were up in the air as the table hurtled at them, their twisting and turning less effective.

One got clipped and was sent spinning aside. A second caught the table under the arm and was taken with it across the room to smash into the far wall. The third, though, landed easily out of a spin and leaped right back in at the demon, his momentum carrying his sword hard into Marilith's lower side.

Malagdorl marked that soldier's name—Turven'di— for a later salute.

The demon shrieked and jerked about frantically, all of her swords coming to bear on Turven'di, overwhelming him and slashing him in short order, driving him back like a pathetic field mouse in front of a hungry fox. To his credit, the drow warrior did manage to parry the khopesh and another blade with his right-hand sword, neatly picked off a third blade with his left-hand sword, and partially deflected a fourth, turning the angle of attack so that it merely stung him as it grazed past.

But the fifth, an underhand cut, got him deep in the thigh, and with his lurch, he had no defense at all against the sixth.

An overhead chop from Marilith's top right arm brought that last weapon, a short, wide-bladed sword straight down into the hollow between Turven'di's neck and left shoulder. The weight and bite of the blow dropped him to his knees, but there he jolted, caught upright long enough for Marilith to sink the sword deeper and deeper, through flesh and bone, through his lung, tearing the side of his heart. A fountain of blood erupted as the blade disappeared into doomed Turven'di. The wound was mortal, but even worse, the poor doomed drow realized, his eyes going wide, this was an Abyssal blade, a soul-capturing weapon. Marilith let go and the sword transformed into a swirl of blackness that engulfed the dying drow, chasing him down to the floor even as the magic ushered his soul to the hopelessness of the Abyss.

It had all happened in a few blinks of an eye, but in the momentary distraction, the remaining elite guards went right back in. Marilith accepted their first strikes, but then met them, three arms sweeping back to engage those from her right, a fourth going at the warrior who had been clipped by the table, as she swung fully around.

Still back a few strides, Malagdorl saw his opening and in he charged, batting aside Marilith's last-moment attempted parry and driving his trident in hard between the demon's breasts. With strength beyond that of any other drow in Menzoberranzan, the nephew of Uthegental crouched forward and bore in, pressing and twisting.

Magical rage burst from the demon—every burning sconce in the room exploded in wild pyrotechnics, more objects came flying in from every angle—and the enraged Marilith sent her swords into purely offensive routines, giving hits to the dark elves around her and accepting strikes without apparent concern. Her tail lashed out left and right, then came forward to snap at Malagdorl, to wrap around him and lift him away.

The coils tightened around him. He felt his bones bending and crunching, but he tightened his great muscles and growled through it, watching his warriors leaping all around the demon, and seeing his trident still stuck deeply into Marilith's chest.

In a great exhale, Marilith unwound her tail, hurling Malagdorl across the room, where he shattered a table and chairs and crashed through the mushroom-stalk planking of the wall. All the other dark elves flew from her as well, her physical shrug accompanied by a burst of telekinesis and a wild sweep of tail and weapons.

Everything seemed to pause for many heartbeats, with Marilith slowly rotating to look at Malagdorl.

"Does it hurt, son of Barrison Del'Armgo?" she asked, blood pouring from her mouth with every determined word.

"You are banished, demon," Malagdorl replied, his voice pained. Every breath sent fire through his surely broken ribs. "A hundred years . . ."

"Not so long," the demon roared, and she laughed wickedly and simply melted away, the great trident of Malagdorl falling flat to the floor with a metallic *clang*.

"I will be waiting for you," Malagdorl threatened, and the voice of Marilith, the demonic spirit still hovering about the room, responded, "I know," and laughed again.

Six drow limped out of the common room and onto the Stenchstreets, dragging dead Turven'di to strap him across the back of his lizard mount. They were all bloody, some with serious wounds, Malagdorl so twisted and broken that he could barely hold himself in his saddle.

But he did, and he managed to straighten a bit with every lizard stride back across the city, his pride overruling his pain.

By the time they reached the gates of the city's Second House, another of the band had fallen unconscious, clearly near death, but the remaining guards and their noble leader spoke only of victory.

They had battled and defeated a major demon, banishing the beast back to the smoke of the Abyss. Indeed was this one a foul beast, especially so in the measure of House Barrison Del'Armgo, because they knew that Marilith served at the pleasure of Matron Mother Quenthel Baenre.

Matron Mother Mez'Barris personally greeted the victorious but battered group with spells of healing, and ordered a great feast in their honor, in honor mostly of Malagdorl, whom she proclaimed openly as the greatest weapons master of Menzoberranzan.

❖ ❖ ❖

"You did not kill the son of House Barrison Del'Armgo?" Lolth asked Marilith when they were together again in the Demonweb Pits.

"He will grimace in pain for many days, whatever spells the priestesses might employ, but he lives," Marilith assured her. "I killed only the one warrior."

Lolth nodded her appreciation. "And Malagdorl of Barrison Del'Armgo will be celebrated in many corners not loyal to House Baenre," she said. "Matron Mother Mez'Barris will be emboldened, surely, perhaps enough to even speak of this at the next meeting of the Ruling Council."

"I wanted to kill them all," Marilith remarked.

Lolth nodded again, certainly understanding and appreciating that this chaotic creature had stayed her murderous hands, had suppressed that which came so naturally to her, and instead had acceded to Lolth's requests—no small feat for a major demon in the heat of combat!

"It will not be a hundred years," Lolth assured her.

"How long?"

"Yes, do tell, Spider Queen of Chaos?" asked a third voice, and the two turned to regard the balor Errtu, striding over to join them.

"When the archmage diminishes the barrier of the Faerzress, you will find your freedom," Lolth promised, looking to Errtu.

"Freedom to kill the weapons master of Barrison Del'Armgo," Marilith said. She cooed, a discordant sound that resembled some strange cross between a purr and a hiss.

"Freedom to crush the son of House Baenre," Errtu growled.

Lolth just nodded and smiled at one and then the other, offering tacit approval. Their tasks would not be as easy as they presumed, she knew. For as chaos grew in her beloved city, the Houses would grow strong once more, ever on alert. Even creatures as mighty as these would realize in the dark elves formidable enemies—enemies aided, of course, by the blessings of the Spider Queen.

Marilith slithered away, but Errtu remained, and Lolth became keenly aware of his penetrating stare. She turned to him at last and noted his toothy smile.

"What do you know, balor?" she asked.

"You strengthened House Baenre under the matron mother," the beast replied. "You foiled me, and the plot against her, with my prisoner K'yorl. You gave to Quenthel the memories of Yvonnel the Eternal, and so tightened her grip on the City of Spiders."

"I needed unity and singular purpose."

"But now the dragons have failed. And now the Weave is beyond you once more, and so . . . you allow your minions to fall back to chaos. Indeed, you coax the city of Menzoberranzan back to a state of nervous chaos."

"Order bores me."

"Great risk."

Lolth shook her head and snickered.

"Will your children of Menzoberranzan not need that unity and strength when demon lords stalk the Underdark?" Errtu asked bluntly, and Lolth's eyes flared dangerously, warning him to silence. The Spider Queen calmed quickly, though.

"For some tasks, the drow are stronger in chaos," she replied. "And beware, always angry Errtu, for the Houses of Menzoberranzan will not suffer the whims of a balor."

That set the hulking Errtu back on his heels, and a simmering growl escaped his toothy maw.

"And beware now," she warned. "I will make of you a demon lord, or I will hang you in a cocoon beside Balor, to be nibbled by spiders until I decide otherwise."

On eight clicking spider legs, Lady Lolth walked away.

◆ ◆ ◆

THE CHEERS FILTERED through the dark and reached the House Baenre compound, where the matron mother and Sos'Umptu stood on a balcony, looking out across Qu'ellarz'orl, the noble section of Menzoberranzan, to the west and the sprawling compound of House Barrison Del'Armgo.

"I liked them much better when they resided in the Narbondellyn," the matron mother quipped. The Second House's move to this plateau in the city's southern reaches was a relatively recent event. "The family Armgo is a collection of peasants, and nothing more."

"They celebrate the triumph of Malagdorl, whom they fancy as the reincarnation of Uthegental now, apparently," Sos'Umptu remarked.

"Of Malagdorl and a company of elite warriors," came the fast reminder.

"Still, Marilith was no minor foe."

The matron mother turned slowly to regard her sister, her face locked in a mask of anger. "Would you like to go and join Mez'Barris in her celebration?"

The high priestess, Mistress of Arach-Tinilith and seated on the Ruling Council, did not shy away from the threat. "We must acknowledge the implications of this unexpected victory for Matron Mother Mez'Barris's fighting dog. Was there a greater demon in the city at this time than Marilith? And if so, if Marilith can be so readily banished, then why not the others?"

"Let them spend their time and blood chasing the demons about the shadows," the matron mother said evenly, her voice low, belying her expressed confidence. "There are other demons awaiting my call." She turned sharply on Sos'Umptu, before the other could remark that there might be, but now there was one less of this particularly devastating type of demon to be summoned.

"I am surprised by the descriptions we have heard of the fight," Sos'Umptu said. "Marilith did not call in any demonic assistance, and her use of magic was limited, apparently. Her pride betrayed her, so it would seem, but still, that one always before seemed more wise than proud."

"Clearly not," said Quenthel, though she wasn't really disagreeing with any heart, for she, too, had entertained some level of surprise regarding that very point. A creature of Marilith's power wouldn't normally fear a squad of seven drow, but Marilith had known Uthegental in centuries past, and so, too, understood well the power of Barrison Del'Armgo warriors.

Across Qu'ellarz'orl, the cheers climbed higher.

Likely there were more drow there than those of House Barrison Del'Armgo, Quenthel knew, and it wasn't hard for her to imagine what other Houses might have scurried through the dark alleyways to join in the celebration.

The matron mother nodded and reinforced her resolve. More demons, she thought.

◆　◆　◆

KIMMURIEL SENSED THE distraction in his student. He continued to guide Gromph through the mental exercises, holding fast his own mental barrier against which the archmage could throw his blasts of psionic energy.

Until this day, Kimmuriel had noted tremendous gains in Gromph's control and power, but psionic energies were contingent upon focus, particularly in novice users.

Gromph was distracted. His waves of energy barely challenged Kimmuriel's mental barriers. Kimmuriel doubted that Gromph could make a goblin stutter in its advance with this pathetic display.

The veteran psionicist didn't relay that disappointment to the archmage. Quite the contrary, his telepathic responses back to Gromph hinted of growing power and an impressive psionic assault.

Kimmuriel felt the acceptance of those compliments, but knew his time here would prove short.

And so, along with the compliments, he sent a suggestion, just a hint, that the psionic powers could be coaxed to work in conjunction with arcane magic. This would be no foreign concept to Gromph. The archmage had deigned to dabble in psionics with this very hope in the forefront of his thoughts—and why wouldn't the greatest practitioner of the Art not hope for such an enhancement from his newest "hobby"?

And with that hint, Kimmuriel gave to Gromph the beginnings of the spell he had been taught in the Abyss, the spell he believed would deliver K'yorl back to Menzoberranzan, where she could wreak her psionic wrath on House Baenre.

"Enough!" Gromph shouted suddenly, breaking Kimmuriel from his trance.

Kimmuriel blinked open his eyes and looked at his student, his expression one of puzzlement. "Archmage?" he innocently asked.

"What kind of fool do you take me to be?" Gromph said with death-like flatness.

A wave of panic rolled up through the normally composed psionicist, and he seriously considered teleporting from that room at once—though of course Gromph would chase him and find him.

"Spare me your false accolades," Gromph clarified, and it was all Kimmuriel could do to suppress a great sigh of relief. "I know I have failed this day." He strode away, to the small balcony of his room here at Sorcere, on the elevated plateau of Tier Breche, clenching and unclenching his fist as he went—and alternately producing a magical flame and crushing the life from it, one after another with practiced ease.

It was a minor spell, surely, but still, the notion that Gromph could enact it repeatedly as such an afterthought, like the magical doodle of a great artist, sent a shiver up the psionicist's spine. He considered again that which he had done in implanting the beginnings of K'yorl's spell—or Errtu's spell, perhaps.

Briefly, Kimmuriel thought himself quite the fool for even attempting such a thing.

"Have you seen them?" Gromph asked, pulling open the decorated door—all black adamantine, but worked with the flare more common to an iron grate, with swirls and spikes and rolling designs. "Have you seen them slithering all about the city?"

"The demons," Kimmuriel reasoned.

"The matron mother's demons," Gromph clarified, leaning on the balcony's railing, limned with purple faerie fire that rushed to engulf his hands as he grasped the bar.

"Can creatures of the Abyss truly belong to any other than their own whim?"

Gromph glanced back over his shoulder to regard the psionicist.

"They serve her simply by going about their business as demons," the archmage explained. "That is the beauty of the matron mother's design."

"Then more glory to House Baenre," Kimmuriel said, and Gromph snickered but didn't bother to look back, clearly not in agreement.

"I will return in half a tenday for our next encounter," Kimmuriel said.

"I will still be distracted."

"Then I will engage with the illithids before we meet again," Kimmuriel improvised. "Perhaps I can gain some insights into the ways of demons, perhaps of controlling them. You might gain advantage over the lesser creatures of the Abyss at least."

This time, Gromph turned to regard the psionicist. The archmage crossed his arms over his chest and leaned back on the balcony rail. The faerie fire engulfed him almost fully.

He didn't flinch. Kimmuriel could sense his intrigue.

"Half a tenday?"

The archmage nodded, and Kimmuriel stepped away, far away, stepped all the way back to the World Above and his private chambers in the city of Luskan along the northern Sword Coast.

Gromph, meanwhile, continued to lean against the rail for a long while in deep contemplation, thinking that perhaps he was beginning to see the greater benefits of this new pursuit of psionic training. The archmage pictured the Faerzress, the source of magical energies within the Underdark, the barrier between the material Underdark and the lower planes that lent this land its dark energies.

Many times before had Gromph pictured this place, and he had visited the Faerzress several times in his long life, and indeed had spent many days there once, when he was adding enchantments to his already fantastic robes.

But now he viewed the Faerzress differently, with a new spark of insight. Now he saw the extraplanar barrier embedded within those glowing stones.

A spark of psionic insight, he thought.

Gromph had not become Archmage of Menzoberranzan, nor had survived as such for centuries untold, by acting rashly, and so he threw aside any foolish notions of incorporating this thought into any such dangerous and formidable spellcasting as that of calling for a major demon.

For now.

CHAPTER 5 ◈

Bang Shields, Clap Flagons, and Sing Songs of War

ER TEMPO INCREASED, HER MOVEMENTS BECOMING sharper and less fluid, but her strikes more deadly.

Doum'wielle couldn't figure out exactly what the sword was trying to do. The sentient weapon was guiding her, telepathically prodding her—thrust, riposte, feint, parry.

Step back! she heard in her thoughts. She had not moved quickly enough for Khazid'hea's liking. Then she sensed the great regret of the sword, as if she, as if they, had failed. Before she could inquire, though, the sword was prodding her once more, the same routine, but now slowly again, and adding in the step. Over and over, building muscle memory.

Doum'wielle still did not question. She came to believe that this sentient weapon was preparing her for a fight with Tiago—or more to the point, she admitted to herself, she desperately wanted to believe that was Khazid'hea's plan.

The Baenre fiend had taken her again the night before, in the forest by the road now beyond the Silver Marches, the violation all the more wretched because she knew it was not wrought out of any honest emotions he held for her— that would still be bad enough!—but simply to remind her that he could take her whenever he wanted, for whatever reason he wanted.

She would love to feel her sword violating his body . . .

A jolt shocked Doum'wielle, startling her and jerking her upright, the weapon lowering as all strength seemed drawn from her arm.

You think in pedestrian terms, the sword scolded.

Doum'wielle took a deep breath and tried to steady herself.

Would you like to kill him?

Yes.

Do you think that would hurt him?

I would make it hurt.

She could feel the sword's amusement, silent laughter mocking her.

Tiago Baenre does not fear death, the sword explained. *But there is something else that he does fear.*

Doum'wielle spurned the obvious question, and instead she considered all that she was doing here, and Khazid'hea's grand plan. "Humiliation," she said aloud, and she felt the sword's agreement.

And she felt the call to get back to her work. Khazid'hea guided her again, thrust and parry, sharp and fast. She moved ahead, but only briefly, then quick-stepped back, holding balance, sword going out left-low and right-high in rapid succession. Though she was alone on the field, she could feel the parries as surely as if her weapon had actually struck steel.

Left and right.

And that clue, left and right, showed her the truth of this exercise. She understood clearly then that her sword wasn't preparing her for any fight with Tiago, who fought with one sword. Khazid'hea was training her to battle a two-handed opponent: Drizzt Do'Urden.

And Khazid'hea knew that drow ranger well, and knew Drizzt's companion Catti-brie even more intimately. She had wielded the sword, which she called Cutter, for a short time, long ago.

And Cutter had dominated her.

A question formed in Doum'wielle's mind, but she blurted it, not wanting to give the sword the satisfaction of reading it from her thoughts.

"Why not return to Catti-brie?" she asked. "You can control her and easily strike Drizzt down."

She felt the sword's seething response.

Doum'wielle dared a little laugh at her pompous weapon's expense.

"She is a Chosen of Mielikki now," she taunted. "She has progressed, grown stronger. Too strong for you, for you are the same. You know this."

Are you enjoying this? the sword asked. *Do you believe that you, too, will grow beyond me? Do you believe that I will let you?*

Doum'wielle swallowed hard. That was as direct a threat as Khazid'hea had ever given her.

Do you believe that you can grow beyond me, that you can succeed without me? the sword went on. *Will you seek your friends, your mother, perhaps? Not your father, surely, for he is a rotting corpse.*

To go along with the telepathic words, Khazid'hea imparted an image of Tos'un lying in the bloody snow, under the glaze of dragon's breath. At first Doum'wielle thought it her own memory—and in a way, it surely was—but then her father began to rot, skin sliding away, maggots writhing.

Wicked Khazid'hea had taken her memory and had perverted it.

One day. Doum'wielle reacted to Khazid'hea's questions before she could think the better of it.

Khazid'hea quieted her thoughts, and she felt as if the sword was leaving her alone then, to reason her way through it all. She truly did not believe that she could survive now without executing the plan, and she could not hope to do that without Khazid'hea.

Perhaps the sword was subtly within her thoughts, but Doum'wielle didn't believe so. She came to see her relationship with the powerful sentient weapon in a different light then, not as a matter of dominance and servitude, but each serving as a tool to help the other attain its desires.

Doum'wielle brought the sword up in front of her eyes, marveling at its workmanship and the sheer beauty of the fine-edged blade. The large flared crosspiece had been worked intricately and beautifully, set with a red gem in the center, like a wary eye.

Doum'wielle's own eyes widened as the pommel became a unicorn's head, then turned dark, the shape of a panther—Guenhwyvar!

Or was it transforming? Was it really, or was it making her see those images?

But it remained a panther. She ran her trembling hands over it and could feel the contours exactly as she saw them.

Her father had told her that when he had found the blade in a rocky valley, its pommel had been exactly this, a replica of Guenhwyvar's feline face. She had thought it an exaggeration, but indeed, the resemblance was striking.

Before her eyes, under the touch of her fingers, the pommel changed again, in shape and in hue, and became white.

"Sunrise," Doum'wielle breathed, and swayed, for now the sword's pommel looked like a pegasus, snowy white save a hint of pink in her flowing manes, with feathery wings tucked in tight and head bowed as if in sleep. Doum'wielle had loved that creature dearly. When Sunrise had grown too old to take flight, Doum'wielle had tended her, and when Sunrise had died, peacefully, a dozen years before, young Doum'wielle had cried for many days.

"She is with Sunset now," her mother had told her, referring to Sunrise's mate, who had been slain in the war with Obould, shot from the sky by the orcs.

A twinge of anger shot through Doum'wielle. How could she have ever sided with the ugly orcs in the war?

The thought flew from her mind—she was too taken with the image to realize that Khazid'hea had forced it away—and she focused again on the image of the pommel.

"As if in death," Doum'wielle whispered.

Peaceful sleep, Khazid'hea quietly whispered in her mind.

She felt contented as she continued to stare at the beautiful pommel—and truly no elf craftsman could have made a better likeness of the beloved pegasus. It was as if the image of Sunrise in her mind had itself formed the artwork now in front of her.

"As if," she said with a self-deprecating snicker. She realized then that that was exactly what had happened. Khazid'hea had found that precious memory and had "seen" it as clearly as Doum'wielle could.

And now Khazid'hea replicated the beautiful pegasus on its malleable pommel.

On the pommel of Doum'wielle's sword.

Her sword. Her partner.

She gave a little laugh as she considered her relationship with Tiago, who thought himself her lover, her master even.

But no. Her intimacy with Khazid'hea was a far greater thing, and one of mutual consent.

She knew that now. The sword would lead her to that which she desired. The sword would keep her alive. The sword would bring her to great glory.

Will you grow beyond me? Khazid'hea asked.

"I cannot," she said, and the words were from Doum'wielle's own heart then. "I will grow with you, and you with me."

I will not dominate you, Little Doe, the sword promised.

Doum'wielle slowly shook her head. *Nor I you,* she thought, and she believed. She stroked the pegasus sculpture lovingly. "You know my heart."

Soon after, they went back to their practice, and Doum'wielle's movements came more easily and fluidly, and she fought better than she ever had before.

Khazid'hea was pleased.

◆ ◆ ◆

EVEN BY DWARF standards, the squat stone buildings tickling the skyline above the tall gray wall of the city of Mirabar could not be considered beautiful. They spoke of utility and efficiency, and that was no small bonus to the dwarf mind-set, but even Bruenor, glancing upon them again from afar, from the field beyond Mirabar's closed gates, could not begin to feel the lift of his heart he might know when standing outside of the cross-walls and angled towers of Citadel Adbar. Even the city of Silverymoon, so reminiscent of elves, could stir a dwarf's heart more than this block of boredom.

But that was Mirabar, where the marchion and the great lords hoarded wealth in personal coffers instead of financing any gaudy displays of aesthetic pleasure. Mirabar was the richest city north of Waterdeep, famously thick in the spoils of vast mining operations. The overcity, what they saw now peeking above the wall, was but a fraction of the marchion's holdings, with a vast array of subterranean housing and mining operations.

"Bah, but we should no' have come here," Emerus said to Bruenor as they looked across the fields to the place—and could see already that the guards of Mirabar had grown animated, running all about.

"Are our brothers in there not Delzoun, then?" Bruenor answered calmly.

"Mirabarran first, I'm thinking, and few friends in there o' Clan Battlehammer and Mithral Hall," said Emerus, and Bruenor knew it was true enough. The marchion and his city had not been thrilled when the mines of Mithral Hall had reopened, nor had they been the best of hosts when King Bruenor had passed through this place on his return to Mithral Hall with the news of King Gandalug's death, more than a century before in 1370 DR.

Bruenor sighed as he thought of the good friends he had made here, though, of Torgar Delzoun Hammerstriker and Shingles McRuff, who had led four hundred Mirabarran dwarves to the cause of Mithral Hall in the first war with King Obould. And the Mirabarran survivors of that war had stayed and pledged fealty to Clan Battlehammer. Many of their descendants—none of whom had ever returned to Mirabar—were on the road now with Bruenor. He thought of Shoudra Stargleam, the human woman, Sceptrana of Mirabar in those long-ago days, who had come to Mithral Hall to fight Obould, who had given her life for the cause.

He thought of Nanfoodle the gnome, and he could not hide his smile as the memories of his dear little friend flooded his thoughts. He remembered Nanfoodle blowing up the entire ridge north of Keeper's Dale, launching frost giants and their war machines into the air in a blast that would have shown a bit of humility to Elminster himself.

Nanfoodle had gone on the road with Bruenor in his search for Gauntlgrym, and had served the dwarf as friend and ally throughout decades of dangerous searching. Many tears had slipped down the cheeks of Bruenor Battlehammer when he had knelt before the grave of Nanfoodle the gnome.

Nanfoodle of Mirabar.

"All them dwarfs o' Mirabar who put their Delzoun blood afore Mirabar came to yer side in the Obould War," Emerus said. "Them that stayed here stayed in fealty to the marchion o' Mirabar."

"That was a hunnerd years ago."

"Aye, and so ye're more removed from them than e'er," said Emerus. "Mirabar's ne'er been friend to the citadels o' the Silver Marches. She's held her love o' trade with the Sword Coast above any loyalty to fellow dwarfs!"

"Bah, they were just knowin' that our weapons and armor were better than they could be makin'," said Bruenor. "And our mithral bars more pure. If them lords o' Waterdeep got a gander o' Adbar mail or Felbarr swords, or the purest mithral that gived me own hall her name, then Mirabar'd become no more than a trading post where east'd be meetin' west!"

"Aye, me friend," Emerus said, and he clapped Bruenor on the shoulder. His smile didn't last, though, and he quickly grew more somber.

"They've not changed their song about ye," he said. "We might still be turning aside, tellin' 'em that our road's to the north and Icewind Dale."

"The dwarfs o' Mirabar're Delzoun," Bruenor said. "They got a right to know. They got a right to come along and fight for our home, for the Throne o' the Dwarf Gods and the ancient Forge that burns with the power of a primordial beast o' fire. A fine Delzoun leader I'm being if I walk aside this place without leavin' the truth!"

His mounting speech fell off when he noted the approach of Drizzt, Catti-brie, Ragged Dain, and Connerad Brawnanvil.

"If ye're tellin' the dwarfs o' Mirabar, ye're tellin' the marchion and all the rest," Emerus reminded. "Them humans in Mirabar ain't much for likin' Mithral Hall or yourself, even if they're not believin' ye're who ye say ye be. They owe ye no loyalty and so ye should be expectin' none."

"I ain't."

"And where're ye thinkin' the news'll go?" Emerus said.

"Right to the Sword Coast," Drizzt interjected.

"Aye," said Emerus. "To Waterdeep and to Neverwinter, and no doubt them dark elves in Gauntlgrym've got spies all about, and agents in Neverwinter. And so if ye go into Mirabar and tell the dwarfs the truth o' yer—of *our* march, then ye're likely tellin' them drow that we're coming for 'em!"

"Aye, and so be it," said Bruenor, and he strode forward to step up a low bluff and better view the distant city. "We got four thousand Delzoun dwarfs standing behind us. Them drow'll know we're comin' long afore we're crossin' the underground lake to Gauntlgrym's top door. And so be it. Once we got the top floor and the throne, we'll chase them into the Underdark."

"It is one drow House," Drizzt said to Emerus. "Powerful with magic, but not numerous."

"How many?"

"They will have slaves to fight for them—goblins and . . ."

"How many drow?" Emerus pressed. "Not much worried for goblins and the like."

"I have not been to Menzoberranzan in more than a century, but from what I knew, perhaps two hundred drow in House Xorlarrin, perhaps three hundred. Many are wizards, though, and no minor practitioners of the Art."

"Couple hundred," Emerus mulled, and he looked to Ragged Dain and chuckled. "Go to Mirabar, Bruenor," he said. "Come on then, I'll be right aside ye."

He waved to the others to follow, but Drizzt stepped back.

"Mirabar will not have him," Catti-brie explained. "Or they would not when last he passed this way."

"Bah, been a hunnerd years!" said Bruenor.

But Drizzt was shaking his head, for it had not been a hundred years since he had last futilely approached Mirabar's imposing, and closed, gates. But it didn't matter anyway. He wasn't about to put his pride and stubbornness ahead of the good of the expedition. "Better that I remain here," he said. "Perhaps I'll scout ahead along the western road while you finish your business."

Bruenor and Drizzt shared a long look of complete understanding, both ways, the dwarf nodding his agreement, the drow responding in kind.

"I'll go with you," Catti-brie said, but Drizzt shook his head.

"Bruenor will need you."

The woman agreed with a sigh. She missed Wulfgar and Regis then—they all did. She didn't like having to leave Drizzt alone with the harsh reality of the prejudiced world lifting its dark wings once more, and she couldn't argue the truth of his statement that Bruenor would need her.

"If the marchion o' Mirabar's speakin' one ill word of ye, or of me husband," she said in her best Dwarvish accent, "then I'm turning him into a frog and squashing him flat on the floor, don't ye doubt!"

She stormed ahead to the southwest, toward the distant city, and all the others were smiling widely as they trotted to catch up.

Drizzt was smiling, too, so glad to have this woman in his life. He grasped the unicorn pendant on the chain around his neck, thinking to call in Andahar, but paused as the rest of the entourage hustled to catch up to the principals.

Athrogate and Ambergris trotted side by side and very close to each other, often bumping and always laughing, and Drizzt was glad for that.

The sisters Fellhammer, Fist and Fury, seemed in a bit of a race to see who could get to Bruenor's side first.

They had been doing that a lot along this march, Drizzt had noted, and he wondered then if his old friend would perhaps find something in this life that had somehow eluded him for most of his last existence.

When the ranger looked at Catti-brie, and considered his own good fortune, he hoped that to be the case.

◆ ◆ ◆

THOUGH FROM A long distance, Drizzt was visible to the two. However, even with the sun far behind them, lowering in the west, and even with some overcast dulling its brilliance, Tiago had to squint hard. He wasn't enjoying the World Above as much now that Tsabrak's Darkening was no more.

He and Doum'wielle crouched atop a hillock and looked back to the east at the vast dwarf army. And now they saw the unicorn, thundering past the ranks as the dwarves set up their encampment, riding out to the southeast toward the road.

"He goes to scout," Tiago said, grinning with every word. "Perhaps it is time to claim my prize." He went up to his hands and knees and began to crawl back from the lip of the hillock, taking great caution even though it would have been next to impossible for any of the enemy force to spot him among the trees at such a distance.

Doum'wielle noted that caution, and wisely mimicked it—wisely, because she saw the intensity of the look on Tiago's face and knew that if she in any way compromised his plans, he would more likely murder her than simply beat her.

And yet, that is exactly what we will do, Khazid'hea whispered in her thoughts, in response to her fears.

"Quick to the road," Tiago instructed. "We can intercept him."

"Astride a great steed that will leap past us or trample us down," Doum'wielle said, hustling to keep up.

"He'll do no such thing to an elf of the Moonwood," Tiago said slyly.

But Doum'wielle was shaking her head. "Drizzt knows me, and knows my mother well. No doubt he has seen much of her these past months of war, and she will surely have told him of her wayward Little Doe."

Tiago's eyes narrowed as if he wanted to strike out at her, and she was confident that he certainly did.

"You will intrigue him!" he said, a bit too desperately. "Disguise yourself as we go. Or tell him that you escaped the clutches of his foul kin. I am sure you could easily offer that lie. Just look into your heart."

The last part had Doum'wielle slowing and staring hatefully at her vile companion, to the point where Tiago skidded to a stop and swung around to face her.

"Faster!" he demanded.

Doum'wielle didn't dare disobey, but Tiago's suggestions rang in her thoughts as a clear warning, and an offering that he knew how much she hated him. Thus, she knew, he was telling her rather clearly that she would not catch him off his guard.

Patience, Khazid'hea's telepathic voice whispered soothingly.

Doum'wielle picked up her pace, running hard and closing in on Tiago. As she neared, though, the drow suddenly skidded to a stop again, and held up his hand to hold her back. She slowed and stopped, and followed Tiago's gaze to the southwest. At first she saw nothing, but Tiago's sniffing tipped her off.

Smoke.

There was a campfire down along the road.

They moved more cautiously, Tiago turning directly south to intercept the road. They hadn't quite arrived there when they heard the passage of a horse—of a unicorn! Drizzt had passed them by.

Tiago continued, but slowly and cautiously. He held out one hand, fingers working in the silent drow language.

A flustered Doum'wielle, with only rudimentary knowledge of the hand language, couldn't keep up, but she thought he was indicating that they'd lay in wait and catch the ranger on the way back.

A shout, then, from not so far to the west, a chorus of dwarf voices, made Doum'wielle doubt that.

◆ ◆ ◆

THEY WERE ALL standing as he neared, close to fifty dwarves, weapons in hands, and all wearing an expression showing that he or she was more than ready to wield a sword, or pick, or battle-axe.

"Far enough!" one barked.

Drizzt held up his hand and backed Andahar a couple short steps. He looked at the group curiously for a few moments, thinking that he recognized more than one.

"Icewind Dale," he said.

"Ah, but it's Drizzt Do'Urden!" said one, a round-bellied, sturdy fellow Drizzt knew to be Hominy Pestler.

"Aye, o' House Do'Urden!" another chimed in, in unfriendly tones.

"Wh-what?" Drizzt stammered and he looked from dwarf to dwarf, noting that few expressions had softened with the recognition. Something was wrong. These dwarves were a long way from home, and this was a sizable fraction of the clan settled under Kelvin's Cairn in Icewind Dale.

And Stokely Silverstream was not among their ranks.

"Why are you here?" Drizzt asked.

"Might be askin' yerself the same question, drow," answered another, a yellow-bearded fellow with a long scar down one cheek and a blue eye dulled by the scrape of a blade, now filmy and barely functional.

Drizzt knew this one, as well. "I am here with King Bruenor, Master Ironbelt," he replied. He swiveled in his seat and pointed back to the east. "With Bruenor and Emerus Warcrown, and four thousand shield dwarves. We have fought a war in the Silver Marches against hordes of orcs and giants, drow of my home city, and even a pair of white dragons."

The dwarves seemed taken aback at that remark—clearly from their reactions, they had not heard of the war—and so another theory Drizzt held of why they might be this far from home was lost.

"Yerself's been fightin?" Master Toivo Ironbelt asked.

"For a year," Drizzt replied.

"We heared rumors in Waterdeep."

"Waterdeep?"

"We had ourselfs a fight, too, elf," Ironbelt said. "A fight with drow. Drow sayin' they come from House Do'Urden, saying they're yer kin."

Drizzt slid off the side of Andahar to the ground and approached the dwarves. "They said the same here," he admitted, holding out his hands, far from the hilts of his deadly blades. "If you think me complicit, then take me as your prisoner back to the west, to King Bruenor."

"We was heading to Mirabar," Hominy chimed in. "To learn what we might o' Mithral Hall."

"Bruenor is there now, meeting with the marchion." Drizzt held his arms out in front of him, crossed at the wrist, inviting a rope if Ironbelt so desired.

"Nah, put 'em back," the dwarf said. "And well met to ye again, Master Drizzt Do'Urden."

"You have a tale to tell," Drizzt said thoughtfully.

"Aye, and not a good one."

"How many of Clan Battlehammer remain in the shadows of Kelvin's Cairn?" Drizzt asked, and he was afraid that he knew the answer.

Still, when Ironbelt confirmed that these were the last of the Clan Battlehammer dwarves of Icewind Dale, save a score who had moved to Bryn Shander and a couple of the other towns, Drizzt found it hard to breathe. An era had ended, brutally, he realized, as Ironbelt detailed the drow raid that had killed so many and taken so many more away into the Underdark.

"We put together a force and followed 'em," Ironbelt explained. "Aye, and the folk o' Ten-Towns came out in force to help us. But there weren't no trail."

"They went back to Gauntlgrym," Hominy added.

"Aye, and dropped the tunnels behind 'em, and we could'no find another way," Ironbelt explained. "We spent a long time tryin', don't ye doubt."

"I do not doubt you at all, of course," Drizzt replied. "And now you've deserted the tunnels beneath Kelvin's Cairn? Seeking Bruenor, I would expect."

"Aye, we went to Waterdeep, and there spent the winter," Ironbelt answered. "We tried to find another way to get back to Gauntlgrym . . ."

"This group alone? You would have been slaughtered to a dwarf."

Some of them bristled at that.

"A drow noble House has entrenched itself in the bowels of Gauntlgrym," Drizzt started to explain, but he was cut off by Hominy's remark.

"House Do'Urden!"

"No, House Xorlarrin, more grand and powerful by far than anything House Do'Urden had ever achieved," Drizzt said. "Thick with magic and soldiers, and with many hundreds of goblin and kobold slaves."

"Don't mean we wouldn't try!" Toivo Ironbelt insisted.

"No, of course not, and I would expect no less from Clan Battlehammer. But you'll be trying with better odds, my friend. King Bruenor has assembled a mighty force, and Gauntlgrym is his goal. Come, I'll take you to your kin, and you can tell your tale to Bruenor."

◆ ◆ ◆

"Curse the gods," muttered Tiago, he and Doum'wielle on a bluff overlooking the road, where Drizzt had just passed with fifty dwarves in tow on his way back to the army.

"We know their destination now," Doum'wielle said, for the dwarves had taken up a cheer of "Gauntlgrym!" right before they had broken camp.

"You didn't know it all along? Fool. Why would such an army of three kingdoms, all fresh from a difficult war, begin such a march? Could there be any doubt?"

He raised his hand as if to strike her, but Doum'wielle shrank away quickly.

Tiago turned back to the road, and the now-distant Drizzt and company. He knew that duty called for him to flee back to Menzoberranzan and warn the city of the dwarves' march on Q'Xorlarrin—but he had known that since first he had learned of the army assembled outside of Mithral Hall back in the Silver Marches.

It wouldn't matter—the extra tendays Tiago might offer to the Xorlarrins and their allies to prepare paled beside the trophy that now rode away from him down the road. Drizzt was acting as a scout for the dwarves, so it seemed, and so Tiago decided to bide his time, to continue to shadow the force.

He'd get his chance at Drizzt before they reached Q'Xorlarrin, he hoped. And if not, he'd find his way inside the complex ahead of the dwarves and kill Drizzt in the tunnels.

He glanced back at Doum'wielle. His first instinct was to go over and take out his frustrations on her. But Tiago realized that he'd need her if Drizzt was out scouting on that magnificent unicorn he rode.

"Patience," Tiago whispered to himself, much the way Khazid'hea had whispered to Doum'wielle.

◆ ◆ ◆

BRUENOR, WHO HAD experience with a similar marchion a century before, wasn't much surprised by the cold shoulder offered him in Mirabar. Indeed, on that previous occasion, those dwarves who had left Mirabar to join in Clan Battlehammer's war with the first Obould had done so as an act of treason against Mirabar, according to then-Marchion Elastul.

Nothing that had happened since those days had given Bruenor any reason to believe that the atmosphere of rivalry and ambivalence between Mirabar and Mithral Hall would be any bit improved.

"Every time a representative of Mithral Hall appears at our gates, it is to ask for help," Marchion Devastul answered when Bruenor and King Emerus had explained their march, after an exhaustive introductory meeting that contained more niceties and nonsense than anything Bruenor had ever imagined possible. "You would have me offer free run to the dwarves of Mirabar to join in with your . . . quest? The cost to Mirabar would be enormous, of course, and you understand that, of course. Are Citadel Felbarr, Citadel Adbar, and Mithral Hall offering to pay me to keep my coffers balanced while my loyal subjects are off playing war with an old king, a young whatever you are, and the soldiers of Adbar, whose ruler thinks so much of this expedition that he didn't deign to join it himself?"

The advisers around the marchion, including the city's newest sceptrana, all had a good chuckle at the preposterous proposition Devastul had just outlined. Mirabar was a rich city, her lords and ladies well luxuriated, and in no small part because of their industrious dwarf workforce, nearly two thousand strong.

"Me kin here in Mirabar are Delzoun," Bruenor said. "I'm thinkin' ye're to find a bit o' wrath if ye're to deny them the chance to march for their ancient home. The warmth o' Gauntlgrym's in the blood o' every dwarf, the hope o' findin' it's in the dreams of every dwarf. And now I found it, and so we're to take it back."

"Of course, and you are the reincarnation of King Bruenor Battlehammer," the sceptrana said with obvious, and amused, skepticism.

"Aye, and Gauntlgrym's a choice for any dwarf that goes deeper than the place he's now callin' home," Emerus added, and there was no mistaking the edge that had come into his voice. "I gived up me crown—or are ye doubtin' me own name as well?"

"Your sanity, perhaps," the sceptrana dared to remark, and Ragged Dain bristled at Emerus's side.

"No, I know you, King Emerus, of course," Marchion Devastul said. "Though yes, I question the . . . wisdom, of your choice. This seems a rather eccentric quest, particularly in this time so soon after war. Wouldn't you agree?"

"What happened before's not to matter," said Emerus. "The road afore us is clear."

"You leave your fortresses vulnerable—"

"Orcs're gone and not coming back," Bruenor interrupted, his voice reflecting his rising temper. "The Marches are blasted, but sure to mend, and there're enough in all the dwarf homes to hold off anything that's coming."

"And two kings, Emerus and Connerad, won't be there to lead if something does come," said the sceptrana.

"Two kings replaced," Emerus replied. "And enough o' yer snickerin' and thin-veiled insults, good woman. We're marchin' to Gauntlgrym, and we're not needin' yer permission. We thinked to stop here that ye might be givin' yer dwarfs the choice to join in—suren this is a quest that every Delzoun lad or lass should—"

"But you did not empty Felbarr, or Adbar, or Mithral Hall," Marchion Devastul declared in a bold tone that stopped the conversation short.

"We bringed four thousand," Emerus replied after a few moments of silence.

"Why four? Why not the twenty thousand of Adbar, the seven thousand of Felbarr, the five thousand of Mithral Hall?" Devastul asked. "Those are the correct numbers, yes? You could have marched past Mirabar with thirty thousand dwarves, yet you arrive with four thousand—and you ask me to empty my city of the great value of craftsdwarves? Are the forges of Adbar cool? Are the hammers of Felbarr silent? Are the picks silent and untended in the mines of Mithral Hall? Is this a quest for Gauntlgrym, or a ruse to gain economic advantage over a rival city?"

"Bah, but ye really are the descendant of Elastul," Bruenor snorted. "Good to see the line's only gotten stupider."

Several fists banged on the table, and more than one of Devastul's guards edged in closer, and for a few heartbeats, it seemed as if a fistfight was about to break out. But then came a calming voice, one that carried more than a bit of magical weight in its timbre.

"Even were all the dwarves of Mirabar to join us, the city would remain defended, the mines tended, and the forges hot," Catti-brie interjected. "What you speak of would be the abandonment of three established cities, something that would be foolish, of course. Adbar, Felbarr, and Mithral Hall have responsibilities to the other kingdoms of Luruar."

"The alliance of Luruar is in ruins," the sceptrana snidely put in, but Catti-brie just talked over her.

"Sundabar has been reduced to rubble. But she will be rebuilt with no small help from the dwarves of the Silver Marches," she said. "The orcs are chased away, but no doubt roaming bands will return to the south to cause mischief—and they will be met and defeated by the elves of the Glimmerwood and the dwarves of Delzoun long before they near the work at Sundabar, or the gates of Silverymoon, or the markets of Nesmé."

That last reference brought a bit of a wince to the marchion, and even to the sceptrana, Bruenor noticed, for while they could so flippantly insult the dwarven citadels, or any of the other kingdoms of the Silver Marches, that little town of Nesmé had become a critical trading post for Mirabar. It was quite clever of Catti-brie to bring the ruined city into the conversation, the dwarf realized.

"Yes, Nesmé," she continued. "The city was flattened by the orcs, with eight of every ten citizens killed. But the survivors have vowed to rebuild, and principal among their backers are Silverymoon and Mithral Hall, even now, even after the march of the dwarves has depleted the numbers in Mithral Hall. You would be wise to help us in those efforts, Marchion of Mirabar, for surely you desire to see the markets of Nesmé opened soon, even this very season, in some manner."

The man had no flippant replies this time, and even nodded slightly.

"It is time to stand together, for all our sakes," Catti-brie said.

"Yet you run off to the Sword Coast," the marchion replied.

"To Gauntlgrym," Catti-brie was fast to answer, before any of the dwarves could respond. "I've been there. I've seen the Forge, and have met the beast that fires it. Know, Marchion, that when Gauntlgrym is reclaimed and renewed, the weapons and armor, and all else that flows from the primordial forges will alter the balance of trade in Faerûn."

All on the Mirabar side of the table stiffened at that prospect, which surely seemed bleak to a city that had made its great wealth through its mining and crafting.

"The dwarves left behind in the Silver Marches are as important to the reclamation of Gauntlgrym as those marching with Bruenor and Emerus," Catti-brie said. "They know it, and we had to hold lotteries to determine which of the volunteers would be granted a place on the march, and which disappointed dwarves would have to remain behind to hold down the homeland in the months or years of transition. Once Gauntlgrym is renewed, Mithral Hall, Citadel Felbarr, and Citadel Adbar will diminish greatly, will become outposts of the Delzoun mining empire."

Not Adbar, Bruenor thought, but did not say. He was fairly certain that young King Harnoth would not soon swallow enough of his overblown pride—or perhaps it was just his enduring scars and grief—to subjugate his family's accomplished citadel to the greater Delzoun alliance. Felbarr and Mithral Hall would indeed become satellite cities of Gauntlgrym. Queen Dagnabbet remained a loyal Battlehammer above all else. Bruenor was quite certain she would surrender the throne of Mithral Hall to him if he insisted. And the dwarves of Citadel Felbarr would never think of anyone but Emerus as their true king, so long as the old dwarf drew breath.

"Quite a claim," Marchion Devastul retorted. "And will the Lords of Waterdeep bow to this empire? Will the great armies of Cormyr—?"

"Gauntlgrym will be no enemy of Waterdeep, or any of the other civilized kingdoms, and those in power will be glad to have the flow of greater goods in their markets," Catti-brie said. "Will Mirabar?"

"We have our own—" the marchion started to somewhat timidly reply, but Catti-brie clearly had the advantage and wasn't about to relinquish it.

"Or will Mirabar now choose to allow her dwarves to partake in the glorious reclamation of Gauntlgrym?" Catti-brie cut him short. "And in so doing, claim her place as a great ally of the fledgling city of the Delzoun dwarves—a fortress that will become the principal buyer of Mirabar's ore, likely, and one that will offer to the marchion fine deals on finer goods. For the memories of dwarves are long indeed, and your help now will not be forgotten in the centuries to come."

She let it hang there, and the marchion said nothing for a long while. Catti-brie had obviously given Devastul something to think about in an entirely new light. Finally, he announced, "I will take your offer to the Council of Sparkling Stones."

And with that, the meeting adjourned.

Bruenor and Emerus exchanged knowing smiles, and as they left the chamber side by side, the former King of Felbarr whispered in Bruenor's ear, "Yer girl's deserving a beard."

The group arrived back at the main encampment just before Drizzt rode in at the head of the fifty dwarves of Icewind Dale, who soon recounted their grim tale to Bruenor and the others.

That night, four thousand and fifty dwarf voices lifted in unison and carried across the hills and valleys, drifting over Mirabar's high wall with such power that the stones reverberated in the melancholy. They sang for Stokely Silverstream and the Battlehammer dwarves of Icewind Dale, for the loss of Kelvin's Cairn, and for the vengeance they would wreak upon the marauding dark elves.

Nearly two thousand dwarves lived in Mirabar. The next morning, more than half of them marched out of the city's gate to join in the quest for Gauntlgrym.

Now more than five thousand strong, all well armed, well armored, and seasoned in battle, the army of Delzoun marched to the west, banging shields, clapping flagons, and singing songs of war.

CHAPTER 6 ◈

Chaos

LONE, HIS BRILLIANTLY DECORATED AND MORE BRIL-
liantly enchanted robes of the archmage whipping about
him, Gromph Baenre moved briskly along the avenues
of Menzoberranzan. He turned for the Stenchstreets,
a place he hadn't visited in many years, a place now
alive with sounds.

Demons danced all around him and fights filled every
alleyway—demon against drow or demon against demon.
The archmage had summoned more than his share of demons
over the centuries, and he could see that these creatures were
under no one's control. His foolish sister was just bringing in
Abyssal beasts, even major demons, and setting them free to
roam Menzoberranzan.

Demons usually went for the weakest targets, and so
House Baenre would be little threatened by the beasts, while
the lesser Houses, including those who might wish to band
together to cause mischief against House Baenre, surely would.
Quenthel's plan to keep the city in line behind House Baenre
seemed solid enough.

But at what cost?

The Stenchstreets, and many of the lesser neighborhoods
of Menzoberranzan, had become an orgy of destruction and
debauchery. Even here, where there was little organization among the
Houseless rogues, the dark elves had gathered together in defensive
groups—what choice did they have?

Gromph pressed into the same common room where Malagdorl Armgo and his entourage had defeated Marilith. A score of drow males started and jumped at his arrival, falling into defensive formations across from the doorway.

He could see the hatred and fear on their faces as they came to recognize him. He could see their uncertainty, their desire to attack him colliding with a very tangible, and very realistic, terror. Oh, how they wanted to kill him! They wanted to rush ahead and stab the Baenre, any Baenre, for this scourge of demons that had been loosed upon them.

But Gromph was the archmage, and they knew that such an attempt would cost them more than their lives, and indeed, would have them begging for the sweet mercy of death.

"Archmage," one young warrior said, standing straight and bringing his weapon to his side. "We feared it was Bilwhr returning."

"Bilwhr?"

"A great and cruel demon—" the young drow began.

"I know who Bilwhr is," Gromph said dryly, and with clear annoyance—both at the impudent fool thinking to school him on the names of the great demons, and at the fact that such a fiend had arrived in Menzoberranzan. Bilwhr was a type of demon commonly called nalfeshnee, named for the greatest of that particular bent of fiend. Huge and incredibly powerful, nalfeshnees ranked high among the servitors of the demon lords, and of all the demons he had ever dealt with, this type was perhaps Gromph's least favorite. For in addition to all the other failings found in demons, these deluded behemoths actually believed themselves just and abiding by the laws of the universe. Indeed, they served as the judges for souls first entering the Abyss and truly believed that what they meted out could be called "justice."

In Gromph's mind, the only thing worse than a psychotic demonic destroyer was a deluded psychotic demonic destroyer.

In other words, a nalfeshnee.

"You have seen Bilwhr?" he asked calmly.

The young drow nodded. "Twice a drow's height and too wide to come through the door, though the beast would surely make its own door with little effort."

"It had the face of a gigantic ape," said another.

"And the body of a great rothé . . ." a third offered.

"A boar," another corrected. "Or half a boar, for it walked on two legs, not four, and with hands that could grip and crush a stone, it seemed."

More than seemed, Gromph thought, but didn't bother to say. He knew the power of a nalfeshnee quite well, and had seen one reshape a piece of cold iron with its bare hands.

"Bilwhr is determining who must be taken away," the young drow added.

"To the Abyss?" Gromph asked.

"To death, at least," the drow answered. "The beast has killed three already."

"At least three," another put in. "Three that we have seen."

Gromph was hardly surprised. The other demons, rampaging though they were, weren't accumulating much of a body count of drow, from all he could tell, though many kobold and goblin slaves had been devoured. Marilith had left a score of drow wounded in her wake by all accounts, but she had only killed the one fighting beside Malagdorl, and that had clearly been a fight to the death or banishment.

But of course, the situation had to devolve to this, especially with a nalfeshnee demon roaming the ways.

"Where is . . . ?" Gromph started to ask, but before he could finish, there came a loud thump and a tremor that shook the mushroom-stalk rafters of the common room.

Bilwhr.

The archmage held up his hand to calm the group, all looking around and clutching their weapons desperately. With a sigh, the archmage went back to the door.

The building shook again under the weight of a thunderous footstep.

Bilwhr.

With a sigh, Gromph motioned for the commoners to stay in place, and he went out into the street.

"The beast," one drow said, an unnecessary warning, when another heavy footfall shook the walls.

"He is the archmage," the young drow reminded the rest. He led the way, tentatively, toward the window on the street side of the common room.

They heard the moans of the manes, lesser demons they knew to be flocking in front of mighty Bilwhr. These were the spirits of the dead consigned to the Abyss in their afterlife, like semi-intelligent zombies formed of Abyssal muck and cursed to serve the major demons throughout eternity, cursed to battle and be destroyed, only to rise again and serve again. They were the fodder of the Abyss in every manner, and so that proved true now. Before the dark elves arrived at the window, they saw such a flash of fiery power that they stumbled back and covered their stinging eyes.

Just outside, the archmage's fireball roiled and burned, taking the rotting flesh from the manes and leaving them as puddles of goo on the stones of the Stenchstreets.

"You are in violation!" they heard Bilwhr roar, and they cowered back even more.

A flash of lightning crackled outside, the thunder of the blast shaking the building once more, and then the mushroom stalk rafters verily bounced under the weight of the charging demon. The young drow saw the huge beast, fully ten feet tall and four tons of power, pass by the window, its small wings flapping furiously behind it—though those strange appendages could never hope to lift the bulky Bilwhr from the ground.

Another lightning bolt sounded, then a great burst of wind shook the building, followed by a tremendous crash.

The wall by the door split and the demon—part of it, at least—crashed through. One arm, one shoulder, and the simian head struggled and twisted, splintering planks.

"Kill it!" the young drow cried, waving his sword and leading the charge. He fell back, as did his companions, only a stride later, though, as black tentacles grew out of the floor, waggling and grabbing, mostly at the struggling demon. So great was Bilwhr's strength, though, that the beast got its thick boar legs planted and simply stood upright, tearing tentacles and floorboards and splintering the wall as if it was no more than brittle paper.

"You dare!" it bellowed, and the dark elves cried out and whimpered and rushed back for cover.

The great demon aimed its ire not at them, but at Gromph, and it burst back out into the street, staggering under the stubborn pull of the remaining tentacles.

Bilwhr had just disappeared from view when there came a blast beyond anything the young drow and his companions had ever experienced, an explosion so violent that it sent them all flying about the room, crashing through furniture and into walls. The front wall by the door all but collapsed under the power of the magical explosion, and shuddered violently as huge pieces of demon splattered against it.

One such chunk of Bilwhr—half an arm, a shoulder, and enough of the back to include one small leathery wing—came flying through the opening to bounce across the floor, and there it melted into black slime.

"The archmage," the young drow said reverently, and the others nodded numbly, jaws open, eyes unblinking as they continued to stare out the window or through the hole in the wall.

◆ ◆ ◆

Gromph retreated to his summoning chamber in the main tower of Sorcere on the plateau of Tier Breche, the drow academy. In a magical bag of holding, the archmage carried dozens of tomes, along with all of the scrolls and notes he could find regarding spells of summoning and demonology.

In the chamber, secured by powerful runes and magic circles, Gromph buried his face in the knowledge. Soon, he once more felt the insight he had noted in his time with Kimmuriel, when first he had considered countering demon with demon, and that led him to one particular black-bound book, *In the Swirling Smoke of Abyss*. In there, he found listings of the demons, the lords, the major demons, the minor demons, with all the known true names.

On a hunch—one implanted by Kimmuriel, though Gromph couldn't know that—the archmage ruffled through some parchments that spoke of the Faerzress, the magical radiation that gave the Underdark its life and magical energy, and that also served as the barrier and door to the lower planes.

It was beginning to come clear to Gromph. His psionic training seemed to blend effortlessly with his insights regarding the spells of summoning. He unrolled many of those scrolls now, and in their words he recognized new possibilities.

He knew that he was close, that soon he could bring in a balor, even—that monster among many other major demons—and fully control the beast.

But not yet.

He found the appropriate references, the appropriate names, and stepped back from his summoning circle. First he enacted some personal wards and surrounded himself with protective glyphs. He was aiming for lesser demons, but powerful creatures nonetheless, and so he would take no chances.

Gromph began to chant, and he fell into his meditation, as Kimmuriel had taught him. He couldn't believe the level of intensity. He felt as if he were in the Abyss, so clear did the image of the place, with its swirling fogs, come into his mind. He could smell the stench.

And he found, too, his targets, and so he beckoned them, then compelled them.

Many, many heartbeats later, Gromph opened his amber eyes to find that he was back in the summoning room of Sorcere.

No longer was it a quiet place of meditation, however. The very stones of the walls shook with the sound of the thrumming wings of several large, hovering demons. They looked like gigantic flies, fully eight feet from the tip of their horn-like proboscis to the stinger that protruded from the back of their abdomens. Their faces were humanlike, save the nose, a curious facet of this particular manifestation of chaos that had led many demonologists to believe that these demons, chasme by name, were created by some vile bonding of demon spirit and wayward soul.

However they came to be, and whatever they were, summing a chasme was no small feat, and summoning a handful, as Gromph had just done, might, as far as the archmage knew, prove unprecedented.

He could hear their telepathic calls in his head, begging for instructions, and he knew that he controlled them.

He could feel it. They would obey his every command.

"Kill that one," he instructed the others, pointing to what appeared to be the most aggressive of the group, and without hesitation, the other four fell over the targeted creature, bearing it to the floor with a tumbling crash.

They tore it apart, appendage by appendage, leaving a smoking, melting husk on the floor.

Gromph felt almost godlike, and he couldn't suppress his grin as he considered the melding of psionics and arcane powers.

He understood the mind flayers much better at that moment, and understood Kimmuriel as well, and wondered how his brother Jarlaxle could possibly control the psionicist of House Oblodra.

This was true power, undeniable and unstoppable.

"Go and watch over the city," Gromph instructed his chasme patrol. "Partake of no murder and no battle. You are spies, nothing more. Engage no one, not even those of your own wretched Abyss, without my permission."

The four began to bob and weave all around each other, and Gromph could feel their mounting excitement and agitation. He sensed that they weren't very happy about his commands, but he felt keenly that neither would they dare to defy him.

"Report to me whenever the height of Narbondel's illumination gains or diminishes a full notch," he instructed. "Every hour."

The archmage began casting once more, and launched a spell into the midst of the magical circle that held the hovering, buzzing chasme, opening a gate that would take them out of tower's low room and into the open air of the city.

Then Gromph sat back and took a deep breath, overwrought from his exertion, and from the realization of the sheer power he had realized in bringing in the group. He spent a long while quieting his thoughts, and compartmentalizing them, for he wanted no probing telepaths, not Methil, surely, and not even Kimmuriel, to recognize the gains in power he was making by mating the magic of the Weave with the strange mind power of psionics.

He gathered up his tomes and scrolls and retired to his room, and once there, put his face right into the black-bound examination of the Abyss. He would fight demon with demon, he decided, but Quenthel's demons, or those brought in by the beasts she had loosed upon the city, would not be in her control.

While his own, like the chasme, like the balors he expected to soon realize, would adhere to his every command.

Lolth had spurned him—he was a mere male after all. Lolth had used him to bring insight and power to Matron Mother Quenthel.

But soon Gromph would help Yvonnel, his daughter, ascend to the position of matron mother, and he would be the power that put her there, and so controlled her.

A power beyond Quenthel.

A power beyond the demons she had set as a plague on the city.

A power beyond Lolth herself?

❖   ❖   ❖

"I ALLOWED HIM to defeat me as you instructed," Bilwhr's bellowing voice informed the Spider Queen and the balor Errtu.

Lolth chuckled at that, and Errtu snickered, a most horrid and shiver-inducing sound, something akin to steel scraping against teeth.

" 'Allowed him'?" Errtu said incredulously. "You 'allowed' the Archmage of Menzoberranzan to defeat you?"

"You doubt my power?" Bilwhr retorted with a threatening growl. But then again, everything Bilwhr said was accompanied by a threatening growl.

"You were obliterated," Errtu said plainly. "Perhaps you meant to follow Lolth's demands and 'allow' it, but by the time you even realized that you were supposed to do so, Gromph Baenre had already blown your corporeal form to pieces."

"My spies were about," Lady Lolth said calmly before the volatile Bilwhr could argue.

"You said that if I was banished by the archmage, I need not serve a century," Bilwhr replied.

"Patience," said Lolth. "I assured you, of course. Patience."

Bilwhr grumbled and growled, but followed Lolth's waving hand and meandered off into the stinky mists.

"Two," Errtu said. "Marilith and Bilwhr. And three if you count me."

"Why would I count you?" Lolth asked. "What have you done to earn my favor?"

A look of panic crossed the balor's face. "The slave, K'yorl . . ." the great fiery beast sputtered in protest.

Lolth laughed at him and waved at him to put him at ease. "You will find your way to the Underdark, perhaps even the surface of Toril, in time," she promised.

"When?"

"Gromph will reach out to the Faerzress with a full demand before the turn to the Year of the Rune Lords Triumphant," she said.

Errtu had to spend a moment considering that. They were now in the sixth month of the Year of the Nether Mountain Scrolls, 1486 by Dalereckoning.

"By the end of this very year?" the balor asked eagerly.

Lolth smiled and nodded. "The archmage is finding his way there as we speak. The first summoning has been completed. Next will be a major demon, a glabrezu likely, and when he is confident that he can fully command the beast . . ."

"One which you have ordered to appear fully under his command, no doubt."

The Spider Queen didn't bother to answer. "From there, he will reach higher. A nalfeshnee, a marilith, a . . ."

"A balor," Errtu growled.

"He will call for Errtu," Lolth explained. "But you will not answer that call."

Errtu winced.

"He will believe that he has called for Errtu," Lolth explained. "In his arrogance and cravenness, Archmage Gromph will reach much deeper. Too deep. Patience, my loyal friend. Patience."

CHAPTER 7 ◈

The Hidden
Smiles

ONGSADDLE," DOUM'WIELLE SAID IN ANSWER TO TIAGO'S question.

"You have been here before?"

The elf woman shook her head. "I have heard of the place, whose reputation is larger than such a hamlet would expect. It is the home of a family of wizards, some powerful but all, by the tales, inept."

Tiago looked at her incredulously. "Inept and powerful?"

"A dangerous combination," Doum'wielle agreed. "The recklessness of the Harpells who rule Longsaddle is the talk far and wide, and has been for centuries."

"Yet the dwarves march to this place?"

"The Harpells are long allies of Mithral Hall," she replied. "They were there, beside the dwarves, when your people attacked. The dwarves still sing silly songs about them, about one in particular—I believe his name was Harkle. I heard these songs often as a child, though I could never decipher most of the words in that heavy Dwarvish accent—some references to his head being where his arse used to be, or some other nonsensical thing."

Tiago looked back to the west, to the mansion on the hill in the distant village, and Doum'wielle followed his lead. Even from here, they could see the line of dwarves running from the gates in front of that house, down the main road of the town, and out to the south, where the rest of the dwarven force had settled in a tight encampment. It looked like a river, Doum'wielle thought, running from the mansion to a living lake of dwarves.

A howl, the call of a wolf, turned the pair's attention to the side, to the forest.

To arms! Khazid'hea screamed in Doum'wielle's thoughts, but even with that telepathic prodding, Doum'wielle did not draw her weapon before her companion had his own in hand, Tiago's magnificent Vidrinath coming up so quickly that the blade seemed to be an extension of the drow's arm. Even so, Tiago found himself immediately hard-pressed, and Doum'wielle nearly run over, when a group of strange hybrid creatures, half-man, half-wolf—werewolves!—leaped out of the brush upon them.

Doum'wielle reflexively pushed her sword ahead, and the fine blade impaled the nearest charging creature, sliding so easily through the werewolf's flesh and even into the bone. With almost any other sword, Doum'wielle's reaction would have spelled her doom. The werewolf kept coming, so hungry for her blood that it simply ignored the wound, and worse, a second creature was even then sweeping in to the side of the first.

But this was Khazid'hea, the blade rightly called "Cutter." Doum'wielle yelped and started to fall back, and started, too, to try to get her sword in line with the second creature, simply by angling it out to her right.

With this sword, that instinctive action proved to be enough. Cutter slashed right through the side of the impaled werewolf, nearly cutting the beast in half, and as Doum'wielle continued across, the vorpal blade gashed the second creature from hip to mid-thigh. Back came Doum'wielle's arm desperately, Khazid'hea cutting as if through air, though again drawing a deep line on the second werewolf, and speeding across to lop the head from the first.

Doum'wielle drew the blade in close, turning the tip down. She hopped back and to her left to avoid the stumbling second creature, and brought the sword across, gashing it across the spine as it stumbled to the ground. And there it writhed, broken beyond repair.

Doum'wielle felt Khazid'hea's admiration and even awe. For a heartbeat, she thought the sword was complimenting her on her double-kill, but she understood differently when she backstepped a bit more and considered her companion.

She had never seen such grace and speed.

Tiago had been closer to the attackers, and so four of the six had leaped at him. One flopped on the ground, blood flying from its multiple wounds.

The other three looked little better.

Tiago went down low under a clawing swipe, his shield—huge now, as it had spiraled outward, widening to his call—going over his ducking head, his forearm braced against his skull. Down atop it slammed a werewolf, arm and shoulder driving, but any balance and leverage the lycanthrope might have had over Tiago was thrown away by a simple tilt of the shield *Orbbcress*, Spiderweb, and it grabbed the werewolf as it tilted. At Tiago's call, the shield let go just as the creature tried to pull back against the stickiness.

And up came Tiago, now beside and behind the beast, and one stroke from the starlight blade of Vidrinath laid the werewolf low.

Already, Tiago was moving to his defensive stance, shield sweeping across to defeat the attacks of the remaining two werewolves.

Doum'wielle thought that she should go to him, but Khazid'hea hit her with a wall of countering demands, holding her in place to watch the spectacle. The veteran sword understood, if Doum'wielle did not, that Tiago was fully in control of this battle.

Behind the shield, the blade named Vidrinath stabbed out, once and again, small cuts on the two werewolves.

Tiago went into a spin, quick-stepping to the right, then back to the left as the werewolves pursued. He leaped into a back somersault, landing gracefully on his feet and in a run right back at the werewolves, but angled to the side.

He went by them to the left, his shield easily defeating the swing of the nearest as he ran past. Easily defeating, and catching with its magical filaments.

Tiago went down to one knee, his drop yanking the werewolf off balance, lurching over. Back the other way went the drow, releasing his shield's grip, turning as he went to sweep his slightly curved sword across the lycanthrope's face.

It howled and fell away as Tiago came together with the remaining creature.

Now one-against-one, Tiago didn't bother with any of his twirling and ducking moves. He fought straight up, his sword and shield darting and sweeping, always ahead of the werewolf, finding its way past the feeble attempts at defense and increasingly putting the beast off balance.

Whenever his movements put him near one of the other beasts, Tiago worked a downward coup de grace into his dancing flow, so effortlessly, so gracefully that it seemed like part of a previously choreographed and rehearsed dance.

And always he was back up against the still-standing werewolf, blocking and stabbing. At first Doum'wielle thought that her drow companion was simply wearing the werewolf down. Its movements began to noticeably slow.

She remembered the name of Tiago's sword. *Vidrinath* was the drow word for "lullaby," or at least, the drow version of the word, which referred to a taunting melody sung to those struck and caught by the infamous drow sleeping poison.

The elf woman just shook her head as the fight continued, as Tiago increased his pace and the werewolf slowed.

An arm went flying, severed at the elbow. Then a hand from the beast's other arm twirled into the air.

Tiago Baenre didn't simply beat the werewolf, he dismembered it, disemboweled it, and ultimately decapitated it as it stood there flailing with stubby arms, ridiculously still trying to battle him.

◆ ◆ ◆

FROM A BALCONY on the northern side of the Ivy Mansion, Catti-brie, Drizzt, and their hosts heard the cries of the werewolves.

"The Bidderdoos," Penelope Harpell explained with a sad shake of her head. "They are so numerous, and so . . ." Her voice trailed off and she shook her head again.

"I knew Bidderdoo Harpell," said Drizzt. "He was a good man."

"A sad legacy he has left," said Penelope.

"Is there nothing that can be done?" Catti-brie asked.

"You are a priestess—a Chosen, it is said," Penelope answered. "Pray to your goddess for inspiration. Many in the Ivy Mansion work their spells and ply their alchemy in search of an antidote, but lycanthropy is a stubborn disease."

"Regis," Drizzt quietly muttered.

"The little one?" Penelope asked.

"An alchemist," Catti-brie explained. "He carries an entire workbench in that magical pouch at his side."

"I do remember," said Penelope. "He showed me. I just assumed that he was out with the dwarves . . . and Wulfgar."

The telling hesitation before she mentioned the giant man had Catti-brie and Drizzt exchanging sly grins, and when their gazes turned back to Penelope, she merely shrugged and nearly giggled, not about to deny the rumors.

"Neither are here, I fear," Catti-brie explained, and Penelope's expression soured just a bit.

"Not killed, I pray."

"They are off in the east, to Aglarond to find Regis's love," Catti-brie explained. "An extraordinarily beautiful halfling, to hear him tell it. Truly, our diminutive friend is smitten."

"They will return, then?"

"We hope," said Drizzt. "Every passing day, we look to the east, hoping to see them riding back to join us."

Penelope sighed. "Well, perhaps they will, then, and perhaps we will find our cure for the poor Bidderdoos, or perhaps Regis will ride in and save the day."

"He has become quite adept at that of late," said Catti-brie, and they all shared a laugh.

"And of course, if there is anything we can do," Drizzt offered.

"We have a Bidderdoo in our dungeon," Penelope explained, and she held up her hand when the others showed a bit of shock at the remark. "She came to us in a moment of lucidity and is being treated well. The brave woman wishes us to do whatever we think may help, and has endured great pain through our failed attempts to cure her. But still, she does not ask for release. She is determined that she will help the pack of doomed souls wandering the forest about Longsaddle. Perhaps you can go to her later, and take your goddess with you," she said to Catti-brie. "If any of the beings we name as gods can help such creatures, Mielikki of nature's domain would seem a logical choice."

"I will do whatever I can, of course, Lady Penelope," Catti-brie replied with a graceful bow. "How much I do owe to the Harpells, and most of all, I owe you my friendship."

Penelope nodded and smiled, then even stepped over and wrapped Catti-brie, once her protégé, in a great hug.

"And what may I, might the Harpells, do for you now?" Penelope asked. "You come to my door with an army of dwarves—such an army that has not been seen beyond the memory of elves, I expect!"

"We have come for respite," Drizzt explained. "It has been a long road, and that after a long and bitter war. We seek the hospitality of Longsaddle, whatever may be spared, while mud-rotted feet heal, boots are mended, and our animals can be rested and shod."

"On your way to the west," Penelope said, a logical conclusion, of course, since they had come from the east.

Drizzt and Catti-brie exchanged another look. "We travel to . . ."

"Gauntlgrym, in the Crags," Penelope finished.

That brought a couple of surprised, but surely not astonished, stares.

"The whispers precede you," Penelope told them. "Did you think you could march an army of five thousand dwarves across the breadth of the North without drawing attention?"

"Perhaps we're simply traveling for Icewind Dale," Drizzt said.

"For a visit?" the clever Penelope asked.

Drizzt shrugged.

"Gauntlgrym sits there in wait, and the Delzoun dwarves march in great numbers," Penelope offered. "One does not need an abacus to add those clues to their obvious answer. And this time, you aren't going to Gauntlgrym to rescue a cursed vampire dwarf, but to rescue the most ancient homeland of Bruenor's ancestors, and those of King Emerus and the twin kings Bromm and Harnoth as well."

"King Bromm is dead," Catti-brie told her. "He fell to a white wyrm on a frozen lake early in the War of the Silver Marches."

"And King Harnoth remains in Citadel Adbar, the lone blood king of the Silver Marches remaining on a dwarven throne," Drizzt said. "Bruenor is out in the encampment, as is King Emerus, who gave his throne to another, as is King Connerad, the Eleventh King of Mithral Hall, who surrendered his crown to a deserving Dagnabbet Brawnanvil that he could join in this greatest quest of the Delzoun dwarves."

"It seems you have quite a story to tell," Penelope said. "And quite a story yet to write. Go and fetch these dwarf kings, Master Drizzt, if you will, and whatever other dwarves they wish to bring in, and you can tell the Harpells your tale in full, and over the finest meal you've had in tendays."

Drizzt and Catti-brie nodded, and turned to the stairs.

"Just him," Penelope said to Catti-brie, who looked back at her curiously. "You and I have so much to catch up on. Please remain."

"Of course," Catti-brie said, and she gave Drizzt a kiss and sent him off. She had barely settled in a comfortable chair beside Penelope when they saw the drow thundering down the hillside on his magnificent white unicorn.

"I'm honored that you and your army chose to come through Longsaddle on your march," Penelope said. "I expect that you played no small role in that decision."

"It seemed a reasonable respite, and one much needed."

"And?"

"You see right through me, lady," Catti-brie said.

"I know you well, Delly Curtie," Penelope replied, using the woman's old name, the one she had worn when first she had come to Longsaddle those few years before. "Or Ruqiah, perhaps?"

Catti-brie laughed. "I do wish to spend some time in the libraries of the Ivy Mansion," she admitted. "And to discuss some thoughts with the greatest of the Harpell wizards, yourself and Kipper, surely, who is so well versed in the matters of teleporting."

"You don't think we can transport an army, I hope," Penelope replied with a laugh.

"No, no," Catti-brie answered, laughing too. "But when Gauntlgrym is retaken, and I have no doubt that it will be . . . the dwarves have responsibilities in other lands."

"Ah," Penelope purred, nodding as she figured it out. "You wish to magically connect Gauntlgrym to Mithral Hall with something akin to a permanent gateway."

"And to Adbar and Felbarr, perhaps Icewind Dale, and perhaps other Delzoun dwarf fortresses," Catti-brie admitted. "How much more secure would my father's people—"

"Your father?"

"Bruenor," Catti-brie explained. "My adoptive father."

"In another life."

"In this one, as well."

Penelope spent a moment pondering that, then shrugged, and Catti-brie got the distinct impression that the carefree woman didn't have a high opinion of that arrangement remaining intact, even through decades of the sleep of death and Mielikki's magical reincarnation.

"So you wish to facilitate a magical portal, through which the dwarves can trade, and can send armies whenever and wherever they are needed?"

"It would be a boon."

"Or a curse," said Penelope. "Even if I could facilitate such an impressive feat as that, you couldn't easily close it down. If one dwarven fortress fell, your enemies would have an open doorway to the other citadels."

Catti-brie mulled that grim possibility for a while. She wanted to deny it, but Penelope had a strong point. If the drow of Menzoberranzan came back to Gauntlgrym and chased out Bruenor, would any of the other kingdoms be safe ever again?

"Something to consider," Penelope said. "So let us explore the possibilities together with Kipper in the coming days. If anyone here at the Ivy Mansion has any idea of how such a gate might be facilitated, it would be him, no doubt."

"I am not so sure . . ."

"Wait until you see the possibilities before you douse the torch, my friend," Penelope advised. "You will gain insight on your choices through this exploration."

"I do not expect that it will be an easy choice if the possibility exists."

"Perhaps we all have some difficult, though exciting decisions ahead of us," Penelope said with a laugh, and she leaped from her chair and held out her hand to Catti-brie. "Come, my nose tells me that you need to bathe, and perhaps we can find, or magically weave, a proper gown for one of your beauty."

"Too kind!" Catti-brie agreed, for she wasn't about to say no to a bath. They had been marching the dusty road through the heat of summer, and Penelope wasn't the only one aware of Catti-brie's fragrance! She took the woman's hand and jumped up beside her, smiling widely. But behind that grin, Catti-brie was trying to make some sense of Penelope's other curious statements regarding difficult and exciting decisions.

◆ ◆ ◆

DAY AFTER DAY dragged by, and Tiago grew frustrated, for Drizzt rarely left the Ivy Mansion, and when he did, it was only to travel the short distance to the dwarven encampment. Tiago certainly wasn't going near to a house of human wizards, and the dwarves presented an equal challenge, for though tendays had passed, through the hottest days of summer, the camp was truly a fortress, with the bearded folk on full alert at all times. It was because of the werewolves. The creatures were everywhere, their howls ever-present in the night.

The couple had found protection from the beasts in an abandoned home—likely a halfling house, for it was more below ground than above. The walls outside the hill that contained the bulk of the place were solid and well fortified. Tiago and Doum'wielle had not been bothered since that first day, though they had on several occasions found tracks near their windows.

Doum'wielle enjoyed the respite, and the training time it afforded her with Khazid'hea. The sword understood Drizzt, and she was being trained specifically to fight him, she knew. She soon came to recognize that she had not been the first one the sentient Cutter had trained in this manner, and for the same purpose.

"You have a vendetta against that particular dark elf," she whispered to the sword one sunny afternoon. Tiago had remained inside the house, out of the uncomfortable sun, while Doum'wielle wanted to bask in the bright sunlight, well aware that she might not again know this sensation for many years, perhaps never again.

I was once wielded by Catti-brie, the sword explained. *She was not worthy.*

Doum'wielle digested the thoughts, not disagreeing, but still unable to make the connection, considering the sword's obvious anger toward the drow ranger. This preparation and training, this plan Khazid'hea had formulated, wasn't just about her, Doum'wielle had come to believe. There was something else here, something personal.

But why would a sword care?

He rejected you, she thought, and the sensation returned by Khazid'hea told her that she had indeed sorted out the riddle.

"You wished Drizzt to wield you when Catti-brie could not properly do so," she whispered.

She felt the sword's anger—not directed at her.

Doum'wielle understood clearly then that she had just confirmed that she was not the first the sentient blade had trained specifically to kill Drizzt Do'Urden. She was about to inquire of that when a noise to the side, along with a warning from Khazid'hea, put her on her guard. She backstepped to the house's door, expecting a group of werewolves, or perhaps a dwarf patrol, to leap out upon her.

But it was not a werewolf that came forth, nor a dwarf, but a drow, and one Doum'wielle did not recognize.

"Well met, Little Doe," he said, but then put his hand to his lips and gasped. "Pardon, Doum'wielle Armgo," he corrected with a low and respectful bow. "Or should I call you Doum'wielle Do'Urden now?"

"Who are you?"

"I am of Bregan D'aerthe," the drow answered.

"The mercenary band?"

"Who serve at the pleasure of Matron Mother Baenre," the drow clarified. "Like your partner, I am Baenre. Beniago, at your service."

Doum'wielle thought she had heard the name before, but she couldn't be sure.

"I am here at the command of the matron mother, and of Archmage Gromph," Beniago went on. "They tasked Bregan D'aerthe with finding you—well, to be honest, with finding Tiago, who is a noble son of House Baenre. But we expected that you would not be far from his side."

"You have come to bring us back to Menzoberranzan?"

"No. Not immediately, at least. I know nothing of that. I was tasked with finding you and delivering to you a gift from the archmage."

He began to approach, and held up his hands as if he were holding something, a cape or a cord, perhaps, though Doum'wielle could see nothing. She shied back a step or two.

He is no enemy, Khazid'hea imparted to her and she let Beniago catch up to her, and only flinched a bit as his hands went up high. He moved them out over her head, as if he were placing a crown, or perhaps a necklace upon her, and indeed as he brought his hands down, Doum'wielle felt the weight of a heavy chain.

"Wh-what . . . ?" she stammered, falling back and reaching up, and indeed feeling a chain around her neck, as thick as a finger, and with a circular pendant hanging low between her breasts.

"With that around your neck, Archmage Gromph can know your place," Beniago explained.

"Know my *place*?"

"The matron mother will send him to retrieve you and Tiago when she so chooses," Beniago bluntly replied. "She is not one to forgive tardiness."

Despite the warning, this whole scenario seemed an invasion to Doum'wielle, and she reflexively went to remove the invisible necklace.

"Do not," Beniago warned, the tone of his voice changing dramatically. "You are instructed to wear it, and to say nothing of it to Tiago, and nothing of this visit at all. To Tiago or anyone else."

At the mention of Tiago, Doum'wielle glanced back at the house, where all was quiet.

"Nothing," Beniago warned her again.

Doum'wielle was about to protest, but Beniago cut her short, and stole any argument she might have offered, by saying, "On penalty of . . ." He paused and smiled. "You can well imagine. The Archmage of Menzoberranzan is already aware of your location, bastard *darthiir* of House Do'Urden. Gromph Baenre is already aware that you wear the necklace. And he will know if you try to remove it."

Doum'wielle understood then that this wasn't a request. It was a command, and one that carried great and deadly consequence if it was not followed. She looked down and cupped the pendant in her hand, trying to make out some slight reflection of the thing. But it was perfectly invisible.

Doum'wielle looked back up, but Beniago was already gone.

She turned back to the house and considered Tiago.

He cannot protect you from the wrath of Archmage Gromph, Khazid'hea said in her thoughts, and if the sword had been reading her mind, it would have known that she understood that truth very, very well.

They have likely been searching for Tiago since he fell from the wyrm, Khazid'hea explained.

Then he should wear the necklace.

You would tell that to Archmage Gromph?

The necklace seemed heavier to Little Doe, then, and its chain, a shackle.

◆ ◆ ◆

"WELL, WHERE WOULD you like to go?" Kipper asked.

"I know not," a flustered and somewhat nervous Catti-brie answered. Old Kipper had just taught her the basics of a spell she feared, one that she wanted to spend some more time studying, and here he was prodding her to give it a try!

"Just think of a place, girl!" Kipper scolded. "Imagine a place of safety and security, a place where you could hide and feel as if nothing in the world could harm you."

Catti-brie looked at him curiously.

"Best for a teleport," Kipper explained. "For there, in your most secure hearth and home, is a place you know best. Every corner, every finger of it is locked into your mind's eye so perfectly that you won't miss with your spell. And so you can trust that you'll never appear too high up in the air and take a nasty fall, or, shudder to say it, magically appear too low, in the midst of stone and dirt!" He paused and scrutinized her carefully. "Mithral Hall, perhaps?"

But Catti-brie's thoughts, spurred by Kipper's description were not, to her surprise, recalling a place anywhere near Mithral Hall. No, she pictured a place she had cultivated, a place of

Mielikki. She had known violence in that place, and had once been discovered there, and yet, to her, the secret garden she had cultivated as the child Ruqiah seemed to her the place of her spirit's warmest rest.

She saw it now, so clearly that she felt as if she could touch it.

She began reciting the spell, though she was hardly aware of the words spilling forth.

She could smell the flowers, she could touch them.

Indeed, she was touching them before she even realized that she had successfully cast the spell, and was then standing in the secret garden in the lands that had been Netheril—and indeed, still might be, for Catti-brie had not been there in several years, and on that occasion had only passed through.

She stood there for a long while, remembering Niraj and Kavita and the Desai tribe. She hoped they were well, and vowed to find them again when she was done with Bruenor's war.

She glanced back at the narrow entrance to the place, through the shielding stones, and thought of Lady Avelyere, who had called to her from that very entrance, angry that her student had so deceived her. Catti-brie smiled, for that was not really a bad memory, though surely she had been startled and afraid when powerful Avelyere had caught her.

But soon after, because of that confrontation, she had come to know that the woman truly cared for her. She nodded, and hoped that Avelyere, too, was well, and thought that she should visit the Coven, Avelyere's school of sorcery, if it could be safely arranged.

Catti-brie remembered that Kipper had placed a contingency spell upon her, one that would return her to the Ivy Mansion in a short while. She let go of external memories and focused instead on the warmth of the place as she made her way through the flowers to the cypress tree shading the far end of the garden. She moved beneath it, under the glare of the Netherese sun, and gently ran her fingers along the light gray bark, tracing the silvery lines that coursed it like veins.

She closed her eyes and remembered the magic she had brought to this place to cultivate it, until it was able to stand on its own—and indeed, it had. She slid the right sleeve of her black robe and the colorful blouse beneath up enough to reveal her divine spellscar, shaped like the head of a unicorn. In this place Catti-brie had truly come to understand her relationship with Mielikki. In this place, she felt whole and warm.

She felt the first tugs of Kipper's spell of return then, and sighed, opening her eyes and scanning the tree so that she could burn its every twist and turn into her memory forevermore.

That's when she noted something very curious.

There was one branch that was not leafy, and seemed like an aberration, a stub. It was as thick around as her wrist, but only extended a few feet from the trunk before rounding off in an abrupt ending. She reached up to touch it, wondering if it had been broken by a strike of lightning, perhaps, or by some animal.

It came free and fell, and she barely managed to catch it before Kipper's spell caught her.

The look of surprise on Catti-brie's face was genuine when she found herself back in Kipper's private library at the Ivy Mansion, the branch in hand.

"Well now, what have you found?" she heard Kipper asking before she properly reoriented herself.

She wanted to answer "a branch," but as she continued to touch the silvery-gray bark, she realized that answer to be a woefully inadequate.

This wasn't just a branch from the cypress tree, she realized, but a gift from the tree—from Mielikki? She clasped it in both hands, like a staff, and brought it closer, and noticed then that the bluish mist of her spellscar was swirling around her forearm, and extending to swirl about the staff, as well.

Catti-brie looked at Kipper and shook her head, at a loss to explain.

Kipper wasn't waiting for an explanation anyway. He was already casting a spell to magically examine the staff. He nodded and opened his eyes some time later.

"A fine item to focus your energies," he said. "I've always said that a wizard should never be without a staff! A young wizard, at least, so that when she errs badly, she can at least knock those laughing at her over the head."

He held out his hand and motioned for the item, and Catti-brie, though she didn't really want to surrender it, handed it to him.

Kipper put it through some movements—sidelong as if in a block, then in one outstretched hand, as if he was loosing a mighty blast of power. He nodded again. Muttering "well-balanced," he examined the head of the item, which was a bit bulbous and also slightly concave.

Kipper laughed and brought his free hand to his lips, glancing all about. He rushed to his desk, fumbled with some keys, and finally opened a drawer.

"A lock?" Catti-brie asked dryly. "A bit mundane, don't you think?"

Kipper laughed again and bent low, rummaging through the cluttered drawer. He came back up holding a large blue gemstone, a sapphire. He brought it to the tip of the staff, settling it into the concave end, nodding. "I can have it properly set," he said, as much to himself as to Catti-brie.

"What is it?"

"It holds spells for you," he replied. "Oh, but it has a lot to offer! I spent many years crafting this one, I did!" He tossed it to Catti-brie.

She caught it easily and held it up in front of her sparkling eyes—sparkling because she could feel the sapphire teeming with energy. It had enchantments upon it, she knew immediately, bringing many spells into her thoughts with only that cursory examination.

"Well, to be fair, I didn't create the orb," Kipper admitted. "It was more in the way of repairing it."

"Repairing what?"

"A staff," he replied. "One that I took from a wizard after defeating her in a duel, and breaking her staff in the process.

Finest lightning bolt I ever threw, I tell you!" He chuckled and nodded, enjoying the memory, apparently. "It's an item of the old magic, before the Spellplague, before the Time of Troubles, even. I'd thought to make it anew, and indeed, even during the Spellplague I managed to repair the orb. But then I never finished, like so much of my life's work. Maybe I just never found a staff suitable for it."

"It sounds like you have great respect for the item this wizard held."

"She was no match for me except for that staff, oh no!" Kipper declared. He looked at Catti-brie more closely. "That blouse you wear, it, too, is from the old times."

Catti-brie looked at the garment—it was more a shift than a blouse, and had been a robe for its previous wearer, a most wicked little gnome named Jack.

"Do you know what it is?"

"I know its properties."

"Its name?"

Catti-brie shook her head, but then answered, "The Robe of the Archmage?" for she had heard it referred to as such.

"Indeed," Kipper replied. "And this . . ." he took the sapphire from her and held it up so she could clearly see it. "This was the heart of a Staff of the Magi. I never finished my work with it, because . . . well, because I am old Kipper and my reputation for distraction is well earned, like so many of my family. And because I never found a suitable staff. Yet here you go, disappearing from me for just a few moments, and *poof*, you return with something I've long wanted, but hardly remembered that I wanted!"

It took Catti-brie a long while to sort that jumble of words out, and she shook her head, mostly in amusement at Kipper's animated state.

But then her expression turned deadly serious. "I cannot," she said, her voice barely above a whisper.

"What, girl?"

"I . . . I cannot give it to you," she tried to explain. "The staff, it is a gift from Mielikki."

Kipper held up the silvery staff. He focused more intently upon it this time. He brought the gem up close to his face and whispered to it, and then his eyes widened indeed.

"It's already enchanted," he said.

"I feel the warmth of divine healing within it," Catti-brie said. "I am sorry, my friend."

"Sorry? No, no, I did not mean for you to give me your staff, of course!" Kipper explained. "No, I meant to complete my work on your staff. For you!"

Catti-brie was taken aback. "I could not . . ."

"Of course you could! Of course you would, and why not? My adventuring days are all but over, and I've little desire to get into any dragon's lairs or troll caves any longer. Why, if I could use you as my protégé and send you forth properly armed—ha!—why then I'd feel as if old Kipper did something truly worthwhile."

"Kipper," Catti-brie said, and she moved over and hugged the man.

He pushed her back, though, just a bit, a mischievous smile on his wrinkled face. He held up the blue sapphire and the silver staff and arched his eyebrows.

"Dare we?" he asked.

◆ ◆ ◆

IT WAS NEARLY midsummer, long into the seventh month of Flamerule, when the dwarves at last broke camp and resumed their march. Their feet healed, their bellies full, their spirits high, the dark tide of dwarven warriors flowed out of Longsaddle, like a river down the road to the southwest, heading with grim determination for the Crags.

Their ranks had not thinned in their long stay, and indeed some new and powerful allies had joined in the march.

Catti-brie was perhaps alone among the army who was not surprised when Penelope Harpell had ridden out to join them, with several other eager young wizards at her side, and one much older one.

For it seemed clear that Catti-brie had intrigued old Kipper with her talk of a functioning gate between Gauntlgrym and Mithral Hall, so much so that the old wizard had decided to investigate the possibilities for himself. The woman looked to her silver-gray staff, the blue sapphire sitting perfectly atop it. She was certain that few in the world could claim an item of this power, infused with both arcane and divine magic, and so fittingly matching the spellscars on her arms.

She nodded, and couldn't contain her smile, so glad to have old Kipper along. For suddenly the road seemed friendlier, suddenly the caverns ahead not so dark, and now, she knew, she would be ready to meet what challenges might come.

◆ ◆ ◆

"THEY GOT A reputation o' bumblin'," King Emerus whispered to Bruenor, the old dwarf full of doubt when the Harpells asked to join in the march.

But Bruenor could only grin. He remembered well the role the Harpell family had played back in the days before the Spellplague, before the Time of Troubles even, when the drow had come to Mithral Hall.

"Aye, and we might find a few of our boys turned into newts, or frogs or dogs, or might be a turnip or two," Bruenor replied.

Emerus looked at him gravely, but Bruenor dismissed it with a laugh. "One thing we're not for matchin' with them drow in Gauntlgrym is wizardry."

"We got a hunnerd priests," Emerus protested.

"*Wizardry*," Bruenor repeated. "Our priests'll be too busy tending burned skin if we can't match them drow wizards, and Drizzt's telling me that this house that's set itself up in

Gauntlgrym is one fat with durned wizards. So now we got some, and aye, them Harpells've earned their foolish reputation honestly. But don't ye doubt the power they're bringin', and this one, Penelope . . ." he paused and looked at the woman, riding easily on a spectral mount and chatting with Drizzt and Catti-brie.

"She's a good one," Bruenor finished. "Me girl says she's a good one."

"As ye wish," Emerus said and let it go at that. He didn't have nearly the experiences of battling dark elves that Bruenor could boast, but he had seen enough of their magical tricks in the siege of Citadel Felbarr, and he had to admit that if these human wizards were at all competent, their presence could only help.

At the very least, Emerus figured, the Harpell wizards would make themselves the first targets of drow lightning bolts, giving him and his boys the chance to get up close to the magic-users.

They kept their pace easy, for this was difficult territory, and since they meant to be battling in the Underdark, in the subterranean halls of Gauntlgrym, they didn't fear the onset of winter. Surely they'd be inside long before the first snows fell.

They moved directly through the wild Crags, fearing no goblin tribes, or barbarians, or any other enemy that might rise against them. Along familiar ground, Drizzt and Bruenor noted that they were near the tunnel entrance that would take them down to Gauntlgrym, but Bruenor pressed the march on beyond that point, leaving only a few scouts behind and taking the army all the way to the city of Neverwinter.

They made camp in sight of Neverwinter's gate on the last day of Eleasis in the Year of the Nether Mountain Scrolls.

◆ ◆ ◆

"All rise for the Protector!" the guard barked, and everyone sitting around the long table in the great building known as the Hall of Justice jumped up from their seats. This was the most impressive structure in the city of Neverwinter, capped with an enormous red and gold dome, and with huge circular windows along the curving ceiling to capture the sky at the true points of the compass. It was a new construction, too, and a testament to the hardy and industrious settlers determined to raise this city from the ashes of the volcano.

A decorated door at the back of the chamber banged open and a young woman of perhaps thirty winters confidently strode in. Her hair was auburn and cut short and made her large blue eyes seem huge, while the blue tint of her vestments and plated greaves made them shine bluer.

"Could be your sister," Drizzt said to Catti-brie.

"General Sabine," Bruenor whispered, nodding, for he had served under her in his short time posing as Bonnego Battle-axe of the Neverwinter Guard.

Behind the young general came a man who appeared just a bit north of middle age, but with youthful vigor, and the musculature typical of a man much younger. His hair and beard, both neatly trimmed, were silver, and his scowl seemed perpetual even at first glance. He wore a golden breastplate carved into the likeness of a lion's face in full roar.

"All hail Lord Protector Dagult Neverember!" the guard called, and around the table came a unified call of "Hail, Neverember!"

General Sabine moved to stand beside her seat, just to the right of the throne centering the back center length of the table. She stood at perfect attention, not even blinking it seemed, though she did move her gaze over to consider Drizzt more than once, and a slight moment of curiosity—recognition, perhaps?—flickered when she scanned Bruenor.

The lord protector came up fast, seeming quite agitated. He brushed past Sabine and verily jumped over the arm of the throne to take his seat, motioning dismissively with his hand to indicate that the others could sit.

"I am roused from my most comfortable bed in Waterdeep with news that an army has camped on the doorstep of Neverwinter," he said as soon as the chairs stopped rustling.

His tone, his posture, and his expression all worked in unison to convey that he was none too pleased.

All eyes of the visitors across the table went to King Emerus, whom they had appointed to speak for them. The old dwarf chuckled a bit at the Lord Protector's cross and demeaning tone—Neverember's reputation had preceded him and he was certainly living up to it.

Emerus planted his hands on the table and slowly rose.

"Me name's Warcrown, Emerus Warcrown, and until this march I was known as the King o' Citadel Felbarr in the Silver Marches and the Alliance of Luruar," the dwarf began. "Ye heared o' me?"

Lord Protector Neverember wouldn't offer the respect of a nod or affirmation, and merely rolled his hands to prompt the old dwarf to keep talking.

"The army afore yer gates, the dwarfs o' Felbarr, Citadel Adbar, and Mithral Hall, did'no come to yer call or with yer permission," the proud old dwarf said evenly. "We come as a courtesy and nothin' more, to let the folk and leaders o' Neverwinter know of our coming and o' what we mean to be doing."

"A courtesy?" Lord Neverember scoffed. "You send an army as a *courtesy*?"

"Well, since we're soon to be neighbors . . ." Emerus retorted.

"To cross my borders without invite? An army? That can be considered an act of war, King Emerus, as you should surely know!"

Emerus started to reply, but Bruenor banged his hands on the table and shot up. "Aye, a courtesy, and so when's it startin' that dwarfs and the folk o' Neverwinter're at odds?"

"Bonnego," he heard from the side. He turned to the end of the table and only then noticed the elderly Jelvus Grinch, who had once been first citizen of the fledgling city, and who had known Bruenor when he had come here in disguise in search of Gauntlgrym.

"Bruenor," the dwarf corrected, but in a friendly tone as he turned to regard the elderly man, and to bow with respect as well.

"Ye knowed me as Bonnego, and aye, I served in yer garrison and on yer wall for a bit," he added, looking then to General Sabine, who now obviously recognized him as well. "But me name's Bruenor, and me family's Battlehammer, and that's a name ye should be knowin' well."

"King Bruenor Battlehammer?" Lord Neverember asked, and he seemed a bit less sure of himself suddenly. "Am I to believe that two dwarf kings have marched to my city's gate?"

"Ye was just telled as much," said Bruenor. "And that we come as a courtesy."

"You are not old enough . . ." Neverember started to argue.

"I am known in your city as well," Drizzt said, and he rose up beside Bruenor. "Indeed, it was Jelvus Grinch, then First Citizen, who asked me to stay those years ago, in the early days of Neverwinter reclaimed."

"Drizzt Do'Urden," the elderly man confirmed. " 'Tis true."

"I speak for the dwarf beside me," Drizzt said. "Know that he is who, and what, he claims—Bruenor Battlehammer, Eighth and Tenth King of Mithral Hall. And beside him is Connerad Brawnanvil, who, like King Emerus with Citadel Felbarr, served as King of Mithral Hall until this very march commenced back in the lands of the Silver Marches."

"Three dwarf kings?" Lord Neverember asked, and he gave a dismissive chuckle.

"They've come for Gauntlgrym," General Sabine soberly remarked, and the lord protector stopped laughing.

"Just figurin' that out, are ye?" Bruenor replied sourly.

Neverember lived up to his short-tempered reputation then, leaping to his feet and yelling, "You have come to my lands to wage war?"

"Nah," said Bruenor. "We're marching to our own land to take it back."

"Land that falls within my borders."

"Then them borders'll be redrawn, don't ye doubt," Bruenor shot back. "Gauntlgrym's a dwarven home, and goin' back to Delzoun rule, and none'll doubt our claim."

"And it's held by drow, by all word that's come forth," Emerus added. "What've ye done to rid yer lands o' that scourge, O Lord Protector?"

Emerus sat down when he finished, and tugged Bruenor's sleeve to get him, too, to return to his seat. Across the way, Lord Neverember leaned on the table with an aggressive posture, staring hard at the dwarves. Finally, he returned to his seat.

"You mean to reclaim Gauntlgrym for the dwarves," he said.

"Aye, and know that we're meanin' to fight any who think to stand afore that end," said Bruenor.

Neverember bristled but let it go. "And re-fire the forges."

"Already runnin'," said Bruenor. "And better that they're runnin' for dwarf smiths."

Neverember nodded and wore an expression that looked as if he was beginning to see things in a different light—no doubt, in a profitable light for Neverwinter, or more important, for himself. Bruenor recognized that clearly, for he had paid close attention to all the whispers along the road regarding the new Lord Protector of Neverwinter. Bruenor had not met the man in his short time in the city previously. But even then the whispers had been quite consistent in tagging the man with some of the mind's deadly sins, and all were on display already in this short meeting: pride, wrath, and now, it seemed pretty clear to the dwarf, avarice.

"We come to introduce ye to yer new neighbors, Lord Neverember," said Bruenor. "Don't ye doubt that."

"Those lands in the Crags are under my control," he countered.

"Not anymore," said Bruenor.

Those seated around Lord Protector Neverember sucked in their breath as one, and the man sputtered as he searched to put his anger into words, but Bruenor wasn't about to let it go.

"Gauntlgrym's dwarf land," he declared, standing again. "If ye're meaning to fight us, ye best do it now, afore we get into the mines. Ye got the belly for that?"

Neverember stared at him incredulously, sputtering still, his lack of options laid bare. There was no way the Neverwinter garrison could be turned loose on the powerful army Bruenor and Emerus had brought to their doorstep. Five thousand battle-hardened dwarf veterans outfitted with the strongest armor and weapons of the finest materials mined in Mithral Hall and Citadel Felbarr and lovingly crafted by the artisans of Citadel Adbar would prove formidable against the very best armies of the Realms, particularly in the open field, where the dwarves' discipline and tight defensive formations could frustrate even heavy cavalry.

Certainly the garrison of Neverwinter wasn't about to leave the protection of the city walls to challenge them, Lord Neverember's bluster notwithstanding.

Exposed now, the Lord Protector of Neverwinter settled back in his chair and stroked his silver beard, managing a smile that was supposed to appear wry, but in reality seemed rather pathetic to Bruenor.

"You have come as a courtesy, you say, but you offer threats?" came the predictable response—the answer of a man trying not to be embarrassed.

"No threats to any who're not trying to stop us from gettin' back our home," said Bruenor. "Are ye sayin' ye like the drow and goblins on yer doorstep more than a kingdom o' dwarfs? If that's what ye're sayin' then say it straight up."

"I said no such thing."

"Gauntlgrym's Delzoun."

"The land above it is under my protection," Lord Neverember said. "Even if you are successful in reclaiming the Underdark of this place you claim to be Gauntlgrym, your kingdom will extend no farther than your front door."

Bruenor chuckled, understanding now. The greedy Waterdhavian lord was angling for a tithe. The dwarves would need trade, obviously, and Neverember wanted his cut.

"Talk for another day," Bruenor said, and he offered Neverember a grin and a nod to show that he understood well what was going on. "First we've got a war to fight and win, and don't ye doubt that we'll be doing just that."

Before Lord Neverember could even respond, Bruenor motioned left and right to his entourage, and they rose and stepped away from the table. The crafty old dwarf, who appeared so young, wanted to make it clear that he and his people were not under the suffrage of Lord Protector Neverember or anyone else, and so he wasn't about to wait for a dismissal from the lord, or even a respectful conclusion to the formal meeting.

He was daring Neverember to take action, perhaps even to detain him and his small entourage.

Because he knew the man would do no such thing, particularly not with King Emerus and Drizzt—who remained quite popular in Neverwinter these days—in that entourage.

They were out of the city soon after, without hindrance, and General Sabine, riding a fabulous warhorse with metal barding, and Citizen Jelvus Grinch on a smaller riding horse even accompanied them back to the main dwarven encampment, chatting amicably all the way.

"Lord Neverember is in a difficult position here," General Sabine told them. "This long-lost complex you call Gauntlgrym . . ."

"Is Gauntlgrym," Bruenor interrupted. "Been there meself more than once. No doubt."

General Sabine bowed to concede the point.

"Gauntlgrym has been a thorn in Neverwinter's side," she explained. "Monsters come forth from the Underdark all the time. And it was from that region, from the very mountain that houses the ancient complex, that the volcano erupted in the first place, destroying the old city."

Bruenor and Drizzt knew the truth of that all too well, and knew the source of the volcano to be the very same fire primordial that fired Gauntlgrym's legendary Forge. Drizzt had watched the eruption from a hilltop not so far away.

"Did ye come out here to tell me how to think o' Neverember then?" Bruenor asked. "I seen what I seen."

"I hope you understand the upset your arrival has caused, and will cause, with the powers that be in the region," General Sabine replied.

"Not just Lord Neverember," Jelvus Grinch added. "I expect that many of the Waterdhavian lords will not be as welcoming as you hope."

"But what would you do if you were still first citizen?" Drizzt asked, his tone revealing that he knew the answer.

"I'd be going into Gauntlgrym beside you to chase the dark elves and the rest away," he answered after only a slight hesitation to glance at General Sabine. His words could be construed as a treasonous act under the court of fiery Neverember. Jelvus Grinch had no authority to speak against the Lord Protector of Neverwinter, and certainly not in the presence of Neverwinter's captain of the guard, and yet he was.

That told Drizzt and the others a lot about Jelvus Grinch, but more importantly, it told Drizzt and Bruenor about the reliability and integrity of General Sabine. Jelvus Grinch would not have spoken so openly if he didn't trust the woman, which in Drizzt and Bruenor's eyes told them that they could trust her as well.

"With the dwarves claiming Gauntlgrym, Neverwinter will be far more secure," Jelvus Grinch went on. "And more prosperous, I would assume, with a mighty trading partner so near. You will want our food and our cloth."

"And our markets for your wares," General Sabine added.

Bruenor nodded, but thought that the dwarves would have nothing to do with Neverwinter's products, craftsmen, or markets if Neverember tried to slap a tariff on the dwarves for bringing their goods out through what the Lord Protector considered Neverwinter land.

As far as Bruenor was concerned—and he was sure that King Emerus and King Connerad felt the same way—in that situation, they'd either tunnel out a new exit farther to the north or to the east, or they'd just disregard any such demands of taxation.

And they'd cut Neverwinter out of any trading partnerships or military alliances.

Bruenor Battlehammer did not march to Gauntlgrym with such a force from the Silver Marches to bow down to the human lords of the Sword Coast.

◆ ◆ ◆

"WE NEED HER alive," the human said.

Jarlaxle sighed. "We did not go to all the trouble of finding the troubled young elf just to see her slaughtered."

"You went to find Tiago at the command of Gromph," the man pressed.

"We went to do both." Jarlaxle turned to Kimmuriel. "A fortunate coincidence that they were together."

Kimmuriel's expression showed that he could not have cared less.

Jarlaxle sighed again, an audible lament to the extremes of his two companions, one who apparently couldn't see past his own immediate desires, and the other, who was so removed from emotion that none of this seemed at all important to him. The mercenary grinned and let it go; this had ever been his role in Bregan D'aerthe, after all, balancing the immediate desires with the long-term implications.

Fortunately for him this time, Gromph's—and by extension, Matron Mother Baenre's—demands that Bregan D'aerthe locate and track Tiago also played into some more important developments and likelihoods that Jarlaxle had expected farther down the line.

Beniago and the human left then, leaving the co-leaders of Bregan D'aerthe alone in the room at the inn called One-Eyed Jax in Luskan.

"We don't need her at all," Kimmuriel pointed out. "Our excitable friend believes that since she, too, is *darthiir*, she will ultimately lead us where he desires to go."

"He sees us as if we all look alike, my friend," Jarlaxle replied. "Are we not guilty of the same prejudices against his kind? Or against Doum'wielle's, for that matter?"

Kimmuriel stared at him for a few moments. "You are," said the ultimately pragmatic psionicist, who spent more time with the otherworldly mind flayers than with his own kind, and when he considered the truth of Kimmuriel's words, Jarlaxle realized that he really couldn't disagree.

Still, Jarlaxle was less inclined toward xenophobia and prejudice than most others of his race, so he could take Kimmuriel's point well without taking it personally.

"When do you meet with Gromph again for his next lesson?" Jarlaxle asked.

"In a tenday, in Sorcere," the psionicist replied.

"We see where this is leading, and I don't think the archmage will approve. Nor will he harbor the risk of knowing our plans without going straight to the wretched matron mother."

"Archmage Gromph has more on his mind than something Bregan D'aerthe might do with a minor House in Menzoberranzan sometime in the future," Kimmuriel insisted.

"He is not removed from this," Jarlaxle reminded him. "He has been tasked with ensuring Tiago's safe return to Menzoberranzan. That puts us side by side, but not with similar end goals."

"He is more removed than you believe," Kimmuriel said. "But I will take great care when I present this to the archmage." He held up a large crystal, one attuned to the necklace Beniago had hung around Doum'wielle's neck.

This item was a psionic creation more than an arcane one, scrying through the sheer power of the mind. If Doum'wielle had been so trained, she could use the gem hanging around her neck to look back the other way, but of course, she'd never recognize such a power. But Gromph, training under Kimmuriel and growing quite adept at the strange psionic powers, would be able to utilize the connection between the gems.

And the great Kimmuriel, holding the third gem, would be able to psionically walk beside Tiago and Doum'wielle as surely as if he were actually standing with them.

"Keep a close watch," Jarlaxle bade him. "If Gromph moves on Tiago and Doum'wielle, we must be quick to act." Jarlaxle considered that closed the business between he and Kimmuriel, and rose from his seat, but Kimmuriel's next words stopped him before he took a step.

"For the sake of your human friend?"

Jarlaxle laughed under his breath at the sarcastic remark, so characteristic of the often too-clever Kimmuriel.

"For all our sakes, as the wider events unfold."

"We find a good profit simply working under the commands of the matron mother," Kimmuriel reminded him.

"Until Quenthel grows tired of us, or wishes to make a point against us."

"Against her brother, you mean."

Jarlaxle spun and glared at Kimmuriel. "You accuse me of using Bregan D'aerthe to further my own designs?"

Kimmuriel shrugged and returned Jarlaxle's look with a disarming grin. "Is that not why we *have* Bregan D'aerthe?"

That stark admission caught Jarlaxle off guard. He had elevated Kimmuriel to co-leader of the band precisely to make sure that he, Jarlaxle, did not wrongly use the band in pursuit of goals that did not serve Bregan D'aerthe.

"In this instance, I do not disagree that your needs and those of Bregan D'aerthe are one and the same," Kimmuriel explained. "When your sister imprisoned you as a guard of House Do'Urden—"

"Along with half of our foot soldiers," Jarlaxle interjected, and Kimmuriel nodded.

"She also sublimated our Luskan operation to House Xorlarrin and their fledgling city," Kimmuriel finished.

"We should remain a proxy group for House Baenre," the psionicist went on, "but only partly that, and only so long as it serves us."

"Keep a close watch, I beg," Jarlaxle said again.

"Of course."

As soon as Jarlaxle exited the room, Kimmuriel pulled forth that third crystal, the one with which he could monitor Doum'wielle and Tiago.

Unknown to Jarlaxle and to the archmage, with this gemstone Kimmuriel would be able to watch Gromph as well.

That breathtaking reality unnerved the psionicist as much as anything he had undertaken in the centuries of his life, for if Gromph Baenre ever got a hint that Kimmuriel was spying on him, his retribution would likely leave Kimmuriel tortured and begging for death next to K'yorl in the prisons of Errtu in the Abyss.

Yes, this was a dangerous game Kimmuriel was playing, and he had to admit to himself that spying on Gromph was as much a fulfillment of his personal desires to savor in the beauty of House Baenre's downfall as Kimmuriel's destroyed House was at long last avenged as it was any hope of practical gain.

The pieces were already in play, after all, and in a tenday, Kimmuriel would quietly insinuate more powerful words of the spell K'yorl had given him to facilitate Gromph's unwitting actions, returning her to Menzoberranzan where she could wreak revenge upon House Baenre.

Kimmuriel didn't have to monitor that—in fact, it was far more logical, and indeed much safer for him to remain as far removed from the coming chaos as he could. Still, despite all of that, despite his life's efforts in remaining purely pragmatic, in being driven purely by reason and not by emotion . . .

Indeed, despite all of that, Kimmuriel Oblodra simply couldn't help himself.

◆ ◆ ◆

OF ALL THE travelers from the Silver Marches, Tiago and Doum'wielle were the first to enter the tunnels that would take them to the ancient dwarven complex, now the drow city of Q'Xorlarrin. Tiago knew this region well, having come forth to raid Port Llast in search of Drizzt, and he knew, too, that he and his companion would almost certainly find the upper reaches of the complex empty of drow.

"Remain alert," he told Doum'wielle when they went into the long approach tunnels. "We will likely encounter enemies, goblins and kobolds at the least, in the upper chambers. Matron Mother Zeerith does not have the resources to secure the whole of the vast tunnels and chambers of the ancient dwarven homeland, particularly after her losses in the Silver Marches War, and I am sure that she remains in the lower tunnels."

"We will go to her?"

"No," Tiago sharply replied. "Once the dwarves are in the Underdark, Drizzt will almost surely serve as scout. We'll find our place, and we'll find him alone. Then we'll go and see Zeerith, and perhaps she will accompany me to the Ruling Council in Menzoberranzan, where I will present the matron mother with the heretic's head."

He should be warning his family of the dwarves' approach, Doum'wielle thought, but knew better than to say. Somehow, the necklace made her bolder about such thoughts.

She felt a sting of disapproval from Khazid'hea, a reminder to her that her own future likely hinged on this expected confrontation with the rogue Do'Urden.

She looked at Tiago and smiled and nodded, then obediently followed him down into the darkness.

Doum'wielle suppressed her wicked smile, secure in the notion that she, not he, would be the one presenting the head of Drizzt Do'Urden to Matron Mother Baenre.

With her father Tos'un dead, this was her only chance to find a place where she was not simply *iblith*, to be abused and discarded by the merciless drow.

PART 2

Seeking Destiny

THE WINDS OF CHANGE HAVE LIFTED THE HAIR FROM MY NECK. They tickle me and tease me, and take me to a place unexpected.

My road has wound in circles these last years, from hearth and home, to the open road, to trying to build anew with a group that was not of my own heart. And now the circle completes, back to where I began, it seems, but not so.

For these friends returned are not the friends I knew. They are very much akin in heart and duty, of course, and surely recognizable to me, but yet, they are different, in that they have seen a new light and way, a new perspective on mortality and death, and on the meaning of life itself. This attitude manifests itself most subtly, usually, but I see it there, in every Bruenor grumble, in every Catti-brie confidence, in every Regis fight, and in every Wulfgar laugh.

And now I see it in myself as well. For these last decades, after the passing of Catti-brie and the others, and even before Bruenor fell in Gauntlgrym, I was restless, and quite content to be. I wanted to know what was around the next bend, any bend in the road, be it the quest to find Gauntlgrym or the years afterward when I led the band of Artemis Entreri, Dahlia, and the others. My home was in my memories—I neither wanted nor needed a replacement. For those memories were enough to sustain me and nourish me. I nearly lost myself in that long and winding journey to that ultimate conclusion, and would have, I know, had I not refused Dahlia on that hillside in Icewind Dale. There, again, I found myself, and so in the end, I survived. Drizzt Do'Urden, this person I strive to be, survived the trials.

And now I find myself on the road of adventure again with Catti-brie and Bruenor, and could anything be better? Ours is a noble quest, as much so as the one that reclaimed Mithral Hall that century and more ago. We march with songs and the cadence of dwarven boots, under the flags of three kings and with the flagons of five thousand grinning dwarf warriors.

Could anything be better?

Perhaps so if Wulfgar and Regis were still with us, and truly I miss them every day. But at the same time, I am happy for them, and hold confidence that we will meet again. I noted the sparkle in Regis's eyes whenever he spoke of Donnola Topolino, and I can only applaud the road he has chosen—and only be happier that mighty Wulfgar walks that road beside him! Woe to any ill-intentioned rogues who cross the path of that formidable pair!

They will come back. I have fretted on this for a while, but now I am convinced. This is not like the time long ago when Wulfgar abandoned us to return to Icewind Dale. Nay, on that occasion, I doubted that we would ever see Wulfgar again, and we would not have, none of us, except that Regis and I ventured to Icewind Dale. Even then, the reunion was . . . strange. For when Wulfgar left us those decades ago, he did so emotionally as well as physically.

That is not the case this time.

They will come back, and we will be victorious in Gauntlgrym. These things I believe, and so I am at peace, and excited and anxious all at once.

And nervous, I admit, and I am surprised by that truth. When we rejoined together atop Kelvin's Cairn that dark night, there was only elation. And as the shock of my friends returned from the dead wore away, I was left simply giddy, feeling blessed and fortunate beyond what anyone should ever expect.

In the early days back together, even when we returned to the Silver Marches and found ourselves embroiled in a war, we all had the sense that the Companions of the Hall survived on time borrowed from the gods, and that our end, for any of us, could come at any moment, and it would be all right, because we had found each other again and had left no words unsaid. Even though my four friends had begun a new life, living two decades and more with new identities, with new family, new friends, and for Regis at least, a new love in his life, our existence was to be enjoyed and appreciated day by day.

And it was . . . all right.

Soon after, Catti-brie, Bruenor, and I had come to believe that Wulfgar and Regis had fallen in the tunnels of the Upperdark on our journey back to Mithral Hall. For months we had thought them lost to us forevermore, that they had journeyed once again into the realm of death, this time not to return.

And it was . . . all right.

The pain was there, to be sure, but still, we had been given the great gift of time together once more, and in the knowledge that our companionship was indeed rooted in mortality! I cannot emphasize that gift enough! Many times, I claim that a person must know he is going to die, must recognize and accept that basic truth of life, in order to defeat his fears and press on with a true sense of purpose in life. My friends knew that, and know that now, better than most.

They have seen the other side.

And when they are called again from this life, they go with acceptance, each, and not because they know a truth of immortality and eternity beyond the mortal coil—indeed, Wulfgar, and even Regis, remain skeptical of the gods, even after their ordeal in the enchanted forest of Iruladoon.

The close brush with death, indeed their decades in the clutches of something other than life, has given them, has given us all, both urgency and acceptance. It is a blessing, twice over.

Perhaps because of the passage of time, perhaps because of our victories and survival in the War of the Silver Marches, but now I have come to sense a change. That borrowed time seems less to me as I grow comfortable with the return of my friends, alive and vibrant, and hopefully with many decades ahead of them—indeed, even discounting the possibility of an enemy blade cutting one of us low, Bruenor could well outlive me in natural years!

Or our end, any of us or all of us, could come this very day, or tomorrow. I've always known this, and make it a part of my daily routine to remind myself of it, but now that the newness of my friends' return has worn off, now that I have come to believe that they are here—they are really here, as surely and tangibly as they were when I first met Catti-brie on the slopes of Kelvin's Cairn, and she introduced me to Bruenor and Regis, and then Wulfgar came to us when he was defeated in battle by Bruenor.

It is new again, it is fresh, and it is, in terms of an individual's life, lasting.

And so I am nervous about going into battle, because now I am seeing the future once more as the comfort of home and of friends, and my Catti-brie, all about, and it is a future I long to realize!

In a strange way, I now see myself moving in the opposite direction of Wulfgar. He has returned carefree, ready to experience whatever the world might throw before him—in battle, in game and in love. He lives for each moment, without regret.

Fully without regret, and that is no small thing. "Consequence" is not a word that now enters Wulfgar's conversation. He is returned to life to play, with joy, with lust, with passion.

I try to mirror that exuberance, and hope to find that joy, and know my lust in my love for Catti-brie, but while Wulfgar embraces the life of the free-spirited nomad, a rapscallion even, finding adventure and entertainment where he may, I find myself suddenly intrigued by the permanency of hearth and home, a husband, among friends.

A father?

—Drizzt Do'Urden

CHAPTER 8 ◈

A Seat of Reverence

THE TUNNELS DID NOT SEEM CRAMPED TO THEM. THE LOW ceilings and tons of stone above them did not bow their shoulders with apprehension. For the Delzoun dwarves, from the moment they entered the tunnel from the rocky dale, traveling down the long and winding subterranean corridor that Bruenor told them would take them to the outer wall of Gauntlgrym, the way, the smell, the aura, all spoke not of danger or foreign discomfort, or the threatening hush of a waiting predator, or the shadows of death fluttering all about.

To the dwarves of Delzoun, the tunnel spoke only of home.

Their most ancient and hallowed home. The home of their earliest ancestors, the hearth that had spawned the smaller fires of Citadel Felbarr and Citadel Adbar, Mithral Hall and Kelvin's Cairn, and all the other Delzoun kingdoms scattered about Faerûn.

This was the home-fire, the true home-fire, the spawn of the dwarven race on Toril, the greatest and earliest Forge that had propelled their kind to unparalleled heights of craftsmanship and reputation.

There were monsters all about, they knew. They could smell the stench of kobolds and goblins, and other, less-sentient denizens of dark places: carrion crawlers with waggling tentacles, and giant cave spiders who would suck the juices from a living victim and leave the pruned corpse for the vermin. The dwarves could smell them, or hear their distant skitters, but the dwarves didn't fear them, any of them.

They were an army of Delzoun warriors, unified in stride and strike, and letting come whatever may come. It didn't matter. They were on the path to Gauntlgrym, and so to Gauntlgrym they would go, and woe to any man or monster who dared to step in their way.

Despite the smells and scat and other goblinkin and monster sign, the dwarves only found a few skirmishes over the next few days, mostly with carrion crawlers, which were apparently so confident in their paralyzing poison, or simply so stupid, that they didn't comprehend the numerical disadvantage. A few dwarves were put into that temporarily paralyzed state by the swatting tentacles, but before the creatures could crawl up and begin a meal, hordes of other dwarves were there to take up the fight and overwhelm the beasts.

So not a dwarf was lost in the trek into the Underdark, and only one injured—and that from a fall, with a wound that the clerics easily mended.

Bruenor remained near the front of the line all the way down, with Drizzt and Catti-brie and the four dwarves that made up his personal bodyguard. Beside Bruenor came King Emerus and his entourage, led by Ragged Dain, along with King Connerad and Bungalow Thump.

So long was the dwarven line that when Bruenor at last entered the lowest chamber, the antechamber to Gauntlgrym's castle-like wall, the trailing dwarves were not even halfway down the long, descending tunnel from the surface.

Drizzt, Catti-brie, Bruenor, and Athrogate all knew this cavern, full of stalagmites and leering stalactites, with many structures hollowed as guard stations, ancient ballistae and catapults rotting in place. They stood on the landing before the tunnel exit, at the western end of the cavern, looking over the low stone wall. Just enough illuminating lichen was scattered about for them to peer through the forest of rock mounds and see the dull reflections off the black water of the underground pond. Across that foreboding water was a small beach of fine sand, fronting the stone wall and the doorway to the throne room.

"Do ye feel it?" Bruenor asked Emerus when the old king moved up to stand beside him.

"Aye," Emerus answered. "In me heart and in me bones. At the other end of this very cavern?"

"Across that water sits the wall, and just inside, the Throne o' the Dwarf Gods," Bruenor explained.

Despite the dim light, King Emerus's eyes sparkled, and he had to work very hard just to draw in his breath.

"We'll be startin' our work right in here," Bruenor told them all. "I'm thinking that we fix these guard posts—and might be buildin' a bridge across that water."

"One easy to drop," Catti-brie offered.

"Aye," said Emerus. "If them drow're up high already in Gauntlgrym, then we'll start our diggin' in right here so they can get the whole o' the army in their ugly faces." He paused and looked at Drizzt, then shrugged and offered a slight bow.

Drizzt, surely not offended, merely chuckled in reply.

"Bring in a swarm o' Gutbusters," Bruenor instructed Bungalow Thump. "Ye take yer boys down first and spread the breadth o' the place to the first mounds. Torch line, with none out o' sight, and all ready to fight for them next to 'em."

Bungalow Thump surveyed the place for a moment. "Wide cave," he said doubtfully.

"Me and me boy'll be with ye," Ambergris remarked, elbowing Athrogate, who snickered and shoved her back.

"Grab them Wilddwarfs from Adbar, if ye need 'em," said Bruenor, but Bungalow Thump shook his head.

"They're all up near the back," he explained.

Bruenor looked to King Emerus, the two of them shaking their heads knowingly. "King Connerad's sure to miss all the fun, and his boys'll find themselves in the back for his absence," Emerus said. He turned to Ragged Dain and nodded.

"I'll have enough o' me boys to take the right half o' the room," Ragged Dain told Bungalow Thump, and the two rushed off back up the tunnel to gather their forces.

With great precision, two hundred hustling dwarves soon stretched along the cavern floor, wall-to-wall in front of the stairway exit. On a call from Bungalow Thump, scores of torches went up in fast order. The long line began its steady move, sweeping clean the cavern in front of them, while more dwarves filled in from behind. Those second ranks formed strike teams, and whenever the leading dwarves crossed a stalagmite mound that had been worked with stairs, one of those strike teams was fast up them to scout the nest and secure the post.

Now Drizzt did go out to scout as well, moving into the shadows in front of the front line, picking his careful and swift way, but never getting too far in front. As they at last neared the water, the drow, with his keen lowlight vision, thought he spotted a pair of figures slipping in through the open door of Gauntlgrym across the way, but he couldn't be certain.

"Secure the bank," Bruenor told them when he, too, came up to the pond's edge. "And keep yerselves ready. Dark things in here, and in the water, too, not to doubt."

"Engineers'll be in tomorrow," Emerus said quietly to Bruenor. "It'll be a bit afore we can get a bridge across."

"And yerself ain't for waiting?" Bruenor asked, and Emerus shrugged. Bruenor pointed down the bank, where the hollowed cap of a giant mushroom sat in the darkness—the boat Bruenor and his friends had made when they had come in for Thibbledorf Pwent a year before. It was right where they had left it, Bruenor believed, and that seemed a good thing.

"Set a ferry?" Emerus asked.

"Dark things in the water, but aye," Bruenor replied.

"The Harpells can get many across in short order," Catti-brie said, moving to join the pair. "Old Kipper is well versed in the art of the dimension door."

The work began immediately, setting a brigade of archers with crossbows on the bank directly opposite the door, while Catti-brie ran back to fetch Penelope, Kipper, and the other Harpells. Skilled craftsdwarves soon arrived with their tools and logs they had dragged down from the forest above. Within a few hours, as more dwarves swarmed into the huge cavern, the Harpells and Catti-brie erected magical gates, and several score dwarves, including the kings and their bodyguards, stepped through the portals onto the beach across the way.

Work on the ferry began immediately, with beams set in place on both sides of the small pond, turnstiles dug in and secured, and with Penelope Harpell taking magical flight, carrying the heavy rope from one side to the other. While the ferry was being completed, with several more mushroom-cap boats fashioned, dwarf clerics cast magical light onto stones and threw them into the water along the ferry route.

Tightly packed schools of fish flitted from the illumination and hovered in the shadows just beyond the light, and those few adventurers who had been this way before understood the danger of those vicious cave fish. And so the Harpells and Catti-brie stood guard, and whenever one of those schools encroached upon the lighted path, a lightning bolt greeted them and sent them scurrying, or had them floating up to the surface, stunned or even dead.

Strong-shouldered dwarves cranked the turnstiles, and tough warriors carried stones across and set to building defensive walls outside the opened door to the upper hall of Gauntlgrym.

Despite their impatience, prudence ruled the day, and it was many hours before the first team of Gutbusters rushed through the small tunnel and into the great throne room—and that only after Penelope Harpell and Kipper had sent magical disembodied wizard eyes into the chamber to scout in front of them.

At long last, King Bruenor Battlehammer and King Emerus Warcrown and King Connerad Brawnanvil strode side by side into that hallowed chamber. They had come not as explorers, as with Bruenor's first journey here, in another time and another life. They had come not in desperation, as with Bruenor's second visit when he sought the council of the dwarf gods, nor to save a friend, as Bruenor and the Companions of the Hall had done to rescue Thibbledorf Pwent.

They had come as conquerors now, heirs to the throne of Delzoun.

Bruenor kept his eyes on Emerus as they walked to the dais down to the right, where sat the Throne of the Dwarf Gods. Bruenor had been here several times, of course, and so he knew what to expect, both with this enchanted and ancient throne he had sat upon before, and with the two graves set not far to the other side of it, the cairns built for himself and for Thibbledorf Pwent when they had both fallen in Gauntlgrym.

He remembered his first journey into this chamber, when he had first come to know for certain that he had indeed found this most ancient Delzoun homeland. He noted the same expression he knew he had worn upon the face of his companion, Emerus, and surely Bruenor understood.

He nodded, and he kept staring at the old King of Citadel Felbarr, and he let Emerus's sense of wonder and reverence bleed back to him, reminding him again of his own feelings on that first journey to this ancient and hallowed ground.

"That's the throne?" Emerus asked, his voice shaky.

"Aye, and beyond it's me own grave, and that o' Thibbledorf Pwent, me battlerager," Bruenor answered. "Ye go and put yer bum in the chair, and ye'll know if yer heart's pleasing Moradin."

Ragged Dain came huffing and puffing up to the pair just before they reached the throne.

"When I put me arse in that seat and me heart wasn't straight with the callings o' the gods, the chair tossed me almost to the wall," Bruenor explained. "Ah but ye'll get yer thoughts sorted out quick enough when ye put yerself in that throne!"

"Can any of us go and sit, then?"

"Royal blood," Bruenor replied. "So I'm guessin'. Though I'm thinking that any who've found the favor o' Moradin would be welcomed . . ."

His voice trailed off when Ragged Dain motioned ahead with his chin, and Bruenor turned to watch King Emerus moving for the seat. Without hesitation, the old king turned and plopped himself down on the throne. He slid back comfortably and placed his hands firmly on the burnished arms, grabbing tightly.

King Emerus closed his eyes. His breath came easy, his shoulders slumped in relaxation, as if all the tension was flowing out of his body.

Ragged Dain put his hand on Bruenor's shoulder, as much to support himself as to comfort the dwarf he had known as little Arr Arr.

◆ ◆ ◆

If King Emerus Warcrown's life had ended at this very moment, he would have died a happy dwarf. Sitting on that throne in these hallowed halls seemed to Emerus to be the crowning achievement of a dwarf life well lived. He felt at peace, more so than ever in his long life, for a sense of divine contentment washed through him.

All of his major life decisions, like abandoning Felbarr to undertake this journey, rolled through him. Not all had been correct, he had learned, sometimes painfully, but he sensed now that the gods of the dwarves, Moradin, Clangeddin, and Dumathoin, were satisfied that Emerus Warcrown had made those choices, right and wrong, with good intent and a proper sense of dwarven purpose.

An image of the Forge of Gauntlgrym came clearly to him, as well as one of the small tunnel leading to the antechamber that housed the fire primordial that gave the Forge its supernatural heat and magical energy.

Emerus wore a wide smile, but only until he sensed, or feared, that the throne had shown him that place in his mind's eye because he would never see it physically.

For he realized then that the dwarves were in for a long and bitter fight here, and that to truly secure Gauntlgrym would likely take them years. Longer than old King Emerus—who felt older now after months on the road—had left to live?

It seemed to Emerus a distinct possibility, but this, too, he accepted, and was content that Moradin and the other gods of his people agreed with his decision to abdicate his throne and journey to this place.

He felt their strength then, in his old and aching bones. And he heard their voices, speaking the old tongue of the dwarves, a language with which Emerus and every other dwarf alive had only cursory knowledge.

Every other dwarf alive except for the one standing in front of Emerus and watching him now, for Bruenor, too, had heard the voices of the ancients, of the gods.

A long time later, King Emerus Warcrown opened his eyes.

"Chan eagnaidth drasta," he said.

"Tha," Bruenor replied.

"What're ye about, then?" Ragged Dain asked, looking to each in turn. "Aye, to what?"

"King Emerus is wiser now," Bruenor explained.

"Tha," Emerus added. "For I'm hearin' the voice o' Moradin."

"And learnin' the tongue o' Moradin, aye?" Ragged Dain asked.

King Emerus smiled wide, then hopped off the throne, a spring in his step, and walked over to the pair. He nodded to his second and met the long gaze of Bruenor. Emerus lifted his hands and placed them solidly on his old friend's shoulders, the two staring unblinkingly for a long time, sharing something they both now knew and understood, something divine and supernatural.

King Emerus couldn't suppress his smile, and he began to nod.

"Lord Moradin's pleased by me choice," he said, his voice a whisper, because if he tried to speak more loudly, his voice would surely break apart with sobs.

◆ ◆ ◆

"You will go out to scout the upper halls?" Catti-brie asked Drizzt, the two off to the side of the entryway, just inside the throne room. They had watched Bruenor and Emerus's solemn walk to the throne, had watched Emerus sit upon it.

"Bruenor stays my hand," Drizzt replied. "The dwarves have decided to take the ground one finger at a time, fully secure that taken ground, then plod ahead to the next room. We'll not leave this room until Bruenor and the other dwarf leaders are satisfied that the chamber outside the wall is secured, or that this hall, too, has proper defenses set in place."

The sound of hammers and stones scraping across the floor lent credence to Drizzt's claims, for work was already underway in the throne room. Sideslinger catapults were already assembled and in place on the walls of the tunnels leading to the mines, and in front of the back door, the main entrance into the formal Gauntlgrym complex, heavy work was underway in constructing defensive half-walls, behind which crossbowdwarves could keep a close watch on the narrow threshold.

"Are you eager for battle?" Catti-brie asked. "Against your own kind?"

"Eager? No. But I accept the journey before us. Bruenor will have Gauntlgrym, I believe, or he will surely die trying."

"And Drizzt?"

"Owes his friend no less than that."

"So you'll die for Bruenor's dream?"

"Did not Bruenor forsake his divine reward for my sake? He could have gone to his gods, justly rewarded for a life well lived, but his duty to a friend turned his course. Is that not the whole point of it? Of it all? If I offer my hand to another and he takes it, do I not also have his hand? We are stronger together, but only if the bond of friendship travels from both hands. I could no more forsake Bruenor in this quest than you could have remained from my side when you knew I needed you. Or Bruenor. This is our bond, our blood, our hands joined. I only wish that Regis and Wulfgar were here, that we five would walk . . ."

He paused as he noted his wife's bemused smile.

"What is it?"

"Nothing," Catti-brie said lightly. "Nothing of much importance. Only that I find it amusing when I consider that Wulfgar labels me as the preachy one."

A flabbergasted Drizzt tried to respond, but his lips moved without making a sound.

"Oh, kiss me," Catti-brie said and moved in close, and pecked Drizzt lightly before moving back with a laugh. "Do you know that I love you?" she asked. "Do you believe that I would rather be here beside you in this dark place, with danger all around and battle looming before us, than anywhere else in the world? Than in any garden Mielikki might fashion to my every sensual pleasure?"

She moved back in front of him again, right in front of him, her blue eyes locking his lavender orbs. "Do you know that?"

Drizzt nodded and kissed her again.

"And we will survive this," Catti-brie insisted. "Our road will not end in Gauntlgrym. We will not allow it!"

"And then where?" The question carried more weight than Drizzt had intended, and the sound of the blunt words gave him pause as much as they stunned his wife. For so many years, in this life and Catti-brie's last, Drizzt and Catti-brie had danced around this issue. They were adventurers, ever seeking the road and the wind in their faces.

But was there more for them?

"When Bruenor sits on Gauntlgrym's throne, does Drizzt remain beside him?" Catti-brie asked.

Drizzt's hesitance spoke more loudly than any words he might have said.

"I do not wish to live again in the halls of the dwarves," Catti-brie bluntly added. "Nearby, surely, but this is not the place for me. I returned in the service of Mielikki, in the love of the open air, to feel the grass beneath my feet, to feel the wind and rain upon my face. I expect that I will spend many tendays in Gauntlgrym, beside my beloved Da, surely, but this is not to be my life."

"Neverwinter?" Drizzt asked, and Catti-brie winced.

"Then where?"

"Penelope has invited us to reside at the Ivy Mansion, or anywhere in Longsaddle," Catti-brie said. "It is not so long a journey for Andahar and my spectral steed."

"And there you can continue your studies," Drizzt reasoned. "No better place."

"But what for Drizzt?"

"The Bidderdoos," the drow ranger replied without the slightest hesitation, and with an honest lightness in his voice. "When we have found an enchantment to relieve them of their lycanthropy, someone will need to catch them and bring them in to receive their cure. Who better suited to such a task as that than a ranger of Mielikki?"

"Noble hunting," Catti-brie agreed, her voice almost giddy with relief now that she had openly expressed her desires, and now that she had seen Drizzt's sincere enthusiasm to share in her choice.

"I will be here, in Gauntlgrym, many tendays as well—many more than you, I expect," Drizzt did say in warning. "The dwarves will not secure this place in Bruenor's lifetime or my own. It will be contested ground by many, from the drow of Menzoberranzan to the Lords of Waterdeep, if Lord Neverember is any indication of the greed we can expect. I intend to stand beside Bruenor and Clan Battlehammer whenever they call, and even when they do not."

"I would have it no other way," Catti-brie agreed. "And I know the Harpells will remain vigilant beside Gauntlgrym."

"Family," Drizzt said.

"And what of your family?" Catti-brie asked.

Drizzt stared at her for a long while, caught off-guard, for he understood the implications of her tone.

"Your wife," she clarified.

Drizzt nodded, but still wasn't sure what to make of her remark.

"In the first fight for Mithral Hall, I was wounded and nearly killed," Catti-brie reminded him.

"I remember it as clearly as you do."

"And from those wounds, I was damaged," Catti-brie said, and Drizzt nodded again. "My days as a warrior were ended . . ."

"And so you turned to the Art."

"My days as a mother would never be ended," Catti-brie went on.

Drizzt swallowed hard.

"In this new life, I am not damaged," Catti-brie explained. "My body is whole. I could take up a sword once more, if I so chose, though I do not."

"Are you with child?"

The woman gave a slight smile. "No," she said. "But if I were?"

Drizzt fell over her with a great hug and a kiss, suddenly wanting nothing more than to share a child with Catti-brie. He had put that thought out of his mind for so long—for in his love's other life, it could not be, and in the decades after she was lost to him, he held no desire to father a child with any other. Certainly Dahlia was not the mother Drizzt would choose for his daughter or son. And there had been no other, no other Catti-brie.

Looking at her now, Drizzt knew that there could never be anyone else for him. Not Innovindil, not Dahlia.

"We will build a wonderful life," he promised her in a whisper.

"When we find the time," she replied, somewhat sourly, but Drizzt put his finger over her lips to silence her.

"We will make the time," he promised.

◆ ◆ ◆

BRUENOR REACHED BEHIND his enchanted shield and pulled forth a flagon of ale.

"Bah, but ye're to put the brewers out o' their living," Emerus said, taking the offered mug.

"Fine ale," Connerad agreed.

"Ale, mead, beer," Bruenor said with a hearty laugh.

"Fine shield, then!" said Connerad, offering a toast, and the three kings tapped their flagons together.

They were on the beach outside of the grand entry hall, the work buzzing around them. All of the dwarves had gained the cavern by then, filling the place and the entry hall. Already, construction on the bridge across the dark pond was well underway, with the buttresses growing tall and solid. The Harpells were out there assisting with the bridge, and old Kipper seemed to be having quite the time of it, easing the heavy burden of the laboring dwarves by magically lifting the heavy beams, which could then be easily shoved into place.

"We should send groups back up to the surface for more logs," Connerad remarked. "Can't have enough ballistae and catapults out."

"Go see to it," said Emerus. "Send some Mirabarrans. Tell them o' the importance."

Connerad looked at the old king curiously, for Connerad, too, was a dwarf king and was not used to being ordered about. But Emerus gave him a solemn nod and Connerad understood. He drained his flagon and handed it to Bruenor, who laughed and threw it over his shoulder to smash against the stone wall of Gauntlgrym. With a wink, Bruenor reached behind the shield yet again to produce another, full to the brim, which he gave to Connerad.

"Ye best be sendin' some Gutbusters with the teams heading back to the sunlight," Bruenor said. "Still might be monsters in the tunnels."

"Ye chose well in fillin' yer seat when ye gived up yer throne," Emerus said when Connerad had gone. "A good dwarf is that one."

"His Da's among the best Mithral Hall e'er knew," Bruenor replied.

"Ye miss it?" Emerus asked after a while.

"Mithral Hall?"

"Aye, and bein' king."

Bruenor snorted and took a big gulp of his ale. "Nah, can't be sayin' that. Don't ye get me wrong, if some orcs or drow took the place, I'd go straight back and kick 'em out, don't ye doubt, for the place's is e'er me home. But I'm likin' the road."

"But now ye're here to stay."

"Moradin called me back."

Emerus nodded, a most serene expression coming over his face. "Aye," he said, several times, for when he had sat on the Throne of the Dwarf Gods, he, too, had felt the infusion of strength and wisdom and ancient secrets, and so he understood.

"All me life I had Felbarr," he said quietly. "Obould took the place and so we kicked him out, and ye know well that he'd come back again to all our misery."

"And all our hope," Bruenor reminded his friend.

"It pained me to watch ye sign that damned treaty in Garumn's Gorge," Emerus admitted. "I know it pained yerself, too."

"Yerself agreed with the treaty . . ." Bruenor began.

"Aye," Emerus cut him short. "Had to be done. And we had to hope. We could'no've fought them damned orcs without the full backin' o' Silverymoon and Sundabar, and they wanted no part o' war." He paused to gulp a swallow of ale then spat upon the ground. "Then they come roarin' back blamin' Bruenor for the new war," he said with a disgusted shake of his hairy head. "Cowards, the lot!"

"Worse," said Bruenor. "Politicians."

Emerus got a loud chuckle out of that.

"Ye done right, me friend," Emerus said. "In the first fight with Obould, back there in Garumn's Gorge, and now again in yer new life. Ye done yer Da and Grandda and all the line o' Battlehammer proud, and know that the name o' Bruenor will e'er be toasted with reverence in Citadel Felbarr." He lifted his flagon and Bruenor tapped it with his own.

"And in Mithral Hall," Emerus went on. "And here in Gauntlgrym, don't ye doubt."

"And yerself?" Bruenor asked. "Ye missing Felbarr?"

"Was me home all me life," said Emerus. "But no, I'm not missin' it now. Wishin' Parson Glaive was with me, but glad he's holdin' the throne in me place. Nah, now," he said, looking around at the grand construction, listening to the fall of mallet and the crank of the turnstiles, looking back at the ancient and solid wall of Gauntlgrym, "now me old heart's tellin' me that I've come home, me friend. Truly home."

Bruenor understood, for he had felt the same way when first he had ventured into these hallowed halls, when first he had sat upon the Throne of the Dwarf Gods. There was something deeper here than even in Mithral Hall for him, some ancient murmur of magic that touched him to the core of his Delzoun soul. He recalled his elation when he had found Mithral Hall those decades and decades ago, marching in with the Companions of the Hall—indeed, culminating the adventure that gave the troupe its name. But this was different. Deeper and more solemn, and less parochial. This adventure to reclaim Gauntlgrym would be shared by all the Delzoun dwarves.

"We're right to be here," Emerus said with conviction.

"Ye didn't see me kicking Connerad to the side and taking back me throne, did ye?" Bruenor agreed. "Aye, I'm knowin' the same, me friend."

Connerad came back over then, the look on his face showing that he had overheard that last comment.

"Bah, but who ye kickin' where?" he asked.

"Yerself!"

"Weren't yer throne to take back," Connerad said. "Was me own to keep or to give."

"Aye," said Bruenor, and Emerus lifted his flagon and said, "King Connerad!" and Bruenor gladly joined in the toast.

"But I hear yer words," Connerad said.

"Glad ye gived yer throne over?" Emerus asked, and Connerad smiled and nodded.

"Only wish me Da might've seen this place," the young king said.

"Ye plannin' to put yer butt on the throne?" Bruenor asked.

Connerad stared at him, seeming unsure.

"Aye, yerself's more than worthy," said Bruenor. "Ye'll see. Go and look at it. Touch it and feel its power. But don't ye sit on it until me and me friend Emerus come in and bear witness."

"Ye're sure?" Connerad asked.

"Sure that it'll be akin to yer first time with a dwarf lass," Emerus said with a laugh. "Ye'll get off it a changed dwarf, and ye'll know. Aye, but ye'll know.

"Don't tarry," Connerad said, turning for the door.

"We'll be right along," said Bruenor.

"He's a good lad," Emerus noted as Connerad again left them. "Hard for me to call him that when he's standing next to yerself, for ye're the one looking so much like a dwarfling!"

"Aye, and good riddance to me old bones!" Bruenor said, toasting yet again, draining his flagon and throwing it, too, against the wall behind him.

Emerus did likewise, but grabbed Bruenor by the shoulder as the red-bearded dwarf started to rise. "I'm jealous of ye, Bruenor Battlehammer," Emerus told him. "Ye'll be the First King o' Gauntlgrym in the new age."

Bruenor stared at him, caught by surprise by the blunt words. He hadn't given the disposition of Gauntlgrym much thought, not beyond waging the war to kick out the drow. There were three dwarf kings here, after all, though Bruenor and Emerus could surely lay claim above the call of Connerad. But

Emerus was as old as Bruenor, and surely as distinguished, and so the claim now that Bruenor would get the throne struck the red-bearded dwarf curiously, and uncomfortably.

Had Emerus seen something on the Throne of the Dwarf Gods to incite that statement?

It was clear to Bruenor that Emerus believed his prediction, and Bruenor saw no reason to doubt the possibility that he would become the First King of Gauntlgrym.

But he and Emerus were wrong.

◆ ◆ ◆

"IT'S HERE," KIPPER said, and his old eyes sparkled at the thought. He reached into his pouch and carefully, with both hands, brought forth that dark gemstone. Kipper lifted the pocked sphere, which was almost as large as a human skull, up for the others to see.

"Are you certain?" Penelope asked breathlessly.

"I can feel it through the stone," Kipper explained. "Just being near the gate excites the magical energies within the orb."

"What gate?" asked Drizzt, standing with Catti-brie, and quite confused by the sudden change in the conversation. Penelope and Catti-brie had been chatting easily about the Bidderdoos and Longsaddle's library, when Kipper had bounded over with his proclamation.

"Gates to connect dwarven homelands," Catti-brie explained.

"There was one here, millennia ago," Kipper insisted.

"Magical portals?" Drizzt asked. "So that one might walk from Gauntlgrym to Mithral Hall . . . instantly?"

"If Mithral Hall had one," Penelope explained. "And if we've the stones to power the portals." She reached into her own belt pouch, which was apparently one much like Regis had worn, a magical pouch of holding that could carry far more extradimensionally than its size and shape would indicate. She drew forth a large tome, bound in some gray leathery material, and locked with silver chains. "As Cattie-brie and I discussed back in Longsaddle," Penelope said, "considerable thought should still be put into the wisdom of opening such magical portals anywhere near a city like Gauntlgrym, which is so well-known to the powers of Menzoberranzan."

Cattie-brie nodded gravely, and when her eyes met Drizzt's he could tell she had decided to proceed.

"Many hints in here about the ancient portals," Penelope went on, patting the book. "And in the other tomes I've brought along."

"I'm surprised you would bring such old and valuable books out of Longsaddle," Drizzt replied.

"Shared extradimensional space," Kipper explained. "The books are in a trunk in the Ivy Mansion, but Penelope can access them through her belt pouch. Quite a clever twist on simple bags of holding, don't you agree?"

"A twist Kipper no doubt perfected," Catti-brie noted slyly, and the old wizard grinned with pride.

"Well, if you have something like that already, could it not be used as a gate?" Drizzt asked. "Could I not crawl through Penelope's pouch and out of the chest in your home?"

"No, no!" Kipper said. "This is not nearly powerful enough for such extradimensional walking. And the risks would be too severe, for the connection is not secured. You might fall into the Nine Hells or some other unpleasant place. Or were you to bring another bag of holding along . . . well . . . if your little friend Regis tried to crawl through, his belt pouch would tear a rift to the Astral Plane and he would be drifting and lost forever!"

"But as you can surmise, Kipper has spent many years mulling over extra dimensions and teleportation and the like," Penelope said. "We have come to Gauntlgrym out of loyalty to our old friends of Mithral Hall, and loyalty to Bruenor and to yourself, and mostly to our beloved Catti-brie there, who lived among us for so many years. But we have also come with good fortune. The possibility that an ancient dwarven gate remains thrills us. Perhaps we will find it and learn from it. Perhaps we will build portals, even minor portals, to connect Mithral Hall and this reclaimed dwarven hall."

She looked at Catti-brie and offered a little wink as she added, "Perhaps a door for Catti-brie to easily visit her adoptive father."

"My hope has now been confirmed," Kipper said, bringing the conversation back to his original interruption. He looked into the stone of power again. "There is a gate here, and the stone can sense it, and that will make finding it, and perhaps even finding another stone to power it, all the easier!"

Drizzt wasn't about to play the contrarian, though he shared Penelope's grave doubts. Perhaps not in the near future, but at some time, surely, the drow would likely find a way to use such a shortcut to attack yet again the Delzoun enclave.

But that was a fear for another day, Drizzt reminded himself.

"The dwarves will be securing the cavern and throne room for a few more days," he told the others. "They will only gradually make their way forward from the throne room to the other chambers of this level. Wherever that gemstone might take you, Kipper, take care not to strike out beyond our forward perimeter. Gauntlgrym is full of enemies—drow, goblinkin, monstrous, animal, and even magical. You will go looking for your portal, but will more likely find yourself in a desperate fight or flight."

"Agreed, Master Do'Urden," Kipper replied. "But do prod your friend Bruenor, I beg." He replaced the stone in his belt pouch and eagerly rubbed his wrinkled old hands together, even giving a small cackle to complete the picture of his giddy energy.

Drizzt was glad of the old wizard's enthusiasm, but he wasn't about to ignore the more immediate problem. Penelope had referred to Gauntlgrym as a reclaimed dwarven hall, but it was no such thing. And with a major noble House of Menzoberranzan dug into the lower levels, such a reality might take years to achieve, if it could be reclaimed at all

CHAPTER 9 ◈

Thinning the Faerzress

IGHTNING FLASHED REPEATEDLY, REVEALING STROBING, startling images of the great cavern that housed Menzoberranzan. On and on, it went, sizzling through the streets and boulevards, frying rothé as they tried to flee, sending dark elves tumbling desperately into alleyways.

At the top of the cavern, similar bolts, some white light, some red, some green, deflected off the thick stone bases of stalactites, illuminating the targets, demonic or drow.

"Impressive," Kimmuriel said sarcastically from the window of Gromph's Sorcere residence. "So chaos reigns supreme in Menzoberranzan. The priestesses must be thrilled, unless of course, that chaos blunts the ambitions of any in particular."

"Order within the chaos," Gromph corrected. "In the madness outside, none can gather in unison to strike back at Matron Mother Baenre."

"How long can she hold the chaos from her own door?" the psionicist dared to ask. He turned away from the spectacle to regard Gromph of House Baenre as he uttered that warning.

Gromph didn't seem upset at all by the suggestion, and reaching deeper, reaching into his student's mind, Kimmuriel understood that the calm facade accurately reflected the calmness inside the archmage.

"There is always that danger when playing with demons," Gromph said with a shrug.

"Powerful demons," Kimmuriel replied. "In my journey through the city, I witnessed every type of demon I know short of balors, and in numbers. A flock of glabrezu? Or should it be called a herd, I wonder? Or a murder, as with the large black crows in the World Above? Yes, that would seem most appropriate."

"Yes, well, we will see where it leads," Gromph replied. "It is all quite above us mere males, after all, for it is in the province of Lady Lolth herself and her chosen Matron Mother."

Kimmuriel detected a background snicker in his voice, an expression of confidence that belied the words he had spoken, and the psionicist nodded and smiled, ostensibly to agree with the archmage. Truthfully, though, Kimmuriel's grin was rooted in his own recognition that his suggestions to Gromph had taken root. Gromph believed that he could control this situation, that he was finding some heretofore unknown combination of psionics and arcane magic that would grant him superiority over even Quenthel in this roiling demon game.

Just as Kimmuriel had hoped, just as his mother had shown him.

How surprised would Gromph be, Kimmuriel wondered in the deepest and most protected corners of his organized and disciplined brain, when he brought forth K'yorl Odran in all her uncontrollable wrath?

The image of K'yorl taking revenge on House Baenre was an undeniably pleasing one to Kimmuriel. He hoped that K'yorl wouldn't destroy Gromph's mind, catching him by surprise as she surely would. For he couldn't wait to witness the flow of unfiltered thoughts in the archmage when he realized his foolish hubris and the ruin he had brought upon his own House.

"Shall we begin?" Gromph ordered as much as asked. "I have much to do this day."

He started toward Kimmuriel, but the psionicist held up his hand to give Gromph pause.

"I have come bearing news from Bregan D'aerthe and Jarlaxle," Kimmuriel explained in the face of Gromph's surprised expression. "A great army of dwarves has entered the upper chambers above Q'Xorlarrin, intent on reclaiming the ancient homeland they name Gauntlgrym."

"What dwarves?"

"From the Silver Marches," Kimmuriel answered, and Gromph sighed.

"They are led by King Bruenor Battlehammer of Mithral Hall, who killed your mother, Matron Mother Yvonnel, soon after the Time of Troubles," Kimmuriel explained. "The same Bruenor, yes, reborn into the world to fight Many-Arrows and for this task, some say. They are formidable and determined, with ranks thousands deep, and Matron Mother Zeerith will not defeat them, Jarlaxle assures me. They will retake the Forge and chase the Xorlarrins and their slaves into the lower tunnels, and the experiment known as Q'Xorlarrin will be no more."

"Jarlaxle believes this?"

"You know enough of him to understand his excellence in predicting these matters."

"I know enough about him to understand that much of what he says is said with motives other than those the message conveys," Gromph replied.

"Take of it what you will. By Bregan D'aerthe's contract and protocol, I should have gone straight to the matron mother, or perhaps even the Ruling Council with this information, but given our . . . clandestine relationship, I thought it wiser to let the archmage deliver this unsettling and startling news."

"Not so startling," Gromph said. "Through the gemstone connection of your own creation, I have seen that Tiago has been moving west, in the direction of Q'Xorlarrin."

"Perhaps to return to his mother and House."

"More likely in pursuit of Drizzt Do'Urden, I assumed," Gromph replied. "Tiago is singularly minded. He will have his day with Drizzt. Nothing is more important to him than that."

"Or Drizzt will have the day."

Gromph shrugged as if it did not matter, and to these two, of course, it certainly did not. Neither Tiago nor Drizzt held any importance to either of them in the long game.

"It is likely that the rogue Drizzt is beside his friend Bruenor," Kimmuriel said.

"I should look in on Tiago then."

Those words revealed a lot to Kimmuriel. If he had been in Gromph's place, he would have been watching Tiago closely, almost continually—as he was with his own scrying stone, of course.

"The scrying wearies you," Tiago said.

Gromph admitted it with a nod. "The power does not come easily. I see it there, just at the edge of my reach. To send my mind through the stone unbalances me, and I return weakened and vulnerable."

"And with powerful demons flying all about your city and tower you cannot afford such vulnerability," Kimmuriel reasoned. "So you look in on Tiago only sporadically and only briefly."

Gromph straightened and squared his shoulders imperiously.

"It will grow easier," Kimmuriel assured him. "These powers of the mind are new to you—I am amazed at the progress you have already made. Such psionic scrying is a difficult task for any, even an illithid, and that you can perform it at all is testament to your mental strength, and offers great hope that you will one day—one day soon, perhaps—attain psionic greatness to rival your arcane prowess."

The compliments performed as Kimmuriel had hoped, and Gromph eased back and visibly relaxed. And the kind words were only partly a lie, Kimmuriel knew, for Gromph was indeed powerful in mind magic—and as intelligent as any drow ever known. Intelligence alone didn't guarantee psionic prowess—the brilliant Jarlaxle was quite fumbling with regard to the psionic powers, after all—but when one had that aptitude, as with Gromph, great intelligence would present great opportunity, a ceiling as high as the sky in the World Above.

"Are you prepared to resume our sessions?" Kimmuriel asked.

"Of course. There are demons all around, but more than a few answer to the demands of Archmage Gromph." He closed his eyes and held his arms out wide, beckoning Kimmuriel to come forth psionically.

And so the son of House Oblodra did, telepathically imparting his lesson into the consciousness of Gromph Baenre.

And while he was there, telepathically imparting some small inflections of the chant he had been given in the Abyss, and putting them just below Gromph's consciousness, in a place where the archmage would find them when next he attempted a summoning, and putting them there in such a way that Gromph would believe them an epiphany, a deeper understanding of the relationship and miscibility of the Art and psionics. Yes, Kimmuriel could feel Gromph's confidence.

The archmage was just arrogant enough to believe that he was exploring new territory in this supposed combination of the two powers, as if such potential had never occurred to the hundreds of brilliant psionicists to come before him, or to the illithids, whose intelligence was beyond question.

When the session ended a short time later, Kimmuriel was quick to take his leave, and Gromph was eager to let him go.

And off Gromph went as well, straight to House Baenre's spidery gate, and to the audience chamber of his sister, Matron Mother Quenthel Baenre.

Quenthel calmly listened to his report of the dwarves' march into Gauntlgrym, her eyes and steady hands not betraying the least nervousness. An army was marching upon House Xorlarrin, perhaps her strongest ally. An army of wretched dwarves, marching from the region where she had initiated a war. An army now preparing for battle against Menzoberranzan's satellite city of Q'Xorlarrin, which granted to Quenthel a trading route to rival that of House Hunzrin.

"You cannot send our House soldiers," Gromph finished. "Not in this dangerous time."

Matron Mother Baenre nodded in agreement.

"Matron Mother Mez'Barris, perhaps?" Gromph said, and he chuckled at the thought of the warriors of House Barrison Del'Armgo being sent forth for the defense of House Xorlarrin, who ranked among their most hated rivals.

"She would refuse, and would be within her rights to refuse," Quenthel answered. "If I demanded this of Matron Mother Mez'Barris, then even those Houses allied with us would fear that they might be next, and no House would willingly spare her soldiers now with the city in such chaos."

"Will you send Do'Urden?" asked the archmage. "Surely you control that House fully, and among its nobles are Matron Mother Zeerith's own two children."

"The garrison of House Do'Urden is made up of too many soldiers from too many Houses—noble Houses who would resent the losses," the matron mother replied, again shaking her head. "Nor would I wish to risk the proxy vote of Matron Darthiir on the council."

She had refused Gromph's every suggestion, yet she was smiling. She clearly knew something, and once again Gromph was reminded of his sister's improved prowess. When he thought of his daughter, blessed with the knowledge and memories of Yvonnel and surely to succeed Quenthel, he felt a tinge of regret at ever having introduced Quenthel to the illithid Methil.

"You have few options," he said.

"I am the matron mother, the voice of Lolth in Menzoberranzan, foolish male," Quenthel answered. "I have every option."

"Matron Mother Zeerith will not withstand the press of King Bruenor and his dwarves," Gromph replied, pointedly using the name of that cursed dwarf, who had split the head of their mother a century before with his fabled battle-axe. He thought to mention his belief that Drizzt Do'Urden would be there beside Bruenor as well. Quenthel knew well the rogue of House Do'Urden. He had killed her once.

But Gromph decided not to twist the verbal blade quite that far. "There are too many dwarves, and by all accounts they came well equipped. It will take much of Menzoberranzan's power to turn them back."

"Menzoberranzan cannot afford to march at this time."

"If the city of Q'Xorlarrin falls . . ."

"It will not fall," the matron mother said with a wry grin. "Not when the dwarves come up against a horde of mighty demons, and that long before they have ever neared Matron Mother Zeerith's position in the lower tunnels."

Gromph stepped back as if struck, and the surprising response had him stuttering in his brain, even if he was too disciplined to let those doubts pass through his lips. Was Quenthel seriously suggesting sending an army of demons to Q'Xorlarrin? An army of demons, led by mighty beasts like Nalfeshnee?

Who could truly control such an army? Bringing those demons together might prove worse for Matron Mother Zeerith if the demons chased off the dwarves than if the dwarves destroyed them to a manes.

"You hold a favored teleport location within Gauntlgrym, do you not?" Quenthel asked.

"I do."

"Then you will—"

"You cannot be serious," Gromph interrupted, and Quenthel's eyes flashed with anger. "My attuned chamber is in the antechamber to the primordial that fires Gauntlgrym's forges. You know this."

"Then nearer the battle."

"The demons will seek to release the primordial," Gromph protested. "These demons you summon are not stupid creatures, and surely they will recognize the chaotic potential of freeing such a force as a fire primordial. They will dance about the explosions as the volcano begins anew!"

The matron mother leaned back and stared at him hard, seeming unimpressed.

"Unless you wish me to bring through simple-minded manes and lesser demons," Gromph clarified, and wisely backstepped. "Chasme, even, who would not be clever enough to defeat Gauntlgrym's magical defenses. Or succubi, who would be too intrigued with playing in the battle to care for an uncontrollable force such as a primordial. Or glabrezu—indeed, the violent hunters would be fine shock troops for the Xorlarrins. They would want the flesh of dwarves for them—"

"Greater beings," Matron Mother Baenre said evenly.

"You wish me to deliver greater demons to the side of the primordial pit?"

The matron mother hesitated, and Gromph could see her inner struggle then. No doubt she wanted to press forward with her ridiculous demand simply to not give her brother the satisfaction of being correct. But she was seeking Yvonnel's advice now, he understood. She was searching those many memories Yvonnel the Eternal could offer in dealing with a nalfeshnee or a marilith, or a balor even.

Gromph knew what that advice would entail, for he knew that he was correct. When such demons moved into Gauntlgrym, Matron Mother Zeerith would have to send her garrison of wizards into the primordial chamber in full force, sealing the area of Abyssal intrusion to protect the lever that kept the magical powers of the Tower of the Arcane in Luskan flowing. Those powers brought in the waters of the ocean, the ancient magic manipulating that aqueduct system, reaching into the Elemental Plane of Water and bringing forth mighty water elementals, which dived down from the ceiling of the primordial's chamber and circled the walls of the entrapping pit in a dance that doused the primordial's volcanic designs.

"The dwarves have only just entered the caverns," Gromph said. "Send forth your creatures—they are tireless and will find the Xorlarrins before King Bruenor has moved from the upper levels."

"Be gone from here," Quenthel ordered, which was her way of admitting that Gromph was right, of course. "Get back to your useless studies before I decide that you should accompany the Abyssal procession."

Gromph bowed and moved off. He had done his duty—twice over. First he had delivered the warning of the dwarves, and second, he had prevented Quenthel from risking utter devastation to the satellite city.

That second thought bothered him. Why had he done that? Why again had he propped up his idiot sister when his daughter waited in the wings to claim Menzoberranzan as her own?

Because this was Quenthel's crisis, and one exacerbated by her greedy action bringing forth so many powerful demons.

"Bide your time," he told himself quietly as he exited the Baenre compound and wound his way across the Qu'ellarz'orl toward Tier Breche and his Sorcere chambers. Had he gone along with Quenthel, knowing the disastrous course for what it was, Q'Xorlarrin would surely have been obliterated. Gromph cared nothing about that, of course, but he cared that the Spider Queen would care, and would seek him out as the one who helped deliver the demons to their source of complete destruction.

No, Gromph's actions had to be more subtle than that heavy hammer. He nodded as his plans came clear—if he could control some of the greater demons that would march for Q'Xorlarrin, he could profoundly wound his sister, perhaps even mortally wound her reputation within the city, and much more important, in the eyes of Lady Lolth.

◆ ◆ ◆

"Do you feel it?" asked the half-spider, half-drow woman with exquisite features and undeniable beauty.

Errtu, the largest of the three demons gathered around the black puddle Lolth was using as a scrying pool, bent low and peered more deeply into the wavy image, taking care that the flames that ever surrounded his massive frame didn't ignite the oily stew.

He could see the rough, natural walls of jagged-edged volcanic stone. It was more porous than what one would expect at this depth, given the amount of pressure upon it from the great weight. It glowed with an inner light, continually shifting within the wall in location and hue. Every pock flared with inner purple or red, as if some wizard had covered himself with faerie fire, then melded into the stone forevermore.

The balor nodded, and had to remind himself not to reach out and plunge his hand into the puddle, for indeed, he felt as if he could grasp the stones, or dive through the puddle, perhaps, and come forth from the jagged stones to walk once more in Faerûn's Underdark.

"The barrier thins," Lolth explained. "The Archmage of Menzoberranzan unknowingly whittles at the protections of the Faerzress."

The Spider Queen laughed, a sound not often heard in the Abyss, and certainly not from her—unless, unlike now, she had a slave lying helpless in front of her, and one worth torturing.

"We will be able to pass through without waiting for some fool to call upon our services?" asked the third of the group, Marilith.

"Not us," Errtu said with a growl, turning to Lolth as he spoke.

The Spider Queen merely snorted and shrugged.

The Faerzress glowed more brightly, a rolling blue to purple to red filling the pool.

"Archmage Gromph, I presume," said Lolth.

Marilith sighed and closed her eyes, drawing the attention of the other two.

"He summons me," she explained. "And I feel compelled to his call. But it cannot be."

"He wishes to confirm the story being put forth by House Barrison Del'Armgo," said Lolth, "that Malagdorl defeated and banished you."

"But I feel as if I can readily answer the call."

"You can."

Both demons turned to the Spider Queen with surprise.

"A hundred years," Errtu said. "The banishment is . . ."

"How do you so break the rules of the cosmos?" Marilith asked. "I was banished by the trident of Malagdorl Armgo. I cannot return to the Prime Material Plane until a century has passed, with rare exception."

"You weren't defeated," Lolth explained. "You did as I instructed. You were sent to lose, and did as you were ordered, so there was no loss. But yes, the Faerzress thins, the boundary between the Underdark of Faerûn and the Abyss is less a barrier, and soon a facilitator."

"And Bilwhr, whom Gromph obliterated?" Errtu said.

"Eagerly awaiting a call to return," said Lolth.

"But I remain banished, by the hand of Tiago Baenre?" From his tone, the balor seemed as if he was about leap upon Lolth in rage. He would not, of course, for she would make short work of him, and would take from him much more than a few decades of freedom.

"You were defeated," Lolth reminded him. "But fear not, for the barrier protecting the Faerzress will continue to diminish, and you will find your way, and perhaps find your vengeance."

Errtu growled. "Tiago Baenre, and then Drizzt Do'Urden."

Lolth laughed again, and she was laughing at him and not with him, though he missed the point of her mirth. Lolth's mockery was one of disbelief as much as anything else. She could not fathom a creature as mighty and intelligent as Errtu wasting so much of his energy plotting vengeance upon a pair of inconsequential mortals.

"My dear Errtu, if a field mouse bit the ankle of Drizzt Do'Urden, do you think he would spend the next century hunting the creature?"

"I will slay Malagdorl before this is through," Marilith said, clearly in support of the balor.

"You will do as you are told," Lady Lolth corrected. "I will grant you much freedom, both of you, and perhaps you will find the opportunity to carry out your desperate revenge. But only, I warn, if it does not interfere with that which I need."

"I have waited . . ." Errtu began to growl.

"And you will wait until I agree with your path," the Spider Queen shot back with equal threat in her tone. "Drizzt has beaten you twice, fool."

"He was not alone!"

"Do you believe he will be alone now? Or that you will find Tiago of House Baenre in solitary combat? A noble son of House Baenre?" She turned to Marilith. "Or that you will similarly find such an opportunity against Malagdorl of House Barrison Del'Armgo? The presence of so many of our Abyssal kin has put the city on its highest guard. You will not likely catch any of your prey alone."

"Drizzt is not in the city," Errtu pointed out.

"On the surface of Abeir-Toril, likely," said Lolth. "And there, you cannot go."

That brought curious expressions to the demons. They looked to each other, Marilith shaking her head, Errtu offering a shrug in return.

"You promised that I would be summoned! I gave you K'yorl, and aided in your plot with Kimmuriel Oblodra—"

"Silence!" Lolth demanded. "The Faerzress will be thinned, and yes, you will be able to pass through *to the Underdark*—whose life and energy is controlled by the Faerzress. Abeir-Toril's sun will not abide you until your century of banishment has passed."

"Never before were such restrictions imposed," Marilith protested. "I have passed between the two, surface and Underdark, on a single summons from a drow wizard, or from a human above! Are you separating the powers, Underdark and World Above?"

"The Faerzress is attuned to the lower planes, which is where it draws its power," Lolth explained. "The barrier of the Faerzress draws its strength from the sunlit lands, and so keeps us at bay."

"And so *kept* us at bay," said Errtu.

"Soon," the Spider Queen promised.

Marilith closed her eyes then and tilted her head back, as if in ecstasy. "The archmage's ceremony nears its end," she explained. "I am called!"

"Go," Lolth bade her. "Go and play. Tell him nothing that will warn him or help him. You remain fully confused that he was able to bring you back after such a defeat. Do you understand?"

"Of course," she said, her voice thinning as her corporeal form thinned, as she melted away to the call of the archmage.

"The stooge Kimmuriel performs admirably," Errtu said when they were alone.

"And Gromph is so eager to bite at Quenthel that he readily accepts this as his own doing."

Errtu nodded, his growl sounding more like a purr then. "When, Lady of Spiders, will the demon lords walk freely in the Underdark?"

"Soon, my pet. Before the turn of Abeir-Toril's year, if Gromph is properly teased."

"He is hungry," Errtu said. He nodded, and Lolth smiled, both confident that their plans were playing out perfectly.

◆　◆　◆

"IT CANNOT BE," Gromph whispered in amazement when the nine-foot tall, six-armed creature materialized within his summoning circle. He knew all of these particular type of demon, called generically "marilith," after the strongest of their kind, as was the custom, and he surely knew this particular specimen as Marilith herself.

But that could not be!

Gromph's thin lips curled in a wicked smile and a chuckle escaped him. "So Malagdorl Del'Armgo lied," he said, and all the possibilities of embarrassment he might now inflict on House Barrison Del'Armgo began to dance in front of him. Perhaps he would parade Marilith into the chamber of the Ruling Council when they were in session, just to watch the blood drain from the face of Matron Mother Mez'Barris.

"How am I here?" Marilith asked, playing the role Lolth had determined for her.

"You are here by my call."

"You cannot . . . but you have," the demon said, appearing quite confused and disoriented.

"Why? What do you know?"

"I was defeated," Marilith explained, "by the weapons master of the Second House and his cohorts. I am banished from Abeir-Toril for a century, and yet barely a tenday has passed! How can this be?"

Gromph's eyes sparkled with astonishment at the possibilities that suddenly danced in front of him.

"Ah, but now I might exact my revenge upon the fork-wielding fool!" Marilith said, her eyes turned to the distance as she played her part flawlessly.

"Malagdorl defeated you, just recently, in a tavern in the Stenchstreets?" Gromph asked.

"Did I not just say as much, Archmage Gromph?" the demon answered curtly. "Though the location is not important, for surely it was on this foul plane full of inconsequential beings." She looked Gromph up and down, scrutinizing him, and seeming not to be much impressed with what she saw. "Why have you disturbed me?" she demanded.

"Did you not just express your elation at being here?"

"Of my own accord and for my own purpose, mortal," Marilith replied. "Unless you tell me that you brought me here to exact my revenge upon weapons master Malagdorl Del'Armgo."

Gromph thought it over for a bit. He had no idea how he had captured Marilith in his summoning, since she just admitted that Malagdorl had defeated her. He had only sought her in the spell on a whim, to test the veracity of Malagdorl's claim. Since that claim was apparently true, there was no way he should have been able to bring Marilith forth.

It was the psionics. He truly was finding the enhancement to the summoning spell through the combination of arcane magic and psionics!

His breath came in short gasps as he pondered just how limitless his powers might soon become. Perhaps he could open half the Abyss to his call, create an army of his own demons and so take power in Menzoberranzan. It seemed a crazy leap, of course, but so, too, did the six-armed demon slithering in front of him here in Menzoberranzan after being so recently banished from the Prime Material Plane. If Gromph could replicate this achievement, he would be revered by the demons and devils weary of their century-long banishments.

If he was the only conduit allowing them to return to the Prime Material Plane before their sentence was served, would they not serve him? Willingly?

Gromph began to chuckle as some other possibilities began to sort themselves out in his thoughts. He believed that he had figured out how he had broken the most ancient code, that his psionics had enhanced his arcane spell of summoning so greatly that Marilith's banishment could not stop him from pulling her forth from the Abyss. But no other drow would know that, or even begin to consider it. Perhaps he could indeed parade Marilith in front of Mez'Barris Armgo and humiliate her in front of the other matron mothers.

"Your call was . . . different, Archmage," Marilith said. "Stronger and more insistent. I lamented it at first, fearing that I could not answer, yet eager to return to Menzoberranzan. But something in the call, some deeper power that I have not felt before, made me believe it was possible, and so here I am."

"To serve me," Gromph said.

Marilith nodded. "That is the price of answering your call."

"Serve me well, Marilith," Gromph explained. "We will together find a most delicious revenge on House Barrison Del'Armgo."

"You will let me kill the weapons master?"

"Eventually, perhaps. But first, we will humiliate them. All of them."

CHAPTER 10 ◈

Kith and Kin

CONNERAD BRAWNANVIL BEAMED WITH PRIDE AS HE STOOD on the bank of the underground pond, having called Bruenor and Emerus to his side. The two had asked Connerad to oversee the defensive coordination of the outside chamber, Bruenor pointedly reminding him that his father had been one of the greatest military tacticians Mithral Hall had ever known.

Now, judging from the younger dwarf's somewhat smug expression, it seemed that Connerad intended to do his father proud.

"We got our shots sighted in at every guard station," he explained, pointing out various stalagmites and stalactites that were hollowed out, either recently or in the original dwarven settlement of Gauntlgrym. "So say we got an enemy on the north wall, creeping for the lake."

He gave a sharp whistle, and a torch flared along the northern wall of the cavern, followed by shouts form various stalactite and stalagmite mounds referencing the "mark."

"Aye, there they be!" Connerad exclaimed, pointing to a pile of stones and sticks set up to resemble a group of goblins or orcs or some other intruders.

Almost as soon as he finished speaking, the dwarf sentinels let fly with their side-slinger catapults and rebuilt ballistae, and the entire area around those targets filled with flying stones and spears, and finally, with burning pitch.

The speed and violence of the attack had Bruenor and Emerus rocking back on their heels.

"Just for that one spot?" Bruenor asked.

"All about the cavern," Connerad replied. "We put our war engines on pivots and sighted in, don't ye doubt, near and far. If it's in here, movin' or not, we can hit it!"

"Well played, young Brawnanvil!" King Emerus said.

"Just as it was in the first days o' Gauntlgrym, and woe to any foe trying to sneak in," Connerad explained. "And I got some boys scraping mica and polishin' silver, working on focusin' mirrors so we can send light from every tower into every crack in the cavern. As it was in the first days o' Gauntlgrym."

"How're ye knowin' . . ." Emerus started to ask, but Bruenor cut him short.

"Ye sat yer bum on the throne," he said, staring at Connerad. The young king didn't argue.

"Bah, but we telled ye to let us be with ye!" said Emerus.

"And I taked it upon meself to do it meself," Connerad replied. "Getting ready for *comragh*!"

Bruenor and Emerus looked at each other then, somewhat surprised and a bit perturbed, but only until they realized that Connerad had used the ancient word for "battle." Aye, he had sat his bum on the throne, and aye, the old ones had talked to him, as they had talked to Bruenor and Emerus. As they had both been leading their respective clans for centuries, it was hard for either of the older kings to think of Connerad as an equal, but by rights, he was just that. He hadn't been Steward of Mithral Hall for the last decades, but King of Mithral Hall, and once again, as with their earlier conversation about Bruenor taking back the throne of Mithral Hall, Connerad had reminded them both that he didn't need their permission.

"The throne showed ye the old designs?" Bruenor asked.

"We're pushin' out into the tunnels beyond, them leadin' back to the rocky dale," he answered. "That's goin' to be takin' some time."

"How many're ye using?" Bruenor asked.

"One brigade only," Connerad answered. "We can't be splittin' our forces with a nest o' drow below."

"Nest o' kobolds not far below," Bruenor reminded him, and the other two nodded.

"Ye plannin' their party?" Connerad asked.

"Aye, and sure to be a good one."

"I'll be expectin' an invitation," said Connerad.

"Right by me side," Bruenor promised, and he clapped Connerad on the shoulder. "Wouldn't be havin' it any other way!" Bruenor turned back out to the wider cavern, impressed by the progress. The bridge was almost finished already, with solid abutments and a center span wired to drop.

"And we've one more thing we're needin' to do afore the fighting starts in full," Connerad said.

The other two looked at him.

"Clangeddin didn't tell ye, then," Connerad asked, "when ye sat yer bums on the throne?"

"Say it clear, lad," Bruenor bade him.

"Deas-ghnaith inntrigidh," Connerad replied.

Bruenor and Emerus turned to each other curiously. These were words neither dwarf had ever heard before, and yet as they stared at each other, each came to understand the phrase, as if they were pulling the wrapping off a present. And more than the words, Connerad's mere recital of the ancient Delzoun phrase, opened in the minds of the other two images of what could be, of what should be, of what must be.

"All th' others need to put their bums on that throne, then," Bruenor whispered, and Emerus nodded his agreement.

"Tariseachd, the Rite o' Fealty, the call o' Kith'n Kin," said Connerad. "Three kingdoms joined as one."

"Aye," the other two said in unison.

A sharp sound from behind startled Bruenor and turned him around to note work on the wall of the complex. Connerad was building nests for archers, and even some war engines back there.

Bruenor thought back to his unpleasant exchange with Lord Neverember, and he couldn't help but grin. Send all of Waterdeep down here, he thought, and watch them limp away, battered, before they ever reached Gauntlgrym's front door.

Because of King Connerad, Gauntlgrym's entry cavern was ready for *comragh*!

◆   ◆   ◆

"THEY ARE JUST kobolds," Tiago grumbled, tugging his shoulder away from Doum'wielle's grip.

"This is their lair and they are many," the half-drow warned.

But Tiago wasn't listening. Kobolds, he thought with disgust—at them and at Doum'wielle for even hinting that these two-legged rats might pose a threat. Menzoberranzan was thick with the vermin, as almost every House used them as slaves. House Baenre kept hundreds, thousands even, tending the gardens, cleaning the compound, and going out into the Underdark to hunt for giant red-cap mushrooms whenever one of the priestesses was in the mood for the delicacy.

Tiago could hardly believe that a colony of kobolds was living here now, in the deeper rooms of the complex's upper tunnels. Why hadn't Matron Mother Zeerith enslaved the beasts by now? Or murdered them?

Or perhaps she had enslaved them, he considered again, and he slowed his pace as he moved along the uneven, cracked stones of one twisted hallway. He could only imagine the force that had so broken this place, as if the whole of the mountain had twisted, turning the hallway as a slave might wring the dirty water from a cleaning rag. At various points along the wide cracks in the walls or floor, Tiago noted volcanic rock. He could feel the heat from it, and that truly unsettled him.

Had the primordial escaped again? While he had been off in the Silver Marches fighting the war, had Ravel's family been blasted by another volcano of primordial power? The last known

211

R. A. SALVATORE

eruption had been decades before, after all. How could the stone still be throwing such heat?

Noting movement in a wider chamber up ahead, the drow put those thoughts aside and picked up his pace even more, breaking into a trot.

He lifted his arm, turning his shield as he did so that Doum'wielle could see, and motioned her ahead, then shifted his fingers in the silent hand code of the drow, side by side.

Doum'wielle hustled to catch up. Before them lay an oval-shaped room, with the wider chamber opening left and right beyond. It was lighter in there, and brightening now, as if the kobolds within might be stoking a fire. A ghostly image drifted past, beyond the oval, and both companions stutter-stepped a bit, caught by surprise for a heartbeat before realizing that it was merely a bit of steam.

"Stay close," Tiago whispered. "We ask once for surrender, then we kill them all."

The drow's eyes sparkled and he couldn't suppress his grin. Too long had it been since he had felt the thrill of battle. Indeed, not since the werewolves haunting the forests around Longsaddle. They had noted the kobold lair upon first entering the complex, but Tiago had stayed away, fearing that these were slaves of Q'Xorlarrin. He did not want to be discovered by Matron Mother Zeerith and the rest of her House.

Not until he had the head of Drizzt in a sack.

Three strides away, ready to leap through the opening, Tiago broke into a sprint and gave a battle cry.

But kobolds appeared from around the edges of the opening at just that moment, each holding a large bucket, which they swept across, throwing forth the liquid contents at the opposite edge of the oval.

Tiago pulled up and spun a circuit to slow, but his momentum was too great, and Doum'wielle pressed him from close behind. He gave another yell, this one in alarm as his mind whirled in fear of what these little rats had thrown at him.

Oil of impact that would explode if he brushed too near, perhaps? Acid to bite at him as he dived through?

Even as his mind tried to sort out the surprise, liquid struck stone and hissed in protest, and a wall of steam filled the opening, glowing red.

Shield leading, Tiago dived through. He hit the ground, tucking that shoulder, waving his sword left and right to fend off any attackers in the opaque veil as he rolled around and came up to his feet.

Doum'wielle came in behind him, not as gracefully and not in a roll, tripping past the threshold and stumbling, but holding her feet as she fell toward Tiago.

Fearing that she'd stagger right past him, Tiago turned and shield-blocked her, jolting her upright and steady.

"What—?" she started to ask, but he hushed her, having no time for her idiocy.

Tiago felt as if sweat was running from every pore in his skin. It was hot in here, and not just from the steam. He noted lines of glowing red and suspected them to be lava.

Uncooled lava, and they could hardly see.

Beware every step! he started to sign, but then, realizing Doum'wielle wouldn't begin to make out the intricate movements in this thick haze, he spoke the warning instead.

His voice had betrayed their position, he realized a moment later, when rocks soared in at them.

Tiago's shield unwound, growing by the heartbeat, and he managed to duck behind it to avoid the volley, though the small stones lobbed his way didn't seem as if they would cause much harm anyway.

But then the first hit his shield, a slight tap. It turned into a more profound one as the ball of stone exploded.

Tiago staggered back even as other missiles banged against the shield, each exploding like the first, driving Tiago back, ever back.

Doum'wielle cried out and went rolling past him to his right, more rocks chasing her, landing all around and pop-popping like the small fireworks and grenades Tiago had used himself at a Baenre celebration, fashioned by the priests of Gond in days gone by, when they had experimented with smoke powder.

These grenades were different, though, for they didn't burst and whistle like those fireworks. They cracked and popped, throwing stone shards, and burning red, bright and angry, but only briefly.

"Forward!" Tiago ordered Doum'wielle. They couldn't stand there and suffer the continuing barrage.

But all she returned were screams of pain. Tiago couldn't see her clearly, but his glance showed him her shadowy form, on the floor and writhing.

The drow tucked his head behind his shield and followed the path of the stones across the room to the throwers. He got hit again, repeatedly, each explosion staggering him, halting him momentarily or even driving him back a step. Tiago reached into his drow heritage, into the magic of the Faerzress that tickled the life-force of his kind, and brought forth a globe of darkness, aiming it in front of him at the far end of the room, where he suspected the kobolds to be.

The barrage slowed, the rocks came in less accurately, and Tiago pressed ahead, shield leading, sword poking forward from all around it. He went into the darkness without hesitation, and thrust more powerfully, scoring a hit.

He dismissed the globe of darkness and found himself faced up with a pair of kobolds, both waving short swords, both holding rocks—missiles that showed the red streaks of contained lava. Behind him, Doum'wielle was still crying out in pain, though it was more a whimper than a scream at that point—a poignant reminder to the son of House Baenre not to let one of those rocks hit him.

The mist thinned, and then he was against not two, but four kobolds, coming at him fearlessly—no slaves these!—and fanning about him, stabbing with short swords, cocking their arms to launch their grenades as soon as an opening showed.

So Tiago gave them that opening—those on his right, at least—as he swept his shield out to the left.

The two on the right let fly, Tiago dropped below the barrage and fast-stepped out to the right, stabbing fiercely, impaling a kobold who fell limp in front of the drow before he'd ever withdrawn the blade.

The mist thinned some more, and Tiago had a better grasp of the room and the grenades. The kobolds stood in front of and beneath a long, slender stalactite, but none like Tiago had ever seen. It dripped red lava, like a leaking, open boil on the skin of the primordial—and onto a mold of solid stone, one that let the lava spread out into a semicircle where it would fast harden and blacken.

So shocked was he by this surprising display of cunning by the miserable little rat-faced kobolds, that Tiago almost forgot that he was in the middle of a fight.

He barely avoided the stab of a short sword from the right, and just got his shield up to deflect the thrust of one of the creatures on his left. He enacted the magic on Orbbcress, his blocker, then, catching the sword fast against the edge. He jerked down and pivoted left, turning the stubborn kobold, who would not surrender its blade.

Bent low, overbalanced, Tiago and Vidrinath turning fast, the kobold surrendered its head instead.

A scraping sound brought the drow back to center, to see a crack opening into a door behind the dropping stalactite, the glowing eyes of a horde of kobolds within.

Tiago felt vulnerable. If that mob held grenades . . .

Movement behind him and to his right almost had him sending Vidrinath out on a sweeping backhand, for only at the last moment did he realize that it was Doum'wielle, come to join him.

To join him and even step past him, her free arm held in tight, her tunic smoking still.

Without hesitation, the elf struck, but not at a kobold. Khazid'hea cleaved the stalactite several feet up from its dripping end.

215

Doum'wielle leaped back, as did Tiago, their elf reflexes saving them as a flood of red lava dropped from the opening, striking the ground and splashing all over, stinging and burning kobold legs and sending the two remaining creatures leaping away, howling in agony.

Both went for the open door in the back, but the one coming from the left tripped over the feet of the other, quicker creature, and down it stumbled right into the splashing lava.

How it shrieked! How it spasmed, with superheated, molten rock grabbing at it, biting at it, melting it . . .

From the opening came a volley of grenades, but Doum'wielle was behind Tiago now, and Tiago behind his shield, the magnificent Orbbcress defeating the jarring and explosive barrage.

Out through the oval went the pair, back into the hallway where they sprinted back the way they had come. In the days they had been in Gauntlgrym, this had been their first encounter with the kobolds, and they hoped it would be their last.

"Clever," Doum'wielle said through a grimace when they had put the enemy far behind. She lifted her left arm from her side and inspected an angry welt and blister where a drop of lava had bit her.

"Too clever," Tiago spat, openly on edge—for he was not used to being chased off by kobolds. "The drow of Q'Xorlarrin have trained them as an upper guard, no doubt, and taught them well."

"You are drow," Doum'wielle reminded him.

"They saw you," Tiago accused. "Were you not with me—"

"You would have faced a dozen lava bombs from the doorway," Doum'wielle interrupted.

The two stared at each other for a long while, and it crossed Tiago's mind more than once to cut the impertinent elf down where she stood. He held his strike, though, and his temper, for he couldn't deny, to himself at least, that Doum'wielle's clever trick with the stalactite had broken them free of the ambush.

Nor could he deny, again to himself, that without Doum'wielle's trick, they would not have survived that assault.

Against kobolds.

More than once, Tiago glanced back in the direction of that chamber. He wanted to believe his own words that Matron Mother Zeerith's soldiers had trained the beasts, but he knew that was not the truth. These kobolds, wretched little creatures though they were, had found harmony with the mountain and the under-chambers—enough so to effectively use the blood of the primordial as a weapon.

Tiago had to remember that.

He glanced about curiously. He had expected Drizzt to come forth to scout for the dwarves, but so far, that had not happened. From his own scouting, it seemed to him that the dwarves were being very cautious, fortifying every inch of ground they had secured.

Or perhaps that would end with the grand entry cavern and the throne room, and once those positions were secured, the dwarves would come forth, and once the dwarves moved along, Drizzt would come forth.

Tiago had to be ready for that, doubly now, for he suspected that if he wanted the kill, he would have to find the ranger before the kobolds did.

Kobolds!

Tiago shook his head and again glanced in the direction of the now-distant ambush chamber. He had never known kobolds to be so clever and industrious.

The chasm called the Clawrift, which split the grand cavern of Menzoberranzan, housed tens of thousands of kobolds, perhaps hundreds of thousands.

Tiago blew a deep sigh, visibly shaken.

◆ ◆ ◆

THEY KNEW A fight was coming. Indeed, they were going to start one! And so Bruenor and the other kings decided that they could not delay the Rite of Fealty. This would bring the dwarves closer together, a bonded force marching in unison.

Bruenor stood at the end of the receiving line, with Emerus first, Connerad to his left, and Bruenor to Connerad's left, all three facing the Throne of the Dwarf Gods. Bruenor held his breath a bit as the first of the dwarves not of royal blood stepped up to the throne. Fittingly, and unanimously approved by the trio, Ragged Dain would be the first.

He moved up to the throne, turned and bowed respectfully to the three kings, closed his eyes, and sat down. Immediately his eyes opened, but the throne did not reject him or wound him, as Bruenor knew it could.

Ragged Dain remained seated for only a few heartbeats, then hopped off and moved down to kneel before King Emerus.

"Ar tariseachd, na daoine de a bheil mise, ar righ," he said reverently, ancient Delzoun for "Me dying fealty, me kith'n kin, me king."

Emerus placed his hand on Ragged Dain's head with genuine affection. The two had been close for more than a century. Then the king nodded and released his hand, and Ragged Dain rose, accepted a kiss on the check from Emerus, and stepped over to kneel before King Connerad.

He repeated his words, and Connerad did as Emerus had done, accepting the fealty, not to himself, but to kith and kin, to Gauntlgrym and the dwarves—all the dwarves—assembled in her halls.

On to Bruenor went Ragged Dain, and it was repeated a third time, and at the end, Bruenor, on sudden impulse, reached behind his shield and brought forth a flagon of ale and handed it to Ragged Dain, waggling a finger to indicate that he should not drink it at that time.

The second dwarf, Oretheo Spikes, was already at King Connerad by then, with the third, Bungalow Thump, kneeling before King Emerus.

And so it went, one after another in fast order, and all walked off to the side with a flagon of Bruenor's ale in hand—there seemed to be no limit to the shield's production this day!

It went on for hour after hour. At the very back of the line, still outside the entryway, Athrogate and Amber fidgeted nervously. Would the throne accept them? Both had committed crimes against their previous kings, Athrogate in Citadel Felbarr, Amber in Citadel Adbar. Would the dwarf gods forgive them, or reject them?

Four hours passed, five hours, then six and they were in the throne room, though still in the back of a long and winding line. Athrogate caught Bruenor's eye, and the dwarf king smiled at him and nodded confidently.

Another hour passed, and now there were only a few score ahead of the couple, with near to five thousand others filling the large hall, many singing softly and using words that those still in line, who had not sat upon the throne, could not begin to understand.

Athrogate lost himself in that song, trying to make sense of it, and so distracted was he that he was caught by surprise when Amber tugged on his sleeve and said, "Here I go, then."

He held his breath as this woman he had come to love moved up to the throne. She bowed to the kings, added a shrug to Bruenor, then took her seat.

With a wide smile and tears flowing from her eyes, Amber Gristle O'Maul of the Adbar O'Mauls hopped back up and verily ran to kneel before King Emerus.

That left Athrogate standing alone in front of the throne, the eyes of all upon him. He bowed to the kings, accepted Bruenor's nod . . .

But still he hesitated.

Athrogate allowed himself a deep sigh. Many of those nearest stopped singing and stared. They wouldn't take him, he knew in his heart. Too far had he strayed. He shook his hairy head and looked at Amber, now holding her flagon, and his tears fell thicker than hers.

Tears of regret.

Tears for a life that had not been lived as well as it should have.

The great hall was silent, not a whisper to be heard. Athrogate looked around at the thousands of faces, and one by one, they began to nod. At the back of the hall, near the exit to the tunnels, he noted Drizzt and Catti-brie, the two beaming at him with wide smiles.

"*Suidh!*" one called, then another, then all of them.

"*Suidh! Suidh!*" and Athrogate understood that they were telling him to sit. But not to judge him, he realized, but rather to welcome him.

So he sat upon the throne.

He was not thrown free.

And he heard the language and then knew their song, and knew, too, that he was kith'n kin.

◆ ◆ ◆

To the side of Tiago, not far away and nursing her wounded arm, Doum'wielle did not miss the noble Baenre's expression of dismay—nor did her sentient sword, which had guided her to strike the stalactite and had warned her to offer a quick retreat after she had.

She watched Tiago's face go through a range of expressions, anger to trepidation to frustration. She understood that he feared for Drizzt's life more than he feared that she would be killed by kobolds.

Nothing else seemed to matter to that one.

Drizzt is Tiago's way of ascendance in the hierarchy of Menzoberranzan, Khazid'hea explained to her. *He envisions no other journey to lift him from the lower environs, where drow males reside.*

"Even as a noble," Doum'wielle whispered, shaking her head in disbelief, and Khazid'hea affirmed that.

I will be stealing his dream from him, Doum'wielle imparted to the sword, given their plans.

You will be saving yourself from a life of slavery and brutality, the sword reminded her.

Doum'wielle nodded in agreement, and her eyes narrowed as she stared back at Tiago, silently scolding herself for even thinking of allowing any hint of sympathy toward her brutal rapist.

The trophy of Drizzt would be all the sweeter knowing the gain to her, and indeed, knowing the cost to Tiago.

◆ ◆ ◆

"Lock!" came the command of General Connerad Brawnanvil, and the ten dwarves leading the square down the wide corridor interlocked their great shields, forming a solid wall of metal.

And not a moment too soon, for even as the shields clanged into place, the first bombs began to rain down upon them from the darkness down the corridor.

"Double-step, boys!" yelled Bruenor, in the middle of the second rank.

Beside him, Drizzt popped up tall, above the shield line, and let fly an arrow that lit up the corridor the length of its travels, albeit briefly—long enough to reveal the horde of kobolds lifting these exploding rocks from a pile, though there was one less monster grenadier when the arrow found its mark.

Drizzt was fast down in a crouch beside Catti-brie.

"Too many," he started to say, but he noted that the woman wasn't listening to him. She moved with her eyes closed, her hand on the shoulder of Ambergris to her other side. She was whispering, but Drizzt could not make out the words, and could not discern to whom she was speaking.

"Charge!" Connerad ordered, and the front rank ran off as one, only gradually decoupling their cleverly designed shields.

Up tall again, Drizzt paced about the second rank while firing off a line of silvery death.

The corridor lit up then in a light more profound than any Drizzt's arrows might achieve, as a wall of rock bombs hurtled down upon the dwarves, smashing against shields and exploding, one after another, with tremendous force.

"Bah!" cried Athrogate, to the other side of Ambergris, when the shield dwarf in front of him was knocked flat and the lava splattered back over Athrogate to strike the dwarves behind him.

Before the bending Athrogate could help the shield dwarf back up, another grenade crashed in just in front of the fallen dwarf's feet, the splash reaching up at his feet and legs—and how he howled.

"Come on, then!" Athrogate yelled, sending his morning-stars into a spin and leaping over the shield dwarf to spur the others forward.

But a second barrage had them all backing and ducking beneath now-dented shields—blockers that dripped with molten lava!

Then came the greatest kobold trap of all, as the ceiling above the front lines of the dwarves cracked open, loosing a river of red liquid stone.

◆ ◆ ◆

CATTI-BRIE WASN'T HEARING Bruenor or Athrogate, or even the grunts and cries of the dwarves in the front line. Her focus remained solely on the ring she wore on her right hand, the Ring of Elemental Power that Drizzt had taken from a drow wizard, Brack'thal Xorlarrin, and then given to her.

She knew these lines of lava to be an extension of the primordial, sending its tendrils far and wide, relishing in the momentary freedom from the water elementals trapping it, a little bit at least. She sensed no kinship from the great and godlike being toward the kobolds, just a measure of acceptance that they would allow the lifeblood lava to drip, drip, drip. For that was the purpose and calling of the primordial, to throw its molten heat far and wide, to consume with liquefied stone. To burn, as the Elemental Plane of Fire itself burned.

Catti-brie felt the flow of lava as surely as she could feel the pulse in her own arm. She sensed it and understood it, and felt it keenly as it pooled in the ceiling just above her and the others.

And so when the ceiling cracked open, Catti-brie was ready for it. The spell came to her lips in an instant. Blue mist encircled her arms, and blasts of water burst from her staff and sprayed upward to intercept the lava. Instead of an immolating, fiery death raining upon her and the dwarves, there came a tumble of hot stones that bounced off helmets and upraised shields. Catti-brie blocked one, painfully, with her upraised forearm, and felt herself stumbling.

But Drizzt had her, tugging her along, and then Athrogate barreled into her, shoving the whole pile back, back.

"To the throne room!" General Connerad ordered, and the dwarves methodically and efficiently pivoted and rushed back the way they had come.

Not all of them, though. Catti-brie grabbed Bruenor by the arm and held him, then pulled back against Drizzt's incessant tug.

"Let's go, girl. Too many!" Bruenor said to her.

"Only because of their trick," Catti-brie argued.

"Aye, and a stinging one!"

"No more," the woman insisted.

"What d'ye know, girl?" Bruenor asked, but Catti-brie was already turning away from him and twisting aside from the driving Athrogate, who fell forward on his face, grunted, and hopped back to his feet.

Catti-brie looked at the ceiling breach, the first stones fallen, and now the rest of the lava pouring out upon them.

Primordial lava, living flame.

She could feel its life-force, though it was no longer part of the greater beast, and she beckoned to it, helping it keep its separate life, fanning the flames to consciousness with her call and her own will.

"Well?" Bruenor said, not understanding what his daughter was doing and wanting an answer—and rightly so, for behind that lava pour came a horde of kobolds, all hoisting grenades.

"Tell her, elf!" Bruenor shouted to Drizzt, but the drow, understanding his wife better than Bruenor ever could, merely smiled and turned a confident look back to Bruenor, even offering the dwarf a knowing wink.

"She got 'em, don't she?" Bruenor asked, and even as he did, the pile of stones and lava in the corridor between them and the kobolds stood up and swung around to face the diminutive monsters, gladly accepting, even being strengthened by, their volley of flaming grenades.

"No, Bruenor," Drizzt corrected, "*We've* got them."

The red-bearded dwarf grinned from ear to ear—there were only a hundred of the beasts, after all.

"Ye ready for some fun, elf?" the red-bearded dwarf roared. Then he banged his axe against his shield and called upon the axe to burst into flame.

Together, the pair ran off past Catti-brie, dodging and diving to get beyond her lava pet.

Drizzt let fly with Taulmaril once, twice, and thrice, and lines of kobolds fell dead as the arrows bored through them, hardly slowing. The drow slung the bow over his shoulder, drew forth his blades, and dodged and ducked and twisted to avoid the shower of explosive, lava-filled stones.

Bruenor just brought his shield up in front of them and weathered the beating. He slowed not at all, plowing into the front ranks of kobolds with wild abandon. He almost grabbed the cracked silver horn hanging around him to summon the spirit of Pwent, but stubbornly refused to give in to the call.

Every swipe of his axe sent a kobold flying left or right, and the roaring flames on the many-notched weapon cauterized the garish wounds even as Bruenor inflicted them. He glanced to his right only once, to see the elf's blades working almost magically, flipping over and around any kobold weapon that neared, reaching forward, prodding and sticking, driving the creatures in front of him. And whenever a kobold stumbled, Drizzt chopped it down

To Bruenor's left came the lava elemental, not even slowing as it hit the first kobold ranks, just stomping through, ignoring the feeble weapons that could in no way harm its rocky flesh.

Bruenor shield-rushed a trio of enemies, too quick for them to escape. He felt their legs angle and buckle in front of him as he pressed forward, his axe, alive with flame, cutting a line in front of him.

"Durned good weapon," Bruenor said, shaking his head, but then he cried out and nearly dropped the enchanted battle-axe when the flame leaping from it took definitive shape, like a living winged creature above the blade, and leaped out from his weapon to engulf a kobold that had broken free in desperate retreat.

Another burst of fire ignited upon his flame-tongued battle-axe, and Bruenor gasped in astonishment before finally solving the riddle. He glanced back over his right shoulder to see Catti-brie calmly pacing him and Drizzt, walking up behind them in all confidence, her eyes half-closed, her lips moving to enact another spell, or to speak with the fire, perhaps.

Farther to the right, Drizzt cut down another kobold, and another.

"Ye'll not get more than meself!" Bruenor shouted at him, and turned to pursue the next nearest group. He paused, though, and shouted out for his girl. From a side passage came a host of kobolds, bearing down on Catti-brie, who looked all alone and vulnerable. Bruenor swung around, but knew he was too far to help her in time.

"Me girl!" he roared.

◆ ◆ ◆

THE CRY OF "Me girl!" sounded behind Catti-brie, but she paid it no heed, her focus solely on the sudden and unexpected threat. In came the lead kobold, spear leveled.

With only minimal movement, Catti-brie turned aside of that thrust and as the kobold stumbled by, she chopped it on the back of the neck with her staff, sending it stumbling and tumbling. And so great was her concentration that she continued her spell and was still able to come up and turn left to face the next attacker, leaping inside its swing so that it could not bring its sword to bear.

With one hand, Catti-brie grabbed the back of its scraggly fur, yanking its snapping maw away, while she pointed with her staff tip, the sapphire flaring, and enacted her spell.

The area right in front of her, under the feet of the charging kobolds, slickened with magical grease, and the creatures suddenly were stumbling all about, flailing and falling.

And then, before Catti-brie could deal with the kobold she was grappling, she felt as if a swarm of bees had entered the fray, and indeed that proved an apt description as Athrogate and Ambergris, Fist and Fury, and Connerad Brawnanvil came pounding by, throwing kobolds aside as easily as a heavy stone could crash through a barrier of thin parchment.

The magic of Athrogate's right-hand morningstar, coated with oil of impact, exploded with a tremendous crash and sent a kobold flying far away, while the dwarf's other morningstar swept across to crush the skull of a second monster. Beside him, Ambergris worked with great sweeping strikes, launching kobolds into the air two at a time with her huge mace.

But neither of these great warriors, amazing as they were, could hold Catti-brie's attention as fully as the two young female dwarves from Citadel Felbarr. Connerad rushed up to Catti-brie's side, but he, too, said nothing, and didn't bother to blink as he watched the deadly play of Fist and Fury.

Both carried swords, neither bothered with a shield. They came up on a pair of kobolds and one of the sisters—Catti-brie wasn't sure which was which!—struck out to the side, distracting the kobold in front of her sister, who then rolled around and dived back down behind the legs of the kobolds.

Ahead came the first dwarf with a vicious burst, and the kobolds, reflexively retreating, tripped over the now-kneeling dwarf behind them, and that dwarf popped up fast and powerfully as they pitched over, launching them up higher into the air. She turned, her back to the kobolds, her hand extended, and her sister took it and she yanked her sister by, launching her like a living missile into the receding mob. In came the other dwarf, and side by side the Fellhammer sisters worked as one, sword left up high, sword right down low, so that the kobold between that vise couldn't duck, couldn't jump and couldn't block.

The leading dwarf turned and reached, and her sister took her hand and now it was her turn to fly into the throng, laughing all the while.

And the Fellhammer sisters caught up to Bruenor, and the three moved like intimate old friends, and fought like intimate old friends, who had trained together for all of their lives.

Like a field of tall wheat in front of the sweeping scythe, the kobolds fell all around them.

Behind Catti-brie and Connerad came the rest of the dwarves, turned by Bruenor's daring charge, shamed now and determined to punish those monsters that had chased them off.

And determined to prove themselves worthy to their king.

There was an old saying in the Realms that "not a dwarf would-could fight like a dwarf angered, but not a dwarf would-could bite like a dwarf shamed."

So it was then, to the great pain of the kobold clan, swept away in a living tidal wave of fury.

Surrounded now by a wall of dwarves, Catti-brie focused once more on the tendrils of the primordial that coursed around her. She sensed the building, concentrated living energy back among the kobold ranks, and understood it to be bits of living flame encased in a multitude of grenades.

The woman called to those flames through her ring, beckoning to them to awaken, to grow stronger, to extend their reach and break free from their tombs.

In heartbeats, popping noises resounded among the kobold ranks, tiny primordial flames bursting from their encasement, exploding in the midst of the kobold grenadiers.

In short order, the whole of the kobold horde was in full retreat, a huge magma elemental in close pursuit, and a host of tiny flames chasing after that beast in hungry pursuit of the kobold flesh they would bite and burn.

CHAPTER 11 ◈

Writing Snakes

AHLIA RAN HER FINGERS ALONG THE SMOOTH METAL OF Kozah's Needle, trying to use the tangible feel of her weapon to bring her back to stability, to a time when she knew a better life.

Somewhere in the recesses of her mind, she believed that she had once known that better life.

She thought of running down a hill, toward a rocky gorge, a drow—a drow friend!—outdistancing her, leaping with amazing balance and grace from stone to rise to stone.

She felt the wind on her face—the wind! She felt herself tumbling, but it was not frightening, for she controlled this movement, her brilliant vault bringing her around to do battle . . .

"How many tendays?" a voice said, and for a moment, Dahlia thought it a memory, until the voice—High Priestess Saribel—spoke again.

"How many tendays have you left to draw breath, *darthiir*?" she asked, and Dahlia opened her eyes to see the woman, resplendent in her spidery laced gown, all purple and black, beautiful and deadly all at once.

So beautiful, so alluring. That was part of their magic, and how could Dahlia resist?

How could she think herself worthy?

"My husband is alive," Saribel said, and Dahlia couldn't begin to understand what that might even mean, let alone who Saribel might be talking about.

"Tiago Baenre," Saribel said, and Dahlia wondered if that name should mean something to her.

An image of mighty Szass Tam flashed in her mind, and she nearly swooned from the overwhelming, almost divine power she felt from him, as well as the incredible malignancy—and Dahlia was sure that she should know who that was. Alarms sounded in her thoughts, echoing and winding, wrapping back under the pile of writhing worms that was her train of thought.

"Tiago has been found, alive and well with that Doum'wielle creature," Saribel said, and she might as well have been talking in the tongue of myconids, for now even the words made no sense to Dahlia.

"When Tiago returns, we together will claim this House Do'Urden for our own. We will be fast rid of you, witch, and I will claim the title of matron mother. Matron Mother Baenre has come to trust me now, and needs not your echo on the Ruling Council, when my own voice would be so much more helpful."

She moved closer, and Dahlia thought she should lash out at the drow, though she couldn't figure out quite how to make her arms do that.

"We will make of you a drider, lovely Dahlia," Saribel said, almost cooing the words, and she raised her hand to gently stroke the elf's face. Lightly, teasingly. And how beautiful was she!

Dahlia closed her eyes, the energy of Saribel's touch filling her body, reverberating through her as a moment of pure sensation and growing ecstasy. She heard herself breathing more heavily, lost herself in the vibrations of the touch, so soft and teasing, moving within her and multiplying.

Saribel slapped her across the face, and in a moment of clarity Dahlia thought that fitting. So beautiful, so alluring.

Yet so horribly wretched and dangerous.

"I will taunt you and torture you for a hundred years," Saribel promised. "When my husband Tiago returns with the head of Drizzt Do'Urden, your time of comfort will end."

Dahlia couldn't make out much of that, but that name! Oh, that name!

Drizzt Do'Urden.

Drizzt Do'Urden!

She knew that name, knew that drow, her lover, her love!

She had felt so safe in his arms, and so wild under his touch. She had found peace there . . . Effron! He had brought her to Effron, her son, her child she thought lost . . .

A tidal wave of emotions rolled over Dahlia then, a flood of memories, all jumbled of course, but relaying so many different emotions all too clearly. She burst into tears, shoulders bobbing in sobs. They had done this. These drow had murdered Effron!

Saribel laughed at her, cackled wildly, taking great pleasure, in thinking her words had terrified the elf.

But Dahlia paid her no heed, had not even recognized many of her words, the sounds nonsensically arranged in Dahlia's ears.

None of them mattered anyway, except for two: Drizzt. Do'Urden.

"Drizzt Do'Urden," she silently mouthed, and she held on desperately to those sounds, to that word if it was a word, to that name if it was a name.

She knew it mattered.

Through all the winding worms within her thoughts, Dahlia became confident that she knew that the name—yes, it was name!—and that it, Drizzt Do'Urden, mattered. So she held it and repeated it as a mantra, a litany against the winding courses of a broken mind.

◆ ◆ ◆

"WHAT HAVE YOU done?" Matron Mother Mez'Barris Armgo screamed at Matron Mother Baenre. The matron mother of the Second House trembled with rage and jumped up from her seat at the council table. "Demons! Too many to battle! Should they all come against any one House—even your own, foolish Matron Mother!—that House will surely perish!"

"Why would they come against any one House?" asked High Priestess Sos'Umptu Baenre from the back of the table.

Matron Mother Mez'Barris swung around to face Sos'Umptu, her eyes narrowing in a clear threat. She knew that Sos'Umptu had been prompted to make that response by the wretched Quenthel.

"Indeed," Quenthel said, following up on that very point. "No one of us controls the demons. Every House has brought forth some—every House seated here has summoned a major fiend to their control."

"Arach-Tinilith, too," Sos'Umptu added, clearly aiming the remark at Mez'Barris. "Our many priestesses have reveled in summoning demons now, with all limitations removed."

All around the table of the Ruling Council, the other matron mothers sucked in their breath at that. Even those Houses of Menzoberranzan most proficient in the arts of summoning, like House Melarn and House Mizzrym, could not hope to match the sheer volume of demons that Arach-Tinilith might bring forth.

Mez'Barris studied her peers, knowing that they were all only then beginning to understand the danger. This demon orgy orchestrated by Matron Mother Baenre could doom any of them, could doom all of them.

Matron Miz'ri Mizzrym rose up then and began to speak, but Quenthel cut her short.

"Sit down! Both of you!" the matron mother ordered. "Pray you, sisters, seek guidance from Lolth, and hold your foolish words, else my scourge will take the tongues from your mouths! We return Menzoberranzan to the early days of the city, when demons shared the boulevards with drow and Lady Lolth was ascendant and pleased."

"Many drow have been murdered by the instruments of the Spider Queen," Mez'Barris reminded her.

"We cull the weak," Matron Mother Baenre answered without hesitation. "And we will be stronger for our vigilance and our experience. As with your weapons master, Malagdorl, who slew

Marilith herself." She paused and flashed a wicked grin, before adding, "Or so you claim."

Mez'Barris felt her nostrils flaring, her eyes widening with pure outrage. Before she could argue, though, the chamber door opened, and in walked Archmage Gromph, and behind him, in slithered Marilith. Not a marilith, but Marilith herself, without question.

Mez'Barris sank back into her chair, her jaw hanging open.

"This is how it was in the earliest days of Menzoberranzan," Matron Mother Baenre said calmly, matter-of-factly, for there was no need to press the embarrassment of Matron Mother Mez'Barris. "And so it shall be again. Look to your prayers, sisters. The Spider Queen is pleased, do not doubt."

Mez'Barris slowly surveyed the table. She saw the surprise, the doubts aimed her way, certainly. She saw the trepidation, even fear, on the faces of these high priestesses who had attained such glory and power, which now, so suddenly, seemed so fragile. They were looking to her now, it seemed to Mez'Barris, and plaintively in the midst of this terrifying confusion, as if pleading with her to serve as some sort of balance to the seemingly out-of-control Matron Mother Baenre.

Matron Mother Mez'Barris covertly scanned the room and met the stares of each matron mother, save Quenthel Baenre and that filthy Dahlia creature. Even in the eyes of Matron Mother Baenre's known allies, Mez'Barris noted some measure of that plea for help. The matron mother of the Second House took heart in that moment. In her insatiable desire to gain full control, perhaps Quenthel Baenre had gripped too tightly.

Mez'Barris let a sly grin appear on her thin lips. She could do as she had hoped now, she was certain. The others, even Quenthel's allies, desired to send a strong message to the matron mother, to back her away from this maddeningly dangerous course. Would they go so far as to covertly join with Mez'Barris in her plans to overwhelm House Do'Urden?

Yes they would, Mez'Barris believed, particularly whenever she directed another's gaze to the matron *darthiir* and noted the immediate sour frown that ugly view elicited of the various matron mothers.

That abomination, the *darthiir* matron mother of House Do'Urden, would soon perish.

And Matron Mother Quenthel would be taught her limitations.

◆ ◆ ◆

LIGHTNING FLASHED AND fires burned in the Stenchstreets, and high above near the cavern's ceiling, and now even in the Qu'ellarz'orl.

Gromph Baenre watched the mounting fight between demons with mild disdain. He was hardly surprised—you couldn't put such numbers of chaotic demons together in one area and not expect wild brawls of magic, tooth, and claw. And there were hundreds of demons in Menzoberranzan now, not even counting the thousands of manes the larger beasts had brought in to serve as fodder.

Gromph moved from his balcony at Sorcere back into his private chambers, for even from the high perch of that tower upon Tier Breche, the archmage couldn't properly witness the mounting carnage.

He waved his hand over a still pool of water in a magical basin, calling forth the images.

He blew a sigh of disgust. Every street, every way, every side region of Menzoberranzan was alive with fighting, it seemed, demon against demon. A gang of glabrezu rampaged across the island housing the city's rothé, the huge demons cutting through the Underdark cattle the way predatory fish might chomp through a swirling school of prey.

Behind the archmage, Marilith hissed with excitement, the view of the carnage teasing her murderous sensibilities. Gromph glanced back, thinking to admonish her, to keep her in line, but she looked past him and gasped once more at some new and greater event in the scrying pool, no doubt.

Gromph spun back just in time to see a swarm of chasme drop upon the glabrezu. In waded another marilith, along with a pair of larger nalfeshnee, and then a monstrous goristro.

This was Matron Mother Quenthel's force.

"A goristro," he muttered, shaking his head. Only certain balors and the demon lords themselves were more powerful. To summon such a creature was always a danger. To summon one and send it forth into battle even more so.

But to summon a goristro and send it out beside a trio of major demons, and with a swarm of chasme besides?

"Madness," Gromph muttered.

The glabrezu gang fled before the superior force, splashing back across the small lake, chasme diving at them every step of the way.

Gromph shifted the image in his scrying pool to a massive brawl right outside the Barrison Del'Armgo compound. Hundreds of manes and other minor demons roiled about the boulevard, clawing each other to shreds. Here, too, chasme buzzed and bit, and larger beasts prowled the shadows and the edge of the battle, no doubt directing their disposable minions.

The pool brightened suddenly in the flash of a massive fireball, followed by a series of roiling balls of fire in the air above the fight. Flamestrikes shot down, turning manes into living candles, the humanoid demons, too stupid to know the pain of the flames engulfing them, running on to ravenous battle, until they fell, one by one, into smoking husks.

Gromph understood then the source of the magic and focused his attention on the Barrison Del'Armgo compound. There stood Mez'Barris's wizards and priestesses, throwing forth their destructive magic into the boulevard beyond. Lightning flashed and manes died. Another fireball erupted, and flamestrikes followed.

The archmage shook his head once more.

"I wish to go and fight," Marilith said from behind him.

"You will stay here," he answered without even bothering to turn around. He heard her hiss then, and was surprised by it, for surely Marilith knew better than to hint at her displeasure with the commands of the one controlling her, particularly when that one was Gromph Baenre.

A wave of the archmage's hand dismissed the images in the scrying pool, and he slowly turned to face his demonic servant. She stood there, towering twice his height, her naked, human-like upper body glistening with sweat, breasts heaving, and with swords held in all six of her hands.

"The battles are glorious," Marilith answered. She seemed apologetic, but Gromph felt the hair on the back of his neck standing up, as if in warning.

"You are here at my call," he said.

"Yes, Master."

"Master . . ." he echoed. "Your master. Your master while you walk the ways of Menzoberranzan. Do not question me."

Marilith bowed her head and turned her blades down to the floor.

"If I dismiss you, you will once more be banished, to serve out your century in the Abyss," Gromph reminded her. "Only I know the secret now of twining the two forms of magic to break the ancient covenant."

Marilith nodded. "Yes, Master."

"Is that what you want?"

The demon looked up at him, her face a mask of alarm. "No, Master! Tell me who to kill, I beg!"

Gromph laughed. "In time," he promised. "In time."

A movement outside caught his attention, and he focused on the view beyond his balcony again just in time to see a ball of flaming pitch go soaring through the air and drop from sight. He moved to the edge of the balcony and saw that it had landed among the combatants in front of Barrison Del'Armgo's gate, though the angle of the shot showed him that it had not come from inside Mez'Barris's compound.

Another House had come to the aid of the Second House.

Not that the Second House had needed any aid. The fight had already greatly diminished, with destroyed, smoking husks of demons thick about the street and the Barrison Del'Armgo wall untouched.

But still, some other House had thought it prudent to join in with one of its war engines.

Symbolically, Gromph realized. That catapult throw was meant to send a message more than it demonstrated any practical aid.

"Conspiracy?" the archmage asked under his breath.

As with the huge demon fight that morning, wise old Gromph Baenre was not surprised.

◆ ◆ ◆

"ARACH-TINILITH OR THE high priestess of House Baenre?" Yvonnel teased in her squeaky baby voice.

Long past the shock at the sight and sound of a tiny child speaking with such sophistication, Minolin Fey considered the question carefully.

"Well?" the impatient child demanded.

"What are you asking me?" Minolin Fey replied. She swallowed hard as she dared to presume. "Are you seeking my preference?"

"Would I have asked if I was not?"

"I did not think either position would . . ."

"You should think more, then," baby Yvonnel interrupted. "In either position, I will need someone capable of thinking, after all."

She was all insults and promises, Minolin Fey thought, and surely not for the first time. All she ever got from her little girl were taunts and teases, and the latter stung more than the former, for Minolin, who was not Baenre by blood, considered the teases as no more than the cruelest taunts of all.

And yet . . .

"High priestess," she said, not daring to not answer, and thinking that her life expectancy would increase greatly if she stayed at Yvonnel's side. If this was truly to be her choice, going out from House Baenre to the Academy would make her a prime target for those who would not accept this child as the matron mother in a time that would surely be marked by great upheaval.

"Good," the baby replied. "I was thinking the same. Sos'Umptu, should she survive, serves House Baenre well from Arach-Tinilith. Were I to bring her in to my side and put you in the Academy, it might embolden your mother to believe that she still commands your loyalty."

The child put on a very sweet smile then and Minolin Fey felt her heart warming at the sight, and all she wanted to do was rush over and hug Yvonnel close to her breast and smother her in kisses.

"I have no desire to destroy your House," the baby said, abruptly tugging Minolin Fey back to the present and throwing aside the warm compulsion. For a brief instant, Minolin Fey thought herself a foolish child, reaching to pat a purring housecat, only to discover it to be a guardian familiar, all teeth and murderous claws.

But then, before she could truly register that Yvonnel was magically toying with her, she wanted to rush over and hug the child, her baby, once more.

"You need to make sure that Matron Byrtyn knows that," the baby said, and it took the confused Minolin Fey a moment to realign her thoughts to the conversation at hand.

"That you wish her and her House no harm?"

"Yes. Her House, which is your House."

"No," Minolin Fey said before she could think better of arguing. Black wings of panic rose up around her, thrumming about the edges of her thoughts.

"No?"

"I am Baenre now," she replied.

"Not Fey-Branche?"

"Baenre!" Minolin Fey declared.

"And who do you serve, Minolin or Baenre?"

"The Matron Mo . . ." Minolin Fey flinched as she heard the reflexive response pouring forth, particularly to this particular audience.

"To all who look, I am the loyal servant of Matron Mother Baenre," she tried to clarify, using the wide caveat and undefined title as she tried to wriggle free.

"And who is that?" the devious little child asked.

Minolin Fey licked her suddenly dry lips. She felt backed into a cage. As far as she knew, Quenthel still held the favor of Lolth and thus, the legitimate title of Matron Mother Baenre. Was this wretched little deviant creature testing her, ready to report her blasphemy to Quenthel should she answer otherwise?

Or would Yvonnel destroy her if she pledged her fealty to Quenthel? And the daughter of Byrtyn Fey held no illusions. Despite the tiny, cherubic little body of Yvonnel, Minolin had no doubt whatsoever that this child, steeped in the knowledge of Yvonnel the Eternal, could easily obliterate her.

"Yv . . . Matron Mo . . ." she stammered, and wicked little Yvonnel turned her lips into an amused smile.

"Whomever Lady Lolth determines is the Matron Mother of Menzoberranzan," poor Minolin Fey sputtered.

"Matron Mother Quenthel Baenre," Yvonnel told her, and then, with that mischievous grin so common with this little one, and so ominous to Minolin Fey, who understood the level of mischief this little one could accomplish, Yvonnel added, "for now."

CHAPTER 12 ◈

Revelations of an Ancient God

ATTI-BRIE CROUCHED BY THE MOUND OF BLACK STONE, delicately running her fingers across the veins of angry red still flaring from the molten lava entombed within. Even with the protection of her ring, the woman felt the heat here, and the power. This was a direct line to the primordial, she knew, and it was still connected to the pulse and strength of the beast, still thrumming with the threat of catastrophe.

She put her ear to the mound and called softly, then listened to the distant voice of the great primordial beast.

Sometime later, she opened her eyes and worked hard not to gasp, for in her communion with the primordial, the woman had been as overwhelmed as in her communion with her goddess Mielikki. The power, the wisdom, the strength of this creature seemed so far beyond her—to think that most would only see the fury and bared power of the thing, would think it a volcano, inanimate and unconscious, a natural firestorm akin to a great tornado or hurricane or any other natural disaster.

But no, Catti-brie had understood for a long while, and knew without the slightest doubt now, this primordial was a preternatural and supernatural disaster, and one full of energy and magic beyond her comprehension.

But not beyond her curiosity.

The woman lifted her staff, the silver-gray cypress branch with its blue sapphire crown, in both hands, hovering the end over the hot mound. She felt a connection of divine powers, and a comfortable communion. Without even thinking of the action, indeed, without even fearing that she would destroy this staff from the cherished garden of her youth, Catti-brie drove the butt end down hard, punching it through the cooling crust and right into the molten lava below. She began to chant, though she knew not the words—*dreos . . . corrachag-cagailt . . . toitean*—as she slid the staff downward into the red liquid stone. The heat assailed her, stinging her eyes, but still she pressed the staff downward, sliding her hands until she was holding only the bulbous, gemmed top of it, the rest submerged. The skin on her fingers reddened, despite the protection of her, but the sting didn't deter her from her . . .

From her what, she wondered? She supposed it was spell-casting, but she couldn't be sure, for all of this was beyond her. Mielikki had given her the staff, Kipper had added a prized possession to it, and now she was dipping it in the blood of a primordial of fire. It made no sense.

She slowly lifted her hand and eased the staff back out. She dared grab it in the middle with her other hand, wincing as the dripping lava bit at her.

Almost immediately, the blue tendrils of her magic, both arcane and divine, came forth from the bottoms of her sleeves, wrapping her hand in healing magic and wrapping the staff in . . . in what, she did not know.

She pulled the staff free and moved it to the side, tapping it on the ground to let the rest of the loose lava fall away.

Catti-brie stared at this enchanted weapon, the gift of Mielikki and of the primordial. No longer was it light gray, silvery, as it had been, but black and streaked with lines of glowing red. And the sapphire was not blue—oh, what had she done?—but rather, glowing an angry red.

And she could feel the staff teeming with power.

And she knew how to get at that power!

But something was lost, she feared, as she stared at the staff, something precious, something beautiful. What had she done?

She glanced at the mound, to see that the top was already cooling to black, then looked at her staff to see that it, too, was cooling. To her great relief, as the red glow dissipated, so, too, did the staff and the gemstone return to its previous colors and textures. She held it up in front of her eyes, clutched it tightly in both hands. She could feel the power contained within.

The power of Mielikki.

The power of the Magi stone.

The power of the primordial.

The power of Catti-brie.

"Thank you," she whispered and she knelt before the mound once more and placed a hand upon it. Her fingers still trembled with the vibrations of power within the stone, and she knelt there staring at the cooling lava for a long while, until she heard someone clear her throat. She turned to see Penelope and Kipper standing behind her.

"What do you know?" Penelope asked.

"More than the rest of us, I gather," Kipper added.

"This vein ties to the primordial being that feeds the forges," Catti-brie explained. "Directly."

"The one you told us about—in the pit beyond the Forge?" asked Penelope, and Catti-brie nodded.

"A being of tremendous power," Catti-brie explained. "A godlike creature that sacked Neverwinter, burying it under a mountain of ash and lava. Were it not for the swarm of water elementals trapping it within the pit, it would do so again, and perhaps send forth its power to consume Port Llast, or Luskan, or even Waterdeep."

"But is it contained?" Kipper asked, moving closer, but quickly retreating, wincing against the oppressive heat.

"Aye, is this a new tendril or an old one?" Penelope asked.

"Old," said Catti-brie, and her two companions offered sighs of relief—short-lived relief, though, as Catti-brie continued, "Old and new. It pulses with new lifeblood, thicker and richer than ever before, save the eruption itself."

Penelope and Kipper turned to each other with concern.

"The containment magic is failing," Catti-brie explained. "The Hosttower of the Arcane in Luskan was destroyed, and its residual magic has fed the water elementals to the pit, entrapping the primordial. But it will not hold forever, likely not even for much longer."

"A vague reply where specifics could save many lives," Kipper complained.

"Centuries more?" Penelope asked.

Catti-brie looked at the mound, unsure, but finally shook her head. She turned back to Penelope. "A decade, perhaps? Less? I can only estimate at how much of the magical containment has eroded in the time since I was last here, and can only wildly guess at when that erosion will allow the beast to break free of its bonds. The erosion seems substantial."

"Then this journey is a fool's errand," said Kipper.

"Let us not dive into grim Kipper's well of eternal darkness," Penelope scolded, and managed a smile at the often dour old mage as she did. "The magic is here to hold the beast, and has done so for millennia. We need only find a way renew that power."

"I have seen the pit," Catti-brie reminded her. "Not all the wizards of the Ivy Mansion could control a small fraction of the water elementals dancing along the walls of the primordial's cage if they did nothing else, not even sleep or eat. It would take all the wizards of the world, Elminster himself and Khelben beside him, and with a renewed Mystra with her hands upon their shoulders."

"So often do we make wide eyes at the ancient relics and powers we uncover," Penelope interrupted. "We gasp in astonishment and awe at that which those long past have made and have done. When really, if we look closer, we oft find that their ways can be replicated, their artifacts reproduced, their marvelous engineering improved upon. Are we to surrender hope now, then? Is this escape a foregone conclusion? For if so, then go to your father, King Bruenor, and tell him that we must be gone from this place."

"That one wouldn't listen," Kipper muttered.

"No," Catti-brie answered. "It has not happened, so it is not a certainty."

"Then lead us, and let us investigate more, discuss more, and reason more, and let us see what we shall see," said Penelope. "Did you come to this particular place at the primordial's call?"

Catti-brie looked around. They were in the same area as where she had helped Bruenor and Drizzt turn the tide on the kobolds, and the monsters had been sent running. Back the way she had come, toward the throne room, the dwarves were hard at work repairing doors and patching corridors, and the other way, deeper into the complex, many dwarves had gone, securing the next steps in the reclamation of Gauntlgrym. Drizzt was out there too, patrolling the corridors ahead of Bruenor's battle force.

"I came to learn what I might now that the region is secured from the kobolds," she answered.

"Not so secure that you should be out alone."

"But I am not alone, am I?"

Penelope smiled. "Lead on, my friend."

Catti-brie turned back to the mound. With a slow breath, she placed her hands upon the glowing pile once more, and followed its tendrils. She visualized the main vein, reaching back to the primordial pit, and noted, too, the tributaries. Most were new, she understood, and tiny and inconsequential—for now—but one seemed quite old to her, a continuation of this same ancient vein that had produced the eruption point.

She nodded to her left, toward the mines, the natural tunnels that ran alongside the area the ancient Delzoun dwarves had carved out as the upper chambers of their homeland.

"They've got the mines blocked just outside of the throne room," Penelope said. "They'll not let us pass through."

As she spoke, though, old Kipper moved to the chamber's left-hand wall. He muttered a few words in the arcane tongue of wizards and brought his hands up, feeling the stone.

"Kipper?" Penelope asked.

"Not so thick here," the old mage replied with a wink.

"And a nest of drow on the other side?"

"Now, now," Kipper teased. "Let us not dive into grim Penelope's well of eternal darkness."

That brought a laugh from both of the women.

"You've a passwall enchantment prepared, no doubt," Catti-brie said dryly.

"Several," Kipper confirmed. "And a few dimensional doorways ready as well. Very handy spells when navigating a maze, especially when one is fleeing hordes of enemies, you know."

Catti-brie shrugged. "I do now."

"Shall we see what we can see?" Kipper asked, rubbing his hands together, and before either had begun to answer, the old mage began his spellcasting. Soon after, a section of the room's wall disappeared, creating a ten-foot deep tunnel that ended in more solid stone.

"Not to worry, the next will get us through!' Kipper assured them, walking forward and beginning a second spell.

As he did so, Penelope conjured a stronger magical light, placing it on the end of her long staff.

Shortly after, the three entered the naturally sloped tunnels of the complex's northern mines. They lingered about the magical opening for a bit, protecting the unexpectedly opened flank of the dwarf workers, and when the passwall effect ended, the solid stone returning, the three made their way, side by side, down into the maze of ancient mines.

◆ ◆ ◆

THE KOBOLD DIED without a sound, and fell to the ground with not a whisper of noise, guided expertly by a strong dark hand.

Drizzt stepped over the body, slowing only a moment to wipe his bloodied scimitar on the creature's ragged fur.

On he went, picking his way from door to door, through rooms that looked as they had millennia before, and others that had been twisted and blasted, ravaged by time, by the eruption of the volcano, and by other mighty denizens of the Underdark. At one point, Drizzt found a tunnel that had most likely been cut by an umber hulk entering a side wall to a narrow room and exiting through the opposite wall. The floor between the tunnel holes showed the deep scratches reminiscent of an umber hulk's powerfully clawed feet, leaving an impression as clearly on the solid stone as a bear might leave on a forest's dirt path.

A closer inspection of the tunnel edges showed Drizzt that this was not a new cut, but neither was it centuries old.

The drow nodded, reminded of the many obstacles the dwarves would find in trying to fully reclaim and reopen this place. Complexes like Gauntlgrym, so vast and far-reaching, tied to mines that wound deeper into other Underdark tunnels, would not remain empty in a land where creatures benign and malignant alike were always seeking security . . . or food.

Drizzt moved along, as invisible as a shadow in a lightless room, so quiet that the skittering of a rat would sound more akin to the scrabbling of a tunneling umber hulk beside him. He kept his bearings at all times, and occasionally heard the ring of a dwarven hammer, another comforting reminder that he was not too far outside the perimeter of the lands Bruenor's kin had tamed.

But then he came upon the remains of a most curious encampment.

Someone had set a cooking fire—Drizzt had never known kobolds to cook their food, or at least had never known them to go to such trouble as to cook their food in an environment with little kindling to burn.

He noted a footprint in some soot residue.

"Drow?" he whispered under his breath, for the boot was too thin, its edges too refined, to be something he would expect from a kobold, and the step appeared far too light to be that of an orc or even a human.

He searched the small room and happened upon a curious parchment, a wrapper, he knew, much like those surface elves used to preserve their foodstuffs when they journeyed the open road.

Some scratches in the wall not far from that caught his eye. No, not scratches, he realized upon closer inspection—someone had purposely and efficiently cut deep lines—letters!—into the hard stone.

Drizzt recognized the lettering as Elvish, surface Elvish and not Drow, though he did not know the word they spelled out.

" 'Tierf,' " he read aloud, his expression quizzical.

He looked back at the cuts, marveling at the sharp edges and clean lines. Some fabulous tool had been employed.

Drizzt stood back up as if he had been slapped.

"Tierflin?" he asked more than said, his thoughts going to Sinnafein's dead son, and by extension, to Tos'un Armgo, whom he knew to be in possession of Khazid'hea, a sword that could so gracefully and easily mar any but the hardest of stones. Was Tos'un Armgo in this place?

No, it could not be. Tos'un had died on the mountainside of Fourthpeak, crashing down with the smaller white dragon sent spiraling to the mountainside by Tazmikella and Ilnezhara and finished off by Brother Afafrenfere. Drizzt had seen that firsthand.

Doum'wielle, perhaps, the daughter of Tos'un and Sinnafein, who had reportedly run off with the sword?

Why would she be in here? How could she be in here? Drizzt shook his head. More likely the dark elves had taken the blade from her—it was a drow sword, after all—but then, how would they know, or care, to so inscribe those letters into the stone?

Drizzt shook his head yet again, not quite certain how it could be. Those were Elvish letters, and they had been cut with a fine tool, such as Khazid'hea, but . . .

He shook his head a third time, thoroughly flummoxed and trying hard to convince himself that he had jumped to errant conclusions. Likely the lettering had been cut into that wall in ages past, and for reasons he couldn't begin to fathom. No matter, though, for the camp was not that old, and it was not the camp of kobolds, but of some form of elves—almost certainly drow.

So they, some at least, were near.

Drizzt drew his blades.

The unseen and unheard shadow crept from the room.

The Hunter went to hunt.

❖ ❖ ❖

"Perhaps it turns, up ahead," Kipper offered. "Or the primal beast's tendril winds about and rejoins later on."

But Catti-brie remained resolute. "No," she said, her hands moving across the side wall of the natural tunnel. The primordial power, the vein of the creature, passed right under them, crossing the corridor beneath their feet.

"A parallel tunnel then, doubling back beside this one," Penelope offered.

Again Catti-brie shook her head.

She felt the stone all around, and noted that one section seemed different, seemed somehow flatter than the more curving walls of the tunnel. "A chamber, hidden," she said, as much to herself as to the others. "Here."

"Hidden?" Kipper asked, moving over. Behind him, Penelope began to cast a spell.

"Sealed, you must mean," Kipper said when Catti-brie directed his hands to the flatter area.

"A summoned wall of stone," Penelope announced a moment later, and both turned to regard her. She nodded her chin to indicate the exact area they had been inspecting. "The magic still resonates, quietly, though it is very, very ancient, I sense."

"The tendril goes in there?" Kipper asked again.

But this time, Catti-brie shook her head. "The tendril ends in there," she clarified, and she was as surprised by the notion as the others.

"Another passwall, Kipper?" Penelope asked.

"I've only a pair remaining, for a quick escape, if needed, or to get us back out the way we came in," the old wizard said.

"Use one," Penelope bade him. "When we are finished, I will summon an extradimensional room where we can rest safely through the night, and you can regain your escape spells for use tomorrow."

Kipper nodded and cleared his throat.

"It won't work," Catti-brie said with certainty before Kipper could begin his spellcasting.

"Too wide a block of stone?" Penelope asked.

"Too heavily warded," Catti-brie replied, and again she was feeling about the stone. "Protected from any magic that might remove it."

"How can you know this?"

Catti-brie thought about that for a moment, then surprised the others—and herself a bit—by replying, "The primordial told me."

"Our girl's gone crazy, Penelope," Kipper said with a snort. "Sure to make herself a proper Harpell, I suppose."

"How can the primordial know . . . ?" Penelope started to say, but she stopped when she noted that Catti-brie was chanting, her voice thick with her brogue and her words unrecognizable, though they sounded Dwarvish.

"Ainm an dee," Catti-brie recited. *"Aghaidh na Dumathoin . . ."*

The young auburn-haired mage closed her eyes and let the words flow through her. The beast was giving them to her! The ghosts of Gauntlgrym, the very memories resonating within the walls of this most ancient dwarven homeland, were offering them to her.

Or perhaps they were fooling her, she worried for just an instant, playing her for a fool so that she would enact a spell that would doom them all.

Catti-brie was in the thrall of the enchantment now. She felt like nothing more than a conduit—and that, too, made her worry that the primordial was using her to facilitate its breakout.

She fell back as the last *"dachaigh fior-charade brathair"* passed her lips, the last syllable resonating about the stones and corridor, hanging in the air magically like the mournful call of a lost age.

The ground began to shake. Catti-brie fell back in fear, and Penelope and Kipper caught her by the arms and ushered her back the way they had come, Kipper crying, "Run away!" with every step.

A great scraping sound echoed around them and the ground trembled more forcefully, but forcefully, too, did Catti-brie break free of the others, skidding to a stop and whirling around. Kipper and Penelope rushed back to grab her again, but then they, too, stopped.

The wall began to rise, dust and debris, and the rock that had formed above the summoned wall of stone over the ages, the natural cladding, broke away and crashed down upon the floor. The summoned stone almost disappeared into the ceiling.

Catti-brie walked to the black opening, unafraid, though truly it seemed the gaping maw of an ancient and massive beast, like the chamber of Gauntlgrym itself was waiting to devour her.

"Well, what did you say?" Kipper demanded.

"I'm not for knowing," Catti-brie admitted, not even looking back. She raised one hand and cast a quick spell, bringing a globe of light up in front of her, beyond the opened portal.

Even with the magical light, the small chamber beyond was not brightly lit, as if its very age was somehow battling the spell.

Catti-brie went in anyway, finding herself in a perfectly rectangular, nondescript room, ten strides left and right, west and east, in front of her, but only half that wide to the other wall, the north wall, directly across from her.

No, not nondescript, she realized when she stepped in and surveyed the whole of the place, for down to her right, deeper into the tunnel, along the short western wall, where three large beams of square stone, two upright and one across the top of them, and slightly askew, like a door jamb that had tilted to the left. They were against the flat wall, either leaning on it or set into it—Catti-brie couldn't be sure.

Hardly thinking of the action, Catti-brie slowly walked toward the strange formation.

"Wait, girl!" she heard Kipper cry, and with such sudden alarm that she heeded his call and even looked back at him and Penelope, who had come into the small room.

"What is it?" Penelope asked.

Kipper blew a deep sigh and reached into his pouch for the skull-sized gemstone. "It's the ancient gate," he said, his voice barely above a whisper—he could not find the strength to lift his voice above a whisper.

"How can you know?" Penelope asked, and Catti-brie asked at the same time, "How can ye be knowin'?"

But then, before Kipper could answer, Catti-brie spoke for him. "The primordial's powering it," she said.

Both women looked at Kipper.

"The beast granted them some magic?" Kipper asked. "Perhaps, yes, it would make sense. The dwarves used it to give them the power for their waygate, and the beast gained a measure of freedom for its troubles—a mutually beneficial arrangement."

"You can't know that," said Penelope.

"We can't know anything for sure," Kipper shot back. "We are speaking of construction and magic that is older than the oldest elves. Millennia, we are talking, not centuries!"

"But your guess is correct," Catti-brie said. "At least partially so."

"The primordial told you that, as well?" Penelope asked, and Catti-brie shrugged and nodded.

"One way to know for sure," Kipper announced, and he moved forward, past Catti-brie, gemstone in hand. He studied the two standing stone beams for a moment, then gave a laugh and set the skull-sized gem into the one on the left.

The space within the jamb burst into flame, and Kipper fell back, yelping in terror. Catti-brie and Penelope caught him, the three watching in amazement as the fires burned and roiled within the confines of the jamb, but then gradually diminished before flying away entirely, as if sucked into the opposing beam.

"The second gem," Kipper realized. "We need the second gem to keep the magic contained within the portal."

"We do not have a second gem," Catti-brie reminded him.

"Well of course not!" said Kipper. "But that is what we need to activate and hold open the portal."

"The fire, you mean," Penelope corrected. "Who would walk into such a thing as that?"

But Catti-brie was thinking along different lines, remembering the clairvoyance spells she had enacted when staring into the flames. Others saw fires as individual events, contained in the stones of an oven, perhaps, or in a campfire, or on a torch.

But Catti-brie, with her ring and with the primordial of Gauntlgrym whispering to her, understood differently. All the flames were alive—indeed, all part of a singular living entity, the Elemental Plane of Fire. They could phase into her plane of existence, coaxed by flint and steel or the strike of lightning, or any other manner, but even though those summoned flames seemed like individual events, they retained their ties to that other plane of existence, where they were all one.

So Catti-brie could look into a hearth in Mithral Hall and see through it, through the Elemental Plane of Fire, and to the hearth of King Emerus in Citadel Felbarr.

So here, a dwarf could enter the portal and travel through the flames to a corresponding gate in another location, could literally step into the Elemental Plane of Fire and step out again back to the Prime Material Plane on the other end.

So the primordial was telling her. So her instincts and her memories of her clairvoyance spell were telling her.

But still she shook her head, not convinced that this wasn't some trick. Would she find a way to empower the gate, only to have Bruenor or another step in and get incinerated?

"Retrieve your gem," she told Kipper, "and let us be gone from here, back to Bruenor and the others to relay our discovery."

"Shouldn't we inspect it a bit more?" Kipper asked, his eager tone showing that he clearly believed they should.

"Me Da will get answers on the Throne of the Dwarf Gods," Catti-brie said. "We have other riddles to solve."

"Like?"

"Like finding the other gem," the young woman said.

Kipper retrieved the gemstone and the three went back into the hallway, Catti-brie turning back to the doorway and casting another spell, her accent returning heavily, a brogue so thick and words so foreign that it seemed to the others, even to her, as if she wasn't actually speaking the words but rather that they were being spoken through her.

The wall grumbled and groaned and slowly lowered back into place, sealing without a seam to be found.

"But the cladding is gone from it," Penelope said when Catti-brie motioned for them to leave. "Anyone coming this way will see the revealed magical stone."

"And none will get through it," Catti-brie assured her.

"None save those who have become intimate with the primordial guardian of Gauntlgrym, it would seem," old Kipper whispered sarcastically, but loud enough for both his companions to hear.

◆ ◆ ◆

"More fightin' in the east," Bruenor said.

"Aye, the boys're battlin' for every room," Emerus agreed. "Kobolds, goblins, orcs, and them damned ugly birdman creatures. Stubborn things. But not a drow yet to be seen."

"They're holding tight about the Forge and the lower mines, not to doubt," said Bruenor.

"Them orcs we caught're sayin' as much," Ragged Dain interjected.

"So fightin' now and tougher fightin' ahead," Bruenor acknowledged. "We never thought it'd be any different, eh?"

"Eh," Emerus agreed.

"Good news coming from th' other way, though," said Ragged Dain. "Connerad's got the tunnel cleared and almost secured all the way to the dale. Once he's done with his fortifyin', we'll get another five hunnerd warriors back to clean the rooms!"

The door to the war room opened then and Catti-brie entered, flanked by Penelope and Kipper.

"What do ye know, girl?" Bruenor asked. "We got many wounded needing yer spells!"

"Aye, I saw Ambergris on me way here," Catti-brie answered, and both Penelope and Kipper turned to regard her curiously as she slipped once more into her Dwarvish accent.

"So where ye been?" Bruenor asked. "Chasin' the durned elf?"

"Chasing the spreading veins of the primordial, more accurately," Penelope replied, drawing concerned looks from all the dwarves in the room.

"A tendril that's been in place since the founding o' Gauntlgrym, I'd guess," Catti-brie quickly added. "And one that's showin' me and me friends here clues about the powers yer ancestors gained from their fiery pet."

"What do ye know?" Emerus asked.

Catti-brie shrugged and shook her head. "Nothing to tell right now. But soon, I'm hoping."

"But we're not to fear this . . . vein o' fire?" Emerus pressed.

"The being's not breaking free," Catti-brie assured him. In her mind, she completed the thought with "not yet, at least," but she held that part silent.

"Just finding a bit of exercise," Penelope added. "The primordial seems to see your girl here as a bit of an ally."

"My guess would be that the primordial isn't happy about having the dark elves holding its home in their thrall," said Kipper. "From what Catti-brie has told us of their altar right in the primordial's chamber, I suspect the ancient being might consider their religious antics akin to a bit of sacrilege."

"Are ye sayin' the beast might be helpin' us, then?" Bruenor and Emerus asked together, and both with equally hopeful tones.

Catti-brie quickly dispelled that notion. "The primordial's not viewing the world as we mortals might. Through some fortunate magic, I been able to gain some insights from the great being—I find meself less inclined to call it a beast!"

"She's talking to it," Kipper explained.

"In fits and starts and nothing much more," Catti-brie added before Kipper had even finished. She wanted no misperceptions, and no false hope. There might be ways in which she could turn her connection to the primordial and to the Elemental Plane of Fire into a benefit in these battles, as she had done with the kobolds, but it was nothing she wished the dwarves to factor into their planning, for indeed it was nothing Catti-brie would even dare depend upon.

She did hold out some hopes, though. The magma elemental the primordial had spat up to her on the ledge in the drow altar room had aided her in turning the battle against Dahlia and the great construct spiders the drow had set out as guards.

"Most help I can be would be looking to the flame, looking into the flame, and looking through the flame to get us a glimpse of what's what in the lower levels," she said. "If other chances come up, like blowing up some kobold bombs, I'll be using them, don't ye doubt."

That seemed to satisfy Bruenor and the gathered dwarves, who nodded their appreciation one after the other.

Catti-brie was glad of that, and glad to leave it at that. She didn't want to get their hopes up. There was a tentative nature to all of this, and a level of power she knew she could never control if it found a way to break free. Most of all, her communion with the primordial had taught her respect for the primal being—it seemed to her as strong as a god! More than helping her, it wanted to escape, to erupt again in all its magnificent and destructive glory.

And Catti-brie knew something else, without the slightest bit of doubt: the magic of the Hosttower of the Arcane was truly failing, and if that erosion could not be stopped, even reversed, the reign of the dwarves in Gauntlgrym, should they retake the complex, would be short indeed, and would end explosively.

CHAPTER 13 ◈

The Sigh of
Two Matrons

K OBOLDS," TSABRAK TOLD MATRON MOTHER ZEERITH WHEN he returned to her in her private chambers, just off Q'Zorlarrin's forge room. "Chased from the upper chambers."

"Yet the kobolds knew we were here," Zeerith said ominously.

"And still they came," Tsabrak agreed. "Some prostrated themselves on the floor and begged us to make of them slaves."

"The dwarves are formidable."

"It is an army," the archmage of Q'Xorlarrin stated. "An army. Not an expeditionary force. An army that could press Menzoberranzan, for a bit at least."

"An army that will overrun us?" Matron Mother Zeerith asked.

"We are formidable with wizards, but it appears that the dwarves have brought more than a few of their own," Tsabrak replied.

"Matron Mother Baenre knows."

"These are the dwarves of the citadels of the Silver Marches, where Baenre waged war. Of course she knows."

"She is waiting for me to call for help."

The Archmage of Q'Xorlarrin nodded.

"To grovel," Matron Mother Zeerith said. She lowered her face and closed her eyes, considering her play. Things had not gone well for her in the last couple years. She had lost Brack'thal, her Elderboy, as well as her powerful daughter Berellip, to a party come to rescue the captives brought to her fledgling city by the impetuous and impossible Tiago Baenre.

She had lost Saribel and Ravel, her other two children, to House Do'Urden where they now served as nobles. Perhaps Saribel would rise to the level of matron mother there in time, as she was married to Tiago, but as of now, neither of the powerful Xorlarrin nobles were available to Zeerith. And she needed them.

"Has Kiriy returned from her communion?" she asked without opening her eyes.

"Not yet. I expect she has much to inquire about with the Spider Queen."

Now Zeerith did open her eyes, and she lifted an unappreciative glare at Tsabrak, hardly in the mood for his quips. His shrug reminded her, though, that his position had become more tentative than her own. Tsabrak had channeled the word of Lolth, enacting the Darkening over the Silver Marches. But that Darkening was no more, and Tsabrak and Zeerith could only take that as a sign that the Spider Queen's defeat in her quest to attain the Weave had left her reeling and retreating from arcane magic.

And that very thing, arcane magic, had been Q'Xorlarrin's play! This House, more than any other in Menzoberranzan or any other drow city, stood to gain the most in the event that Lolth continued to turn her attention to the Weave and the domain of Mystra. The Xorlarrin family had long embraced wizardry, and had elevated the male wizards to stations equal to the roles of the female priestesses—privately, of course.

But were they now falling out of favor with Lolth, Matron Mother Zeerith had to wonder? Was it an accident that the dwarf army now appeared in the upper chambers of their fledgling city?

"What word from Faelas and Jaemas?" she asked, referring to the two Xorlarrin nobles who had continued to serve as Masters of Sorcere back in Menzoberranzan and had not yet been called to Q'Xorlarrin.

"The same word. Demons roam the city. All of the Houses are bringing them forth, and in great numbers. Archmage Gromph has recalled Marilith, though she was reportedly recently slain by the weapons master of House Barrison Del'Armgo and should have remained banished." Tsabrak shook his head, having no answers. "It is all chaos."

"The matron mother tightens her grip," Zeerith surmised. "And with Lolth's favor, so it would seem, if her brother wizard can so warp the ancient rules as to recall defeated demons."

"You have to call to her," Tsabrak dared to say.

"To Lolth, or to Quenthel Baenre?"

"Yes," Tsabrak answered.

Matron Mother Zeerith sighed and nodded, offering the wizard a sympathetic shrug. He had recently held onto hopes for a great ascension, for himself and for his family, in the new domain of the Spider Queen.

"Should we summon demons of our own?" Tsabrak asked. "Is this the way of the dark elves now?"

Zeerith shook her head. She would do no such thing until Kiriy brought her answers. If Lolth was done with the Weave and House Xorlarrin's aspirations had been crushed, and so Lolth would not now favor the Xorlarrin family or their fledgling city, filling their corridors with demons might facilitate their own doom.

"Has there been any word from Hoshtar?"

"Nothing to help us," Tsabrak answered. "The last he determined was that Jarlaxle had managed to slip away from House Do'Urden, along with most of his trusted minions, replacing them with new recruits to Bregan D'aerthe. He is likely on the surface, though the possibilities range from coast to coast with that one. Kimmuriel, though . . ."

"Not Kimmuriel!" Matron Mother Zeerith replied. "I'll not deal with that one—I would rather crawl on the floor in front of Matron Mother Baenre herself and beg her to take our city as her own."

"I understand your reluctance."

"He fornicates with illithids," Zeerith spat. "With his mind, if not his body. To trust Kimmuriel is to trust a creature we cannot begin to decipher. Why Jarlaxle elevated him to lead Bregan D'aerthe, I will never understand."

"Perhaps Jarlaxle believes that he understands Kimmuriel."

"Then Jarlaxle fools himself."

Tsabrak accepted that outwardly with a nod, though Zeerith knew that he—and that she, for that matter—did not honestly believe that the too-clever Jarlaxle ever fooled himself.

"Find Jarlaxle, my friend," Matron Mother Zeerith said. "In the end, he may prove our only salvation. Only he possesses intimate knowledge of our enemies in the upper halls . . . and of those back in Menzoberranzan. He is the broker."

"He is always the broker."

"And never the honest broker," Zeerith admitted, as much to herself as to Tsabrak. She hated her position. She had worked with Bregan D'aerthe often in the past—her nephew Hoshtar's greatest achievement was the relationship he had quietly woven between Q'Xorlarrin and Bregan D'aerthe—a potential alliance and trading route the new city would need if they were to compete with House Hunzrin.

Other than that, however, Zeerith had little use for Hoshtar. He was a mediocre wizard at best, who spent more time worrying about the set of his ridiculous red veil than he did his skill in the Art. It was likely, Zeerith knew, that Hoshtar's incompetence was exactly why he had found some measure of success in dealing with Jarlaxle, for surely Hoshtar could be easily controlled by that one.

"We will find our way, my blessed matron mother," Tsabrak said with a bow.

Matron Mother Zeerith offered a calm smile and waved him away.

She looked anxiously to the room's other door, the one leading to the private chapel she had fashioned. Kiriy wasn't in there, having gone to the main chapel in the primordial chamber for her most important commune.

Perhaps it would do Matron Mother Zeerith good to go and pray as well

◆ ◆ ◆

"House Do'Urden," Gromph said to the matron mother. They stood on the balcony of House Baenre, staring across the city to the newest outbreak of demonic violence, along the western wall of the great cavern, at the gates of House Do'Urden.

"It is not a coincidence, I expect," Gromph added sardonically.

Quenthel stared and contemplated. This was a move against her, by proxy, and some of those major Houses aligned with her, and supporting her on the council, were surely involved. They were testing her, and more than that, testing the level of support House Baenre would offer to the puppet House Do'Urden. And doing it all with demons, beasts that couldn't be traced to any one House or another.

"Go there, and take your pet demon," Quenthel instructed.

"I have sent the Xorlarrin cousins from Sorcere to Ravel's side," Gromph replied. "Both are masters, their ranks honestly earned. That is a formidable trio of wizards."

"With their leader, Ravel Xorlarrin, standing to gain if the Matron Darthiir is destroyed," Quenthel said. "Ravel would like nothing more than to see his sister Saribel ascend to the throne of his new House. Go . . ." She paused.

"No," she said, shaking her head as she changed her mind. "Go back to Sorcere. Use your powers to find your safe room in Q'Xorlarrin. Check in on Matron Mother Zeerith."

"Collect her plea for help, you mean."

Matron Mother Baenre grinned. She walked from the balcony and pointedly shut the door behind her, letting Gromph know that he should be gone immediately, through magical means.

◆ ◆ ◆

"Glad I am to see you, cousins," Ravel said to Faelas and Jaemas when the two appeared, quite unexpectedly, in the audience chamber of House Do'Urden.

"You have demons at your gate, cousin," Faelas said.

"The archmage supposed that you might welcome our help," Jaemas added.

"More than at our gate," Saribel said, entering the room. "The bottom floor is thick with manes, and chasme have gained the balcony."

"Where is the Matron Darthiir?" Jaemas asked.

"Hopefully being chopped into mounds of sludge by the axe-wielding balgura that commands the manes," Saribel said, hardly hiding her sneer.

"Dear cousin, High Priestess, she is the matron mother of your House," Jaemas dared to say, his impertinence drawing wide eyes from the astounded Saribel.

The woman stuttered a few times, as if futilely trying to fashion a response. "Rid this place of demons," she ordered, and stormed back out of the room.

Ravel considered his older cousins carefully. These two were no minor wizards. Both were Masters of Sorcere, and had been for decades—Jaemas since before the onset of the Spellplague. Most accountings had Jaemas third on the list of successors to the position of Archmage of Menzoberranzan, with Faelas closely behind. Only Tsabrak and Brack'thal had been thought of more highly among the House Xorlarrin cadre of powerful wizards, and then only Tsabrak, when the Spellplague had taken most of poor Brack'thal's mind.

Still, for a male of any standing, short of the archmage himself, to speak to a high priestess in such a manner, openly, was quite shocking to Ravel.

"Where is the Matron Darthiir?" Jaemas asked Ravel.

"In her chambers, as always, other than her jaunts to sit at the council table when High Priestess Sos'Umptu Baenre comes to fetch her."

"Show us," said Faelas.

Ravel turned a puzzled expression on the younger of the masters. "We have demons inside the compound . . ."

"Inside the *house*," Faelas corrected. "So take us to the Matron Darthiir."

The trio moved along the corridors, walking calmly while drow warriors rushed to and fro. Ravel took careful note of the House guard here, suspecting correctly that those warriors associated with the city's Second House might well be seeking to avoid the fight.

He had no doubt that Barrison Del'Armgo had quietly arranged for this battle.

The corridor leading to the matron mother's room was strangely empty, but not quiet, as sounds of battle could be heard behind the central, ornate door.

Ravel stopped with surprise, but Jaemas grunted and cursed and rushed ahead, Faelas close behind. As they neared the door, there came a thunderous retort. The doors flew open, and a host of manes came flying out, crashing onto the floor, where they lay twitching and smoking, melting away.

A flying chasme demon, a gigantic ugly housefly, sputtered out the open doors, trailing smoke as it crashed hard into the opposite wall. It, too, fell to the floor and there died.

The wizards turned the corner, eyes wide with surprise—and none were more surprised than Ravel, when he, too, glanced in upon Matron Darthiir Do'Urden, battling ferociously, her metallic quarterstaff spinning gracefully in her hands, darting left and right and swatting aside the demon manes.

◆ ◆ ◆

IN DESPERATE BATTLE had Dahlia found clarity. The worms writhing inside her head could not distract her now, not with demons clawing at her from every angle. Kozah's Needle was her salvation, building another charge as Dahlia sent it prodding hard into the chest of a manes, then swung it about and tapped it hard on the floor, then broke it into a tri-staff and launched it into an overhead twirl, smacking aside another chasme.

All of her focus stayed on that remarkable weapon, breaking it through its myriad motions and combinations. It was a staff, a tri-staff, bo sticks, flails, at her command and with the subtle workings of her skilled fingers. And she used all of her weapons and repertoire, for in that demanded focus, Dahlia found mental clarity and kept the writhing worms of confusion at bay.

A lightning bolt shocked her, sizzling out to her left and dropping a line of manes.

She noted the drow at the door, noted the second wizard in his spellcasting, and noted his angle.

His lightning bolt shot in as well, to the other side, destroying some manes, but before it could plow through as had the first, Dahlia's magnificent weapon prodded near it and gobbled up the bolt.

Now she felt the power of the lightning within Kozah's Needle, and she sent it forth with renewed enthusiasm. She worked it out to the left, then left again, inviting those manes pressing her from the right to push in, clawed fingers reaching for her.

Across came Kozah's Needle, slamming the two, and Dahlia let free some of the lightning energy, the blast lifting the manes from the floor, throwing them up and back, right over the next in line.

Jaemas and Faelas gawked.

Ravel's lightning bolt followed, dropping another line of the least demons, and once again swallowed up by Dahlia's hungry weapon.

Without hesitating, Dahlia rushed forward, leaped into the middle of the pack, and stamped her weapon on the floor, releasing the energy in a mighty circular electrical blast that hurled the manes aside, far from her, where they became easy targets for the three drow wizards with their magic missiles and gouts of flames, and were quickly, summarily destroyed.

Dahlia stood there, then, breathing hard, trying to hold on to the clarity as the worms writhed once more.

"The weapon," she heard the one called Ravel explain to the others.

"These demons were allowed in here," said one of the others.

"To destroy your matron mother," said the other.

And they kept talking, but Dahlia was falling away once more. She felt the drow grab her by the arms and usher her away, still talking amongst themselves, but now seeming far, far distant.

◆ ◆ ◆

MATRON MOTHER MEZ'BARRIS Armgo was not happy as the reports began to filter out of the Do'Urden compound. Not at all. The fight had ended, all the attacking demons destroyed, banished, or driven from the scene.

Marilith was about the place now, stalking the grounds with her contingent of lesser guards. And so, Mez'Barris understood, Archmage Gromph was not far behind.

And the most recent report indicated that Matron Mother Baenre was there too, along with that wretched Sos'Umptu and all the priestesses of the Fane of the Goddess—indeed, those very priestesses had banished many of the demons sent against house Do'Urden.

Worst of all, Matron Darthiir had escaped unharmed. The *iblith* abomination lived, and would sit again at the table of the Ruling Council.

"Let me go and slay Marilith once more!" Malagdorl grumbled at Mez'Barris's side.

"Shut up," she replied without even bothering to turn and regard him, and in a tone that had even the impetuous and prideful weapons master swallowing hard.

Mez'Barris knew that she had to regroup and quickly. Her alliance—the other noble matron mothers who had agreed to go after House Do'Urden—would not be reconstituted. For all their efforts and plotting, only a handful of Do'Urden House guards had been slain—and half of those had been low-ranking warriors Mez'Barris's own House had provided.

But Matron Darthiir, this Dahlia creature, had survived.

Terondarg Del'Armgo, one of Mez'Barris's most capable scouts, rushed back into the room, and on her nod, ran up to her and began conversing with her secretly, shielding his hands with his wide cloak and flashing the matron mother the information in sign language.

Mez'Barris dismissed him with a wave and closed her eyes.

"What news?" High Priestess Taayrul, Mez'Barris's daughter, asked tentatively.

"Go to Melarn and tell Matron Zhindia that she and I need to parlay," Mez'Barris replied curtly, and she waved her daughter away.

Her wince was telling, though, and all in the room understood that the spy Terondarg had not delivered welcome news.

All in the room wisely followed Priestess Taayrul out of Mez'Barris's chamber.

The matron mother of the Second House moved over and flopped into her chair, trying to sort out her next move—any move—that would somehow repair the damage of this day. She had known that the demons would inflict little pain to House Do'Urden with the Baenres and Bregan D'aerthe so near, but the critical point to the assault was to facilitate the death of the abomination, the surface elf posing as a matron mother of Menzoberranzan.

But Dahlia had escaped, and worse, Mez'Barris now had learned that her spies within the Do'Urden compound, the guards to Matron Darthiir Do'Urden who had allowed the demon encroachment to her chamber, had been discovered. Those Barrison Del'Armgo warriors had admitted their crimes.

"The mind flayer," Mez'Barris muttered under her breath, solving the riddle, for surely the matron mother's pet illithid had aided in extracting the information. What couldn't Quenthel Baenre find out? Mez'Barris wondered—and feared.

"She will make a spectacle of it," Mez'Barris said. Terondarg had told her that the trial would be public, as would the transformation.

The transformation.

Her warriors would be turned into driders in full view of the city, in full view of those who had dared conspire with Matron Mother Mez'Barris to bring about the fall of Matron Darthiir. Those driders, no doubt, would become the core guard for the abomination, a poignant reminder to Mez'Barris and to all who would quietly stand with her of the consequences of going against Matron Mother Quenthel Baenre.

It had not been a good day.

CHAPTER 14 ◈

To the Call of a
Wicked Sword

SHE STAYED CLOSE TO THE BACK WALL, ALERT AND READY, BUT with no weapon in hand, staring across the low-burning fire to the open door across from her. There was movement out in the hall. Doum'wielle could sense it, and Khazid'hea did as well.

Soon, my Little Doe, the sword promised. *You will regain your leverage.*

The priestesses will interrogate me, Doum'wielle reiterated, the strong fear that had kept creeping into her mind as this pivotal day moved nearer to reality.

I will protect you from their inquisitions. The day is ours!

A black feline face appeared in the doorway, peeking in from the right, and before Doum'wielle could react, the huge panther leaped around the corner and into the room, ears flat, fangs bared.

"Guenhwyvar!" Doum'wielle said, as happily as she could manage.

The panther paused, ears coming up.

"Oh, Guen, dear Guen!" the half-elf, half-drow said, clapping her hands together. "You must save me, please!"

She knew this cat fairly well, and recognized that Guenhwyvar, so intelligent, understood most of what she was saying. The panther padded a step forward, silently, sniffing the air.

Then Guenhwyvar whirled when Doum'wielle yelled, "Behind you!"

But it was too late, and the stone door slammed shut. The panther hit it hard, clawing and pressing to no avail.

And Doum'wielle slipped out the secret door behind her, and closed that, too, securing the locking bar, trapping the panther in the room.

She moved down a side hallway and around a corner to find Tiago, smiling widely, coming to meet her.

"He is mine," the drow declared, and led the way back toward where they knew Drizzt was scouting.

◆ ◆ ◆

In a tower in Menzoberranzan, Gromph watched the trap spring. The archmage shook his head, not thrilled with the timing here—too much was at play in Menzoberranzan and the last thing he needed now was more complications.

He tried to imagine how the return of Tiago might help with the situation, but he couldn't see much to gain, particularly with that wretched half-elf Armgo creature along beside him.

At least House Do'Urden was secure for the time being, and Quenthel would not soon call on him.

Gromph waved his arms and barked out a sharp chant. A few moments later, he disappeared, arriving securely into his prepared chamber in Q'Xorlarrin. He stepped out of the small room to consider the main chapel of the city, across the way and over the primordial pit. Gromph's second spell created a disembodied orb through which he could see while a third rendered that orb invisible, and off it flew at tremendous speed.

A fourth spell turned Gromph into a floating wisp, ghostly and barely tangible, and a fifth made him invisible. Off he went, passing locked doors as if they were open portals, gliding through the forge room where several drow craftsmen and wizards looked up curiously, sensing something.

But while the hair on their necks might have stood up in warning, even the greatest of the dark elves in that room could not begin to decipher the wards against detection the archmage had enacted, and he was beyond them before any even realized that something had passed.

◆ ◆ ◆

"THE ARCHMAGE IS in Q'Xorlarrin," Kimmuriel informed Jarlaxle only moments later.

"Good," the mercenary leader replied. "I have long grown bored of this game. Let us finish it."

"Our play must be subtle," Kimmuriel warned.

"Have we a play to make?"

"Jarlaxle always has a play to make."

The mercenary leader reset his eye patch to his right eye and shrugged and grinned, clearly accepting that as a compliment. In this one particular case, however, both truly hoped that Kimmuriel was wrong. Better for them all if it played out perfectly without any intervention.

"I do not expect to find the archmage in a good mood," Kimmuriel said.

"My brother is never in a good mood. That is his weakness, and why he is so predictable."

Kimmuriel didn't often sigh, but he did so now. Jarlaxle might be taking Gromph lightly, but the psionicist could not afford to do so. If Gromph found them in Q'Xorlarrin at this critical time and in that critical place, would he consider it a coincidence? Or might he figure out that Kimmuriel's scrying gemstones included a bonus to Kimmuriel that allowed him to also spy on Gromph?

In that instance, the consequences would likely prove rather unpleasant.

◆ ◆ ◆

DRIZZT CREPT ALONG from shadow to shadow, scimitars in hand in these close quarters. He had seen little sign of anyone about, or anything amiss, but his warrior sense told him differently.

And where was Guenhwyvar?

He moved to the doorway of a wider room, the ancient furniture inside broken and cast about. He noted the absence of cobwebs, which were prevalent in many of the other rooms. He wrapped his fingers anxiously around his scimitar hilts.

He heard a call then, a low and long roar, more sad than excited, he thought. He clutched the blades tighter.

Then came a tapping noise, rhythmic and determined, from across the way, in the corridor beyond.

Drizzt held his position at the side of the door, his eyes widening when a dark elf—Tiago Baenre!—stepped into the room through the opposite door.

"Well, Drizzt Do'Urden," Tiago said, obviously perfectly aware of Drizzt's position. "Shall we end this at last?"

The brash young warrior stepped into the room. Drizzt could have pulled Taulmaril and let fly, but he did not. Instead, he marveled at Tiago's shield and sword, which seemed to him as if made of star-stuff, with glittering diamonds encased in the nearly translucent blade and all about the buckler, which resembled, too, a spider's web. He thought of the dragon fight, when he had seen Tiago up in the darkened sky, when he had first looked upon that sword, and the shield that had unwound to defeat his lightning arrows.

He reminded himself that this was a Baenre, and so the armor Tiago wore and the quiet magical items set on his person were likely superior to anything Drizzt had faced in many a decade.

The ranger stepped into the room to face his nemesis.

"How many years have you pursued me now, Tiago of House Baenre?" Drizzt asked.

"Decades," Tiago corrected. "Did you ever believe that I would stop? Did you secretly hope that this day would never come, cowardly rogue?"

"Yours is a foolish endeavor and a worthless quest."

"I'll not think it worthless when I hand your head to the matron mother."

Drizzt sighed and shook his head. They were doomed, his people. Doomed forever to their stupid traditions and dishonorable manners. The drow would war upon the drow until time's end. They would waste their talent and potential, their ability to truly do good for the world, in their endless pursuits of gaining the upper hand, of personal aggrandizement, of petty revenge.

"If only . . ." Drizzt mumbled, and not for the first time. "I had no desire to fight you," he said instead.

"Then surrender and save yourself the pain," Tiago replied. "I will be as merciful as you deserve." With that, he started walking toward Drizzt, but veered off to the ranger's left, circling, and Drizzt, too, began to move, keeping himself square with Tiago.

"*Had* no desire," Drizzt emphasized. "For truly your quest seems a silly thing. But then, you see, I only thought of the pain you brought to the people of Icewind Dale, to the people of Port Llast, and . . ."

"And to the dwarves of Icewind Dale?" Tiago finished. "Ah yes, what fine slaves they make! Until they are worked to their miserable deaths, of course."

Drizzt narrowed his lavender eyes. He focused on his enemy's weapon and noted the delicate curve of that starlit blade. It wasn't quite as curved as Drizzt's own blades, but it was as much scimitar as straight long sword, leading Drizzt to believe that Tiago fought in circles, much like Drizzt, rather than the straight ahead and straight back routines more common among the drow who used long swords.

They continued to circle and Drizzt kept making mental notes of this mostly unknown opponent, who had likely studied many of the tales of Drizzt's fighting style and exploits. Tiago had the edge, Drizzt knew, because Tiago had not ventured into a fight with the unknown.

"Leap upon me, O great Drizzt Do'Urden," the noble son of House Baenre taunted. "Let your hatred flow to your blades. Let me prove who is the stronger."

When Drizzt didn't accept that invitation, Tiago took it upon himself, leaping wildly into the air, flying for Drizzt, falling over Drizzt, his shield spinning and widening and sweeping clear of his flank as he burrowed in behind it, Vidrinath slashing hard.

Drizzt was too quick for such a straightforward attack, of course, and he quickly dodged, first to his right, as Tiago surely anticipated, but then fast back to his left, in front of the sweep of the shield. He took Tiago's sword down harmlessly to the side with his right-hand blade, Icingdeath, leaving him in a half-turn that aligned Twinkle perfectly with the younger drow's exposed side.

But Tiago landed in a spin, with amazing speed and balance, and he came all the way around to bring his shield to bear in time to block the counter.

Out came Vidrinath with three quick stabs, low, high, and low again.

Up went Twinkle to lift the first harmlessly away. Drizzt hopped back from the second, and down came Twinkle to crash against the third strike, driving Tiago's sword down to the side, across Tiago's body. Drizzt went out to the left behind the parry, and Tiago spun again and wisely went down low in a crouch so that Drizzt's stab came in high.

Tiago slashed across with his shield.

Drizzt hopped it and came down with both blades, but Tiago's shield was too large now, and the skilled young warrior brought it up deftly from the slash to cover above.

Twinkle and Icingdeath struck solidly on the shield, and seemed to hold there for just a heartbeat, allowing Tiago to come up fast and hard, stabbing out his sword from under the lifting, horizontal shield.

Drizzt wasn't quite sure what had just happened, or why he hadn't disengaged his blades fast enough to properly respond. That question followed him through his desperate backstepping.

Desperate, but not quite fast enough. Tiago's brilliant sword caught up to him and stuck him, just a bit, until Drizzt could bring his scimitars to bear in driving the biting blade away. He was hurt, in the belly, and he felt the sting.

But that was hardly the worst of his problems, Drizzt realized. He felt something else within that sting: the familiar burn of drow sleeping poison. The sword was Vidrinath, after all, the drow word for lullaby.

Drizzt grimaced and fought against the poison, one whose sting he had suffered many times before. A lesser drow, a lesser warrior, would have been slowing already from the dose that sword had inflicted, but when Tiago came confidently on, he found a flurry of scimitars blurring in his path and inevitably driving him back.

Drizzt took the offensive, fearing that time might work against him as the poison seeped deeper into his body. His scimitars rolled over each other, stabbing and slashing from many different angles. He felt the same frustration as he had that day on the dragon. Tiago was simply too good with that shield to allow for any clean hits—and now Drizzt had learned the hard way to be wary of that shield, suspecting that it had grabbed his blades, allowing Tiago the strike.

He had to formulate some new attack routine, had to piece together a strategy in the middle of the frenzy to somehow separate the Baenre warrior enough from his shield so that he could slip one of his blades past the guard.

Drizzt reached into his innate magic, the reverberations of the Faerzress still within him despite his many decades on the surface. Tiago's frame lit up in purplish flames of faerie fire, harmless except that they outlined him more clearly for his opponent.

Tiago skidded to a stop, glancing at himself with incredulity, then did likewise to Drizzt, limning him with angry red flames— dark elf warriors in Menzoberranzan hardly bothered with the faerie fire when engaged in melee with each other.

For Drizzt, though, the pause gave him a moment of clarity, which was the whole point, and in that moment, he searched for answers. He came on furiously once more, red and purple flames licking each other as the two combatants passed and turned.

Vidrinath came out in a solid thrust, and across came Icingdeath to drive it wide to Drizzt's left.

But Tiago rolled with the blow, his shield sliding back into alignment to slow any pursuit Drizzt might have intended. And then Tiago swung back the other way, suddenly and powerfully.

Up came Twinkle to block, a ringing blow—one heavier than Drizzt had anticipated, telling him that Tiago was likely in possession of some item, a belt or a ring, that granted him magical strength beyond his musculature and training.

Drizzt only fought the heavy blow for the blink of an eye, thrusting Twinkle vertically to intercept before collapsing to the right, falling into a roll. Sparks flew as Tiago's sword crashed against Twinkle, and unknown to the combatants, so, too, flew a piece of Drizzt's left-hand scimitar, compromising the integrity of the blade.

The greatest power of Vidrinath wasn't its poisoning bite, but the simple craftsmanship of the weapon. It had been created in this very complex, at the Forge of Gauntlgrym, with primordial fire and by the greatest drow weaponsmith of the age, using an ancient recipe reserved for this one special blade.

Few weapons in all the Realms could match the strength of glassteel Vidrinath, and so it was with Twinkle.

But Drizzt was too engaged in his plotting, in moving the fight to where he needed it to be, to notice. He rolled to his feet and went right back in, slapping Icingdeath hard into Tiago's shield—and retracting too quickly for that equally impressive blocker, Orbbcress by name, to get a firm hold on it.

But Drizzt did feel that pull, just for a moment as he retracted, and he understood.

And now his plan took clearer shape.

◆ ◆ ◆

OUTSIDE THE ROOM, Doum'wielle dared to peek in.

Her breath was stolen away.

She saw Drizzt and Tiago, each outlined in flames, rushing to and fro, each leaping in flying somersaults, vaulting the debris of old furniture, or the other's attempted strikes. Scimitars scraped and rang out with each passage, or a dull drumbeat sounded as Drizzt rolled his blades and Tiago got his shield up to block.

At one point, Drizzt broke free and dived aside, rolling up to one knee with his bow in hand instead of his scimitars, each laid neatly on the floor in front of him. Tiago yelped, and Doum'wielle almost cried out—and would have, had not Khazid'hea shot a warning through her mind before she uttered the gasp. For surely she thought Tiago doomed as the lightning arrow shot toward him.

But somehow the young warrior had brought his shield to block the lightning.

Doum'wielle felt her courage waning in the face of this display. The three blades moved faster than she could follow—either of these magnificent warriors could cut her apart with little effort. Hardly even thinking, Little Doe began to rise, perhaps to run away.

Take heart! Khazid'hea screamed in her thoughts. *The moment of your salvation is at hand!*

I cannot defeat them!

You do not have to, the sinister sword reminded her. *In their obsession, they will defeat each other.*

Doum'wielle's eyes spun as she tried to keep up with the frenetic, beautiful movements. Tiago went down in a slide, his blade coming out wide to cut at Drizzt's thighs.

But over that blade went Drizzt in a graceful dive and spin, and he broke out of it wide-armed and wide-legged, landing lightly on his feet.

Go! Khazid'hea implored Doum'wielle, for that sword, knowing the tactics of Drizzt so well, knew what was coming.

◆ ◆ ◆

DRIZZT WENT IN with Twinkle leading with a low thrust. But that was the feint, and Icingdeath went up above and over the sister scimitar, which Drizzt suddenly retracted, and swooped down from on high, left to right, smashing solidly against Tiago's shield.

The shield grabbed Icingdeath, as Drizzt had hoped, and he darted out to the left, tugging and turning, and flipping Twinkle in his hand. His left went up high, and as he stepped and turned his back to the twisting Tiago, he drove his hand down and back, a reverse thrust the Baenre noble could not hope to block with his shield.

Drizzt had him!

But Twinkle was hit as someone darted in the other way, and parried up high—and Drizzt nearly lost the blade.

"Hah!" Tiago cried with clear glee, surely thinking victory at hand.

But the ranger was quick, and Drizzt pulled Icingdeath free and completed his spin. Flipping Twinkle, he fell back a step defensively. He wore a curious expression when he came around, to see Doum'wielle, her parry complete, thrust ahead with the blade. But she stabbed at Tiago's exposed flank and not at Drizzt!

The Baenre noble howled and groaned and fell away, clutching his side, as Doum'wielle, her blade bloodied, spun back on Drizzt.

"Little Doe," Drizzt said, in both relief and surprise—and ending with his surprise multiplied as the daughter of Sinnafein, her face a mask of rage, swept her deadly blade across at Drizzt.

For this was the plan of Khazid'hea, the redemption of Doum'wielle, who would claim the head of Drizzt Do'Urden as her trophy when she returned to Menzoberranzan!

Twinkle came up in a vertical block once more, perfectly timed to intercept the slashing sword.

But Twinkle had been compromised from the earlier hit, and Khazid'hea had coaxed every ounce of strength Doum'wielle could manage into that brutal strike. The fine edge of the sword that could cut stone snapped the blade from Twinkle and continued across, shearing Drizzt's leather armor and mithral shirt with ease, opening a line across the ranger's chest from his left shoulder to the midpoint of his ribs.

Blood erupted from the garish wound, pouring freely onto Drizzt's torn shirt. He stood there, mouth agape, staring into the wicked smile of Doum'wielle, of Little Doe, of the daughter of his dear friend Sinnafein.

He couldn't retaliate. He couldn't even lift an arm to block as Doum'wielle lifted the awful Khazid'hea yet again. Drizzt knew his wound to be mortal.

He knew he was dead.

He got slammed hard and darkness fell over him.

He felt as if he were flying sidelong, or perhaps tumbling over to the ground, and he crashed against the stone and got hit again, with brutal force, and knew only darkness and weight, as if the stones of the floor had swallowed him up, or the ceiling had fallen upon him.

There was no breath to draw.

PART 3

The First King's Death

In the moment of my death, will I be surprised? In that instant? When the sword cuts my flesh, or the giant's hammer descends, or the dragon's flames curl my skin?

When I know it is happening, when I know beyond doubt that Death has come for me, will I be surprised or calm, accepting or panicked?

I tell myself that I am prepared. I have surrounded the question logically, rationally, removing emotion, accepting the inevitability. But knowing it will happen and knowing there is nothing I can do to stop it from happening is a different level of acceptance, perhaps, than any actual preparation for that onetime, ultimate event.

Can anything be more unsettling to conscious thought than the likely end of conscious thought?

This notion is not something I dwell upon. I do not go to my bed each night with the worry of the moment of death climbing under my blanket beside me. In merely asking this question—in the moment of my death, will I be surprised?—I suspect that I am entertaining the notion more than many, more than most, likely.

In many—in each—of us there is this deep-seated avoidance of, even denial of, the undeniable.

For others, there is the salve of religion. For some it is a false claim—more a hope than a belief. I know this because I have seen these faithful in their moment of death, and it is a terrifying moment for them. For others, it is a genuine, sanguine acceptance and belief in something better beyond.

This religious salve has never been my way. I know not why, but I am not so arrogant as to demean those who choose a different path through this muddled life and its inevitable end, or to pretend that they are somehow lesser of intellect, of moral integrity, or of courage, than I. For among that last group, those of deep faith, I would include my beloved wife, Catti-brie, so secure in her knowledge of what awaits when the scythe falls and her time on Toril is at its end.

Would I see it differently had I been in that altered passage of time and space beside my four dear friends?

I honestly do not know.

Wulfgar was there, and he returns anew, unconvinced of that which would have awaited him on the other side of that pond in the forest of Iruladoon. Indeed, Wulfgar confided to me that his certainty of the Halls of Tempus is less now than before his journey through death to return to this world. We live in a world of amazing magic. We assign to it names, and pretend to understand, and reduce it to fit our purposes.

More importantly, we reduce the beauty of the universe around us to fit our hopes and to chase away our fears.

I know the day will come. The enemy's sword, the giant's hammer, the dragon's breath. There is no escape, no alternate course, no luck of the draw.

The day will come.

Will I be surprised? Will I be prepared?

Can anyone be, truly?

Perhaps not, but again, this will not be that which chases me to my bed each night. Nay, I'll worry more for that which I can influence—my concern cannot be my inevitable demise, but rather, my actions in my waking life.

For before me, before us all, lie choices right and wrong, and clear to see. To follow my heart is to know contentment. To dodge the edicts of my heart, to convince myself through twisted words and feeble justifications to go against what I know to be true and right for the sake of glory or wealth or self-aggrandizement or any of the other mortal frailties, is, to my thinking, anathema to the concept of peace and justice, divine or otherwise.

And so to best prepare myself for that ultimate mortal moment is to live my life honestly, to myself, to the greater deeds and greater goods.

I do this not for divine reward. I do this not in fear of any god or divine retribution, or to ensure that there is no place for me in the Abyss or the Nine Hells.

I do this because of that which is in my heart. Once I gave it the name Mielikki. Now, given the edicts made in that name regarding goblinkin as relayed through Catti-brie, I am not so certain that Mielikki and my heart are truly aligned.

But no matter.

Am I prepared for the moment of my death?

No, I expect not.

But I am content and I am at peace. I know my guide, and that guide is my heart.

More than that, I cannot do.

—Drizzt Do'Urden

CHAPTER 15 ◈

A One-Handed Catastrophe

HE MARCH WAS METHODICAL AND COMPLETE, CLEARING room after room, corridor after corridor. Occasionally, a few of the dwarves and their allies would break free of the lead ranks, bursting through doors, pursuing fleeing kobolds or the avian humanoids called dire corbies, or whatever other monstrous inhabitants they had sent running.

Hoshtar Xorlarrin, magically invisible and magically tiny, watched from afar as a trio of dwarves crashed through one door, careening down a corridor. A pair of dwarf women led the way, swords waving, grabbing each other hand to arm and launching each other along. Oftentimes they fell, but it hardly seemed to matter, for they just bounced or rolled or twisted about, and always came back to their feet, in full speed and ready to chop down the nearest fleeing kobold.

Behind them came a red-bearded dwarf carrying a shining shield with the foaming mug standard of the clan, and banging it with an old battle-axe that had surely seen its share of battles. He laughed wildly, though he kept shouting his discontent, for the two women were tearing the place apart—and tearing apart the monsters, long before he could get near to them.

The powerful Xorlarrin wizard contemplated destroying the three fools as they passed along the corridor below his secret perch. He could summon an earthquake, perhaps, and tumble the walls upon them. Or invoke black tentacles from the floor to grab at them and occupy them, then blast them dead with fireballs and lightning bolts.

Yes, it all seemed perfectly delightful.

More sound from the back put an end to that fantasy, though. These three had broken free, but they had not gone too far in front, clearly, and now another pair of dwarves appeared at the doorway far back up the hallway. Another female came first, carrying a mace that seemed more fitting in the hands of an ogre. She was followed by a sturdy-looking fellow, black-bearded and muscular, with wild eyes and a ready laugh, and spinning a pair of heavy morningstars with practiced ease.

Hoshtar's eyes widened at the sight of Athrogate, Jarlaxle's ugly little friend. Hoshtar, who had long served as Matron Mother Zeerith's liaison to both Bregan D'aerthe and House Melarn, knew who the dwarf was with certainty. But what was the annoying fellow doing here? What was Bregan D'aerthe doing here, in any capacity, unless that capacity served the matron mother? Hadn't Matron Mother Baenre just effectively enslaved Jarlaxle as a House guard in her ridiculous reincarnation of House Do'Urden?

Hoshtar's mind leaped in a dozen different directions as he tried to sort it all out. Perhaps when the main forces of Bregan D'aerthe had been recalled to Menzoberranzan, Jarlaxle had set the dwarf free. Jarlaxle would not want Athrogate in the City of Spiders, after all. The rhyming, smelly creature wouldn't survive a tenday in the city before some aggravated drow laid him low! Or was Athrogate now spying, perhaps on behalf of Jarlaxle—and if that was true, perhaps it might ultimately serve Matron Mother Zeerith.

But no, Hoshtar knew, his first impression seemed the most reasonable, and now he played it to a logical conclusion. These dwarves, this army, had come to Q'Xorlarrin at the behest of the matron mother. She was pressuring House Xorlarrin to plead for her assistance so that she could garner Matron Mother Zeerith's unwavering fealty.

"Yes, that must be it," Hoshtar said under his breath, and he found himself disgusted and intrigued all at once.

And worried, for what might Matron Mother Zeerith's reaction be when he passed along this terrifying information?

That moment was fast approaching, Hoshtar realized, when more sounds followed Athrogate and the woman into the corridor. This entire section of the complex would fall to their small hands in short order, and his escape routes would be few and far between.

The Xorlarrin wizard adjusted his red veil over his face and quietly mouthed a spell. Fortunately for him, Athrogate, who was not so far away, launched loudly into a bawdy song, covering his spellcasting.

Hoshtar became an insubstantial cloud of fog and wafted away.

◆ ◆ ◆

"No ye don't, girlie!" Tannabritches Fellhammer yelled as she went skidding on her knees down the hallway past her sister, launching herself at the kobold line.

She almost got the next swing in, but her sister Mallabritches leaped over her, head down, and crashed into the monsters, driving them back.

"Ah, ye cheatin' daughter of an ugly orc!" Tannabritches howled, putting her feet under her and charging ahead. She shouldered Mallabritches aside and stabbed out with her sword once and then again, dropping a pair of kobolds.

"And ye're me twin!" Mallabritches reminded her. "So who's the orc?"

"Hah!" Tannabritches cried in victory, and started ahead, her sister growling and matching her charge.

But then Tannabritches was flying backward, tugged by a strong hand. She started to question it, but heard a familiar laugh and saw a familiar one-horned helmet atop a mop of wild red hair.

"Bah!" she cried, and Mallabritches grunted and offered a resounding "oof!" as Bruenor bulled past her.

Bruenor's shield rush drove into the kobold ranks, the dwarf leaning hard, shoulder to buckler, his powerful legs pumping and driving. Every now and then, Bruenor reached his axe up and over his shield, smacking at the beasts, and whenever one managed to get a foothold to slow his press, the dwarf turned and cut low, taking out its legs.

"Duck!" the Fellhammer sisters yelled in unison, and Bruenor reflexively scrunched lower. He felt a boot on his left shoulder, another boot on his right shoulder, and over went the sisters, using him as a springboard to lift them high above the front kobold ranks and drop into the middle of the swarm.

"No!" Bruenor cried. "What're ye thinkin'?"

His last word came out as a grunt, though, as another boot stomped atop his shoulder, and another on the other side.

"Bwahaha!" he heard, and he knew that Athrogate and Ambergris had come.

The kobolds knew it, too.

Painfully so.

◆ ◆ ◆

Reconstituted in his corporeal form once more, Hoshtar Xorlarrin glanced back over his shoulder, hearing the approaching battle. He was in the last tunnel now, moving for the large chamber that joined the lower levels with these upper portions of the complex.

The kobolds were running out of room.

The dwarves would be here soon, in this tunnel, and the upper complex would be theirs.

There remained some monsters between them and Hoshtar's clan, and surely the drow could bring in some more to hinder the progress of these bearded ruffians.

Hinder, but not stop, for it was only a matter of time now, and not much time at that.

Hoshtar reached the end of the corridor, moving through a door to a landing that opened high above the vast chamber and the deep darkness below. With a last glance back up the corridor, the mage touched his House emblem, enacting an enchantment of levitation, and stepped from the ledge, drifting down.

Matron Mother Zeerith would not be pleased, for he had nothing good to tell her. The dwarves had made tremendous progress, securing room after room after tunnel, and fortifying everything in their wake. When Hoshtar had secretly crossed through the front warrior ranks of the enemy, he had found the industrious dwarves behind hard at work, building traps and secure doors of stone and iron, even reshaping corridors in meticulous detail, setting up kill zones with their clever war engines. Even if House Xorlarrin fought off the initial assaults and defeated the front lines of dwarves, claiming these upper tunnels of Q'Xorlarrin would be costly.

And without these upper tunnels secured, Matron Mother Zeerith's designs on trade with surface-dwelling partners could not be easily realized.

Hoshtar thought of Athrogate, Jarlaxle's ugly little friend.

"Oh, clever Jarlaxle," he said, drifting down into the darkness. Might Jarlaxle, and not the matron mother, prove to be the impetus behind the dwarves' reclamation of the upper halls? Jarlaxle knew these dwarves, obviously, and had spies among them—Athrogate at least. With these devious developments, with an army of dwarves holding fast to the upper complex, only Jarlaxle could facilitate the necessary trade between the city of Q'Xorlarrin and the World Above.

Was this Jarlaxle's way of ensuring himself a larger profit?

"Or is it truly the work of the matron mother?" he asked himself as he lightly touched down beside the huge spiral staircase that could be, and now was, retracted halfway to the ceiling.

Aware then that many eyes and bows were trained upon him, Hoshtar held up his hands unthreateningly and offered his name.

"Beware falling kobolds," he warned the drow sentries, moving past into the deeper tunnels, moving toward the unenviable task of informing Matron Mother Zeerith on the successes their enemies had already realized.

"Dwarves," the delicate and fashionable dark elf muttered repeatedly during that long, long walk to the royal chambers. "Ugly, hairy, filthy dwarves. Oh, why must it be dwarves?"

◆ ◆ ◆

"Haha, but ye've picked yerself a band o' bluster an' bustin'!" Athrogate said to Bruenor a bit later, when the five had turned into a series of side passages and found—to their disappointment—a few moments of much-needed respite. "Don't know that I've e'er seen a one-hander so quick to clobber!" he added, using an old dwarven nickname, "one-hander," to describe a five-dwarf patrol group.

Bruenor had a hard time disagreeing with the sentiment. Fist and Fury were truly a rolling disaster from any enemy's viewpoint, and Bruenor, with his supreme skill, centuries of experience, and mighty gear, knew how to complement them perfectly. And no less devastating were Athrogate and Ambergris, particularly Athrogate. Never in his life had Bruenor witnessed a more capable dwarven catastrophe—indeed, this one was on a par with Thibbledorf Pwent!

"If I didn't have ye with me, I'd not be out in front o' the group," he replied, and dropped a friendly hand on Athrogate's shoulder.

"Aye, and an added pleasure it is that th' other three are lasses," Athrogate said, lowering his voice so that the trio, who were not so far away, couldn't hear. "I know ye're me king here, and know that ye've got me allegiance, but I'm beggin' ye to keep yer charms from me girl Ambergris. I've ne'er known a sturdier lassie, and oh, but she's taken me heart in her hands!"

Bruenor just stared at him curiously.

"What?" Athrogate asked when he finally caught on to that expression. "Were ye thinkin' o' takin' her from me, then?"

"I'm yer king?" Bruenor asked, seeming genuinely surprised.

And Athrogate seemed genuinely wounded. He stuttered about for a response for several heartbeats, then whispered, as he had in the Rite of Kith'n Kin, *"Ar tariseachd, na daoine de a bheil mise, ar righ."*

"Ye're here because Jarlaxle sent ye here, and no pretendin' other," said Bruenor. "Ye're not serving me, Athrogate, and I'm not to hold any fancies on it. Ye serve Jarlaxle and his band o' drow, and ye serve yerself, and so ye have since when first I met ye."

That statement seemed perfectly logical, given the history, but it clearly caught Athrogate by surprise and rocked him back on his heels, and put on Athrogate's face an expression caught somewhere between surprise and sadness.

"I'm not judgin' ye," Bruenor was quick to add. "I've had Jarlaxle aside meself, as well."

Athrogate winced.

"What, then?" Bruenor asked.

"I came to Nesmé as Jarlaxle's spy," Athrogate answered. "I'm not for denyin' that. Never did." He paused and looked at Ambergris. "But me spyin' showed me more than I was thinkin'."

"Jarlaxle's band'll accept yer girl, if that's yer worry," Bruenor assured him.

"Nay," Athrogate said. "Not me worry."

"Then what?"

"Not a life for a dwarf," Athrogate said, and he seemed genuinely choked up by then.

"What're ye sayin'?" Bruenor prompted. "Speak it straight out."

"I'm hopin' to call ye me king. So's Amber Gristle O'Maul o' the Adbar O'Mauls."

Now it was Bruenor's turn to rock back on his heels. Despite the Rite of Kith'n Kin, despite even that the Throne of the Dwarf Gods had accepted Athrogate, Bruenor's surprise at the level of

Athrogate's intensity and pleading here was genuine, his eyes wide, his jaw hanging slack until he could fumble around in his thoughts enough to find words for his shock. "Ye think Jarlaxle's to just let ye go?" he said, because he had nothing else to say.

"Why's it got to be one or th' other?" Athrogate replied. "I . . . we, me and me girl, will be Jarlaxle's eyes, ears, and mouth in Gauntlgrym."

"Serving both?" Bruenor asked, his tone showing that he was none too pleased by that prospect. Was Athrogate asking him to willingly accept a spy in Gauntlgrym's midst?

"Serving the king o' me clan," Athrogate replied without hesitation, and with sincere conviction. "Tellin' Jarlaxle only that what ye're tellin' me I can be tellin' him! And I'll be lettin' him know that right up front, what, and if that's not good enough for him, then good riddance to him!"

Bruenor stared at him hard, and found that he truly believed every word.

The other three came over then, Fist and Fury obviously eager to be on their way.

"More . . ." Tannabritches began.

". . . to hit," Mallabritches finished, and the two punched each other in the shoulder.

"Lot o' trust, ye're askin'," Bruenor remarked.

Athrogate shrugged.

Bruenor nodded. For some reason he couldn't quite sort out at that moment, it all seemed to fit. He had thought that Bungalow Thump would become his new Thibbledorf Pwent. Both had headed the Gutbuster Brigade, after all, and both could fight in the manner of a tornado.

But this seemed more appropriate to him. The fit was right. Other than Drizzt, and perhaps Pwent, Bruenor could not think of anyone above Athrogate he would rather have beside him when battle was at hand.

He had no reason to trust Athrogate now. The dwarf had been a fine fighting partner throughout the campaign, and particularly of late in Gauntlgrym, but asking Athrogate to fight well was like asking a fish to swim. If Athrogate's loyalties remained with Jarlaxle, wouldn't he have spoken the exact words Bruenor had just heard?

And yet, Bruenor knew better. Perhaps it had been the surprised expression, which appeared so genuine. Perhaps the hours of close-combat battle, joining these two as comrades.

Or perhaps because it just seemed to fit, and just seemed to make sense.

Bruenor silently cautioned himself against overthinking his feelings. He had led his people for centuries by relying on his gut, and his gut's reaction to Athrogate now was clear.

"Welcome home, me friend," he said quietly.

Athrogate grinned widely, so widely! But that was just to cover up the moisture that had come to his dark eyes, Bruenor realized. He could see that Athrogate wanted to respond verbally, but that he wouldn't dare, afraid he would break out in an open sob.

"What're we missin'?" Ambergris asked.

"Me axe ain't missing nothing," Bruenor replied. "So let's find it something to hit!"

"Aye!" the Fellhammer sisters said together, with such enthusiasm that Bruenor almost expected them to launch into aerial somersaults.

Off went the one-hand catastrophe.

◆ ◆ ◆

SOMETIME LATER, A scratching sound, like a spear tip against stone, alerted them that they were not alone, and a quick survey placed the sound behind a barred door in a perpendicular corridor.

Tannabritches slid past the door on her knees, skidding to a stop just to the far side of the jamb. Mallabritches came right behind, skidding up to the nearer edge.

"Might be a wizard," Bruenor whispered to Ambergris, the two and Athrogate back at the corridor corner, just a few strides from the kneeling sisters. The priestess nodded and quietly began preparing a spell.

Bruenor motioned to Athrogate and the two moved up to stand in front of the portal and between the sisters. Tannabritches and Mallabritches slowly grasped the locking bar.

Bruenor glanced back to see if Ambergris was ready before he took up his shield and axe and motioned to the pair.

Off went the bar, thrown aside. Athrogate leaped up and kicked in the door.

Then he screamed in shock and fell away, a tumble of thick limbs and bouncing morningstars. Before they could begin to react, before they could properly fill the void left by the diving dwarf, the Fellhammer sisters, too, were knocked aside by a huge living missile. And they, too, screamed, or seemed as if they were crying out, but Bruenor couldn't hear a sound.

Ambergris's magical spell of silence filled the area.

So Bruenor's scream, too, was no more than a facial expression. In front of him, the Fellhammers tumbled, but he hardly noticed, falling instead behind his shield to try to brace—futilely, though, as he was hit hard and sent flying into the wall across from the door, which smashed in and crushed down. He felt the huge claws scraping against him as his attacker set its powerful legs and sprang away.

Bruenor twisted and tried to unwind himself from the awkward position. He saw the blackness flying away, saw, but couldn't hear, Ambergris crying out in surprise. The priestess fell to the floor as the missile—as *Guenhwyvar*—twisted and hit the wall beside her and hit it running, going around the corner right above her and speeding off down the hall.

The four dwarves fell all over each other trying to get back down the hall.

". . . th' elf's cat?" Bruenor heard Athrogate finish as he, too, came out of the area of silence. Bruenor turned the corner first, in a full run, extending his hand to Ambergris and yanking her upright as he stumbled past.

"Guenhwyvar!" he cried, but the cat was already out of sight, around a right turn up ahead.

The dwarves ran in swift pursuit, turning corners so fast that they rebounded off the far walls of the new passageways.

Guenhwyvar always seemed just ahead of them, enough for them to catch a glimpse of a black tail retreating around another bend.

Bruenor called out to her repeatedly, but she wasn't slowing to his call. And when they finally caught up to her, a gasping, horrified Bruenor understood why.

Chapter 16 ◈

Vortex

OUM'WIELLE STOOD THERE, STARING BLANKLY, SHOCKED and not understanding.

Now! Khazid'hea screamed in her thoughts, but the poor young elf was too surprised, stupefied even, to begin to move.

Her golden hair swept out behind her as a sudden wind appeared from out of nowhere. She heard a groan behind her and managed to turn just a bit, just enough to see Tiago, struggling to rise and holding his bleeding side.

Her eyes widened in horror as she looked past him to the wall, where a swirling vortex had appeared, like a black tornado spinning on its side, black smoke roiling and twisting ominously.

"Doum'wielle!" Tiago cried desperately, reaching out for her.

She grabbed at his hand, but a blast of wind rose up and slammed Tiago away, sending him tumbling, lifting him right off the stone floor, bouncing and rolling.

The vortex ate him, swallowing him into darkness.

Doum'wielle didn't know how to react. She couldn't understand the directional nature of the wind, and the . . . purposefulness of it! Was this roiling vortex some living creature? Had it *inhaled* Tiago?

Panicked, she spun, leaning against the wind that continued to buffet her, determined to run away.

And then she saw him, terrible and powerful, standing opposite the sidelong tornado, with her between him and it.

She knew this one to be the source of that incredible power, knew then that the tornado was no living thing, but was, rather, a tool for the Archmage of Menzoberranzan.

Now! a desperate Khazid'hea implored her. The sentient sword found its plans unraveling, saw the target of its wrath slipping away.

Hardly thinking of the movement, Doum'wielle lifted the blade, and Gromph lifted his hand.

A sharp burst of wind tore the sword from her grasp and sent it bouncing back, to disappear into the vortex.

"I killed . . ." Doum'wielle started to say, but her words became a shriek as a blast of wind as tangible as a giant's punching fist hurled her backward. Instinctively she braced, or tried to, certain she was about to collide with the stone wall.

But she did not.

She fell, instead, speeding along a tunnel of dark clouds, rolling and tumbling over and over.

◆ ◆ ◆

JARLAXLE SIGHED.

"He must be the center of all creation," he said with great lament, he and Kimmuriel watching Gromph's victorious walk across the room, to his own enhanced dimensional tunnel. The archmage paused only briefly to consider the splatter on the far wall, the boots hanging, waggling a bit in the continuing wind from his spell.

He, too, sighed, and no doubt at his brother, Jarlaxle knew.

Gromph stretched out his arms, his great robes flapping in his own magical wind, catching him like a kite and sending him into the tunnel.

Jarlaxle and Kimmuriel followed, the mercenary pausing only to scrape some goo onto his hand. Kimmuriel went in first, Jarlaxle close behind.

Jarlaxle was still wiping that sticky goo from his fingers when he passed through the dimensional tunnel to exit into the audience chamber of House Do'Urden right beside Kimmuriel, where Archmage Gromph held court.

Ravel Xorlarrin and his sister Saribel were there as well, along with Dahlia, who sat on the throne looking very much like a mannequin—or a corpse, perhaps. The image pained Jarlaxle greatly, but alas, what was a rogue to do?

"Archmage," Ravel breathed. He had been trying to help the injured and confused Tiago up from the floor, but now let his friend fall and backed away deferentially—terror often resembled deference.

Gromph didn't bother to look at him. His eyes stayed locked on Doum'wielle, who was splayed on the floor, her fine sword not far from her.

She looked back at the archmage, and she felt, and seemed to all around, so tiny and small. For some reason Jarlaxle couldn't understand—surely she didn't intend to try to stand against Gromph!—her hand crept out for that lost blade.

Gromph lifted his hand and began to circle it in the air in front of him. "That is a Baenre blade!" he warned her, his voice booming with grand magical enhancement—so grand that even the near-comatose Dahlia started in surprise and looked at him.

Gromph thrust his hand forward at Doum'wielle, launching his spell past her, and another vortex appeared, a sidelong tornado on the room's far wall. And this one seemed lighter in the eye, bright and sunlit, perhaps, but there was a coldness associated with that light.

"A Baenre blade!" Gromph roared just as Doum'wielle foolishly reached for Khazid'hea. The sword flew from the floor to Gromph's waiting hand.

Doum'wielle stared at him, terrified and lost . . . so lost!

But there was no mercy to be found in the amber flame of Gromph Baenre's eyes.

"You do not belong here, *iblith*," Archmage Gromph declared.

A great howl of wind sounded, shaking the room, focusing on Doum'wielle. Her eyes went wide with terror, she clawed at the floor so desperately that she tore her fingers, and left more than one fingernail behind when the wind finally caught her and lifted her, and flipped her, somersaulting, into the vortex.

Jarlaxle winced and whispered, "Poor girl."

The vortex spun faster and faster, its diameter shrinking, the storm's eye becoming a dot. Then it was gone, as if collapsing in upon itself, leaving only the blank wall there in House Do'Urden's audience chamber.

"Tend to your husband, foolish priestess," Gromph told Saribel. "And know that if he dies, you will quickly follow him to the grave."

◆ ◆ ◆

"THE UPPER LEVELS are lost," Hoshtar said with finality. "Even were you to throw every drow, every spell, every slave up above, it would be to no avail. They are mighty, led by capable warriors and with clever generals in support. And they are securing every footstep of ground they gain. My Matron Mother, they'll not be easily dislodged."

"Nor easily stopped," Matron Mother Zeerith said, staring at the spy.

Hoshtar merely shrugged, not about to deny the obvious truth.

"How long can we fend them off?" Matron Mother Zeerith asked.

"Their journey to the lower city will be difficult," the spy answered. "The drop to the main entry cavern of the lower levels is considerable and the stairway cannot be raised, of course. The stair is down, folded and secured, and will remain so. I expect that the dwarves will employ magic to get them down to the lower level, but doing so will give us ample opportunity to sting at them with arrows and magic."

"Considerable magic," Tsabrak promised from the side, and Matron Mother Zeerith nodded in appreciation.

"There are other ways to access the lower levels," Matron Mother Zeerith reminded him.

Hoshtar nodded. "All narrow and easily defended."

"See to that defense."

"My Matron Mother," said Hoshtar, bowing, and he rushed from the room.

"They will find their way down here," Tsabrak said when he and the matron mother were alone. "Do not underestimate the resilience and cleverness of dwarves. Matron Mother Yvonnel did so a century ago and the price she paid was her very life."

"I understand the danger," Matron Mother Zeerith assured him, her voice dead, defeated.

"You have no choice," said Tsabrak.

"You ask me to beg Matron Mother Baenre."

Tsabrak didn't bother to answer.

"Facilitate the conversation," Matron Mother Zeerith instructed, and Tsabrak nodded and moved to a scrying pool.

Soon after, the image of Matron Mother Baenre appeared in the still waters, and Matron Mother Zeerith moved into her view.

◆ ◆ ◆

JARLAXLE AND KIMMURIEL followed Gromph across the city to his tower abode in Sorcere. All along the way, Gromph continued to point out the damage the demons had caused, including one scene where several drow bodies lay strewn along a side street, torn apart, limbs asunder, as if clipped by the pincers of a glabrezu.

"Bregan D'aerthe might soon expect a command from the matron mother to clean up the streets," Gromph told them when they entered his private chambers.

"Of bodies, or rampaging demons?" Jarlaxle asked, seeming unamused.

"Both, I would expect," said the archmage.

"Bregan D'aerthe is not a—" Kimmuriel started to protest.

"Bregan D'aerthe is whatever the matron mother tells you it is," Gromph interrupted. "Have we not already seen as much?" he added, looking to Jarlaxle. "House guards, perhaps?"

Jarlaxle remained unamused.

Gromph got a curious expression on his face then, seeming somewhat surprised. He reached down to his belt, putting a hand on the hilt of the Baenre sword he had just taken from Doum'wielle Armgo.

"It calls to me," he explained, drawing the fine-edged blade and holding it up in front of his eyes.

"Are you its new wielder, then?" asked Jarlaxle, who of course was no stranger to Khazid'hea.

"Hmm," Gromph mused. "Perhaps I am." His expression turned skeptical, and quite amused then. "Or perhaps not, if the sword has any say in the matter."

"Khazid'hea is not pleased to be held by a wizard," Jarlaxle surmised. "The blade wants to taste blood."

"What Khazid'hea wants is irrelevant," Gromph replied.

The archmage started then, as if hit by some unseen force, wincing like someone who had been flicked by a finger under the nose, or some other stinging but harmless disrespect.

"It would seem that the sword does not agree," put in Kimmuriel.

Jarlaxle looked at Kimmuriel and noted that he had his eyes closed. He was intercepting the telepathic protests the sword was launching at Gromph, Jarlaxle realized.

"Truly?" Gromph said with a snort, and he was clearly talking to the sword then, as he lifted it higher in front of his sparkling eyes. He studied the pommel, shaped so beautifully into the likeness of a curled and sleeping pegasus. "No," he said, shaking his head. "That will not do."

Gromph pressed the pommel against his forehead, closed his eyes and scrunched up his face.

Jarlaxle looked to Kimmuriel, who glanced back and nodded, clearly impressed—impressed by the psionic assault that Gromph was leveling at Khazid'hea.

And Jarlaxle, too, was impressed, as he watched the pommel of Khazid'hea shift and change, going black, then adding red speckles. Jarlaxle barely contained a laugh as he considered it more closely. Gromph had turned the pommel of mighty Khazid'hea into the likeness of a mushroom!

The archmage moved the sword back to arm's length, gave a nod at his handiwork, and said, "Better."

"Not very appropriate for a Baenre blade," Kimmuriel remarked. "But a proper insult to such a crude instrument as a sword."

"And so I doubt that Khazid'hea will try to impose its will upon you again," Jarlaxle remarked.

"It is a minor item," said Gromph. With a look from the sword to the mercenary leader, he casually tossed the sword to Jarlaxle, who caught it easily.

"It is a Baenre blade," Gromph explained. "And you are a Baenre. And a Baenre warrior, at that. Fitting that you carry the sword, if you are strong enough of will to control it."

Jarlaxle returned an amused, if somewhat bored stare at the open challenge. He could hear the frustration of Khazid'hea in his thoughts, but only if he concentrated on the very distant murmur, and blocking it out entirely was no more a challenge for him than it had been for Gromph. Even without his magical eye patch, which prevented psionic intrusions and commands, Jarlaxle held no fear whatsoever regarding the sword's willpower and ego against his own.

He nodded to his brother, offering a look of appreciation—and one that was only half-feigned. Jarlaxle loved his magical toys and knew that he had a powerful one in hand with Khazid'hea.

"Where is the half-drow girl?" Jarlaxle asked, sliding the sword into his belt loop. "The daughter of Tos'un Armgo?"

"Why do you care?"

Jarlaxle shrugged. "Perhaps I do not, not excessively at least. It is my curiosity, nothing more."

"I honestly do not know," said Gromph. "Freezing to death on a cold mountainside . . . somewhere. The Spine of the World,

I expect, and likely somewhere near to the lair of Arauthator. Why do you wish to know? Do you intend to fetch her?"

Again Jarlaxle shrugged. "She might prove useful at some point."

"If I ever lay eyes on that half-*iblith*, half-Armgo creature again, I will transform her into a jelly and serve her at the next feast I attend," Gromph said, and there wasn't the slightest hint in his tone to suggest that he was exaggerating.

"Fortunately, I am in the possession of many things you will never see, then," Jarlaxle replied with a tip of his great-brimmed hat. He turned to Kimmuriel. "To Luskan," he instructed. "I have no desire to be discovered by the matron mother here in the city."

"But the streets need cleaning, brother," Gromph said.

"That is why the gods gave us magic, brother," Jarlaxle replied in the same smug tone. "To perform the mundane tasks of life."

Wisely, Kimmuriel didn't hesitate, and a moment later, he and Jarlaxle stepped into the Bregan D'aerthe audience hall in Illusk, the undercity of Luskan.

❖ ❖ ❖

SHE LIFTED HER wet face, trying to regain her wits and strength after the spinning, flying ride through the archmage's rough portal. She didn't note the cold at first, not until she managed to pull open her eyes to realize that she was facedown in deep snow.

Doum'wielle knew the season, knew that the snows had not yet started to fall anywhere but in the high mountains.

She propped herself up on straight arms and slowly swiveled her head about, taking in the grandeur of the scene in front of her. Mountains, huge and tall, with dark rocky spurs prodding forth from the thick blanket of snow, loomed before her—she realized from her posture that her head was higher up the mountain than her feet.

To the left and right, the mountains went on beyond her sight. The Spine of the World, she realized. Though she didn't recognize any specific peaks from this different perspective, she knew of no other mountain ranges in Faerûn of this magnitude and majesty.

She lay in the snow, the cold beginning to creep in.

The weight of her troubles only then began to creep in with it.

Doum'wielle looked around. She slapped at the snow desperately, shoving it aside, throwing it far from her. She jabbed her hands down through it, grabbing, grasping, looking for something to catch onto, and only after she began to tire did she take a heartbeat and remember that for which she was searching.

Her movements slowed then, and she was relieved to know that she still had all of her fingers, for if she had plunged her hand through the snow to strike against the impossibly sharp blade of Khazid'hea, then surely she would have left some fingers behind.

She pulled herself up to a kneeling position and took a different tack, calling out telepathically for her missing sword, pleading with Khazid'hea to guide her search.

She heard nothing.

Panic swept over her. She cried out audibly now, screaming "Cutter!" repeatedly. She forced herself to her feet and staggered about.

"Cutter!"

Her cries echoed back to her from the mountainsides, and those echoes brought her desperate, pathetic tone to her ears and mocked her. The vastness of the Spine of the World laughed at Little Doe.

The sun shined brilliantly upon her, bright in the snow, but the air was cold up here in the vast white sheets.

Doum'wielle had not often been in the mountains. Where could she go? How could she protect herself from the cold and the wet?

And the prowling monsters? Yes, she knew enough of the environment to realize that the cold might be the least of her problems.

Khazid'hea! Doum'wielle's thoughts cried out once more, one last time.

The sword was lost.
She was lost.

◆　◆　◆

"WHEN YOU ARE of the mind to taunt the archmage, I would prefer you do so after a proper warning to me, that I can be far away," Kimmuriel scolded his dangerous companion.

Jarlaxle drew out Khazid'hea and turned it over to examine the pommel. "An impressive feat," he asked as much as stated.

"More so than you understand," Kimmuriel replied. "The sword tried to dominate him. A sewer rat would have a better chance at ordering about the matron mother."

Jarlaxle nodded and stared at the mushroom-shaped and speckled pommel, muttering, "Impressive," and he was talking more about Gromph in general than about this particular feat of willpower.

Khazid'hea was no minor magic item, after all. It was possessed of its own sentience and a great ego. The sword had dominated powerful warriors in the past, even Catti-brie, and even, albeit only for a very short time and only until he had properly understood the threat, Artemis Entreri.

The mercenary considered Gromph's words when he had given Jarlaxle the prize. He was reminding Jarlaxle of his heritage, and openly, in front of Kimmuriel. Jarlaxle began to nod, sorting it out. Despite the insulting look of the pommel, this sword wasn't a gift for Jarlaxle as much as an offer. Gromph knew that he was walking on dangerous ground back in Menzoberranzan. It didn't take one of Jarlaxle's perception to recognize the archmage's outrage over Lolth's loss of the Weave, and worse, over her continuing disrespect to the male wizards, even to Gromph, when all believed that she would come to include the Web of Magic in her domain and should respect its users.

Gromph had given Jarlaxle the sword to buy an out for himself, should that necessity come to pass.

ARCHMAGE

The—former—Archmage of Menzoberranzan as a member of Bregan D'aerthe? Jarlaxle's eyes widened at the possibilities.

Possibilities that Jarlaxle subsequently dismissed, for in that circumstance, did he really believe that Gromph Baenre would serve him and Kimmuriel? More likely, he knew, Gromph would demand servitude of them.

Gromph Baenre did not make offers that one could refuse.

Kimmuriel walked off to see to some other matters, and Jarlaxle wasted no time. He removed his eye patch to better communicate with the sword, then nodded as the pommel went fully black and became feline in form—a panther. For a moment, Jarlaxle almost abandoned his course and thought to make it look like Guenhwyvar—perhaps he could use it as a gift back to Drizzt. But no, he decided, and said, "It is a Baenre blade."

A pair of tentacles sprouted from the panther's shoulders, transforming the figure from that of a great cat of the World Above to an Underdark displacer beast, a formidable foe indeed, and a symbol worthy of a blade hanging in the belt loop of Jarlaxle.

Those tentacles seemed to come to life for just a moment, magically wrapping around Jarlaxle's hand, securing his grip.

In his mind, Jarlaxle could feel Khazid'hea's appreciation.

Yes, they would get along splendidly.

CHAPTER 17 ◈

The Lonely
Cadence

B RUENOR FLUNG HIMSELF THROUGH THE OPENED DOORWAY
and nearly pitched headlong to the floor in surprise, realizing that he had caught up to Guenhwyvar. The great
panther stood there in the room in front of him, staring at
the wall—and what a curious sight that was.

"By the gods, but them drow've come," Bruenor muttered under his breath, staring at the swirling, cloud-like vortex
spinning against the wall, or within the wall, as if the very stones
were malleable and part of the sidelong tornado.

The other dwarves bobbed in behind Bruenor, bumping into
him in their rush, but held their ground. All of the four started
to ask what was what, and all of them bit back the words even
as they started to utter them, caught by the same incredible sight
that held Bruenor and Guenhwyvar.

The vortex spun tighter and tighter, the wall seeming to
solidify around its retreating edges. And then it was gone, and
the room went perfectly silent.

A low growl from Guenhwyvar broke that stillness.

Bruenor moved past the panther, on edge, glancing all about.

"What d'ye know?" Tannabritches asked.

"Been a fight in here," Athrogate said. The black-bearded
dwarf motioned for the Fellhammer sisters to fan out to
the right, then nodded to Ambergris to go with him to the
left flank.

"I'm smellin' the blood, or I'm a pretty goblin," Athrogate added.

Bruenor smelled it too, more so because he was closer to the center of the battle, where blood stained the floor. And as he was drawn to that, he found something else besides.

"Elf?" he asked weakly, lifting a very familiar blade—not the whole scimitar, but just the broken blade of Twinkle—from the floor.

"That cyclone!" Ambergris cried, rushing over. "They taked Drizzt!"

Bruenor started for the wall, thinking to shoulder right through it if need be, but Mallabritches's cry of "No, here!" spun him back the other way. He looked curiously at the sisters, who stood in front of some discoloration on the wall, some malformation that Bruenor couldn't quite make out. He moved closer, scanning.

The dwarf's eyes went wide when he glanced at the bottom of that malformation, to see familiar boots hanging below it.

"Drizzt!" he cried. "Oh, me elf!" And he leaped forward at the viscous goo, reaching with his axe as if to cut at it, retracting, dropping the weapon, grabbing at the substance—he didn't know what to do!

"His nose! His nose!" Tannabritches said, hopping up and down and pointing to a place just above, where it looked as if someone had pulled the slime away from Drizzt's face, clearing his nose, at least, that he could draw breath.

Bruenor threw down his shield beside his axe and leaped for the spot. "Peel him out!" he shouted, and he began clawing at the glob which had pinned Drizzt against the stone. It came free, but grabbed at Bruenor's hands so hard that he could barely shake it from his fingers, one stubborn piece at a time, and even then only after rolling it in on itself repeatedly. With Fist and Fury's help, though, he soon had Drizzt's head cleared, and the drow's face lolled forward, Drizzt clearly not hearing the dwarf's frantic calls, and not reacting at all when a desperate Bruenor slapped him across the face.

"Come on, elf!" Bruenor yelled, cradling the drow's face, looking at him closely, pleading with him to open his eyes.

Tannabritches and Mallabritches bore on, tearing free the goo, and Athrogate joined in, but Ambergris came up more cautiously. She carried the broken blade of Twinkle, alternately examining the cut along the base of the severed scimitar blade and staring at Drizzt, shaking her head.

It went on for a long while, when finally Tannabritches said, "Oooo," and stepped back. She had peeled the goo down over Drizzt's collarbone, down to his chest, and blood poured out.

"What?" Mallabritches demanded.

Tannabritches held up her bloodied hands.

"Stop! Stop!" Ambergris cried, leaping forward to grab at Athrogate and pull him back. "Stop!"

"What, girl?" Athrogate demanded, and all eyes turned to the priestess.

"The glob," she said, "it's holding Drizzt together. Keepin' his blood in! Ye pull it down and he'll spill all over ye—all over the floor!"

"Like a bandage?" Mallabritches asked.

Bruenor, verging on panic, for it seemed very much to him that Drizzt was already dead, looked from Drizzt to the cleric and back again. Ambergris walked past him to press her hand against the exposed portion of the dark elf's garish wound. She felt around, put on a pained expression, then said to Bruenor, "It's a deep one."

"Well heal him, ye dolt!" Bruenor finally shouted.

Ambergris nodded, but then shook her head and replied, "Ah, but this one's beyond me."

"Well try!" the frantic Bruenor screamed.

"Ye go and get his wife," Ambergris told the Fellhammer sisters. "Go now, and quick."

"We can't wait!" Bruenor frantically shouted, but Ambergris was already beginning her first spell, and when he realized that, the dwarf calmed somewhat.

Ambergris pressed her hand in tighter against the drow's torn chest and brought forth her healing magic. The blood flow slowed its trickle from that small, uncovered part of the wound, but the cleric looked to Bruenor and shook her head.

"Me spells won't be enough for this one," she lamented. "Be sure that he's been killed to death in battle, and only the goo's keeping him a bit alive."

"Aye, and smotherin' him at the same time!" Athrogate said.

Bruenor was shaking his head. Someone had cleared Drizzt's nose, and Bruenor realized that it was probably the same person who had hit him with the syrupy glob in the first place. "Jarlaxle," he muttered, nodding. He had seen this trick before from that one.

But why would Jarlaxle just leave Drizzt here like this? The dwarf looked to the wall, where the vortex had been. Another Jarlaxle trick, he wondered?

But had Drizzt and Jarlaxle battled? It didn't seem possible to him. He could not begin to imagine those two going at each other with blades.

None of this made sense to him, but Bruenor figured that the only way he was going to get the answers was to get Drizzt healed.

He looked to Ambergris, who was deep into casting another spell, and this one elicited a groan from Drizzt as the healing waves entered his torn and battered body.

"Come on, girl," Bruenor muttered, looking to the door.

"Come on, get his other leg, then," Athrogate called to him, and Bruenor turned to see the black-bearded dwarf clearing the goo from Drizzt's shin. "Just a bit at a time, so we're not for opening any more cuts! Elf's bled enough!"

"Too much," Bruenor replied, going at the other leg. He winced as he did, wondering suddenly if this determined expedition was worth it to him. If he recovered Gauntlgrym, but at the price of Drizzt and Catti-brie's lives, say, would he consider that a victory?

"Aye," he said with determination, but without much conviction. And he added, "Come on, girl."

◆ ◆ ◆

MATRON MOTHER BAENRE sat quietly for a long while after Sos'Umptu's prayer, which called the meeting of the Ruling Council to order. She let her gaze settle on each of the rival matron mothers, her withering look telling them that she understood well the true power behind the attack on the Do'Urden compound, and the coordination it had required. Even those matron mothers who had not participated directly shifted uncomfortably in their seats under the weight of that stare, for certainly all had known of the whispers, the shadowy nods and look-aways that had led to the coordinated assault.

And behind them, seated at the back leg of the table, Matron Darthiir Do'Urden sat impassively.

"Are we to believe this was anything less than an attempted assassination?" the matron mother asked. Several shifted uncomfortably, Matron Mother Mez'Barris let out a little growl, and other matron mothers nodded at the sentiment. Such accusations, if that indeed was where Matron Mother Baenre was going, were not acceptable in the city of backstabbing dark elves.

"Or the will of the goddess?" the matron mother continued, giving them an out for their protests, and turning away from the course that would have inexorably led to direct and violent confrontation.

"A signal, perhaps, that Matron Darthiir should not be seated here at the Ruling Council," Matron Mother Zhindia Melarn offered.

"Or perhaps that she should not be a matron mother at all," Mez'Barris added.

"Or that she should not be suffered to live," said Zhindia.

"Yet here she is," said Matron Mother Baenre. "Alive and well."

"Foolishly rescued . . ." Zhindia started to interrupt, but Quenthel slammed her fist down on the table.

"Matron Darthiir fought brilliantly, so say the Xorlarrin nobles who happened upon her," Matron Mother Baenre declared. "Shall I bring them in to confirm? Matron Darthiir was assaulted by a horde of demons, but she battled them away and left them melting on the floor."

She turned to Mez'Barris, locking stares with her rival. "What say you?" Quenthel demanded. "Are we to believe that Lady Lolth ordered forth the demons to destroy a matron mother of the Ruling Council, and believe even more so that those demons failed in the Spider Queen's task?"

With no answer forthcoming, Quenthel stood up and towered over the others. "And if so," she went on, "then why would Lady Lolth allow Matron Darthiir back here to sit beside us on the Ruling Council of this, her city? Go and seek guidance, Zhindia Melarn, I beg, before you blaspheme the Spider Queen with your ignorance and prejudice. And rest assured, if the Spider Queen had wanted Matron Darthiir dead, then Matron Darthiir would be dead by my own hand!"

"Are we to celebrate her great victory?" Matron Mother Mez'Barris asked sarcastically. "Perhaps you would elevate House Do'Urden to a place of greater rank to properly acknowledge that a matron mother successfully killed a handful of manes."

The matron mother turned a perfectly wicked smile over Mez'Barris as others snickered.

"Perhaps House Do'Urden will find its own ascent under the guidance of its heroic matron mother," Matron Mother Baenre calmly replied, and she glanced sidelong at the sneering Zhindia Melarn, whose House was ranked one above Do'Urden, and so seemed the most likely target of any such attempt.

"Perhaps the bastard House, so favored by Lady Lolth, will find its way to your seat," Quenthel added to Mez'Barris, an absurd proposition, of course, but surely a threat the matron mother did not try to veil.

"This is all for another day," said Sos'Umptu at the back of the chamber. "This meeting was not convened to applaud or decry the battle at the compound of House Do'Urden, nor the valiance of Matron Darthiir Do'Urden."

"Indeed," agreed Quenthel, who had demanded the meeting. "Matron Mother Zeerith of Q'Xorlarrin is in dire need. It would seem that an army of dwarves have come to reclaim the citadel they know as Gauntlgrym."

"That was ever a possibility," Matron Mother Byrtyn Fey replied.

"I will spare no warriors to go do battle for the sake of Q'Xorlarrin," Matron Mother Mez'Barris said bluntly, and more than a couple of gasps were heard following that declaration.

"We cannot," Matron Mother Miz'ri Mizzrym added. "Not with a city full of demons scratching at our doors."

"And now you understand the beauty of my call to the Abyss," Quenthel calmly replied. She let that hang in the air for a short while, all the others staring at her curiously. Quenthel took great pleasure in seeing the epiphany flash on each drow face, one by one, as they came to understand.

"I have already spoken with the archmage," Quenthel went on. "Marilith, whom he fully controls, will lead their march to Q'Xorlarrin, Nalfeshnee at her side, to the defense of Matron Mother Zeerith."

"You will send an army of demons to Matron Mother Zeerith's door?" Zhindia Melarn asked, incredulous. "She would fare better battling the dwarves!"

"I am sure that you hope your words prove true," Quenthel replied, and Zhindia narrowed her hate-filled eyes, clearly recognizing the not-too-subtle implication that Quenthel had sorted out the secret alliance between the Melarni and the traders of House Hunzrin, who hated the very idea of the satellite city of Q'Xorlarrin. "I have assured Matron Mother Zeerith of our allegiance, and so our demons will serve her, by the will of Lolth."

Zhindia Melarn sat there simmering, with Mez'Barris Armgo looking no less miserable, and Quenthel basked in their frustration. Every time they thought they had gained the upper hand, Quenthel had snatched it back from them. They thought they had House Do'Urden destroyed, or Matron Darthiir murdered, at least. And yet here she was, seated beside them at the table of the Ruling Council.

They had conspired and fumed over Quenthel's decision to summon demons to the City of Spiders, and yet now those demons seemed the salvation of the satellite enclave of Q'Xorlarrin.

Armed with the memories and reasoning of Yvonnel the Eternal, Matron Mother Quenthel was always one step ahead of them.

Later that same day, all across the huge cavern that housed Menzoberranzan, nobles looked out from their balconies, nodding, sighing with relief as they watched the ghastly procession, hundreds of demons and thousands of manes and lesser Abyssal beings, filtering out of the city, marching to the command of the Ruling Council.

And what a council it had been, so said the whispers filtering throughout the city, rumors that seemed confirmed by the noticeable increase in guards around the Barrison Del'Armgo compound.

◆ ◆ ◆

THE HAMMER RANG out, slow and steady, like the heartbeat of a dying man, or the tears dripping from a broken woman's eyes.

"Ye stay with him, then," Connerad Brawnanvil said to Emerus Warcrown after one ring of hammer on metal.

"Aye, but we're near to taking the whole o' the top," Emerus replied.

The hammer rang again.

"The entry cavern's work is all in order," Connerad explained. "They're not needin' me shouts now. I'll get Bungalow Thump aside me and the Gutbusters'll finish the task Bruenor started."

"An uamh," Emerus said, nodding, the ancient Dwarvish words for the "under way."

"Tha," Connerad agreed, and he clasped wrists with Emerus. "Hold faith that I'll call for ye afore we take the Forge."

Emerus nodded and Connerad started away. The young dwarf king flinched, but didn't turn, though Emerus surely did, when another ring of hammer on metal echoed along the halls.

"Ah, me friend Bruenor," both dwarves independently and quietly whispered, and both, though they weren't looking at each other and hadn't heard each other, shook their heads in dismay.

◆ ◆ ◆

FLANKED BY A pack of glabrezu, the six-armed Marilith led the demonic procession. Tireless, brutal, unstoppable, the chaotic beast traversed the tunnels of the Lowerdark, many weaving down side passages, seeking prey. And any before them—goblin or myconid or umber hulk, it did not matter—was torn asunder and consumed, pulled down in a sea of manes, borne down under a flight of chasme, torn apart by a flock of vrock.

It did not matter. The very stones of the Underdark reverberated under the stamp of demonic feet and hooves.

Unseen by Marilith, but surely felt, the magical emanations of the Faerzress fed her and promised her freedom. She could feel the truth of Lolth's promises now, away from the city. It was obvious to her that the barrier had thinned. She felt no pull to return to the Abyss, felt as welcome and secure here as in the swirling gray stench of her home plane.

She would serve as instructed by Gromph now, and serve him well, and that, in this situation, meant adhering to the demands of the matron mother.

Marilith was amenable to that, for those demands included the spilling of buckets of blood, a liquid she relished as decoration.

◆ ◆ ◆

"PUT HER IN place, boys!" Oretheo Spikes yelled to the hauling team as the great stone slab began to twist out of alignment. "Don't ye be lettin' her crash the buttress, what!"

The Wilddwarves on the bridge crew grunted and pressed with all their considerable strength, tugging and digging in their heels to twist the great center span back in alignment.

"Ah, but there ye go!" Oretheo cheered.

"Can't none be sayin' that them Adbar boys can't build a bridge," he heard behind him, and he turned to see the approach of Connerad. The two shared a hug and a heavy clap on the back. "All done but the pretty bas-reliefs!"

"Aye, we'll have a full bridge by the end o' the day," Oretheo replied. "Might that yerself and meself'll name her, eh? Got a fine handle o' Baldur's Gate Single I'm thinkin' to drain, right there on the middle o' the span!"

"Well lift one in toast to me, then," Connerad replied.

Oretheo looked at him curiously.

"Ye heared o' Bruenor?"

"Heared o' Drizzt the elf," said Oretheo. "Guessed as much about Bruenor afore I e'er heard. Sad day."

"We're nearin' the under way," said Connerad. "Bruenor'd almost got there."

"Aye."

Connerad paused and shrugged.

"Aye," Oretheo said again, nodding as he figured it out. "So ye're to be leading the way down, then."

Connerad nodded.

"Well, let me get me boys," said Oretheo. "We'll follow ye to the Nine Hells, King Connerad o' Mithral Hall, don't ye doubt!"

"Ah, but I'm not for doubtin' ye," Connerad assured him, his tone comforting—too much so, and that brought a puzzled expression to the face of Oretheo Spikes.

"What're ye sayin'?" the Wilddwarf leader demanded. "Ye're off for the front and fightin', but me and me boys're stayin' here? Guardin' the backside?"

Connerad shrugged apologetically.

"Bah! But did we not go through *deas-ghnaith inntrigidh* with all our hearts, then?" Oretheo cried. "We gived ye three kings *ar tariseachd*, our dying fealty! Are me and me boys lesser, then? Is that our place fore'ermore in the tunnels o' Gauntlgrym? And the Mirabarran dwarfs, too?" he added, sweeping his arm back across the cavern to the far end and the tunnels beyond, where the dwarves of Mirabar worked the defenses.

"Nay, and ye're fealty's a treasured thing, by meself and me fellows, Bruenor and Emerus." Connerad put his hand on Oretheo's sturdy shoulder. "Yerself and yer boys're as much Delzoun as any here, don't ye doubt. But ye're knowing the defenses here in the entryway—ye built 'em!—and aye but they got to stay strong now."

"Because ye're pressin' down to the drow."

"Aye, and might that them trickster drow come slitherin' up behind us, eh?"

Oretheo Spikes didn't seem very convinced, but he did nod his agreement. "Wilddwarfs ain't for guardin'. Not when there's a road leadin' straight to a real fight."

"Not me call, me friend," Connerad explained. "Bungalow's got the lead group with his Gutbusters. Yerself was given the cavern, the boys o' Mirabar the back end and the tunnels beyond, and aye, but ye've all been a blessin' to us all with yer work."

Oretheo Spikes heaved a great sigh.

Connerad nodded, not disagreeing, and certainly understanding.

"Then Moradin walk with ye, boy," Oretheo Spikes said, and he clapped Connerad on the shoulder.

The young dwarf king replied with a similar movement before he turned and headed for the throne room to collect his entourage, and from there to the front lines, to the breach to the under way.

No sooner had the former King of Mithral Hall walked away when another of the Wilddwarf commanders came up to stand beside Oretheo.

"Ye heared?" Oretheo asked.

"I heared," the other replied, his voice thick with anger.

"Don't ye be aimin' that ire at Connerad or the others," Oretheo told him. "Can't be blamin' them for taking them they know to the fight. Were it King Harnoth leading that march, then we'd be flankin' him."

"Aye," the other agreed. "And so I'm thinking me king choosed wrong, what."

"King Harnoth should be here," Oretheo Spikes agreed.

"Good choice, that one, to lead the march," the other Wilddwarf remarked, nodding to Connerad as the former King of Mithral Hall entered Gauntlgrym. "Good as any. I'm hearin' whispers that he'll make a play for the throne when all's done, and I'm not for saying that King Connerad o' Gauntlgrym'd be a bad choice."

Above Emerus and Bruenor? Oretheo Spikes thought, but did not say, for even as the notion formulated, it didn't seem all that outrageous to him. Certainly King Bruenor Battlehammer and King Emerus Warcrown remained as legends among the dwarves of Faerûn, and surely so in the Silver Marches. But who could deny the fine work of King Connerad Brawnanvil?

And now Emerus was looking old to all, and Bruenor?

Well, who might know of King Bruenor with his elf friend lying near to dead? Surely he seemed a broken dwarf at that time.

◆ ◆ ◆

"How's he restin'?" Emerus asked Catti-brie when he entered the small room they had set up as an infirmary. The woman sat on a chair beside Drizzt, who lay very still, his eyes closed.

"I done all I can," she replied, and she almost laughed at herself as she heard the words spill forth, for it seemed that whenever she was speaking with dwarves now, she instinctively reverted to the brogue. "His cuts're tied, but sure that he's bled more than any should, and the shock of the hit . . ." She paused and lowered her gaze.

Emerus rushed over to her and dropped a hand on her shoulder. "He'll come back to ye, girl," he said.

Catti-brie nodded. She did believe that, though she wasn't sure of what might be left of Drizzt when he did. She recalled her own injuries from a giant's rock in defending Mithral Hall. Never had she been the same, despite the tireless efforts of many dwarf clerics.

"Been talkin' with the Harpell lass, Penelope," Emerus said. "She's tellin' me yerself and her got something to show me and Bruenor."

"Aye," Catti-brie replied. "And the sooner the better."

"Connerad's taking the lead in the forward press. No better time than now."

Catti-brie nodded and rose, then bent over and kissed Drizzt on the forehead. "Don't ye leave me," she whispered.

Emerus was at the room's door, holding it open, and so the next ring of that solitary hammer carried to Catti-brie's ears, reminding her that Drizzt wasn't the only one in need of help. She went with the old dwarf king through the maze of corridors, following the lonely cadence of the solitary hammer.

They found Bruenor bent over a small forge, tapping away on the broken scimitar of his dearest friend.

"We got work to do, me friend," Emerus said as they entered the small chamber.

Bruenor held up the rebuilt scimitar for the others to see. "Been workin'," he replied.

"Ye fixed it!" Catti-brie said happily, but Bruenor merely shrugged.

"I put the blade back on, but can'no put the magic back in her," he explained.

"When we get to the Forge o' Gauntlgrym, then," Catti-brie offered, and Bruenor shrugged again.

"Yer elf friend's restin' peacefully," Emerus said.

"Still asleep," Catti-brie was quick to add when she saw the sparkle of false hope ignite in Bruenor's eyes.

Bruenor snorted helplessly.

"We found an ancient portal," Catti-brie explained. "Meself and the Harpells. Ye're needing to see it, me Da. It's a great tool, but might be a great danger. For the sake of all who've come to Gauntlgrym, I ask ye to come with me and Emerus now to view the thing and judge what we're to do with it."

Bruenor looked at Twinkle, sighed, and nodded. Clearly, he'd done all he could with the scimitar. Catti-brie, who had spent so long trying to repair broken Drizzt, and possibly with the same partial effect, understood his pain.

Was the magic of Twinkle lost forever?

Was the magic of Drizzt lost forever?

Bruenor tossed his hammer on the table and sent his gloves onto it behind. He carried Twinkle to Catti-brie and bade her return it to Drizzt after they got back from wherever it was she intended to take them.

"Better for yerself to take it to him," she replied and tried to hand back the scimitar.

Bruenor balked and shook his head and would not take the blade back. He had made it quite clear, with voice at first, but with his actions since, that he didn't want to see Drizzt lying helpless and near death on a cot.

Catti-brie, however, wasn't about to let this go. Not now. She pushed the blade out to Bruenor, and scowled at him when he began to shake his head once more.

Reluctantly, Bruenor took the repaired scimitar and slid it into a loop on his backpack.

"Lead on, then, and let's be done with it," he grumbled.

Catti-brie paused for a few heartbeats, staring at her adoptive father, at the pommel of Twinkle sticking up from behind his left shoulder. For some reason, that image resonated with her. Seeing that Bruenor had taken the blade, and so would return it to Drizzt, reassured her that her father, at least, would soon enough be all right.

Any victory seemed a major victory at that dark time.

CHAPTER 18 ◈

Comragh Na Uamh

VERY PATROL LED BACK TO THIS CENTRAL CORRIDOR, ONE that ran to a great gap in the floor of the upper complex, and more important, ended in a thick door that opened to a landing set just below the ceiling of a vast cavern of the deeper levels.

In darkness and silence Bungalow Thump was down at the end of that corridor, lying flat on the landing floor and peering over the rim into the deep gloom below. Quietly, young King Connerad crept up beside him and similarly gazed into the vast darkness. The two dwarves exchanged looks and a shrug, then Connerad motioned Bungalow back.

They went a long way along the tunnel and down a side passage before they broke their silence.

"Get yer Harpell friends and put some light down there?" Bungalow Thump asked.

"She's a vast one," Connerad said. "Got to be a hunnerd ogre feet from here to the floor, if there's even a floor to be found." He considered Bungalow's request for a bit, but couldn't agree. "We drop a magic light down there and sure that every drow in the lower levels'll be ready for us. Shinin' bright in deep tunnels brings them all in for a what-to-do, and not sure I'm liking that with just this one way down. Ropes and slides and all we can put in are still to be leavin' us hanging high and open if they're waiting for us."

"Aye, figured as much, but I had to ask," said Bungalow Thump.

319

"Suren that yer duty's to put it all out afore me, and for that, ye got me gratitude," Connerad replied.

"Are we knowing where the stair's at?"

"Right below and folded over in half," Connerad replied. "That's what Athrogate told me o' the place, at least. The durned drow've done a great job in building themselves a stair that can be taken down fast, but not so fast to put back up, so I'm hearin'. So no, me friend, we won't be slippin' a few fellows down to the stair and getting it set up for us, if that's what ye were thinking."

"All of us fast down on a slide rope then," said Bungalow. "I'm not feelin' good about puttin' me boys on ropes to rappel a hunnerd feet and more to the dark floor. Not with a horde o' damned drow below shootin' at us all the way."

"Silence and darkness and two set o' three ropes abreast," Connerad replied. "And know that I'll be right beside ye."

Bungalow Thump patted Connerad on the shoulder, never doubting for a heartbeat that his king wouldn't send him and his boys into a danger that Connerad wouldn't face right beside them. Connerad's family name was Brawnanvil, but for all that he was Battlehammer, through and through.

"We got them young Harpell wizards, too," Connerad reminded.

"Wishin' we had the old one," said Bungalow. "And the woman who's leadin' 'em. Both can throw a bit o' lightning and fire, so I'm hearin'."

"The one girl with this group—said her name's Kenneally," Connerad replied, "she's a flyer and a floater, and with more than a few tricks for such. Might be that she can give us wings, me and yerself, and so we'll chase our boys down the hole, eh?"

"Kenneally Harpell," Bungalow reminded him, emphasizing that legendary family name. "So she'll likely turn us into bats, what!"

"Ha!" said Connerad. "Aye, her and the skinny fellow . . . Tuck-the-Duck?"

"Tuckernuck," came the correction from the doorway and the two dwarves turned to see the two in question, Kenneally and Tuckernuck Harpell.

"Rest assured, King Connerad, that we two and the others will be of great assistance in getting your force swiftly to the bottom, if that is your wish," Kenneally Harpell said.

"I've a new spell to try for just this purpose," Tuckernuck added, and the dwarves looked to each other doubtfully, having heard, and seen, much of the leftover effects of "new spells" tried at the Ivy Mansion in Longsaddle, including more than half the statues in the place. More than a few brilliant Harpell wizards had mastered a spell to turn himself or herself into such a statue, and of course, did so knowing the words to reverse the spell but without realizing that as a statue, he or she wouldn't be able to mouth those words.

"Do tell, boy," Connerad gingerly prompted.

"Field of Feather Falling," Tuckernuck replied.

"You fall into it, you float out of it," Kenneally replied.

The dwarves exchanged skeptical looks once more.

"We put it down near the floor, perhaps," said Tuckernuck. "A long and fast fall into the field and a short float to the fight!"

"Or quick surprise turned into a quick splat, eh?" Bungalow Thump said dryly.

◆ ◆ ◆

MATRON MOTHER ZEERITH sat on the altar stone in the chapel of Q'Xorlarrin, fidgeting nervously. More than once, she imagined taking just a few steps and leaping from the ledge to the fiery maw of the fire primordial.

It was just a passing thought, and nothing she seriously considered.

Not yet, at least, but she could well envision a day not too far off when such a suicidal leap into utter oblivion might prove to be her best course.

She spun around on the altar stone then and leaned forward to peer into the pit, its sides swirling with water elementals rushing about in their cyclonic frenzy.

"Matron Mother?" she heard from behind her, and she turned to see High Priestess Kiriy and the wizard Hoshtar entering the chamber.

"I do not wish to disturb your communion, Matron Mother," Kiriy said respectfully, and she bowed low.

"What do you want?" Matron Mother Zeerith snapped in reply. She turned a threatening glare over Hoshtar, who similarly bowed, and had the wisdom to remain low.

"They near the lower positions," Kiriy explained. "I thought it important that you greet them personally."

Matron Mother Zeerith winced. "Already?" she whispered under her breath, though she knew she shouldn't be surprised, for demons were tireless creatures.

"They are to be allowed nowhere near this room," she said to her daughter. "Or the forge room."

"It will take one of your supreme station to deter them, Matron Mother," Kiriy explained. "Mighty Marilith herself leads the throng."

"A marilith . . ." Matron Mother Zeerith said with a sigh. She was hoping that a nalfeshnee, with its strange sense of law and order, would be at the head of the demonic column, or perhaps even some weaker type of major demon, one that she could easily dominate. The six-armed mariliths, though, were exceedingly cunning, and could warp any command to their advantage.

"Not a marilith," Kiriy said, interrupting Zeerith's train of thought. "Marilith herself."

"Under the suffrage and domination of Archmage Gromph Baenre," Hoshtar added, and Matron Mother Zeerith felt as if he were twisting a knife in her back. By all reason, Gromph Baenre should be a friend to the Xorlarrins, a family so strong in male wizards. But whether it was his jealousy, or his fear that one of

322

the Xorlarrins would usurp his high station, such an alliance had never come to pass.

Zeerith sighed again. "Let us go," she said. "I wish to greet our . . . reinforcements as far from this room as possible."

Deep in the mines, past the slave miners from Icewind Dale and those few remaining that had been taken from Port Llast, the drow contingent met up with the lesser demons in front of the march from Menzoberranzan.

Matron Mother Zeerith barred their way, and ordered several back to gather Marilith.

Demons continued to press, looking for a way past Matron Mother Zeerith. It wasn't until she cast a spell of banishment, sending a large vrock back to its Abyssal home, that the others fell into order—at least, as much order as chaotic demons could manage. Still, they all knew that they might soon wash their bodies in mortal blood, and the threat of banishment proved incentive enough to keep them at bay until at last the giant Marilith slithered up to face the Matron of Q'Xorlarrin.

"I am here by the word of Archmage Gromph Baenre," Marilith stated flatly. "Sent to kill dwarves."

"There are thousands to kill, I am told," Matron Mother Zeerith replied.

"Show me," Marilith said, and her voice sounded very much like a purr, while the fingers of her six hands eagerly tickled the hilts of her belted weapons.

"There are many tunnels," Zeerith replied, and she turned and motioned up the sloping corridor. "The first right-hand passages lead to Q'Xorlarrin. The place is secure, do not doubt, and any demons you send down that way will be destroyed or banished, at the least, by my defenses."

Marilith let out a little growl, clearly wanting to go down those tunnels simply because of the overt threat. "And where do the others lead, Matron Mother Zeerith?"

"This way and that," the matron mother of Q'Xorlarrin replied. "This most ancient dwarven complex is indeed a vast compound, much of it still unexplored by my family. Any time you are climbing nearer the surface, know that you are moving closer to the dwarves who have come to this place, for they have not gained the lower corridors."

"Then they shan't," Marilith decreed, her red eyes flaring, and now her six weapons slid free.

Matron Mother Zeerith wisely used that moment to begin her return to Q'Xorlarrin, her entourage hustling beside her, and with other dark elves ordered to collect the slaves—who would surely have been devoured by the demonic procession—and retreat within the main compound area.

By the time Matron Mother Zeerith had returned to her altar room, Q'Xorlarrin had more sentries guarding the lower entrances than those in the areas where the dwarves might come down.

The first good news of the day greeted Matron Mother Zeerith in that altar room, for she found her nephews, the powerful Masters of Sorcere Jaemas and Faelas, waiting for her.

"Well met again, Matron Mother of Q'Xorlarrin," they said in unison, both bowing deeply and respectfully.

"It has been too long since your beauty has graced our eyes, Matron Mother Zeerith," Faelas Xorlarrin added.

"Menzoberranzan is a lesser place without you," Jaemas added.

"Enough of your insipid flattery," Matron Mother Zeerith replied, though it was clear from her tone that she was indeed a bit flattered. Behind her, High Priestess Kiriy caught that little fact, too, it seemed, for she chortled, drawing an evil glance from her mother.

"Have you spoken with any since your arrival?" Zeerith asked.

"Out in the forge room," Jaemas said, pointing past her.

"Then you know that I have been off to greet a column of demonic reinforcements. One led by Marilith, who serves . . ."

"The archmage, yes," said Faelas. "He brought her to Menzoberranzan after her defeat at the blades of Malagdorl

Armgo, and so shamed House Barrison Del'Armgo, or cast doubts upon the tale woven by their weapons master, at least."

"Matron Mother Baenre chose Marilith to lead the column above even the goristro that now serves her . . ." Faelas started to explain, but Zeerith cut him short.

"To further irk Matron Mother Mez'Barris," she said with a shake of her head—one that wasn't full of the glee expected from one of her high station when learning of such diabolical intrigue, but rather, one of disgust.

The two wizards didn't miss it, and they glanced at each other, puzzled.

"Help to organize the attack groups," Zeerith bade her nephews. "Take Hoshtar with you. When the demons engage the dwarves and wound them as I expect, we must be ready to finish the task, and so not allow Gromph and the matron mother all of the glory."

The wizards nodded.

"That would be wise," Jaemas agreed, "but first . . ."

He let that hang ominously for a moment, until Faelas added, "We have been to the great stair in the main lower hall, Matron Mother, and have witnessed the tunnels directly above it. You have more immediate problems."

◆ ◆ ◆

"You are sure it will work?" Kenneally asked Tuckernuck.

The other Harpell nodded. "It won't be large, perhaps a score of strides to a side, but all who fall through it will float gently to the ground. You know how long I have been preparing this."

Kenneally couldn't miss the flash of anger in his tone, or defensiveness at least.

"It is well over a hundred feet to the floor of the lower cavern," she reminded him, and indeed, Tuckernuck had flown beside her, invisibly, to scout the room, and so this was not new information to him. "Even a dwarf . . ." She shook her head and let that unsettling thought hang in the air for a moment. "They'll be down from the landing to your feather fall field in under a three-count, and will be falling fast."

Tuckernuck nodded. "I know."

"How high will you put your magic field?"

"Twice my height, no more," he answered confidently.

"They will be falling fast."

"And floating the moment they touch the enchantment," Tuckernuck assured her. "If we put it up too high, the dwarves will be helplessly floating about in the air for too long."

Kenneally brushed her long brown hair back from her face. She seemed as if she were about to say something, but cut it short before she made a sound.

Tuckernuck smiled at her reassuringly, even reached out and patted her on the shoulder. "It will work," he said quietly. "We'll get five hundred battle dwarves in that cavern in short order, including the whole of the Gutbuster Brigade."

"I should anchor—"

"No!" Tuckernuck said to his powerful cousin, for indeed, Kenneally Harpell was considered among the greatest of their wizards, with mastery of some of the most powerful spells known at the Ivy Mansion. "No. They will need you in other ways, of course. We'll find battle soon after the first dwarven boots are on the cavern floor, do not doubt."

The two heard the rumble of marching dwarves then, and so Kenneally nodded and motioned for Tuckernuck to go and prepare the battlefield. The younger cousin pumped a clenched fist and ran off to find his trio of cohorts. After a short confirmation of the positions and plan, they began checking their components and rehearsing the words of the magical ritual.

The youngest of the group cast a spell of flying on herself, became invisible, and flew off for a quick scouting of the cavern to mark the spot.

The others crouched on the platform, staring, looking for the signal. Tuckernuck flexed his fingers repeatedly to allay his nerves.

Back from the group, through the door and in the hallway, Kenneally stood with Connerad and Bungalow Thump at the head of the dwarven force. "You are sure?" she asked the young king, and not for the first time.

"Will the damned spell work?"

Kenneally glanced back at the four Harpells on the landing and nodded. "I do believe in Tuckernuck, yes. But there might be many enemies waiting for you."

"Then we're sure," Bungalow Thump answered for Connerad. "Ye just get us down there, girl, and get out o' our way so ye're not slippin' in drow blood!"

Out on the landing, Tuckernuck and his assistants cast spells of flying and fell from their perch, disappearing from sight.

"You tell your warriors not to run and leap," Kenneally warned him. "Just walk off and fall straight down. We marked the spot carefully. Don't miss it!"

"Aye, we told 'em," said Connerad.

"Gutbusters!" Bungalow Thump added. "Crazy as ye might be thinking 'em, none're fightin' smarter!"

Behind the two leaders, the next dwarves in line turned and passed down the reminder.

Kenneally led the way onto the platform, lay down, and peered over, awaiting the signal.

"Groups o' ten at a time, boys," she heard Bungalow Thump whisper, and the first leap team moved into position. "Three count and the next're off!"

Connerad and Bungalow Thump were among that first group, and it occurred to Kenneally that if Tuckernuck's spell didn't work, his failure would splatter a dwarf king and the leader of the famed Gutbusters all over the stone.

She saw the signal then, a brief pulse of red light, and heard herself saying, "Go!" before she could even think about the grim possibilities.

And so they did, fearlessly, ten dwarves simply stepping off the landing and plummeting blindly into the darkness of a cavern whose floor was more than a hundred feet below.

Kenneally held her breath as they disappeared from sight, hoping, praying, that she didn't hear a crash. Already the second group hustled into position around her, and before she could be sure the first group had even reached the bottom, those ten dwarves fell fearlessly away.

◆　◆　◆

FROM THE MOMENT he stepped off the ledge, Connerad Brawnanvil feared that he was being foolish, his confidence inflated by the Throne of the Gods and his fine work in the entry cavern up above.

And inflated by the whispers, the young dwarf had to admit. Many were talking about him as the First King of Gauntlgrym, and the fact that he was being considered by some to be worthy of even being mentioned as a possibility for that title along with Emerus Warcrown and Bruenor Battlehammer, overwhelmed Connerad.

Had his pride overplayed his hand?

Those nagging doubts followed the dwarf down into the darkness, plummeting from on high. The cavern was not well lit, with only marginal illuminating fungi nearby, but he saw then the floor, hard stone, rushing toward him.

He noted the Harpells, too, though, the four standing as the corners of a square some twenty paces across, and even as he and several others started to yell out, he noted a shimmer in the marked-off field between them.

Then, before that could even fully register in his thoughts, Connerad was floating, touching down gently a moment later with nine Gutbusters beside him.

"Move out!" Bungalow Thump ordered and the group leaped away, two to each side of the square, with four, including

Bungalow and Connerad, at the side nearest the circular stair-well. Barely had they made their positions and caught their collective breath, when ten more warrior dwarves came down behind them, breaking immediately, as practiced, to properly reinforce the perimeter.

Out moved the dwarves with ten more down, then another group and another, and with fifty battle-hardened Gutbusters now beside him, Connerad couldn't suppress his grin.

Another ten landed.

Huzzah for the Harpells and the clever Tuckernuck!

◆ ◆ ◆

BRILLIANTLY PLAYED, JAEMAS signaled to Faelas in the silent hand code of the drow.

Or would be, had we not discovered their intent, Faelas's fingers flashed back at him.

Enough? Jaemas asked, and Faelas nodded.

Jaemas lifted his hands and clapped loudly. In response to the signal, stones scraped and doors slid open and a host of enemies leaped out from concealment to charge at the dwarves. Slaves, mostly, goblins, orcs, and kobolds by the score.

More than a hundred dwarves were down by that point, with several times that number of monstrous foes flooding in to do battle.

But these were battleragers, with fine arms and armor, and neither of the Xorlarrin wizards held any notion that the slave force could overwhelm the dwarves.

Then came the first bolts of lightning, crackling above the heads of dwarf and orc alike. The drow were not aiming at the dwarves, but at the four wizards they knew to be in the air above them, the four human mages that Hoshtar's spell had revealed.

Faelas looked at his cousin and smiled and nodded, and the two began their spellcasting in unison.

A few heartbeats later, a pair of small flaming orbs sailed across the darkness, arcing over the monstrous horde, and settling in the area where the leaping dwarves were touching down, right in the midst of the dwarven perimeter.

Two fireballs stole the darkness.

◆ ◆ ◆

"OH, NO, NO!" Kenneally Harpell cried out when she saw the lightning, when she realized that the lightning was not aimed at those dwarves already on the ground.

"Stop! Stop!" she cried at the dwarves on the landing, but these were battleragers, and they weren't about to listen with a fight so near and their kin being hard-pressed by monsters and magic.

Ten more came rushing through the door. Kenneally leaped up to block them, screaming for them to halt.

And at that moment, they heard the crashes as the first group of unfortunate dwarves passed through the level of the flying Harpells—just three now, with the fourth having been driven off by a lightning stroke—and the now failed Field of Feather Falling.

The second group, the ones Kenneally had futilely tried to stop, hit next, crashing and groaning, and still several of the newcomers to the platform leaped away.

"Oh, no, no," Kenneally Harpell lamented. She knew that she had to do something here, but had no idea at that moment what it might be.

"Get yer ropes!" the dwarves around her cried down the line through the door, and more than one cast a disparaging glance Kenneally's way.

"Oh no, no," she whispered yet again, staring into the darkness. And with a resolute shake of her head, she leaped away.

◆ ◆ ◆

THE SWORD OF King Connerad felled the first orc to approach the perimeter, a swift and deadly strike right between the creature's ugly eyes. Not Connerad, nor any of the Gutbusters around him, cried out with worry when the monstrous hordes appeared and charged in at them. Nay, they welcomed the fight, and when they noted the monsters as goblinkin, relished it all the more.

The trio of goblins following that orc met the gauntleted fist of Bungalow Thump, a wild head butt—one that would have made Thibbledorf Pwent himself proud!—by the same, and a twist, kick, trip, and stab movement by Connerad.

All around them Gutbusters fought wildly, and goblins died horribly.

And more dwarves descended, touching down and leaping wildly into the fray. Within heartbeats, though they were outnumbered, the dwarven perimeter widened.

Then came the lightning bolts, and Bungalow Thump laughed at them and chided the enemy wizards for missing the mark.

But a wounded cry from up above warned Connerad that such was not the case, that he and his boys weren't the targets. With the immediate threat in front of him writhing and dying on the ground, Connerad managed to step back and spin, determined to take command.

Another group of dwarves touched down, several with armor smoking from the lightning bolts—but such a tingle as that would hardly slow a Gutbuster!

Still, Connerad hoped that it had been one of the dwarves on the ground who had cried out.

A heartbeat later, when ten good dwarves crashed down in free-fall to the floor, the young king knew better.

The field of magic had been eliminated.

"No!" Connerad yelled out to a pair of dwarves who turned and rushed to their fallen comrades. The young king grimaced and looked away as the next ten came crashing down, burying those two under them in a tangle of broken bones and spraying blood.

Another dwarf hit the floor, and several more behind him.

"Form and fight!" Connerad shouted to his boys, for what else could he do? More than a hundred were down on the cavern floor, with no way to retreat, and with no further reinforcements coming . . . at least, he hoped not.

◆ ◆ ◆

"STOP THEM!" TUCKERNUCK screamed, soaring back up, even as Kenneally came flying down from the landing.

"We have to get them out of there!" the woman shouted, moving in close. Two of the other Harpells came soaring up beside them.

"They hit Toliver!" one exclaimed.

"They broke the ritual!" said the other.

Kenneally looked to Tuckernuck, who could only shake his head, his expression horrified.

"Is Toliver dead?" she started to ask, but the answer came not from one of the three flying about her, but from below, where a lightning bolt split the darkness—one originating in the air above the battle and not the recesses of the cavern.

"Toliver!" Tuckernuck said.

"Fetch him," said Kenneally. "We have to get the dwarves out of there. Fetch him and fly back up near the landing and prepare to set your feather fall once more."

"Too high," Tuckernuck argued. "The dwarves will float for a long while, easy targets . . ."

"Do it!" Kenneally yelled at him. "And allow no more dwarves to come down. Not on their ropes and not with your magic. Be quick!"

She flew off then, diving down to the cavern floor. As she moved lower, she only confirmed her idea—Connerad and his Gutbusters were being sorely pressed by monstrous hordes of goblinkin.

And soon to be joined by demons or devils or some other extraplanar menace, Kenneally saw, noting a band of lumbering four-armed, dog-faced beasts moving through the slave horde, tossing aside the goblinkin with abandon.

The woman stopped and hovered, surveying the area, noting mostly the movements of the two Harpells flying down to retrieve Toliver.

"Hurry," she whispered under her breath, and then, having no choice in the matter, Kenneally began to cast a powerful spell.

◆ ◆ ◆

ANOTHER PEA OF flame arced in. Connerad and Bungalow Thump dropped to the floor and covered just in time before the fireball erupted, immolating several goblins they were battling and igniting a dwarf behind them.

"Put 'im out!" Bungalow Thump shouted to the others, but all nearby were too engaged in desperate battle to break off to the aid of their burning friend.

"Go!" Connerad told his friend, and he shoved Bungalow Thump along. The dwarf sprang over the burning fellow, bearing him to the ground and rolling him about, smothering the flames.

Behind them, Connerad met the incoming enemy, bracing himself to the charge of a pair of orcs.

But those creatures never made it, caught suddenly by monstrous pincers, to be so easily hoisted and flipped aside.

In waded the gigantic glabrezu. Connerad got his shield up in front of a snapping pincer. He slashed across with his sword, but the glabrezu's reach was too great and the blade cut across short of its mark.

In came the second pincer and Connerad had to throw himself backward and to the side, executing a perfect shoulder roll to come back to his feet just in time to spin and duck behind the shield as the pincer came in once more.

A familiar voice sounded then, a magical call from above. "Get to the landing area! Now!"

The dwarves didn't know what to make of it, and weren't sure the call was even aimed at them, or from where it had come.

Connerad couldn't begin to react to the command anyway. The demon pressed him hard, pincers snapping all around him. He got his shield up to block one, but the powerful demon pressed in with the claw anyway, and Connerad winced as the shield cracked ominously under the great weight of the press.

The demon held on and twisted and the young dwarf king found himself easily yanked off balance, and thought his life at its end as the second pincer came across for his midsection.

A living missile intercepted it as Bungalow Thump flew into the glabrezu, knocking aside the arm and driving the beast backward. It let go of Connerad's shield, and the overbalanced dwarf king tumbled back and to the ground.

Bungalow's cry of pain had Connerad back up immediately, though, and seeing Bungalow Thump hugged in close, the demon's maw chewing at the dwarf's neck, he fearlessly charged in.

Connerad Brawnanvil leaped high, both hands gripping his sword for a mighty two-hand chop aimed at the glabrezu's neck. At the last moment, the demon stood taller, though, and so the cut came in low, driving just below the shoulder.

Not a mortal blow, perhaps, but a vicious one, so much so that the glabrezu's top left arm fell free, cleanly severed.

The demon's howl echoed across the cavern, and many combatants—dwarf, goblin, demon, and even drow—paused to consider the sheer horror of that shriek.

The glabrezu threw Bungalow Thump at Connerad, the dwarves colliding and tumbling in a heap.

But Connerad went up and hauled the bleeding Bungalow Thump up beside him. Before the Gutbuster could argue or resist, Connerad shoved him hard and sent him stumbling back to the landing area.

"Ye heared Kenneally Harpell!" Connerad called to all the dwarves. "To the landing area, I say!"

Easier said than done for Connerad, though. The wounded, outraged glabrezu leaped in at him.

"Go! Go!" he roared at Bungalow Thump even as the demon began knocking him back. He knew the Gutbuster wouldn't leave him. "I am right behind! Form the defenses!"

But Connerad Brawnanvil wasn't right behind. The glabrezu's pincer caught him by the shield again, and this time the compromised buckler folded under the tremendous pressure.

Connerad grimaced and growled as the pincer came in hard across his forearm, pressing in through his fine mail. He tried to bring his sword to bear, but the demon caught his arm and held him at bay.

In came the biting maw, and Connerad timed his headbutt perfectly to intercept the toothy jaws with the crown of his helmet.

The glabrezu staggered, and Connerad wriggled free his sword arm and stabbed straight ahead. He felt his fine blade sink into demon flesh, and felt the hot Abyssal blood spurting out over his arm.

◆　◆　◆

NOT FAR FROM the floor, Kenneally Harpell watched the dwarves scrambling, trying to get back to the landing area—which was easy to locate with nearly thirty broken dwarves lying in a tangled heap.

The woman forced the gruesome image out of her thoughts and looked up, trying to see if Tuckernuck and the others were in position, and with their spell enacted once more.

But to no avail, for they were in darkness too complete. But Kenneally knew she couldn't wait. She began casting her spell, a powerful dweomer known to only a few at the Ivy Mansion, aiming it right at the dwarves clustered about their fallen kin.

◆ ◆ ◆

"No, YOU HOLD!" Tuckernuck shouted at the dwarves on the landing. He had figured out Kenneally's desperate plan and knew what would soon be coming his way. "They're coming back, all of them, and you need to be ready to catch them and pull them to safety! Grapnels, I say! Ropes and grapnels!"

Many dwarves shouted questions back at the flying wizard, and many more shouted curses.

Tuckernuck ignored them. He had to lead the ritual—nothing else mattered. He understood the carnage that would ensue should he fail Kenneally, should he fail the dwarves now.

The other three Harpells returned to him, and he motioned them into place. Clearly injured, Toliver barely managed to get near to his spot diagonally across from the leading wizard, and Tuckernuck wasn't sure that one could bring forth his part of the ritual.

The dweomer needed four participants.

With no options available, Tuckernuck continued his casting, then reached his arms out left and right, forming his corner of the square. From his fingertips shot tiny filaments of light streaming out to be caught by the casters at those corners, the two of them then redirecting the energy to Toliver.

But Toliver only had one arm up to receive the light. He remained lurched over to his left. There was nothing Tuckernuck could do—he couldn't even shout out for Toliver or he would ruin his own casting.

But how he wanted to, and even more so when he heard the sudden commotion below him, and glanced down to see the tumbling, spinning charge of a score of dwarves flying up at him.

No, falling up at him, he realized, for they were caught in Kenneally's spell of inversion, where up was down and down was up.

"Flip!" he did yell at the other wizards when the dweomer reached them, and they did, except for Toliver, righting themselves upside down, which was now upright!

The falling dwarves drew near, but the Field of Feather Fall wasn't complete, and the ceiling, now the floor, loomed just above.

"Toliver!" Tuckernuck and the other two shouted, for now their spells were complete.

And from the landing, which was not in the area of effect, the dwarves began to scream and curse.

◆ ◆ ◆

DEAD DWARVES TUMBLED upward beside living dwarves. Pursuing goblins were caught in the spell and went falling upward in the line. More dwarves came in, leaping, then flailing as they were caught in a free fall as surely as if they had leaped off a cliff.

But many other dwarves weren't going to make it, Kenneally realized. Nearly a hundred and fifty of the sturdy folk had leaped down, the last three groups falling to their deaths almost to a dwarf. But the Harpell wizard realized that of the six-score who were already on the floor, less than half were going to find their way back. Yet another group of several Gutbusters were pulled down by the goblin horde, overwhelmed by sheer numbers.

Kenneally spotted King Connerad of Mithral Hall staggering away from a skewered demon, the beast spouting blood from its gut but still stubbornly pursuing.

And more monsters—like great bipedal vultures—swept in from the sides, cutting off the young dwarf's retreat.

Connerad fought valiantly, but Kenneally shook her head in despair. She began casting a spell, a fireball, thinking to put it high enough to catch the heads of the tall monsters. She took hope when one of those vulture-like demons screeched and staggered back, its beak shattered by a mighty stroke of Connerad's sword.

But the four-armed behemoth leaped in, pincers leading, and Kenneally lost the spell in her throat as the beast extracted

Connerad from the commotion and lifted him up into the air, both pincers grasping tightly around the poor dwarf's midsection.

"Bah, ye dog!" she heard Connerad cry, and he lashed out with his blade and managed to clip the huge beast's canine muzzle.

With a yelp of protest and rage, the demon thrust its arms out wide, and Connerad Brawnanvil, the Twelfth King of Mithral Hall, was ripped in half at the waist.

Kenneally's fireball spell was lost in her throat then, and all she could do was fly up for the ceiling, her eyes wet with tears, and gasping for breath she could not seem to find.

She took some heart as she rose, though, to see her four kin maintaining their dweomer. Toliver had straightened and completed the square just in time. Upward fell the dwarves, then upward they floated, to land lightly on the ceiling.

And dwarves on the landing threw them ropes, which fell up to them, that they could be hauled to safety.

And upward fell the pursuing monsters, too, then upward they floated, and not one got to the ceiling before a dwarven crossbow launched a bolt into its torso, and the dwarves already up above were ready for them anyway, cutting the disoriented and confused goblinkin apart in short order.

"Hurry, pull them in!" she heard Tuckernuck commanding. "Kenneally's spell will not last much longer! We will lose any not on the ledge!"

Kenneally nodded agreement and focused on the task at hand. She was more than halfway to the ceiling, the jumble of falling dwarves and monsters just in front of her. Now she concentrated on that tumbling mess, picking out monsters.

A line of magic missiles shot out from her fingertips, striking a goblin, killing it, and taking out the one beside it as well.

Kenneally chanted the spell for a lightning bolt, and when she executed it, she perfectly angled it to blast several enemies, with not a dwarf singed. The power of the bolt jolted one large demon too, sending it spinning out of the area of her reverse gravity, and as soon as the beast went out of the dweomer, it fell back the other way, more than fifty feet to the floor.

And so Kenneally realized a new and deadly tactic, and one executed by a simple spell she could cast quickly and repeatedly. She picked out her targets with gusts of wind, blowing them out of the reverse gravity field, sending them falling back for the cavern floor, living bombs to drop upon the sprawling horde below.

She would avenge Connerad, she determined, and she narrowed her eyes and sent a dozen goblins flying free of her enchanted area.

◆ ◆ ◆

TUCKERNUCK HARPELL LOOKED up, or rather down, nodding approvingly of Kenneally's exploits.

But noting, too, that fewer and fewer dwarves were among the dozens falling upward, and that little fighting continued on the floor.

He glanced the other way to see most of the living dwarves already out of the enchanted area, scrambling on ropes with their crowded brethren grabbing at them and hauling them over the lip of the landing.

He looked back the other way, back to the floor. He saw no dwarves, none living at least, but now more and more monsters were taking the leap.

Tuckernuck could only hope that he wasn't killing more dwarves then, but he flew backward and dropped his arms, ending the ritual enchantment of the Field of Feather Falling. He flipped back upright, and waved his three fellow Harpells back as monster after monster tumbled past to crash against the ceiling, or, soon, to crash against the bodies of those that had already crashed against the ceiling.

He looked down again to Kenneally, and he gasped and cried out. A pair of ghastly creatures, like giant houseflies with human faces, flew upon her at either side, biting and tearing at her.

"Kenneally!"

He began to dive, but a fireball below stopped him before he ever truly moved.

Kenneally's fireball dropped right upon herself.

The flames cleared and the chasme demons, their wings burned away, tumbled for the floor, bearing poor Kenneally with them.

Again Tuckernuck began to dive, and again he stopped short, for Kenneally's powerful dweomer ended then, and a host of monsters and dead dwarves fell from the ceiling, and those falling upward in the field paused, then went tumbling back the other way.

So enthralled by the strange sight was Tuckernuck that he didn't notice a swarm of chasme demons soaring up at him until it was too late.

◆ ◆ ◆

COVERED IN BLOOD, much of it his own, Bungalow Thump was the last dwarf holding the landing, and the one who hauled Toliver, the only Harpell to reach the landing, over the edge. The powerful dwarf sent the wounded man skidding back through the door, then his eyes widened in horror to note the other two nearby wizards caught suddenly by the horrid, insectoid demons.

Bungalow fell back in shock, barely avoiding yet another of the darting chasme. He would have been caught and surely killed, but a dwarf within the doorway grabbed him by the shoulder and hauled him back and to the ground—and the pursuing chasme caught a swarm of crossbow bolts right in its hideous face.

The door slammed shut and *Comragh na Uamh,* the Battle of the Under Way, came to an abrupt and disastrous end.

Chapter 19 ◇

Comragh Na
Fo Aster

ORETHEO SPIKES HARRUMPHED REPEATEDLY AS HE PACED across the bridge over the small pond in Gauntlgrym's entry cavern. The veteran Wilddwarf had grown quite fond of Connerad and missed the young king, but even worse, in Connerad's absence Oretheo had been given control of the finishing touches for the defenses of the vital cavern.

Oretheo Spikes was a fighter, as fine a warrior as Adbar had ever produced, and not a yard boss!

And there was a battle soon to begin, he knew, if it hadn't already, for the whispers said that Connerad and his boys—almost all from Mithral Hall and Felbarr—had pushed into the final reaches of the upper level of the complex and expected to breach the lower caverns in short order. By all expectations, there would be dark elves waiting for them.

And Oretheo wouldn't be there. He looked around as he moved across the bridge yet again, this time heading back for Gauntlgrym's castle-like wall. He noted the many engineers, masons, and blacksmiths hard at work, finalizing the triggers and springs that could drop the bridge from a single command point.

He turned his gaze wider about the huge cavern, where a thousand dwarves worked or watched from the stalagmite towers that had been hollowed and set up as guard posts. Even out in the hallway, the dwarves labored with defensible positions—anyone coming in here would fight for every inch of ground.

341

That thought bolstered him, but he couldn't shake off the notion that almost all of the dwarves in this rear guard area were from Citadel Adbar. As were almost all of the dwarves working in the throne room and adjacent chambers.

Because of King Harnoth.

Despite his earlier protestations to the contrary, Oretheo Spikes truly wanted to blame king Emerus and King Bruenor, and even King Connerad. He wanted to pretend that this was Mithral Hall's fault, or Citadel Felbarr's. But he could not, because he understood the truth and the way of dwarves.

He and all his boys had participated in the call of Kith'n Kin with all their hearts, had given their fealty wholly to their Delzoun heritage and the rebuilding of Gauntlgrym, and he knew that their pledge had been accepted honestly and with open hearts, open arms, and a mug of magical ale courtesy of Bruenor's marvelous shield.

But this snubbing of the Adbar dwarves was not an emotional decision by the kings of the other clans, as was proven by the fact that the thousand dwarves who had joined in from Mirabar were also here in this cavern, or scattered about at other tasks in securing the ground they had gained. The decision to take the dwarves of Felbarr and Mithral Hall was purely a practical one. In any expedition to the as-yet unconquered reaches of Gauntlgrym, the mission would be led by a dwarf king. And no king would spearhead his battle group with the boys of another clan when his own trusted warriors—in Connerad's case, the famed Gutbuster Brigade—were readily available.

If King Harnoth had come to Gauntlgrym, Oretheo Spikes would be at the front of the column pushing into the lower chambers. Two thousand of the five thousand dwarves who had come into Gauntlgrym were Adbarrim, easily the largest of the four contingents. King Harnoth would have stood at the end of that reception line in the Rite of Kith'n Kin, instead of Bruenor. Despite his youth, he, Harnoth, would have determined the place for the Adbar dwarves.

He might have even made a play to wear the first crown of Gauntlgrym, and wouldn't that have warmed the bones of King Harbromm in his cold grave?

"And wouldn't that've avenged the death o' his brother, King Bromm?" Oretheo Spikes remarked as he stepped off the bridge onto the beach in front of the castle wall. He turned a sharp left, moving along the bank to check on some fellows arguing about the placement height of their side-slinger catapult.

"Aligned to the top o' the bridge!" roared one yellow-bearded dwarf, who looked very much like Oretheo, though with a much more modest beard.

"Bah! But if we're needin' to shoot the durned thing, the bridge'll be turned and the enemy'll be in the water, ye dolt!" his orange-bearded opponent countered.

Oretheo Spikes shook his head, certain that this disagreement, like all of the foul moods he had witnessed in the cavern this day, stemmed from the same frustration that twisted his own belly. Heading over to arbitrate, he was about to shout out to the two to shut their traps, when suddenly they went quiet of their own accord, both turning to the dark waters of the pond. The young yellow-bearded dwarf scratched his head and the other looked at him and shrugged, clearly at a loss.

Oretheo Spikes, too, turned to that water, and now he noted the first small ripples running toward the bank, and the strange undercurrent of the waves. He continued on his way, and glanced back just as a sizable freshwater fish leaped out of the water and sailed at the yellow-bearded dwarf. That fellow reacted quickly enough to bat the biting thing aside, but another came out, and another.

Oretheo Spikes started to run to the fellows, but skidded to a stop and threw himself back a stride, narrowly avoiding his own leaping fish missile.

"How're they seein' us?" the red-bearded dwarf yelled, but before any could even consider the question, they realized that it was moot, and simply coincidence, for the only fish they had noticed were the ones coming at them, but now that they had taken note, all three of the dwarves saw the truth and fell back in shock.

Dozens of fish were leaping out of the pond, flying onto the beach and flapping wildly.

Nay, scores of fish, on both sides of the pond, from one end to the other.

Just off the shore, some dozen feet, the water stirred and broke, and Oretheo Spikes and the rest of the dwarves watching the spectacle quickly came to understand why the fish were fleeing. They knew at first glance the horrible nature of the demons walking toward the shore, walking toward them.

An army of misshapen humanoids, pallid and decrepit and bloated, like ugly little fat men with flaming red eyes . . . an army of manes.

"Shields and pointy things!" Oretheo Spikes shouted, and he fell all over himself scrambling from the bank.

He nearly tumbled to the dirt when out in the middle of the pond a swarm of chasme broke the surface, the buzz of their wings filling the cavern with strange echoes.

Whistles sounded at every end of the cavern, along with cries of "Battle groups!"

"Here, Oretheo!" one dwarf by the wall cried, and Oretheo Spikes glanced that way to see a gathering of shield dwarves already forming their line at the base of the castle wall.

Above them, side-slinger catapults cranked back and let fly, clusters of sharp stones spinning over Oretheo's head, splashing into the water and crashing into the approaching demons. So, too, did the ballistae fire, huge spears whipping away, skewering manes two at a time. But perhaps most damning of all to the demons came the spells of magical light from the many clerics at the wall, illuminating all the beach areas on both sides of the pond.

Oretheo staggered for the shield line, and glanced back, nodding at the holes already punched into the approaching horde. He sucked in his breath, though, for bigger things than manes appeared in the pond. Crawling out the other way, into the main cavern, went a pack of four-armed—and two of those with fearsome snapping pincers—greater demons. And vulture-like creatures—huge and terrible, and with beaks that seemed as if they could surely punch through a breastplate with ease.

The cranking catapults brought him hope, and before he had ever reached the shield line, which parted to let him in, a second volley of heavy stones flew for the pond and the monsters.

"Ah, good boys!" Oretheo Spikes congratulated. "We'll hold 'em here and let the wall-sitters thin 'em to nothing, eh!"

The dwarves, their shields hooked together as one solid wall, reached over in unison and banged their hammers, maces, and swords on the strong metal blockers. And those about Oretheo Spikes in the second rank readied their longer weapons, the spears and pikes they would prod above that solid wall of shields.

Oretheo Spikes continued to call out commands, but he knew that he needn't have bothered. This group knew their jobs and did them well.

◆ ◆ ◆

THIRTY FEET UP from the floor in the middle of the large entry cavern, in a wide, round room cleverly carved to give optimal views—and thus, optimal lines for shooting—Nigel Thunderstorm leaned on his heavy ballista, thinking of what delicacy he might prepare for his Ma, Nigella, when she arrived in Gauntlgrym. And aye, she would soon enough be here, the dwarf master chef was certain, for Nigella still resided in Citadel Felbarr, whereas Nigel had gone to live in Adbar. King Emerus understood the grandeur of this place, and he'd allow as many from Citadel Felbarr as desired to come here to settle.

"What ho?" cried another of the dwarves in that stalag-mite guard station, a strapping young lass named Carrinda

Castleduck, who braided her long yellow hair under her chin in a "beard" that would make a grumpy old metal-pounder proud. "Oh, by the hairy-arsed gods!"

"What do ye know?" asked Ogden Nugget, the third in the room, and he and Nigel scrambled over beside Carrinda to gaze out over the battlement.

"Demon beasties! And what a horde!" came a cry from the lower level of the tower even as the three artillery dwarves began to register the monsters crawling out of the pond, so clear to see under the magical illumination of the enchantments thrown about the pond by the dwarf clerics.

"Line her level!" Nigel cried, running to the missile rack set against the opposite end of the chamber. He first lifted a thick-ended bolt, the shaft filled with oil that could be set aflame, but put it back and pulled forth a black metal tri-spear instead.

Carrinda and Ogden had already turned the ballista, which was set on a circular base that could swing it in a full circle, before Nigel had the tri-spear in place.

"Put 'er down a fat fist," Nigel instructed, one eye closed, the other looking through the crosshair sight set atop the weapon. He held up a hand when the tip lowered just enough, accounting for the expected drop to the pond—one they had measured many times—and nodded.

"Ah, but just a pinky-finger to me left," he begged, for he had a particular target in mind. This was their first shot, after all, and Nigel wanted it to count. Staring through the sight, the dwarf gave a rather eager chuckle and nod, noting the top crown of an avian behemoth.

Nigel yanked the lever and the ballista let fly, the spear arcing out beautifully and breaking into three separate missiles.

The spear on the right disappeared into the water with a splash, and perhaps hit something just below the surface, given the strange way it didn't immediately sink. The missile on the left drove into the hip of a vrock, drawing a great screech from the beast. And the third, the center spear, impaled the target, another vrock, right through its massive chest.

Unlike its counterpart, that one didn't cry out, but simply flew over backward into the water.

"Huzzah!" Carrinda cried, turning back to Nigel—and finding him already back at the caisson, drawing forth another tri-spear.

"Find another group!" she told her partner, and she grabbed the crank at the side of the ballista and began drawing the heavy wire once more.

The stalagmite shook then, as the side-slinger catapult mounted in the lower level let fly, and then again as the conventional catapult out on the balcony joined in.

"Find the biggest!" Carrinda ordered. "Aye, but we're the prime bombers, so let's make 'em count!"

◆ ◆ ◆

THE BARRAGE POUNDED the lake and the demons coming forth, spears and stones and burning pitch flying in from many guard towers, while those artillery batteries set in the castle wall focused their devastation on the back of the horde pressing the shield dwarves.

How wonderful the light was, Oretheo Spikes realized, seeing that it clearly marked out the targets.

But with that thought, the Wilddwarf leader saw a bigger problem. Across the way there was no such clarity, and there, into the wider cavern, went the biggest of the monsters coming forth—the biggest and the smartest, no doubt.

And from those shadows, he saw a group strike, huge four-armed glabrezu demons appearing as if out of nowhere to assault one of the stalagmite guard positions. That tower was lost in short order. The demons had been clever in their assault, using the mound to shield themselves from any other batteries that might have struck out at them.

The focusing mirrors were not yet in place in the stalactite and stalagmite towers, and without them, the shadows would greatly limit the artillery.

The dwarf shook his head. Though this side of the pond already seemed as if it would hold, and so this monstrous horde would find no easy entrance into Gauntlgrym, he had no desire to surrender the rest of this cavern, particularly not with nearly eight hundred of his fellows out there across the pond.

"All right, boys," he told the spear-wielding dwarves at his side, dwarves furiously stabbing as monsters tried to reach over the shield line, "our brothers'll be pouring out o' the throne room in a heartbeat, not to doubt. Ye gather 'em and make yerself a wedge and push to the bridge. Ye take the pond bank, one wall to th' other, and nothing gets out on this side!"

"Ye goin' somewhere?" one of the dwarves asked, and Oretheo Spikes smiled with resignation.

"Aye," he replied. "And don't ye let none forget me!"

He hopped up and tapped the two shield dwarves directly in front of him on the shoulder. "On me word," he instructed, and they grunted, shoulder-blocked back the press of manes, and nodded.

Oretheo turned to the wall and called up to the nearby batteries. "Ye open me a line to the bridge!"

"The bridge?" one dwarf yelled back. "Bah, but th' other side's crawlin' with the damned things."

"Aye," Oretheo Spikes agreed, and he hunched up his shoulders, shook his head wildly, banged his axe against his shield, and laughed boisterously.

"Open it!" he roared.

That command echoed up and down the line on the wall and many of the batteries concentrated their fire then on the monsters between Oretheo's position and the entrance to the bridge.

"Clear the closest," he told the spear-wielders, and as soon as they began to drive the most immediate monsters off, he yelled, "Shields!"

The shield wall parted and out leaped Oretheo Spikes, chopping and twirling, and sprinting for the bridge. Others wanted to follow, of course, but the shield dwarves knew their place and immediately sealed the line once more, leaving Oretheo Spikes out there alone.

"Cover him! Oretheo!" dwarves yelled and from above came a volley of crossbow bolts, ballista spears, and a pair of beautifully placed catapult throws that blew free the ground in front of the running Wilddwarf leader.

Oretheo Spikes made the base of the bridge, but monsters rushed around the large buttresses in close pursuit.

And so many more hulking monsters loomed in the shadows across the way.

"Clangeddin's strength to ye," more than one of the dwarves at the wall muttered, and there was little more to say.

◆ ◆ ◆

"Nothing clear to hit!" Ogden Nugget cried, leaning out the long window and looking down from their position.

Carrinda and Nigel shared his frustration, for they could hear the raucous battle not far from their tower, where a large square of dwarves, a brigade or more, had begun a sweep toward the pond. But demons had come from the shadows in a coordinated manner, and the square found itself surrounded on all four sides, with nearly two hundred battle dwarves fighting for their lives.

But the line was too tight and too mingled for ballistae and catapults to help.

Ogden pounded his fist on the stone sill and turned back.

"Let it go, friend," Nigel offered. "Take what we can . . ." He stopped short as Ogden's eyes popped open wide in shock. Nigel figured it out and spun to see the ugly, bloated human face of a chasme only a hand's breadth away as the monster landed on the sill.

Nigel cried out and threw his hands up and threw himself back, thinking he was surely doomed.

But even as he retreated, a spear flew past him and drove right into that ugly demon's face.

"Bah! But who's needin' a ballista, what?" Carrinda Castleduck proclaimed, shaking a fist at the chasme as it fell away.

"Well flung!" a relieved Nigel congratulated her. "Now, ye find me something big to skewer!"

"I'm seein' naught but the little ones," Ogden replied, collecting his wits and spinning about. "Big ones're all skippin' about the shadows."

"Bah!" Nigel roared. "Then shoot for the pond!"

He set another spear and Carrinda began to turn the swiveling ballista once more.

◆ ◆ ◆

THAT FRUSTRATION WAS exactly what Oretheo Spikes understood and expected. They weren't going to win this fight by battling the coordinated efforts of the small demons. There were simply too many of the ugly things. And the big ones, the smart ones who were coordinating it all, weren't about to make targets of themselves until most of the stalagmite and stalactite batteries had been shut down.

Those artillery batteries needed a spotter.

The Wilddwarf sprinted across the bridge and threw himself into a horde of manes that had clustered there at the far end, his wild sweeps with his vicious axe driving them back or gutting them where they stood. The dwarf leaped and spun sidelong, a downward swing splattering a manes's misshapen head.

He tore his axe free and used the momentum of the pull to sweep it across again, gutting another, then brought the weapon up and into a tight spin and let its weight carry him around to take the face from the nearest manes that had pursued him across the bridge.

Pure fury drove him—shield bashing, shield rushing, axe sweeping—and that same fury nearly got him killed, for only at the last moment did he note another horrible demon, a pile of goo slithering across the floor. With a desperate yelp, Oretheo threw himself over the monster, landing with a thud. He rolled frantically, not daring to stop, and as he came around and looked back, he blanched with horror.

A few of the manes had chased him but had not leaped, and now they tried to wade through the jelly-like demonic creature, and smoke wafted up from their dissolving legs.

"Oh, but lovely," Oretheo said with a sigh, and he hopped up and ran off to the base of the nearest guard tower. All of them had been stocked for exactly this purpose, with torches and with a pile of burning embers glowing under a stone hood.

He drove the torch into the orange-glowing pile and pulled it back, the end igniting and flaring to life. He took it in his shield hand, hoisted his axe once more, and ran off, waving the flaming torch to gather attention.

◆   ◆   ◆

"We got ourselves a marker!" Ogden Nugget called, pointing to the running dwarf with the waving torch.

"Aye, and it's Oretheo Spikes hisself!" Carrinda said. She punched her fist into the air again. "Just stay at the window and guide me turns!" she instructed Ogden even as she leaped back to the ballista and grabbed the handles.

"Just stay with him," she added, as Nigel pointed left and up, then down and back to the right, accurately following the movements of Oretheo Spikes. Powerful Carrinda and Nigel turned the ballista in line.

"Fourth north pocket!" Ogden called out, and that same shout was echoed in a score of similar towers all across the cavern, and on the lower floor of this one as well. The call was more than a description of a place, it was one of the common marks to which all of the weapons on this side of the cavern had been sighted, and it told every artillery dwarf exactly where to align his weapon.

"Bugs!" Carrinda shouted then, and all three turned and gasped to see a swarm of chasme flying in at them.

But just below them on the balcony, their brethren saw it, too, and they were well prepared. Even as the three in the ballista room braced for the incoming fight, the catapult below let fly, a basket full of small caltrops that tumbled and spread wide as they flew off.

"Bird shot," the dwarves called it, for such a load could take a flock of geese from the sky.

Or a swarm of chasme, the ugly things sent spinning and tumbling all in a rush.

Carrinda, Nigel, and Ogden went right back to work.

"Fourth north pocket again!" cried Ogden, seeming somewhat surprised that Oretheo Spikes had apparently backtracked.

"Ah, but he found somethin'!" Carrinda said, eyes gleaming in anticipation. "Something big!"

◆ ◆ ◆

OH, ORETHEO SPIKES had indeed!

The dwarf ran faster than he ever had before in his entire life. Only twice in his years had Oretheo Spikes truly known fear: first near a frozen lake when the source of that unseasonable ice, a great white dragon, had exploded through the pack to join in the battle, and now, when in his run, he had nearly tumbled into a pack—a pack!—of gigantic glabrezu.

He just lowered his head and ran for all his life, a dozen of the beasts close behind, and with a flock of giant vrocks right behind them.

"Third pocket!" came the cry from every tower, and as Oretheo Spikes passed that mark, he skidded to a stop and spun, pointing back with his torch.

A signal the disciplined Adbar dwarves knew well.

Oretheo saw the demons rushing for him, towering over him. And he heard the creak and whoosh of the great weapons of war.

"Bah, but yer mother's a bunny!" the Wilddwarf roared, certain that he was doomed, seeing great pincers already coming his way.

A score of ballista spears crashed just in front of him. A score of catapult loads and twice that number of side-slingers—bird shot, larger rocks, burning pitch, and one with a pile of stones soaked in oil of impact—let fly for that sighted area just in front of Oretheo Spikes, the place the dwarves had named "third pocket north."

The cavern shook under the weight of the barrage, and trembled with the explosion of the magical oil.

Oretheo Spikes was barely aware that he was in the air, but he felt the hard stone when he crashed down.

He felt it because he was, somehow, alive!

Looking back, he saw the jumble of demons and spears and rocks large and small, and the smoking husks of fallen fiends and the cracked wall of the cavern.

Another catapult load smashed in, throwing a vulture beast into the wall.

And more followed, relentless and punishing.

"Bah, but yer mother's a bunny!" Oretheo Spikes roared once more, pulling himself from the floor. And off he ran, torch waving.

And now, he noted, he wasn't the only marker, as other dwarves on this end of the large cavern had taken up torches. Far across the cavern, he heard "Second pocket south!" and a few heartbeats later, a similar devastating barrage went out from the southern guard towers.

"Well done, King Connerad," Oretheo Spikes mumbled under his breath, truly glad that the young dwarf had so brilliantly organized this defense, and blissfully unaware that at that very moment, King Connerad Brawnanvil was being torn in half by the powerful pincers of a glabrezu very much like the beasts Oretheo's gallant efforts had just destroyed.

He began his run anew, but blowing horns gave him pause.

He looked back to the pond and took heart, for the rest of Adbar's force had come forth from the throne room, and now more than a thousand battle dwarves had pushed to the far bank of the pond, and no more beasts would get free of that water.

And the Adbarrim were coming across the bridge as well, a great wedge of dwarven fury and dwarven muscle and dwarven metal.

And on the near side, the boys of Mirabar had poured into the chamber from the outer caverns. Dwarven squares had used the support artillery to join up in stronger formations and had begun an irresistible march back toward the pond. Nearly three hundred Mirabarran and Adbarrim would die this day in the entry cavern of Gauntlgrym, but so be it.

When the pond's water stilled once more, Oretheo Spikes, Nigel Thunderstorm, and all the remaining dwarves looked about at the carnage and knew that *Comragh na fo Aster,* the Battle of the Cavern, had come to a glorious and victorious end.

CHAPTER 20 ◈

Comragh Na Tochlahd

RUENOR AND EMERUS STOOD BESIDE THE OUTLINE OF THE stone door the wizards had identified as the ancient portal connecting dwarf lands. Over and over, the dwarf kings ran their hands along the ancient stonework, nodding as if they could feel the power thrumming within the stone—and likely they could feel it, Catti-brie and the others realized. Ever since they had sat on the throne, these two and Connerad seemed more attuned to this place than any non-dwarf could ever hope to understand.

"Where'd it go?" Emerus asked, his gravelly old voice filled with wonder and awe.

"Another dwarf kingdom, they're saying. And aye, but I'm thinkin' that's the truth of it," Bruenor replied. Then he added slyly, "If they were thinking o' what might be the greatest place to go of all, they'd've had it set in line with Mithral Hall, eh?"

"Aye," Emerus said without missing a beat, "that hole'd be a great musterin' field for them dwarfs heading over to Citadel Felbarr."

The two kings smirked at each other, both glad for the levity, and Bruenor truly needing it with his dearest friend lying so broken back in the main complex.

Behind them, Ambergris and Athrogate began to laugh, then to howl, drawing curious looks from Ragged Dain and Fist and Fury, and a curious glance back from the two kings.

Shaking her head, Catti-brie walked past the onlooking dwarves, Penelope and Kipper beside her.

"So if we're to get it working, then how're we to know where we're going?" Emerus asked them. "Could be anywhere. I'm not knowing o' any other dwarf homes as old as Gauntlgrym, and I'm guessing this was put in early on."

"Right after they got the Great Forge fired, I'd wager," Catti-brie agreed. "Might be that it opened into Waterdeep—or whatever city was thereabouts back in the day o' Gauntlgrym's making. Easy journey for trade."

"No," Kipper Harpell insisted. "It opened to another dwarven complex, likely in a mine not far from the other complex, but not readily accessible to the place. Certainly not in any city not of dwarves."

"Aye," Bruenor said, and Emerus nodded, coming to agree that his off-the-cuff theory really didn't hold up. Even to this day, in the Realms dwarves were clannish—Bruenor's choices in assembling the Companions of the Hall had raised more than a few bushy dwarf eyebrows over the years, and when Bruenor had appointed Regis as Steward of Mithral Hall, even King Emerus had gasped with surprise.

But still, despite that obvious xenophobia, by all accounts and historical text, the dwarves were much more tolerant of the other races now than they had been in the days of Gauntlgrym's glory.

"If you were given a choice of where to place a complementary gate, good King Emerus, would you choose Waterdeep?" Kipper asked.

"I'd be sticking it up Moradin's hairy bum afore I'd be doin' that!" the dwarf said, and the point was made.

Emerus looked to Bruenor, but the red-bearded dwarf was immersed in the contours of the ancient portal once more. Perhaps he was sulking, perhaps deep in thought, but in any case, he had clearly stepped out of the conversation.

"Wait, are ye sayin' that we might be choosing the location o' th' other gate, the exit?" Emerus asked, his thoughts sharpening with the possibilities.

How grand might it be to connect Gauntlgrym to the tunnels under the Silver Marches, a place easily accessible to all three of the dwarf kingdoms of the North? If the dwarves could have easy transport back and forth, all four fortresses would be more secure by far, with combined armies ready to muster at a moment's notice.

"We do no' even know if we can power the durned thing," Catti-brie reminded them all. "She's an old magic, like the one firing the Forge, like the magic keeping the primordial in its pit."

"But it is possible!" Kipper jumped in quickly and enthusiastically. "I have been studying this for decades, my friend, and this gate! Oh, but how long have I searched for such an opportunity as—"

The tunnel shook then under the force of something weighty, some resounding thud that rolled through the stone and right up the legs of the ten standing in front of the ancient gate.

"That ain't sounding good," Ragged Dain remarked as he moved closer to Emerus and set himself defensively to protect his friend and king.

"I'll go and have a look," Athrogate offered and he sprinted back through the secret doorway to the portal room, with Ambergris close behind. They paused in the outer mine tunnel for a moment, glancing left and right, and when another heavy thud resounded, the pair took off to the right.

"We should be getting this place closed, and quickly," Ragged Dain offered.

"Aye," Emerus agreed over Kipper's protestations. "Keepin' this room secret's more important than the lives of all."

The eight started for the doorway, but before they even neared the open portal, Ambergris came rushing back in, Athrogate right behind her.

"Can ye close the door from in here?" Ambergris asked Catti-brie. "Lock us in, then?"

"Aye, and be quick about it!" Athrogate added.

Both looked terribly unraveled, and both were gasping for breath, as if they had come back in a sprint.

"I canno'," Catti-brie replied.

"Out, then, out!" Athrogate ordered. "Don't ye get caught in this corner!"

"Caught by . . . ?" Penelope asked, and she was answered by a bellowing roar. It is not an easy thing to describe a sound as "evil," but to the ten in the small room this rumbling, raspy, screeching combination of noise, all blended in one discordant note, surely seemed to be just that.

"Out! Out!" they all began shouting together, and they tumbled all over each other to get to the door. Before they had all even come through and out into the tunnel beyond, Catti-brie began her chant to the ancient magic of the fire primordial to close the secret doorway.

"Demons!" she heard Penelope gasp before the door even started coming down, but the woman wouldn't stop now, determined that their enemies would not get into the special chamber beyond.

She heard the dwarves calling for formations, and was glad to hear Bruenor's voice lifting above the others. If anything could get Bruenor Battlehammer out of his worrying malaise, it would be a good fight!

Finally, the door began its downward slide, and the woman spun around—and nearly lost all hope.

Demons indeed, she saw and heard, the ravenous beasts coming at the group from both directions in the long tunnel. She noted manes—so many of those disgusting lesser Abyssal creatures—leading the charge left and right, but mostly she noted the leaders of the beasts, a hulking glabrezu to her right, back the way they had come, and an even greater beast, massive and thick, with short wings beating crazily, but with no hope of lifting the tremendously fat demon from the floor. And others, too, scrambled for the fight: vulture-like creatures she knew to be vrocks, and thick and short beasts that looked like a rough carving of human, only with dwarf-like proportions and a huge head set upon broad shoulders that seemed to be conspicuously missing a neck.

"You stay with us," she heard Penelope tell Emerus and Ragged Dain. Out to the left in front of the Felbarrans stood Athrogate and Ambergris, setting their feet and ready to brawl.

Out to the right, Bruenor and the Fellhammers similarly waited.

The demons came in an organized fashion, the disposable fodder, the manes, filtering to the front.

Catti-brie wasn't waiting. She stamped her staff upon the ground, shouting *"Syafa!"* and the silvery wood turned black again, streaked with red, while the blue sapphire became a red sapphire.

"What in the world?" asked the surprised and clearly impressed Kipper, standing by Penelope and readying his own magic.

But Catti-brie wasn't about to answer. She was deep into her spell then, and the red lines along the black staff began to glow more angrily, as if it was filled with fire that begged for release.

Indeed.

The demons came on in a rush, but Catti-brie struck first. She lifted her staff out to the right, launching a ball of flame out past Bruenor and the twins. Before that fireball had even landed, she swung the staff out the other way and sent a second ball flying off down the tunnel.

The first fireball exploded, and a blast of hot air swept down the tunnel to wash over the companions. The second exploded almost immediately following, and now the hot wind came from the other direction.

When the smoke cleared, far fewer manes were moving, most lying on the ground as smoking husks. The vrocks screeched in protest, the huge nalfeshnee beat its little smoking wings furiously, and the glabrezu drove in harder.

"I see the end of the line!" Penelope said to Kipper, who began tracing an outline in the air. "Keep in the midst of the five dwarves we're leaving here, Catti-brie," she instructed.

"And where are you going?" Catti-brie asked.

"Go!" Kipper shouted at Emerus and Ragged Dain, and he pushed them at the magical portal he had just constructed.

"I ain't leavin' me friends!" Emerus protested.

"Neither are we!" Penelope shouted. And she had to shout now. The battle had been joined on both ends of the line, Athrogate and Ambergris smashing the leading lesser demons, Bruenor and the Fellhammer sisters battling a pair of vrocks.

Kipper went into the portal and seemed to step into the same tunnel, but far afield, behind the demons to Catti-brie's left.

"Well, go!" Penelope said emphatically, and Ragged Dain leaped into the gate, Emerus close behind.

"Hold the line and we'll thin that group in short order," Penelope said with a wink to Catti-brie. She leaned over and kissed Catti-brie on the cheek then, smiling widely, evidently enjoying it all—and indeed, hadn't she professed to Wulfgar her adventurous side? With a battle cry that would make a Battlehammer proud, Penelope leaped into the portal and disappeared.

Catti-brie started to call to the five dwarves still around her to tighten up their ranks, but she thought the better of it, realizing that this crew, deep into their fighting now, probably wouldn't even hear her.

She did yell out anyway, a simple warning of "Light!" and called out *"Alfara!"* and stamped her staff, which reverted to its silver-gray hue with the blue sapphire. She launched into a quick spell and held the staff aloft, using it as a focus for her magical energies. Once more blue mist wafted out of her sleeves, this time from the right arm, from the spellscar of the unicorn of Mielikki.

And from that magic, Catti-brie brought forth a light, brilliant and warm and full of comfort to her allies, and full of stinging, unwanted pain for the beasts of the lower planes.

Catti-brie stayed halfway between the dwarf lines, looking left and right, ready to cast a spell of healing through the conduit of her magical staff.

The mist from her left sleeve, the symbol of Mystra, began to curl, too, the woman eager to set loose some more destructive arcane magic.

◆　◆　◆

"TRUST HIM," PENELOPE told Emerus and Ragged Dain. "Kipper knows this spell better than any alive, I expect!"

The dwarves shook their hairy heads doubtfully. Kipper had asked them to stand five feet back from a wall, a bend in the corridor, and face it, though the demons were back the other way.

"They've taken notice!" Kipper said. "And here they come!"

Emerus glanced back over his shoulder to see one of the human-height demons, thick as any dwarf, rambling down at them, vulture-like beasts close behind and others pressing in from behind. Emerus's expression twisted when the hallway seemed to shimmer, and the huge dwarf-like creature disappeared.

And reappeared immediately, stepping through Kipper's newest gate and exiting right in front of Emerus and Ragged Dain, but not facing them. It was clearly disoriented, stumbling away from them.

"Ho!" Ragged Dain yelped in surprise when the thick-limbed beast appeared right in front of him. He managed to strike out at it and clip it just a bit—and he almost pursued, as did Emerus, but Penelope had told them not to travel farther down the corridor for any reason.

They both came to understand why, as the vulture beast charged through the gate to crash into the turning beast, stopping it short, and now both dwarves got in clean hits. More demons piled through, disoriented, looking the wrong way, crashing into those who had come through before.

The dwarves just kept swinging, their weapons smacking against demon skin and cracking demon bones.

A streak of lightning cut between the dwarves, slicing into the tumbled mob. Behind Penelope, the dwarves heard Kipper laughing.

They just kept swinging.

Hot flames blew back their beards as Penelope's fireball landed in the midst of the confused and tangled mass of demons, and that only spurred the two Felbarran dwarves on more, their weapons, wet with blood and gore, whacking away with abandon.

◆ ◆ ◆

BACK BY THE main fight, Athrogate and Ambergris didn't notice the trailing ranks of the demon mob turning back. Many of the little ones were already dead from Catti-brie's fireball, but of the ones that remained, many were huge beasts, including one behemoth nalfeshnee that seemed more angry than injured.

"Ah, but I'm saving a fun trick for that one," Athrogate remarked, and across came a morningstar to intercept, turn aside, and crack open the sharp beak of a vrock. The battered creature tried to fall over him, its leathery wings crowned out wide, but Athrogate's second weapon was already spinning in and those open wings presented him with a most wonderful target.

The vrock's screech came out as a breathless gasp as Cracker's heavy ball crushed its ribs, and as the beast lurched, Ambergris stabbed her huge mace, Skullcracker, straight out, driving back the manes ambling toward her, and whipped it across to smack the vrock in the side of its head just at the same moment that Athrogate's Whacker came back in on the other side.

The vrock's thick skull could not resist the press of those two weapons coming together with such force and coordination. The sound of bone snapping echoed off the tunnel walls.

The vrock fell straight down over Athrogate, or would have if the dwarf was not possessed of giant strength. He dropped his weapons and caught the falling creature and sent it flying back into the next demons in line.

The dwarf squatted fast and scooped up his devastating morningstars. He meant to grab them and burst ahead to pummel the demons, but Ambergris tackled him before he ever really started. And a good thing she did. A wall of fire appeared right in front of Athrogate, lining the left-hand wall of the tunnel and running down almost to where Penelope and the others had gone. Flames leaped out from the conflagration, filling the corridor, and terrible shrieks came from within the roiling flames as demon flesh curled.

Athrogate and Ambergris had to fall back a couple of steps, almost to Catti-brie, who stood with her staff upraised, the gem glowing an angry red, reflecting in her eyes. She seemed a part of the weapon and it a part of her, one being bathed in communal magic, controlling the flames, bringing forth the flames, reveling in the cleansing fires.

"Girl," Athrogate breathed, hardly believing the strength of the wall.

Catti-brie didn't blink, her focus pure. She was drawing straight from the primordial then, her own arcane magical powers enhanced greatly by her kinship with the preternatural godlike creature, and by the powerful weapon it had helped her to fashion.

"Guessin' our work is done," Ambergris said, shaking her head with similar disbelief.

Even as she spoke, though, the giant nalfeshnee strode out of the flames and roared.

"Guessin' not," Athrogate said, and with a wink at his girl, he launched himself at the behemoth.

He swatted the giant demon with a swinging morningstar, and it grunted as it swatted him with its own club, a black, metallic, evil-looking thing. The weight of the blow threw Athrogate against the right-hand wall.

Right behind the departing Athrogate came Ambergris, though, Skullcracker smashing against the nalfeshnee's forearm before it could pull back.

Another grunt escaped the beast and it charged forward, kicking out, and Ambergris had to throw herself backward so that she wasn't launched halfway up the tunnel.

The demon paid Athrogate no more heed as it continued for the woman, apparently figuring Athrogate to be crumbling against the stone.

It wasn't the first monstrous enemy to underestimate this particular dwarf.

Athrogate came out from the wall swinging, and now with one of his weapon heads coated in liquid. He struck with his other flail once and again, forcing the behemoth to turn toward him, and as soon as it did, around came the coated ball, squarely into the demon's knee.

The oil of impact exploded on contact.

The nalfeshnee's knee exploded on contact.

How the demon howled!

And now the dwarves struck wildly, in perfect harmony, Ambergris cracking the beast on the other hip, Athrogate's morningstars spinning in a blur and whacking the demon wherever the furious dwarf found an opening.

At one point, the demon bent over and swept its heavy club around in a wide and low sidelong sweep, cleverly trying to drive Athrogate farther down the corridor and into the still-burning wall of fire.

But Athrogate, recognizing the deadly aim, caught the club with a great "Oof!" and held it at bay, stubbornly, mightily, holding his ground.

The behemoth pressed on, and the dwarf, for all his strength, found his feet sliding on the blood- and brain-slickened floor.

"Girl!" he cried.

He needn't have bothered. The demon was so focused on Athrogate that it remained in its crouch, bent low and over, hands engaged.

Whether or not Athrogate had called out, Ambergris wasn't about to let that beautifully presented target go to waste. She ran back up the hall several steps, turned, and charged, leaping high, Skullcracker up and over her head. The huge mace came over as she descended.

The demon looked back just in time to see the weapon's descent.

That blow would have shattered the skull of a hill giant. It did drive the demon to one knee, staggering it, but only temporarily.

Long enough for Athrogate to press back against the shoving weapon, though, even to wrench it from the demon's grasp.

The nalfeshnee started to rise, but Skullcracker hit it on the head again. Stubbornly, the beast growled through the blow and tried again, but now came Athrogate's morningstars, one after another.

And the nalfeshnee was dazed again, and now the dwarves were climbing all over it, striking and leaping, climbing and striking again and again, battering the beast with an incessant rain of heavy blows, any of which would have felled an ogre.

Soon enough, the demon spent less time trying to stand up to its full height than in trying to grasp at the troublesome dwarves.

But it couldn't catch up to them, in their coordinated fury, and anytime the beast got near to grabbing Athrogate, Ambergris changed its mind with a crushing blow from Skullcracker. And anytime it got near to grabbing Ambergris, Athrogate introduced its ugly face to Cracker and Whacker yet again.

Demon blood and ichor splattered the floor all about the hunched creature, and that only spurred on the ferocious dwarves.

By the time they had finished—and that only when Catti-brie cried out in horror—the creature hardly resembled a nalfeshnee demon, seeming more like a mound of boneless jelly.

◆ ◆ ◆

"Break!" Bruenor yelled and the Fellhammer sisters caught each other by the wrists and whipped about left and right, each flinging the other aside. And through that gap leaped Bruenor, and through the vrock's outstretched arms, as well, as the confused creature grabbed at the two fleeing dwarves it had been fighting.

Inside its defenses, Bruenor had one clear attack, and he struck true and struck hard, his powerful axe burying deeply into the vulture demon's chest.

Its screech came out as a blood-filled gasp, and the destroyed vrock fell away.

Another took its place, coming at Bruenor but catching a faceful of Mallabritches instead, the furious dwarf leaping high and battering it with her fine sword.

Across the way, Tannabritches dispatched a manes with a stab and a twist, then flung herself across in front of Bruenor just as Mallabritches landed on her feet and leaped at the vrock again. The creature was more ready for her this time—or would have been, except that Tannabritches barreled into the back of its legs just as Mallabritches hit.

Over went the demon and over went Mallabritches atop it, living up to her nickname of Fury as she continued her assault, using an offense of pure fury to keep the demon from beginning to counter.

Bruenor turned to follow the tumbling duo, but stopped short and set himself in a defensive crouch. The glabrezu rushed in, pincers leading. Bruenor called to Tannabritches, but too late—she was well on her way to leaping upon the downed vrock. Into the air she flew, and from the air she was plucked by the powerful glabrezu.

"No!" Bruenor roared, leaping forward, axe swinging for the pincer arm that had caught his dear friend Fist. He scored a clean and deep hit, but on the demon's chest and not its arm.

He brought his shield up as the demon's left hook pounded home, the balled fist hitting Bruenor's buckler with the force he would expect from a mountain giant.

The blow sent him skidding, his feet churning to send him back the other way.

His progress halted when the demon's free pincer caught him by the shield and began to tug him all around, his feet flying off the floor.

He was in trouble, off-balance and seemingly overmatched.

Then Tannabritches cried out in pain as the pincer closed around her waist.

"No!"

Bruenor's roar came from somewhere inside of him, came from a place of utter denial and utter outrage. He felt the dwarf gods then, as he had on the ledge on that long-ago day when he had battled a pit fiend in the primordial chamber.

The pincer yanked Bruenor's shield arm out to the left, opening his defenses, and a heavy punch came in right behind it, hitting him squarely in the face. His head snapped back from the devastating blow.

But he accepted it and countered cleanly, turning, his axe chopping across his body to hit the forearm of the pincer limb grasping his shield.

The shield was freed, the pincer fell free to the floor.

Tannabritches screamed in pain, the remaining pincer arm digging at her waist.

A lightning bolt from Catti-brie flashed above Bruenor, striking the glabrezu and sending it staggering back—not fast enough to evade the howling Bruenor, though, the dwarf charging in.

Again the glabrezu punched at him, this time striking the shield once more. But this time, the weight of the blow did not halt the dwarf or move him backward. The strength of Clangeddin flowed through him now as he swelled with rage and terror for poor Tannabritches.

The demon threw Tannabritches at him and he instinctively ducked, then winced as he realized the truth of the missile. With a roar of denial, he crashed into the glabrezu and sent his axe spinning forward and up, then right back over his shoulder.

The pincer snapped down at him, catching only shield, and the axe came around and up, right between the demon's legs and into its crotch, driving the beast up high on its clawed toes.

Bruenor bore in, cursing it, bashing it. He stopped and sent his axe across, chopping the inside of the glabrezu's right knee. He reversed his swing, spinning the axe in his hand as he went and bringing the weapon back across to strike at the left knee, but now with the weapon's head farther back, behind the leg.

The glabrezu was still backing, but Bruenor went the other way, tugging powerfully, the axe-head catching behind the demon's knee and twisting it off balance.

Bruenor came back in again, behind a second lightning bolt cast by Catti-brie, crashing into the demon and sending it tumbling backward to the floor.

Bruenor also fell, face first, and fell hard. His nose bleeding and broken, Bruenor just kept on charging, using his axe as an ice-climber might use a pick, repeatedly chopping it into the demon and tugging himself forward.

By the time the axe descended into the demon's chest, the glabrezu was no longer defending, and by the time the next swing came down on the creature's canine face, the husk was already beginning to smoke and disintegrate, the destroyed thing melting back to the Abyss.

Hot winds buffeted Bruenor as he tore his axe free, scrambled up to his knees, and lifted the axe in both hands up above his head to hit the thing again. For a moment, the dwarf thought another demon had come.

But no, it was instead another devastating fireball from Catti-brie, filling the corridor farther along, melting the next group of demons and opening the way to where the tunnel wall neared the inner complex, the place where Kipper's passwall had brought them through: the way home.

But Bruenor couldn't think of that then. He drove his axe down on the already destroyed demon, and used the leverage of the embedded weapon to help him hop back up to his feet. He ripped the axe free with a sickening sound as he leaped around, calling out to Catti-brie to call the goddess to Tannabritches's side.

His words stuck in his throat as the scene in front of him took shape.

Mallabritches cradled her fallen sister in her arms tenderly. The blue mist already swirled around Catti-brie's right arm as she reached for healing spells for the fallen dwarf. Farther along the corridor, Athrogate and Ambergris had turned sidelong, waving at Emerus, Ragged Dain, and the Harpells to hurry along.

Other than the footfalls and Mallabritches's sobs, the tunnel was silent once more, and Bruenor knew that *Comragh na Tochlahd*, the Battle of the Mines, had ended.

Looking at Tannabritches, though, at sweet Fury, a teary-eyed Bruenor couldn't rightly declare victory.

CHAPTER 21 ◈

Delzoun

W HEN THEY RETURNED TO THE MAIN RECAPTURED complex in the upper halls, the group from the mines found Drizzt resting a bit more easily, though he remained far, far away, his eyes closed, his fingers not responding when Bruenor or Catti-brie took his hand. Still, after a quick check on him, measuring his breathing and sensing the peace within the darkness, Catti-brie took hope that her husband would survive, though whether he would ever again be a great warrior, none could know. Catti-brie had learned from bitter personal experience in her previous life how debilitating some injuries could be, no matter how much magical healing the priests might apply.

She had never been the same warrior after the defense of Mithral Hall, when that giant-hurled stone had caught her. She had survived, but could not bear children, and could not hope to fight as well with the sword as before.

But she had survived, and she had thrived for years afterward, turning her thoughts to arcane magic. Perhaps it could be so with Drizzt, she pondered, and a smile found its way onto her pained face as she fantasized about having Drizzt as her student, reading the texts beside him at the Ivy Mansion in Longsaddle, laughing at him good-naturedly when his first spells fizzled—much as he had taunted her in the early days of her martial training.

"It will be all right," she said to Bruenor, squeezing his shoulder and bending low to peck him on the hairy cheek. "The sun will rise."

Bruenor's stubby fingers patted her hand and he nodded. He was too choked up to respond, though, and so Catti-brie kissed him again and left him alone with Drizzt in the room.

"Ah, elf, it's harder than I thinked," Bruenor said to his friend when she was gone. "I'm needin' ye, elf. But ye get yer sleep, aye, and when ye come back, a dwarf'll be on the throne o' Gauntlgrym, don't ye doubt!"

He glanced around, noting Drizzt's weapon belt hanging over the back of a chair, along with the rest of the drow's equipment. Bruenor went over and slid the repaired Twinkle back into its sheath. He paused before the scimitar went all the way in, inspecting his handiwork. He had to nod, for it had been a solid repair.

But of course, the formerly magical weapon would never be as powerful.

Bruenor glanced back at Drizzt and wondered the same for his friend.

The dwarf's hand slid down the weapon belt to a pouch, and from it he lifted a familiar onyx figurine.

A twinkle came to Bruenor's eye as he brought Guenhwyvar up for closer inspection. Might he take her with him? Would she come to his call and serve him as she had so well served Drizzt? Or perhaps he could give the cat to Catti-brie.

But it didn't seem right to him.

He shook his head and moved to the bed, placing Guenhwyvar down gently on Drizzt's chest, then lifting the drow's arms up to hug the panther. This was where she belonged. Only.

"Ye come back to us, elf," Bruenor whispered. "Ain't ready to say farewell to ye just yet!"

He gave a last pat to Drizzt and left the room, considering the dark road in front of him and wondering if he'd get his wish, because it seemed very possible to Bruenor that he'd never speak to his dear elf friend again.

In the next room over, he heard the quiet voice of Mallabritches Fellhammer, whispering encouragement to her fallen sister.

Tannabritches was in far worse shape than Drizzt, and Catti-brie, for all her efforts, could not give Bruenor any assurances that the young dwarf lass would survive her brutal wounds. The glabrezu's pincer had crushed and gashed her midsection. If Catti-brie hadn't been right there with powerful healing magic, Tannabritches would never have gotten out of those mines alive.

Even now, her hold on life seemed tenuous indeed, her breathing shallow and raspy, her only sounds profound groans that came without conscious thought.

Bruenor pulled a chair in from the hallway outside the room, placing it right beside the chair holding Mallabritches, the two of them close enough to Tannabritches as she lay on the small bed to hear her labored breathing and the quiet, pained sounds.

"Not wantin' to lose her," Mallabritches said quietly past the obvious lump in her throat. "All me life, been me and her, Fist'n'Fury. Not wantin' one without th' other."

"Aye, girl, but she can't be leaving," Bruenor said, and he snorted as he did, his emotions pouring forth. He couldn't stand seeing Tannabritches like this. His head and heart careened back to Citadel Felbarr, to the early days of his second life when he had trained beside the wild Fellhammer duo, when he had served beside them, when he had fought beside them—beside Tannabritches in particular, in one wild battle in the Rauvin Mountains.

Tannabritches had been badly wounded in that fight, too, struck in the chest by an orc spear. All she had thought about as she fell was the safety of the others, of Bruenor, whom she knew as her friend Little Arr Arr. She had told him to get the others and run away, to leave her to her grim fate.

"Bah, but I didn't save ye then to watch ye die now, girl," Bruenor growled in a harsh whisper. "Ye don't be leavin' me, ye hear?"

Mallabritches took his hand and squeezed it tightly.

He looked up at her, meeting her gaze, and tears streamed from his eyes.

Mallabritches shook her head, overwhelmed.

"I can't be lettin' her go," Bruenor gasped, and surely he was overwhelmed then, with Tannabritches lying here and Drizzt in the room next door. He was as surprised by his reaction as was Mallabritches, for the depth of his pain cut straight to his heart. He really could not stand the thought of losing Tannabritches now!

When Emerus had given over the Fellhammer sisters to serve as part of Bruenor's elite guard, the red-bearded dwarf's heart had leaped—more than he had truly understood. But now, seeing Tannabritches lying there, so pale and near to death, he did understand, and surely his heart broke as he came to believe that she was slipping away from him forever.

"Ye got yer Gutbusters," Mallabritches said, but in a leading way that told Bruenor she was fishing deeper. "King Bruenor's to be surrounded by fighters, eh?"

"Not about that!" Bruenor snapped. He sucked in his breath to steady himself, shook his head ferociously, and leaned forward, staring at the wounded lass, silently imploring her to live. "Not about fightin'," he said. "About needin' her aside me when the fightin's done."

"When ye take the throne, ye mean?"

The shock of Mallabritches' words jolted Bruenor upright, and he turned to regard her curiously.

"It'll be yerself," she said. "Aye, but ye're the proper choice, I'm sayin'. The great Emerus is so old, and even if ye gave him the throne, he'd not hold it for long. We'll be rid o' the damned drow, don't ye doubt, and Bruenor'll be King o' Gauntlgrym one day not far along."

Bruenor didn't respond, but neither did he blink.

"Ye're thinkin' her yer queen, ain't ye?" the Fellhammer girl asked.

Again, her words shocked Bruenor, for he hadn't carried his thoughts and his pain that far along. His initial reaction was to shake his head in denial. The whole proposition sounded ridiculous to him. He was a long way from claiming Gauntlgrym's throne, after all.

But as he considered Mallabritches's question, which sounded more like an accusation, Bruenor's biggest surprise was that he came to recognize that she wasn't wrong. He stammered something undecipherable under his breath and his head swiveled back to consider the poor lass lying on the bed.

"Do ye love her, Arr Arr?" Mallabritches asked.

"Aye," Bruenor said, surprised by his honest answer.

"And yer heart's breaking in seein' her in the bed like that, eh?"

"Aye," he weakly answered.

Mallabritches grabbed him by the shoulder and yanked him around, forcing him to look her in the eye once more. "And ye tell me true, me friend, what if it was meself in that bed, and me sister sittin' here with ye? Where might Arr Arr . . . where might Bruenor Battlehammer be then, I'm askin'?"

Bruenor's face started to twist up in confusion, but his answer came from a place of clarity when he said, "Same place."

His gray eyes opened wide as the weight of his words sank in, as he came to realize that he had just professed his love to Mallabritches—and to her sister.

Mallabritches yanked him closer then, and put her arm around his shoulders, lifting her hand to press Bruenor's head onto her own strong shoulder for support.

"Don't ye be worried, me friend," she whispered in his ear. "Fist ain't leavin' us. She just ain't."

◆ ◆ ◆

"I DONE ALL I could," Bungalow Thump pleaded to the two dwarf kings and the others gathered in the throne room.

Word of the disaster in the lower chambers had preceded him, but few details had come forth, other than the deaths of a hundred Battlehammer warriors . . . and the Twelfth King of Mithral Hall.

Bungalow Thump, himself wounded and battered, had come to the throne room to offer a full recounting to the leaders. Toliver Harpell stood behind him, head bowed respectfully, with Penelope and Kipper beside him.

Bungalow Thump didn't leave out any details. He glanced back at Toliver Harpell and offered an apologetic shrug before he told of the failure of the Field of Feather Fall, as he described poor dwarves bouncing onto the stone floor, or onto the bodies of their fallen comrades.

The dwarf's voice soared as he recounted the heroics of those trapped on the ground, and again, he didn't exclude the Harpells, taking great pains to accurately describe Kenneally's brilliant improvisation.

"Aye, but she saved the lot of us," Bungalow Thump said. "And gived her own life in doin' it!"

"Huzzah for Kenneally Harpell, then!" Ragged Dain offered, drawing a stern look from Bruenor—but one that didn't hold, and indeed, Bruenor joined in the cheer for Kenneally.

"It seems as if it was more demon than drow opposin' ye," Emerus Warcrown offered at that break.

"More demons and hordes o' goblins and orcs," Bungalow Thump confirmed. "Saw a drow or two from the shadows and throwing spells, but none other."

"Goblins and orcs," Bruenor muttered, for surely he had seen his fill of the wretched orcs in recent months. "Slaves o' the damned drow!" As he said that aloud, he realized that much of it was likely true for the War of the Silver Marches, as well. His thoughts careened to Lorgru, of the line of Obould, and those orcs who once more rallied around that name and their professed desire to live in peace.

Might the treaty of Garumn's Gorge have held if not for the damned drow?

Bruenor shook the thought away.

"And them demons?" Oretheo Spikes offered. "Demons in the entry hall, demons in the mines! Durned Gauntlgrym's more full o' demons than dwarfs and drow together!"

"I ain't seeing much difference between demons and drow, meself," Emerus growled.

"Aye, to the Abyss with 'em all!" Ragged Dain added, and a great cheer went up all around the throne room, one rolling from bravado to a muted confusion, it seemed.

The starkly mixed results of the three battles fought this same day had them all off balance. They had won in the entry hall, slaughtering demons by the score. Every defense had held strong and every plan had been executed to near perfection, and the hero of that battle, Oretheo Spikes, deserved every cheer and honor offered to him.

And Connerad Brawnanvil, too, would garner much of the credit for that battle in the entry cavern, for the defenses of that hall were his doing, offered with insight he had gained on the Throne of the Dwarf Gods.

But they had been defeated badly in the lower chamber, and it simply could not continue that each side could hold its own ground. For the drow had the Great Forge.

That could not stand!

As the cheering died away, Bruenor rose and approached the throne, nodding, but with his expression grave.

"Ropes, I say!" Emerus called. "Yerselves should've used the rappel to the cavern floor and not some wild magic!"

"You cannot lay the blame with . . ." Penelope Harpell started to protest, but Bungalow Thump held up his hand to silence her, and did it for her.

"Nay, King Emerus, and sure to know that I'm yer loyal servant here, pledged in fealty and acceptin' o' yer judgments," he said. "But I can'no agree—nay, for the plan was a good one, and oh, but we were hitting the floor in full charge."

"Until the magic fell away," Emerus reminded.

"Aye, but we could no' know the power o' the enemies below us," Bungalow Thump replied. "Ah, but they were thick with wizards and thick with demons. Big demons by the score. By rope or by Harpell magic, we'd've lost many of our boys today, and we'd've ne'er gained the lower hall."

"Well said, Master Thump, and I'd not expect less o' ye than that," Bruenor replied before Emerus could—and with almost exactly the same words Emerus would have used.

All eyes went to Bruenor and many bushy eyebrows, Emerus's included, lifted in surprise to see him sitting on the throne once more, hands solidly on the burnished arms of the great chair, eyes closed, and his whole body slowly swaying back and forth.

And nodding, as if he was in a conversation with some unknown beings—given the throne upon which he sat, he likely was.

"But now we're knowin'," Bruenor said at length, his gray eyes popping open. "Aye and they be thick in the lower tunnels, eh, and with hordes of demons and a swarm o' goblinkin."

He swept his gaze across the room, a sly smile creasing his fiery red beard. That stare settled on Emerus, who nodded his approval then swerved to lock stares with Bungalow Thump.

"And we got an army o' dwarves with blood kin to avenge," Bruenor explained. "So tell me, me boys, which corner's getting yer bettin' pouch?"

That brought the biggest cheer of all, of course, and Penelope Harpell put her hand on Bungalow Thump's shoulder, squeezing tight. For Bruenor had just absolved the Harpells and the force Connerad had led below of any blame for the defeat, accepting Bungalow's explanation without question.

And now Bruenor had sworn vengeance, and woe to those below.

"Huzzah and heigh-ho!" the cheering went on, all in the room joining in exuberantly—save two.

Bruenor just sat there on the throne, listening to the whispers of Moradin carried in on the song of dwarven cheering, and Catti-brie stood off to the side, staring at her adoptive father, recognizing that Bruenor had turned the corner on his grief and worry.

The woman had worried that Drizzt would not return to her, but so, too, had she worried that Bruenor would not—not in time, at least. But now that latter fear washed away. There was her Da, King Bruenor Battlehammer, his eyes full of fight.

There was no time for moping about, not with an army of drow and demons and goblinkin lying in wait below.

No, now was the time for preparation, and for vengeance.

Catti-brie saw it clearly on Bruenor's face. He meant to avenge Connerad and the Gutbusters. He meant to make them pay for the injury to Tannabritches Fellhammer.

And he meant to make them all pay dearly for the wounds they had inflicted upon his dearest friend.

"Woe to the drow," Catti-brie whispered under her breath, and she ended with a knowing smile and a nod.

For King Bruenor Battlehammer was coming for them.

◆ ◆ ◆

"SEEN HIM LIKE this before," Emerus whispered to Ragged Dain as they made their way along the upper tunnels of Gauntlgrym, part of a grand procession, four thousand of the dwarves geared for battle. "Ain't good for his enemies," the old king said with a snort and a nod.

Ragged Dain couldn't disagree. Bruenor led the procession, Mallabritches Fellhammer at his side, Athrogate and Ambergris close behind. The solid stride of the red-bearded dwarf bespoke his determination. He was angry—outraged, even—with his dear friends lying gravely wounded. But Bruenor hadn't let that outrage take him to a place of recklessness by any means—his method for vengeance was clear-sighted and truly inspired. He had devised the plan of attacking the lower levels in careful consultation with King Emerus, Bungalow Thump, Oretheo Spikes, Catti-brie, and the three Harpells.

He had devised the plan while sitting on the Throne of the Dwarf Gods.

King Bruenor was purely focused and determined to get his revenge and to claim his prize, but every dwarf marching behind him went with full confidence that Bruenor would lead the army onto the battlefield of his proper choosing, giving them the best chance of a great victory.

The army divided into battle groups as they neared the last corridor, the same corridor that led to the landing where the first battle of the lower levels had gone disastrously wrong. Among all the ranks, clerics ran, casting spells of protection from fire and from cold, spells to mitigate wounds, and spells to bless the ranks.

Bruenor and his battle group, made up mostly of the Mithral Hall dwarves, including the remaining Gutbusters, veered into a side corridor along with the three remaining Harpells and Catti-brie. All along the journey, the spellcasters remained busy creating small stones with enchantments of light. Now they went along the lines of Battlehammer dwarves, handing those light pellets out to every commander and with all the leftovers going to predetermined foot soldiers.

If all went as planned, this battle group would not begin the attack in the lower cavern, but would be the first to reach the floor of that battlefield chamber in any significant numbers.

Oretheo Spikes led the second group, the largest and most prominent force, fronted by the Wilddwarves of Citadel Adbar. They carried long lines of rope as they made for the main corridor and the landing, ready to rappel, six at a time, to the darkness below. Two thousand warriors and clerics formed this force, with more than a thousand ready to hit the floor below and the rest supporting the battle from the landing and the corridors above. If the drow or their demonic allies found a way to get up behind the dwarves in the lower chamber, they'd find nearly a thousand Adbarrim and Mirabarran warriors ready to show them the error of their ways.

King Emerus, Ragged Dain, and the third group held back. They would be the last to the fight, but perhaps the most important, and the most daring.

"There are a lot of them," Kipper Harpell remarked to Bruenor and the others, looking at the mob of dwarves filling the side corridor and the antechambers that lined it. "How many will get through before the exit is dispelled, I wonder? Is this plan not simply going to trap you in the cavern as just happened with poor King Connerad?"

"Only way down," Bruenor replied. "Our enemies are below and so we're going below. We're counting on yerself and th' others to make sure it won't happen."

"But once you are on the floor—" Kipper started.

"No running from this fight," Bruenor interrupted, and there was no debate to be found in his tone.

Kipper, with a glance at a shrugging Penelope, conceded the point. Kipper Harpell was the master of magical gates, dimensional doors, and the like, but Bruenor had several hundred dwarves with him, all trying to negotiate quickly through the tight quarters of this side corridor. Perhaps they should have done this part of the attack from the throne room after all, as had been suggested.

But no, despite his reservations and his very real fears that this fight would end up eerily similar to the one Kenneally and Tuckernuck's magic had led, Kipper had to admit this tactic offered the best hope. He was close enough to the targeted area to use lesser spells to create his portal, and so he could quickly enact replacements if the initial one failed.

"Once you're down there, I won't easily be able to get you out," he reminded Bruenor.

"Once I'm down there, only ones who'll be wantin' me out're the damned drow," Bruenor replied without the slightest hesitation.

Kipper took his place at the end of the side corridor and rubbed his hands together, awaiting the signal. Similarly, Catti-brie and Penelope, both readying the same dimensional gate spell as the old Harpell, found appropriate locations nearby, where they could channel supporting lines of dwarves into the cavern.

Toliver Harpell, meanwhile, cast his own spell, and a disembodied wizard eye floated back out of the corridor and into the main passageway, flitting past the lines of Wilddwarves preparing their ropes and harnesses and out to the landing, where Oretheo Spikes and his best fighters stood ready.

The Adbarrim warrior nodded and grinned at the approach of Toliver's enchanted orb. That wizard eye served as the "go" signal.

"For King Connerad, for Citadel Adbar, for the Silver Marches, for Gauntlgrym, for Delzoun!" Oretheo Spikes whispered, and so it began, with Oretheo and five others taking up their ropes and rolling off the landing, sliding down for the floor.

And six more dwarves went right behind them.

From the landing, the wizard eye went down alongside the dwarves, with Toliver noting the landmarks and locations. Kipper launched into his casting.

The first drow lightning bolt reached out to blast at the dwarves. The first demon howls echoed below as the lower level came awake to the threat.

Oretheo Spikes was the first dwarf to the floor, five others beside him, six more coming fast, and six more right behind them.

But on came the goblinkin and the demon hordes, ready for the expected battle, and surely expecting to overwhelm this puny force in short order.

Toliver called out to the others, "No surprise! Our enemies were waiting for us."

"Aye, and that's the way we knew it'd be!" Bruenor roared. "Who's to stop a dwarf charge, I ask ye?"

And the cheering erupted all along that side corridor, and dwarves began banging their weapons against their shields, and all crowded in on Kipper, who was in the thrall of spellcasting.

Old Kipper prayed that he had the location correct, that Toliver was relaying the information properly, as he at last completed his spell, connecting this corridor to the floor just to the right of Oretheo Spikes.

◆ ◆ ◆

"FOOLS," JAEMAS SAID, shaking his head in disbelief. "We repelled them last time, and now they come down even more slowly? And more vulnerably?"

He looked to his cousin Faelas, who was just completing his next lightning bolt. The spell shot off, and Faelas nodded in satisfaction. The flash of his first bolt had shown him the target, and now this second streak of lightning had hit the mark, the magic slashing through one of the rappelling ropes far up from the floor.

The lowest dwarf on that rope was just jumping the last few feet to the ground. The next tumbled fifteen feet or so, bounced and rolled back to his feet. The third on the rope fell from twice that height. He hit, buckled, and groaned, grabbing at his legs.

The fourth, the fifth, and the sixth crashed hard onto the floor. One of them was moaning, the other two lying silently and very still.

Faelas looked to Jaemas and shrugged, as much at a loss as to why the foolish dwarves would try something so obviously desperate as this after the first catastrophe, and indeed, among the piled remains of their dead kin. Drow would never be so stubborn or stupid as that, after all.

But then the cousins heard a sudden onslaught of cheering and the cavern brightened, a brightly glowing square of light just to the side of the main fighting.

"What is it?" Faelas asked.

"A gate!" Jaemas yelled, and indeed it was.

Through that portal came the Battlehammers, led by Bruenor himself, pouring out into the cavern just to the side of Oretheo Spikes's position. Many of those dwarves came out bearing a small light stone, and they flung those illuminating orbs as prescribed, scattering them sequentially throughout the reaches of the huge cavern.

The drow shied in pain and surprise. The cavern became as bright as daylight, brutal to Underdark eyes.

Demons and goblinkin hunched away and shielded their eyes, and the wall of Battlehammers crashed into them like a stampede of crazed rothé, stomping over them, smashing and slashing at them, burying them.

Bruenor ran right up the side of one vrock, his axe whacking away with wild abandon, driving into the demon, pounding it down bit by bit.

Standing atop the broken, destroyed thing, Bruenor glanced back at Oretheo Spikes, the two sharing a knowing nod.

"Vengeance," Bruenor Battlehammer muttered quietly, but loud enough for Fury Fellhammer, Athrogate, and Ambergris to hear and echo the sentiment.

◆ ◆ ◆

"BE QUICK!" KIPPER Harpell implored the dwarves still pouring through his portal, and to the other wizards who were only then enacting their spells. "They are trying to dispel the gate!"

Across the way, Catti-brie and Penelope focused on the sight through Kipper's gate, using that to aid in the placement of their own dimensional doorways. Neither was prolific enough with these types of spells to safely do as Kipper had done, locating and opening a gate merely on the words of Toliver, but now with the target area clearly in their view, both had their spells successfully away.

At that very moment, Kipper's gate went away, but it didn't matter. Two portals were in place now, and soon enough three, as the old mage opened yet another to replace the first.

Several hundred Battlehammers would be in that cavern before the drow or their demon allies could hope to close the gates.

"Go! Go!" Catti-brie yelled to the other wizards, and all three rushed around the charging dwarves and back out into the main corridor, pausing to cast as they went.

"You remember the ritual?" Penelope asked, and both Cattie-brie and Kipper nodded.

The Adbar dwarves, still rappelling along the ropes—five now, but with a new sixth line soon to be in place—moved aside for the magic-users, and for the royal procession, King Emerus and Ragged Dain and a host of elite Felbarran warriors close behind them.

As soon as they passed through the last door, Catti-brie and the three Harpells flew away, Toliver leading them down to the correct position near to the floor.

Up on the landing, King Emerus, Ragged Dain, and the others chanted out a battle song, using the cadence to count as instructed.

And when the second verse ended, fully confident in the wizards and their timing, the Felbarrans leaped out into the open cavern, plummeting to within ten feet of the floor before passing through the newly enacted Field of Feather Falling, then floating down to begin solidifying Oretheo Spikes's left flank.

The shield walls were formed in the blink of a trained dwarf's eye, the dwarf ranks thickening precisely in the well-lit cavern. Drow darkness spells took some of that light away, but there weren't many Xorlarrins in this cavern and it was a feeble attempt indeed against the overwhelming number of lighted stones the dwarves had brought to bear.

And now they were the tide, breaking waves made of rolling dwarves, following the leads of Bruenor Battlehammer, Oretheo Spikes, and Emerus Warcrown.

Goblins, orcs, and demons died by the score, and the shield line would not be broken.

Drow lightning and fire came at them, but so quick had the Felbarran assault filled the cavern that Catti-brie and the Harpells, too, began to focus on more offensive spells.

Thick ran the blood. Goblins and orcs piled deep in death, scores of manes lay smoking and melting on the floor, and many dwarves went to Moradin's Hall in those early moments of wild battle.

But the line held, frustratingly so for those hungry demons who could not get to their bearded enemies, and so began attacking the other living creatures, the allied goblinkin, to satisfy their undeniable hunger.

◆ ◆ ◆

THEY WERE WINNING. Bruenor understood that as again the dwarven line rolled forward and engulfed their enemies, curling up and down the length of the cavern like a breaking wave on a long beach, as inexorable and undeniable as the tide itself.

They were winning, and it seemed to Bruenor that the fight was quickly turning into a rout. Once they had this hold on the lower levels, with easy resupply from above, they could not be denied. The Forge and the adjoining primordial chamber, the heart of Gauntlgrym, would be theirs for the taking.

Gauntlgrym would be Delzoun once more, as Moradin had demanded.

But something was off-kilter, Bruenor felt, some emptiness within him that muted his joy at the moment of supreme victory.

Drizzt was not beside him now to share in his greatest triumph. For all their decades together, in this, the culmination of Bruenor's achievements, Drizzt Do'Urden was not there, and perhaps would never again be.

His dearest friend, the greatest warrior he had ever known.

He remembered his own dying words in his previous life, when he had looked into the eyes of his dear friend and whispered, "I found it, elf." Aye, he had found Gauntlgrym, the most ancient dwarven homeland, the greatest dwarven treasure of all, yet not because of dwarven help but because a dark elf had stood beside his journey for decades, had suffered his wrong turns, had helped him through near-disastrous battles, and in the end, had led the way to put the primordial back in its captivity.

Drizzt had done all of that. For Bruenor. For friendship. Selflessly.

Drizzt, who now had paid, at long last, for Bruenor's dwarven needs.

The red-bearded dwarf winced, feeling again as if this victory might prove hollow after all. In defiance, Bruenor blew his cracked silver horn. Let the wild spirit of Thibbledorf Pwent come forward, he decided, wanting to ultimately punish those who stood against him.

◆　◆　◆

FAR FROM THE roar of battle, the explosions of fire and lightning, the whipping ice storms of Penelope Harpell and the latest shield rush led by Bruenor Battlehammer, the drow ranger lay quietly in the darkness.

His first sensations of semiconsciousness came from his fingers, playing over a familiar shape as they shifted across the onyx figurine of the panther.

Somewhere distantly, Drizzt felt the warmth and heard the name of Guenhwyvar echoing in his thoughts.

Memories would not come back to him—nothing specific at least. Just a feeling of companionship and joy. Images of his friends flashed in the recesses of his mind, of Catti-brie and Bruenor, mostly.

And of Guenhwyvar, the panther, the figurine that served as her beacon so tangible in Drizzt's weak hands.

He could not hear the cries of dying dwarves, and could not know the battle raging far below, a battle then looking like victory to his friends.

Somehow, though, Drizzt knew better. A pair of great demon leaders, Marilith and Nalfeshnee, were waiting in the shadows and would soon come onto the battlefield and rally the demonic forces and the drow to turn back the tide of dwarves.

Where the hopes and expectations of victory in his dearest friends would suddenly turn to dread.

Another image flashed in his mind, but did not flutter aside. Instead it held him and called to him, demanded of Drizzt that he shake off the irresistible darkness, that he wake up.

He saw Jarlaxle in his thoughts, and when he at last did open his weary eyes, Drizzt saw Jarlaxle once more, standing with Kimmuriel beside his bed.

"Welcome back."

CHAPTER 22 ◈

The Gray Fog of Death

"ORETHEO SPIKES'S A GOOD ONE," BUNGALOW THUMP assured Bruenor.

"He's got 'em in line, aye!" Bruenor replied, glancing down to his left where the large Adbar contingent centered the dwarven line, with Bruenor and Mithral Hall holding strong on the right flank, King Emerus and the Felbarran leapers holding the left.

It would have been easy for Oretheo Spikes and his Wilddwarves to press too far ahead, and surely that would prove oh-so-tempting to the ferocious band. They were nearest the huge structure that housed the circular stair to the upper levels, the centerpiece of this cavern, the symbol of control of the chamber. And they were Wilddwarves, so akin in attitude, indeed patterned after, the Mithral Hall Gutbusters, who never met an enemy they didn't eagerly punch, leap upon, shake apart, or bite.

The enemy was weaker there too, in the middle, with the stair dispersing the demons and what few remained alive of their goblinkin fodder out to the left and right.

But Oretheo was keeping his boys in line, and the long front ranks of the dwarven charge kept rolling in practiced unison. Inexorable, unstoppable, a rolling, swallowing wave. And as they had planned up above, Bruenor's end of the line initiated the roll of each wave. King Bruenor alone paced the assault, keeping his own formations tight, keeping his cadence solid and straight.

Magical explosions shook the chamber from all around, coming in from dark elf wizards or demons skulking in the shadows, and going out from Catti-brie and the Harpells. The demons, other than the manes and other lesser creatures, didn't seem overly bothered by the magical barrage, but neither were the tough dwarves, secure behind their armor and shields, as solid as the stone they mined.

Behind the initial line of fighting, Bruenor noticed something else—and he laughed out loud at the sight. Back there, the demons, who couldn't get into the fight fast enough to satiate their hateful hunger, had turned on the slave fodder, pulling down goblins and orcs and tearing them to shreds.

"Keep it slow and keep it steady, me boys!" Bruenor yelled. "Let 'em eat their own a bit afore they're tastin' me axe for dessert!"

And the cheers rolled down the line, and the dwarven wave rolled on across the cavern floor.

But far down to the left, there came a new commotion, and when Bruenor and the others turned that way, it seemed to them as if the dwarven advance, that metaphorical wave, was suddenly breaking against huge rocks.

Or huge demons, to be more precise.

A six-armed female beauty towered three times the height of the unfortunate dwarves facing her, and an even larger beast, much like the one Athrogate and Ambergris had killed in the mines, only bigger, and, given the dwarves flying and dying in front of him, surely meaner.

Bruenor shouted over to Bungalow Thump, who had scurried back to his line of Gutbusters. "Send Adbar reinforcing to the left!"

Even as he called out, though, a wall of fire appeared down that way, far to the left, down by the Felbarrans. One of the demon leaders had done that, Bruenor guessed easily enough, and behind the roiling flames, King Emerus and his charges had no choice but to fall back.

And worse, all around those two demon leaders, the rest of the horde was suddenly rallying and falling into order. From the beginning of the fight, much like in the halls above, the Abyssal creatures had fought as individuals, each taking any opening to leap forward and attack—and so, out there alone, without support, those too-eager demons had been easy prey for the teamwork of the disciplined dwarves.

But now all of that was fast changing, right in front of Bruenor's surprised and worried gaze. He heard a low buzzing sound, and knew that this, too, was coming from the demon leaders, from the six-armed female behemoth it seemed. Under that drone, the demons all the way down to this far-thest end of the line reformed their ranks, suddenly ready to battle in unison.

The leaders had brought discipline, and powerful magic, and now Bruenor wasn't feeling that the victory might be hollow. He was wondering if he had led three thousand dwarves into a death trap.

"Fight on, boys!" he called to rally those around him. "Hold close to yer fellows! None o' us're to move out to get catched and pulled off!"

He turned to Catti-brie and the Harpells. "Them big ones're controlling it all."

"Marilith and Nalfeshnee," Penelope Harpell replied, shaking her head, her face a mask of dread. She knew of demonkind and understood the great power that had unex-pectedly come upon them. "They are demonic nobility in all but title. Mighty leaders have joined our enemies!"

"Ye get me down there," Bruenor told them. "We'll be cuttin' the head from the snake or I'm a bearded gnome!"

"Huzzah!" roared all those dwarves who heard the claim.

But the middle of that cheer seemed to carry on for a long while, a great buzzing drone, and now a swarm of chasme, scores of the flying beasts, swept into the cavern in tight formation.

And those chasme carried barrels of oil heated in the nearby forge, so their bombs began to fall, and great blasts of biting flames erupted all around the dwarven lines.

◆ ◆ ◆

"THEM TWO'RE CONTROLLING it!" King Emerus yelled to Ragged Dain, both of them coming to the same conclusion as Bruenor. "We got to get to them!"

But the two in question seemed far beyond the reach of the Felbarran leaders. They loomed as ghostly silhouettes behind the great magical wall of flames that licked and bit at the dwarven line and drove them back.

King Emerus spun and called for the priestess Mandarina Dobberbright.

"Ye get me through that wall!" he ordered her.

"Ye canno' go alone!" she cried back at him, staring through the roiling flames at the beastly demons beyond.

"Do it!" Emerus ordered. "And send others to help me as ye can!"

Still shaking her head, Mandarina launched into her spell-casting, putting an enchantment upon Emerus that would protect him more fully from the biting flames than the minor protections that had been offered before the onset of battle.

"Now meself," Ragged Dain demanded as soon as she had finished.

But King Emerus didn't wait for his shield dwarf. As soon as he felt the enchantment washing over him, he spun and ran off, plunging into and through the wall of fire, and coming out the other side with a roar and a leap.

"Be quick!" Ragged Dain cried, and Mandarina pressed on, as other dwarves tried to breach the wall in pursuit of their daring king, only to be turned back by the unbearable heat.

"Priests!" many yelled, seeking similar enchantments to get them through, or something, anything, that might bring down that wall. And indeed, many dwarf clerics were already approaching the task, attacking the magical fire with dispelling enchantments, a few even creating water to fall upon the flames and dim them.

Ragged Dain began his run even before Mandarina finished her spell, and he only felt the enchantment washing over him as he entered the fires. He didn't care, though, for at the same time, he heard the ring of metal and knew that King Emerus had joined in battle.

When he burst through the other side of the fire wall, Ragged Dain could only wince, for that battle Emerus had found was with the six-armed demon herself, and her blades worked in a blur all around him. No novice to battle, indeed as great a warrior as Citadel Felbarr had ever known, old King Emerus fought back valiantly, trying to block, trying to dodge, trying to parry, even trying to counterstrike.

And he seemed to be holding his own. Ragged Dain knew his guess had been correct when the wall behind him dimmed and flashed out. Emerus had taken Marilith's concentration off her enchantment, and so she could not counter the spells of the many dwarf priests.

"Me king!" Ragged Dain proudly yelled, sprinting to join Emerus.

But then Emerus came staggering backward, and a swarm of hulking demons, many vrocks and glabrezu among them, rolled around Marilith and Nalfeshnee to shield their leaders.

Ragged Dain caught his king in his arms and fast retreated. Other dwarves similarly rolled around Dain and Emerus to meet the demon charge.

"Me king, oh, me king," Ragged Dain breathed, and he kept stumbling backward. He soon had to ease Emerus Warcrown down to the floor and as he did, he saw that for all his brilliant efforts, Emerus hadn't blocked all of those swings. Blood covered his chest and belly, with more spilling fast. "Priests!" Ragged Dain shrieked desperately.

But he knew in his heart that it was too late.

• ◆ •

"Ye hold the line," Bruenor told Bungalow Thump. "Whate'er ye do, ye keep the flank solid!"

"Aye!" the Gutbuster replied, nodding. He, like all the others around, saw the gleam in Bruenor's eye and understood what the dwarf meant to do.

When Obould's minions had descended upon Mithral Hall a century before, King Bruenor had left his bed and charged out into Keeper's Dale. Atop a stone that long-ago day, Bruenor had been the guidepost, the rallying point, the immovable object that would not allow the orcs passage. So it would be again. With these greater demons on the scene, the dwarves would be overwhelmed, would die here by the thousands.

The reclamation of Gauntlgrym would die here, too. Perhaps forevermore.

"Pwent!" he called to the specter he had sent out from the ranks, thinking to bring the spectral warrior along for the fun. But Bruenor then realized his error in calling in Thibbledorf Pwent too soon in the battle. The dwarf was nowhere to be found, and very likely the spirit had been defeated, and so sent back into the enchanted horn. Bruenor growled and shook his head.

"Come on, then," Bruenor told Mallabritches, Athrogate, and Ambergris, and off they ran, Catti-brie close behind.

"Crossbows up!" Bruenor ordered as he made his way down the ranks, pointing at the chasme and leaving no doubt about the first order of business for every crossbowdwarf. Along with those missiles went lightning bolts, the Harpells trying to blow the ugly creatures out of the air.

By the time Bruenor's entourage made it past the Adbar contingent, they found King Emerus lying in the arms of a sobbing Ragged Dain. The wall of fire was down, and the Felbarr dwarves were into the battle with the demons once more—but not with the demon leaders, Bruenor noted, for those two giants remained in the back, directing the fight from behind a shield wall of vrocks and glabrezu and other hulking and ugly beasts.

Bruenor was fast to the spot of the fallen king, sliding down beside Ragged Dain. He was surprised to find Emerus still alive.

"Girl!" he called to Catti-brie. "Put yer healin' on him!"

Emerus reached up and grabbed Bruenor's forearm. "I tried," he whispered.

"We're all knowin'," Bruenor assured him.

"Ye kill her," Emerus said with a bloody gasp. "Ye kill 'em both dead. Head o' the snake."

Bruenor bent low and kissed his old friend on the forehead, then leaped to his feet, shouted for Catti-brie once more, and charged for the front of the dwarven line, his three battle companions close beside him.

"Get me to 'em!" Bruenor yelled. He leaped upon a giant vulture demon, his axe working furiously, pounding the creature down. He felt the strength of Clangeddin, the wisdom of Moradin, the whispers of Dumathoin. When desperation reared up around him, so, too, did the spirits of the dwarf gods, and his final swat sent the vrock tumbling aside.

The dwarves around him rallied greatly, none more powerfully than Athrogate, with devastating swings of his enchanted morningstars.

But the shell around Marilith and Nalfeshnee was solid, with ranks of mighty creatures, and fight as they may, with the king lying near death, the Felbarrans and Bruenor's group could not make much headway.

Drow lightning and fire reached out at the mass of dwarves. Chasme rained death from above. All along the line, the demons moved in coordination to Marilith's buzzing call.

And for all his power and all his strength, for all the spirits of the dwarf gods within him, this time, Bruenor came to realize, it would not be enough. Soon he and those around him were being driven back, and he saw the six-armed demon note him and grin wickedly.

She knew.

And she knew that he knew.

It would not be enough.

◆ ◆ ◆

CATTI-BRIE WORKED FURIOUSLY over King Emerus, the blue magical mist pouring from her sleeve, the divine healing bathing the fallen king. The whole time, though, Catti-brie was shaking her head, fearing that the wounds were too deep and too wicked.

Shouts around her, not from the fighting up front, but from behind, demanded her attention, and even Ragged Dain looked up.

The dwarves in the back were diving aside every which way, some screaming "Poison!" others warning of some Abyssal beast about to materialize in their midst.

Ragged Dain saw it first, a concentrated gray fog sliding through the ranks, coming straight for him, and with a gasp he fell away, throwing his hands up defensively.

Catti-brie, too, let out a gasp, but as it passed them by, the fog didn't leave her and Ragged Dain on the floor writhing, nor did it pause as it continued its apparently focused sweep beyond them.

The woman leaped to her feet and followed it as it closed on Bruenor and the others. Behind her, Ragged Dain shouted out a warning to the last standing king. Bruenor turned, Ambergris began a spell, and Athrogate took a wild and futile swing at the fog as it went past.

Still it did not stop. And it crossed through the glabrezu and the vrocks, who seemed not to notice.

Then it stopped, hovering for just a moment before it became a swirling vortex of gray mist right in front of the demonic commanders.

And from that swirl came Guenhwyvar, leaping far and high upon Nalfeshnee even as she materialized.

And from that swirling mist came Drizzt Do'Urden, scimitars in hand.

◆ ◆ ◆

I STILL HOPE they kill Marilith, at least, the fingers of Jaemas Xorlarrin signaled to his cousin Faelas in the silent hand code of the drow, as if he was too fearful to speak those words aloud—and indeed, he was.

The more demons who fall now, the better, Faelas agreed. The drow wizards were thrilled at the turn of the battle, of course, for now it seemed clear that the dwarves would be driven back, perhaps slaughtered to a one. But if that victory came with the added benefit of thinning the demonic ranks enough to ensure that Matron Mother Zeerith could properly control the remaining horde, then all the better.

"Cousin!" Faelas then added vocally, though breathlessly, as he noted the newcomer to the battle, a scimitar-wielding dark elf who set upon Marilith with wild and brilliant abandon. Her six weapons spun and stabbed and swept all around her, but always a scimitar was there to block, or the agile drow warrior was quick enough to dodge, and quick enough in behind the attack—impossibly quick!—to riposte.

"By Lolth's eight legs . . ." Jaemas agreed.

"That's the Do'Urden rogue!" Faelas realized even as he began readying a spell, turning his sights on the grand trophy that had come unto them. He noted, though, that Jaemas wasn't similarly focusing, and indeed, was shaking his head. "Cousin?"

Don't strike out at him, Jaemas replied—or more accurately, Jaemas relayed, for a voice in his head warned him against any such actions.

"Let Marilith have the kill?" Faelas asked, clearly confused.

"We must be gone from this place," Jaemas said.

"The dwarves will not win," Faelas replied.

"It matters not," said Jaemas. "We must be gone. All of House Xorlarrin, and now!"

"Why?"

Jaemas could only shake his head. He wasn't sure who was in his thoughts, but the telepathically imparted suggestions were undeniably powerful and beyond debate. If they stayed, they would die, and horribly, the inner voice promised.

"I do not understand!" Faelas scolded.

And neither did Jaemas, who could only shake his head.

"Why must we be gone?" Faelas demanded.

"Because this is quite beyond you now," came a voice behind him, and he and his cousin turned to see Jarlaxle, sitting comfortably on a ledge above the nearby tunnel exit.

"Where did you . . . ?" Faelas asked.

"How?" Jaemas asked at the same time.

But Jarlaxle merely turned and motioned for them to follow, and indeed, they saw that others of their family were coming to them then, looking as confused as they.

Faelas glanced back at Marilith and the warrior he knew to be Drizzt, and gasped aloud to see that rogue drow in full fight now, running to the side of Marilith, easily leaping the sweeping tail of the naga-like creature, ducking the sweep of one long sword, sidestepping the downward stab of a spear, throwing himself back from the sweep of a second sword.

But in behind that sword he came, with a sudden burst of speed that stole Faelas's breath, too quick for the turning Marilith to bring her other three arms and weapons to bear.

He ran his blade right up her torso and slashed her hard, then vaulted over her shoulder, landing with amazing grace, and leaped again above the sweep of that deadly tail.

Faelas swallowed hard, Jarlaxle's advice suddenly sounding so much wiser.

◆ ◆ ◆

THE MAGIC LASHING out at them from the shadows slowed greatly. The dwarves didn't know why, but the battered, bearded folk were surely glad of it.

When they came to trust that the diminishment of drow magic was real, the three Harpells turned their focus more directly to the grotesque chasme above, lighting bolts and fireballs brightening the air above the battle.

And the frontlines of the dwarves were holding their own again. It seemed as if the demons pressing them were no longer covering for each other or working in unison. It didn't take long for the dwarves of Felbarr to understand why, and their cries of "Drizzt!" were taken up by the Adbarrim, and echoed all the way to the other end of the line, to Bruenor's clan.

Every dwarf tried to get a glance at the brilliant battle, at Drizzt and the six-armed she-demon, eight weapons ringing in a continual song.

Or to the side of that titanic battle, to get a glance at the legendary black panther, raking and biting, taking brutal hits from the huge demon and tearing its gray skin into loose flaps in reply.

"Huzzah and heigh-ho!" became the call once more as the dwarves rallied, and none greater than Bruenor Battlehammer and his entourage of three, leaping about each other and swatting at a glabrezu, determined to clear the way and get to the side of the dark elf ranger.

◆ ◆ ◆

DRIZZT SAW NONE of that, heard none of the cheers, and didn't even register the battle right beside him, where Guenhwyvar and Nalfeshnee traded such brutal strikes. His focus was narrow and fully on the six-armed demon. He was not unfamiliar with this particular type of beast, for he had battled a marilith before, in another time and place.

But not Marilith herself, not this creature, so huge and powerful.

He had come in with the element of surprise, had been upon the demon before she even knew he was there, had struck hard and true with both his blades, the repaired Twinkle, and Icingdeath, the frostbrand, which feasted on the flesh of creatures of fire and the lower planes.

That advantage had proven short-lived, however, and now Drizzt found himself in the fight of his life against a foe mighty and indomitable and unshakable. His focus was perfect because it had to be perfect, because anything less than that would get him cut down in short order.

His body moved somewhere beyond simple consciousness, in some almost ethereal state where conscious thought simply could not keep up. He was the Hunter, because to be anything less was to be dead.

His blades moved as they had to move to intercept and deflect deadly strikes. His legs propelled him to and fro, just ahead of strikes. It was all a blur to him, and to those watching, surely, as he just let himself flow with the battle, let the sounds and movements, the smells and the rush of air even, guide him along. Conscious thought was his enemy—even considering the motions and consciously trying to anticipate the next, would get him killed.

He just let the battle flow, trusting his instincts and reactions without thinking of them at all.

Somehow he had not been hit, though a hundred strikes had come his way. Somehow, he did not tire.

Because he could not tire.

Somehow.

◆ ◆ ◆

THE BULKY WINGED demon could not begin to keep up with the sheer speed of Guenhwyvar's movements, and even the beast's thick hide could only partly deter those incessantly raking claws. Again and again, Nalfeshnee slapped a huge hand to try to catch the cat, and almost always wound up just hitting himself. And on those few occasions when the demon managed to get some grasp on the elusive panther, quick as lightning, Guenhwyvar spun about and bit a demon finger hard.

But these two demon leaders were not mere warriors, brilliant as they were in combat, and for all the tribulations of the early battle, Nalfeshnee was more frustrated than worried.

And so the Abyssal behemoth drew a symbol in the air, chanting guttural sounds to enact the magic.

The glowing symbol hung in front of the beast, and even those dwarves battling the demon line, and those in the ranks behind, had to shy and squint, the unholy power of the magical symbol stinging them and burning them.

For Drizzt and Guenhwyvar, the effect was more pronounced, and the panther issued an agonized growl, and the drow ranger fell back from Marilith and lurched over in pain. So it was that both personal battles would have ended right there, with the major demons crushing their puny enemies.

But in just a few heartbeats, a shimmering wave rolled back and forth around the combatants and the demonic symbol sparked and disappeared. One woman stood tall against the unholy power.

Behind the initial dwarven shield wall, behind her adoptive father and his battling entourage, Catti-brie would not be bowed by demonic magic. She stood with her silvery staff upraised, the blue sapphire glowing fiercely, throwing forth disenchanting waves, inhibiting the Abyssal magic.

And so when Nalfeshnee paused to consider her, a relieved Guenhwyvar leaped upon the beast's massive shoulder and bit down hard, igniting a fountain of demon blood.

And when Marilith moved forward fast to bury the lurching Drizzt, he came up straight in front of her, and fast turned the tables, driving her back yet again with flashing ripostes.

"Ah, good girl!" Bruenor congratulated her, and he and Athrogate worked in powerful unison to topple yet another vrock, the black-bearded dwarf hardly pausing to consider the win before sweeping out his morningstars to swat away another trio of manes.

"Bwahaha!" he roared happily. "We're coming Drizzle-Elf! Ye just hold yer ground!"

Bruenor looked to Catti-brie, thinking to ask her for some evocations of her own to help blast clear the way to the drow and his cat, but he found the woman fully engaged, looking at Drizzt, her stare purely focused as if she were expecting some signal.

Catti-brie knew her husband better than any, and understood the flow of the battle he now waged, and so indeed, she was looking for a specific cue.

◆ ◆ ◆

DRIZZT HAD BATTLED a marilith before, and knew one great trick this demon could play: a quick teleport spell to land her behind her opponent.

He knew, too, the disenchantment that had come over the area, and understood the source of it. So when Marilith came at him only to find him relieved of his pain and ready to counter, then found herself in a desperate backslide, Drizzt guessed what to expect.

The huge demon hissed and brought all of her blades in for complete parries, then threw them out wide, rearing away from Drizzt—and thinking to teleport behind him.

But she could not, and so he got her with a sudden leap and thrust, Icingdeath puncturing her belly.

And chewing hungrily at her life-force.

The demon went into a berserk rage, driving Drizzt back, three arms sweeping across one way, then back again, followed by the other three with the cruel weapons they held. Around came her snakelike tail, trying to sweep the feet from the drow, and he only barely stayed ahead of the sudden, brutal assault.

And in one dodge, he glanced back and caught an opening in the demon-on-dwarf battle to catch a glimpse of Catti-brie. He found her staring back. He only had time to offer a slight nod, but that was all she needed.

Drizzt sped out to the side and reached into his innate drow magic. Purple flames of faerie fire covered the demon. Marilith's own magic suppressed that almost immediately, but Drizzt hadn't evoked the dweomer for any reason other than to verify that he could, that Catti-brie had correctly dismissed her disenchanting wave.

Marilith came on, and Drizzt stopped running away, turning back to her and charging abruptly.

He led with a globe of impenetrable darkness, covering the huge demon, and into it he sped. Even as his vision failed him, he heard the cries, the collective gasp, from his friends and allies behind.

It was a daring move, to be sure, and never in his life before had Drizzt put this much trust in his anticipation of his opponent's actions—and in truth, he didn't really know where that anticipation had come from. How could he know?

But yet again, this was not conscious thought guiding him, only instinct and confidence and trust.

He just knew that Marilith was already moving to counter. Perhaps it was the press of the air, the tiny currents from her arms and blades. She was leading with her left arms, and so her left hip was forward, and in that pose, her blades would come across up high.

And so Drizzt fell flat to the floor, and felt the rush of air above him.

He was up almost instantly and knew the backhand follow was coming fast, and from all the little things he had just subconsciously noted in the last back-and-forth of battle he knew, too, that Marilith would be shifting her left hip to an even posture, and as he understood her general positioning, so, too, must she know his.

So he leaped and turned horizontally in the air, and Marilith's low blade went beneath him, scraping the floor. And her middle blade, too, was too low, but perilously close. The third blade slashed across so near to his face that if Drizzt hadn't wisely turned his head, it would have taken his nose.

He rolled as he descended, even as the blades passed, twisting, driving his legs down, catching the floor in a crouch. Three more blades were right behind, but Drizzt went forward still, springing forth inside the demon's reach.

Springing forth with one scimitar out in front of him, one blade hungry for demon flesh.

He felt Icingdeath enter the demon's skin in the hollow between her breasts, and he kept going forward, and the material body of the Abyssal creature could not resist or repel the bite of the frostbrand.

◆ ◆ ◆

THE HOWL FILLED the vast cavern. From behind the dwarves, Catti-brie cried out in fear. On a ledge above Faelas and Jaemas, very near to the lower exit, Jarlaxle, too, cried out, seeing Drizzt leap into that darkened globe where Marilith surely waited.

"Elf!" Bruenor cried, and he and all around him held their collective breath in the agonizing heartbeat it took for the combatants to clear the darkness globe.

Marilith charged in a frenzy, Drizzt up against her. She bit at him and slapped at him, tried to turn her weapons and stab at him, and seemed impossible that he had not been badly hit yet, and it was impossible that he would not soon be—particularly when Marilith threw aside a pair of her weapons and hugged him tight.

"Elf!" Bruenor cried again, and he started to add, "Girl!"

But Catti-brie didn't need the prompt. With no other choice, she had already raised her staff to the demon and let fly a great forked lightning bolt, one that hit both Marilith and Drizzt, a stunning, jolting blast that rocked the demon back over her serpentine tail and sent Drizzt tumbling and flying from her grasp.

The agile drow hit the ground in a roll and came up spinning back in a defensive crouch to face the demon, neither of his blades in hand.

Icingdeath ate at the demon, but not quickly enough, and on she came.

But an axe, an old, many-notched axe, newly reforged in this very place and burning with the enchantment of flames, appeared spinning out of nowhere to embed itself deeply into the face of the great six-armed demon.

Marilith stared at Drizzt hatefully from either side of that battle-axe. She held there, leaning back over her snake tail, her other weapons falling from her grasp, her hands reaching for the hilt of the scimitar that was buried deep in her chest. She wanted to grab it and tear it free, but she simply could not.

Icingdeath ate.

◆ ◆ ◆

"By THE GODDESS," said Faelas Xorlarrin, shaking his head in disbelief. He and his cousin looked up at Jarlaxle to find him smiling widely and nodding knowingly.

He sensed their looks and held out his hand, inviting them to note that Drizzt was already on to other things, though Marilith remained in place. In his roll and rise, he had replaced his scimitars with his bow, the deadly Heartseeker, and now took a bead on the other demon behemoth.

The panther leaped up from Nalfeshnee, straight into the air. The demon reached high and roared.

An arrow entered Nalfeshnee's mouth.

A second, following before the first ever struck, entered the demon's left eye, and a third took Nalfeshnee in the right eye.

Drizzt had to be perfect, and so he was perfect, and Guenhwyvar dropped upon the demon's head and shoulders and tore mercilessly at the flesh.

Marilith shrieked again in protest, but she was still leaning back over her tail, and even farther now, and she simply collapsed, acrid smoke, her life's essence, flowing from the wound around the hilt of Icingdeath, her body withering, her essence retreating to the Abyss in true banishment.

"What do we do?" Jaemas Xorlarrin asked Jarlaxle, who glanced down from his perch, seeming quite amused.

"You go to Matron Mother Zeerith and tell her that the cavern is lost," an unexpected voice answered, as Kimmuriel Oblodra walked out of that exit tunnel to stand beside the two wizards.

Jarlaxle looked back to the battle, where the coordination of the demon line was already beginning to fail, the dwarves rallying, and Drizzt cutting down everything near to him with a volley of silver-streaking arrows. He looked at the smoking husk that had been Marilith, Drizzt's scimitar protruding from her withered chest, King Bruenor's axe creasing her once-beautiful face.

Jarlaxle could not disagree with Kimmuriel's assessment. Indeed, the rout was on once more.

As it progressed, as more and more of the drow abandoned the cavern, as demons turned on demons in a mob of senseless murder and frenzy, Jarlaxle looked to Kimmuriel.

"Methinks it is time that we, too, are gone from this place," he said. He smiled widely. This was the outcome he preferred.

"Long past time," Kimmuriel agreed.

The psionicist was not nearly as interested in this battle as Jarlaxle was, of course, and mostly because he had another matter to attend, one where he would at long last impart the last pieces of the powerful summoning to the archmage who would unintentionally free his mother.

So he errantly believed.

CHAPTER 23 ◈

Goading Catastrophe

"YOU MEAN TO GO TO HIM NOW?" JARLAXLE ASKED INCREDU-lously. He and Kimmuriel stood alone in a side chamber just off the Forge of Q'Xorlarrin, which they both expected would soon enough be known as the Great Forge of Gauntlgrym once more. The dwarves had secured the main lower chamber, had even put the staircase back up, and were already fortifying their foothold and constructing war engines to sweep clear the lower level.

Neither Jarlaxle nor Kimmuriel were convinced there would soon be anything left to sweep, however, for the demons were once again acting very much like . . . demons. Orc slave, goblin slave, rothé, or even dark elf, it did not matter. With the fall of Marilith and Nalfeshnee, the Abyssal beasts had turned. Any creature of the Prime Material Plane was now prey, and even the lesser demons shied from their larger, insatiable Abyssal kin.

And so the Xorlarrins had retreated to this very small area around the Great Forge and the primordial chamber, their wizards nervously readying spells of banishment or evocation—anything to be rid of rampaging demons.

"It is the appointed time," Kimmuriel calmly answered. "The archmage is not forgiving of my tardiness."

"The enclave of Q'Xorlarrin will likely be wiped out before you return," Jarlaxle pointed out.

Kimmuriel shrugged as if he hardly cared. "This city will find its fate whether I am here or not."

"When the dwarves come, perhaps I will need you."

Kimmuriel scoffed. "Jarlaxle, you have more friends among their ranks than in Q'Xorlarrin," he said, and he closed his eyes, opened his distance-warping mental gate, and stepped far, far away, to the antechamber of Archmage Gromph in the distant city of Menzoberranzan.

He found Gromph in the other room, sitting at his desk and tapping his fingers together pensively.

"Ill news will soon arrive from Q'Xorlarrin," Kimmuriel warned.

The archmage nodded, seeming unsurprised. He had felt the fall of Marilith, his demon.

Are you prepared? Kimmuriel telepathically reached out to his student.

No reply.

Perhaps we should forsake your instruction this day, the psionicist offered, and he was reading the archmage's mind as he imparted that thought.

Gromph did a good job in feigning only limited interest in pursuing the lesson when he responded, but Kimmuriel knew better. The archmage had nearly panicked at the thought of foregoing the lesson, and understandably so to Kimmuriel, who knew that Gromph believed that psionics were giving him the edge in summoning extraplanar creatures, an edge he'd likely need soon enough with Quenthel Baenre holding a goristro at her side and with Marilith now banished back to her Abyssal home.

Yes, Kimmuriel mused, Gromph would be very receptive to his quiet background impartations this day.

And so he would give to Gromph all of the missing words and inflections, the completed spell, and let chaos reign—and let catastrophe rain upon Menzoberranzan and House Baenre.

◆ ◆ ◆

MATRON MOTHER ZEERITH sat upon her altar in the primordial chamber of Gauntlgrym, the open pit steaming behind her, the wall in front of her covered in webbing. All of her principals advisers were there—Archmage Tsabrak, High Priestess Kiriy, Hoshtar, Jaemas, and Faelas among them.

"We must be gone from this place," Faelas advised. "To remain is foolhardy."

"Nay, we must kill the dwarves," the often-fanatical Kiriy argued. "The Spider Queen demands no less of us!"

"They will overrun us," Jaemas flatly stated.

"We will turn the demons back—"

"No, we won't," a clearly defeated Matron Mother Zeerith interrupted.

"Then call out to Matron Mother Baenre," the high priestess begged. "She will grant us allies as we continue the fight."

"Even if she sent a second army, even if it was led by a demon as powerful as Marilith once more, they would not arrive in time to save Q'Xorlarrin."

"Then what do we do, Matron Mother?" Hoshtar asked, and his tone showed that he knew well enough.

"The tunnels below will shield us," Matron Mother Zeerith said. "The dwarves will not chase us far beyond their precious forge and the beast that powers the furnaces of this place. So we will leave. Let the dwarves and the demons battle to the last."

"And then we will return," said Kiriy, and the matron mother nodded and smiled, but unconvincingly to any who cared to study her more closely.

Zeerith waved them away then, telling them to gather together the family and begin the retreat. She motioned for Tsabrak to stay behind with her, though.

"Bring to me the newest prisoners," she instructed when she was alone with the wizard. She nodded to the webbing.

"You mean to greet the invaders?" Tsabrak asked skeptically. "Dwarves are not known for their mercy, Matron Mother."

"I have enough with which to bargain," she assured him.

Tsabrak shook his head. "We could just . . ."

"Do as I say," Zeerith cut him short. "I'll not have an army of dwarves chasing my House through the Underdark."

Tsabrak started to argue yet again, but Matron Mother Zeerith's scowl chased him away.

"Well played, Matron Mother," said the only other person in the room, the one whose presence had been known only to Zeerith.

"That's just what I meant to say to you, these last days, Jarlaxle," the matron mother answered. "Do I congratulate you? Or is there another who would lay claim to the credit?"

"You wound me, truly," said the mercenary, moving over and casually sitting upon the altar stone, one leg dangling off the far end, the other foot comfortably settled on the floor in front of him. "I did not orchestrate the events, but do pride myself on being the first to understand where those events will lead."

If his words convinced Matron Mother Zeerith, she surely didn't show it. She glanced at the room's main exit, her expression revealing her desire to take her leave.

"You guarantee my safety?"

"That was the deal," Jarlaxle replied.

"A deal I am sure to regret, of course."

"The best deal you will be offered."

"I am a matron mother of Menzoberranzan!"

"You were," Jarlaxle corrected. "Would you bring your tattered House back to the City of Spiders? Where will you now rank in that hierarchy, I wonder?"

"Xorlarrin was the Third House, and—" she protested.

"Was," the clever mercenary said again. "Can you claim the favor of Lolth?" He laughed, and it sounded very much like a mocking snort. "My dear Matron Mother Zeerith, were you ever truly in the favor of Lolth?"

"Third House," she replied.

"We know the truth of the familial rankings, so please, do not take that as confirmation. Lolth rarely meddles in such minutiae, and hardly cares beyond the identity of the Matron Mother of the First House."

"I grow weary of your chiding," she said. "Be warned."

"I am doing no such thing!" he earnestly protested. "Now is the time for honesty, for your sake more than mine, so let us speak the truth. My fondness for you goes back many years. You know this. You alone among the matron mothers value the men of your House as greatly as the women."

"Barrison Del'Armgo . . ."

Jarlaxle snorted. "The witch Mez'Barris uses her men as she would a pack of guard dogs, biting instruments to bring glory to the priestesses of her House, herself paramount. But you've never been like that."

He spoke the last words quietly, and after a proper glance around to ensure that no one had entered, he reached out and gently and intimately stroked Zeerith Xorlarrin's cheek.

And she let him, for the touch was not unfamiliar to her, though it had been years.

"Lolth will punish me if I do this," she said.

"She has not punished me," Jarlaxle argued. "And I have been doing this for centuries!"

"But she will see my desertion . . ."

"It is not a desertion!" Jarlaxle insisted. He shook his head. "My old friend, do not give in to the fear that the Spider Queen oversees our every move. Or that she cares! Her ambitions are quite beyond us, I assure you. Archmage Gromph summoned Marilith and sent her here, under his direct command, and yet the rogue Do'Urden slayed her!"

Zeerith's eyes flashed at the mention of Drizzt.

Jarlaxle shook his head and gave her a stern glance, silently but clearly warning her to forget that obvious thought. Every drow in Menzoberranzan seemed to believe that bringing the head of Drizzt would somehow garner great fame and stature and the favor of the Spider Queen, but Jarlaxle knew better, knew that it was a fool's mission. In Menzoberranzan, there was no bigger fool than Tiago Baenre, and his obsession with the rogue Do'Urden had already cost him greatly.

"As you come to understand Drizzt Do'Urden the way I do, you will learn," he promised.

"You will introduce me to him," Matron Mother Zeerith said.

"In time," was all that Jarlaxle would offer, and to his thinking, that might be a very, very long time. Though, of course, Jarlaxle expected that Drizzt might well meet Zeerith this very day.

"This is difficult for you," Jarlaxle said.

"I am the matron mother of a powerful House."

"Your family will survive, and so your House will survive."

"Under the suffrage of . . . ?"

"I promised you a great measure of autonomy," Jarlaxle reminded her.

Matron Mother Zeerith seemed unconvinced, and even shook her head.

"You pretend that you have options," Jarlaxle reminded her. "It would be easier for me to abandon you here and let you play out your story in the Underdark, or back in Menzoberranzan with my unmerciful sister. If Quenthel Baenre finds advantage in having you murdered, know that your death will not be painless."

"And what might Matron Mother Baenre think of your designs, should I go to her?" Zeerith asked, a rather pitiful attempt to take back the upper hand.

"She would applaud." Jarlaxle let his smile linger for a moment, before the sound of a distant door caught his attention.

"Tsabrak returns," he said. "You have time to consider the wider reaches of my offer, of course. Quite a bit of time once this immediate crisis is averted, and your safety is my guarantee. For now, your best play is to remain."

Matron Mother Zeerith stared at him for few long moments, then nodded, and Jarlaxle disappeared once more into the shadows of the webbing, right before Archmage Tsabrak arrived with the prisoners in tow.

◆ ◆ ◆

GROMPH WASN'T SURPRISED by the next visitor to his quarters this day. The matron mother entered with hardly an announcement, and with a scowl that told him that she, too, knew of the failures in Q'Xorlarrin.

"Your demon has fallen," she said in greeting.

"Along with many, it would seem," Gromph calmly answered. "Matron Mother Zeerith will not hold for long, I presume."

"The dwarves will reclaim Gauntlgrym, but they will never hold it," the matron mother vowed.

Gromph did well not to laugh out loud at that pronouncement. He found this whole adventure rather silly. How many resources would Quenthel squander in trying to evict the formidable dwarves? And for what practical gain?

"Because next time, I will be wiser than to rely on the foolish Gromph for such important matters!" the matron mother added, and she sounded so small and petulant at that moment. Had she abandoned the wisdom of Yvonnel?

The archmage just stared at her, unsure as to what any of this could mean. The satellite city of Q'Xorlarrin had been brought down, or soon would be, it seemed, but in the end, most of Matron Mother Zeerith's House would escape and so the loss would be minimal to Menzoberranzan. In fact, such an event might even strengthen Quenthel's hold over the Ruling Council, for it would remove a very sharp thorn from the side of House Hunzrin and the Melarni fanatics, and that alliance was one that Matron Mother Mez'Barris Armgo could actually use to weaken House Baenre.

"Your demon led the defense," the matron mother spat. "This failure falls upon your shoulders. Be cautious, wizard, for Tsabrak Xorlarrin will surely survive this, and he remains in the graces of the Spider Queen."

She spun and swept out of the room and Gromph fell back in his seat, his fingers tap-tapping once more. He tried to dismiss

Quenthel's overt threat, but he began to see some troubling possibilities. Would his sister cut a deal with Matron Mother Zeerith to absorb House Xorlarrin into House Baenre? Where might the Xorlarrins go if the dwarves gained an unshakable foothold? They would not be welcomed back into Menzoberranzan as a rival House, particularly not now with so many backroom alliances being formed among the ruling matron mothers.

And perhaps Quenthel would spread the whispers that Gromph had failed, that the archmage had, in fact, been the cause of the loss of Q'Xorlarrin. In that event, would Quenthel be in a stronger position to offer Zeerith one of her most coveted trophies: a Xorlarrin as Archmage of Menzoberranzan?

Nay, this was not a threat Gromph could easily dismiss, and in that realization, so came his outrage.

Barely had Quenthel left the tower of Sorcere when Gromph began his spellcasting, twining in the psionic insights to heighten the spell—or so he thought.

In truth, the archmage was obliviously casting Lolth's spell, given to him through Kimmuriel in the guise of the captured K'yorl Odran.

Gromph's long-developed sense of caution should have clarified the truth to him, but his anger and ego overruled his common sense, and so he pressed on.

"Omminem dimti'ite'spem," he chanted, words he did not know, a language he did not know, but he somehow understood—or that he believed at least, that this chant aligned perfectly with his usual vocalizations for his spells of summoning. This was the perfect joining, psionics and arcane magic, perhaps the greatest and purest call to the lower planes any mortal had made in centuries.

He would replace the fallen Marilith with something bigger. With a balor, likely, and one to match and exceed Quenthel's current pet. Or perhaps several of the major demons would come to his call, bound and allied under the sheer power of his will.

"Ovisin trantes vobis ohm!"

He had to work hard to keep a bubbling chuckle out of his voice when he felt the power growing within him. He could visualize his hand reaching for the Faerzress, prodding through the boundary between the planes, demanding an answer to his call.

And he felt the presence! A balor? A great one indeed—the strength of the demon resonated within him.

He reached deeper, unwittingly wounding the boundary of the Faerzress. He reached for the great power that lurked there in the shadows, just out of sight, only barely beyond his grasping thoughts.

But he could stretch . . .

"Dimti'ite spem!"

CHAPTER 24 ◈

The Prince

RUENOR'S STRIKE LANDED WITH AN EXPLOSIVE SOUND, the vrock's skull disintegrating beneath the tremendous weight of the blow.

Another room, another corridor, secured.

"I'm thinking they runned off, elf," he said to Drizzt.

The drow ranger could only shrug, for indeed, there was no sign of any other dark elves about. They had encountered a few demons—nothing bigger than the vulture-like vrock—and various groups of orcs or goblins, but all of those had seemed more interested in running away than in fighting.

And no drow.

"They are either laying a trap for us, or you are quite correct," Drizzt answered.

"The Forge is clear," Catti-brie said, coming into the room to join her friends. "Toliver's wizard eye entered and swept through the entirety of the area, and more than once."

Drizzt was about to suggest that they should go and take the place, but he found he didn't have to, for as soon as the woman's message became clear, Bruenor ran off, growling with determination.

Within a very short while, Bruenor's strike force burst into the all-important Forge of Gauntlgrym, with Drizzt, Catti-brie, and the Harpells close behind. Oretheo Spikes and a brigade of Wilddwarves fanned out to one flank, Bungalow Thump taking the Gutbusters the other way.

"King Emerus should be here," Bruenor decided as soon as they determined that the room was clear of enemies. He motioned to Mallabritches, who had served her beloved King Emerus for all her life, and she ran off for the main chamber where the gravely wounded dwarf lay.

"Send an eye to the primordial chamber," Catti-brie bade Toliver, and she pointed out the side door that led to the nearby cavern.

"No need," Bruenor insisted, and he walked right to that side door, pulled it open, and started in. Drizzt, Athrogate, Ambergris, and the wizards followed close behind. "I'm bringing three gods with me."

"Why thank ye, me king," said Athrogate.

"Not yerself, ye dolt!" Bruenor roared, and Athrogate howled with laughter.

Down the tunnel they went, full of confidence. Bruenor didn't even hesitate as he strode into the main chamber. Near the center of the ledge on this side of the pit, past a gigantic, inanimate jade spider—one that Catti-brie focused her attention on, for she had seen these guardians attack before—Bruenor, Drizzt, and the others found quite a surprise waiting for them.

A beautiful drow woman sat upon the altar stone, seeming quite at ease—though an occasional wince betrayed the hatred that was in her heart.

Bruenor's entourage fanned out wide, while Drizzt and Catti-brie remained close to the red-bearded dwarf's side, Catti-brie alternating her wary glance from the drow female to that jade spider, and to another gigantic green arachnid statue standing guard across the way, near the collapsed tunnel where Catti-brie had struck down Dahlia a couple of years earlier.

"And you are the famous Drizzt Do'Urden," the beautiful drow said, not hiding her contempt. "I congratulate you on being alive, though I doubt it will last all that long."

All the dwarves and Harpells went deeper into their crouches then, expecting some catastrophe to erupt.

"Short when measured against the lifespan of a drow, I mean," the matron mother clarified. "Fear not, Drizzt Do'Urden, or you, King Bruenor Battlehammer. There is no battle to be found. You have won back Gauntlgrym. My people, House Xorlarrin, are gone."

"You are Matron Mother Zeerith Xorlarrin?" Drizzt asked.

The woman stood and bowed.

"And ye waited here to be catched?" Bruenor asked doubtfully.

"I awaited your arrival that we might come to terms," she replied.

"Terms o' yer surrender?"

She bowed again. "It is a simple matter," she said. "I will leave you, the members of House Xorlarrin beside me, and we will not return . . ." She paused and smiled. "Let us use the terms of demonic banishment," she added slyly, "for that seems fitting at this time. We will not return to challenge you for this place you call Gauntlgrym until at least a century has passed."

"From where I'm looking, I got me a prisoner that's worth the peace," Bruenor replied. "For one what's been beaten, ye're asking a high price, even in just thinking I'm to let ye go."

He meant every word, all knew, and why would he not? King Connerad was dead, along with many Gutbusters and hundreds of dwarves from the Silver Marches who had given their lives to drive the drow from Gauntlgrym. King Emerus lay near death, and none of the priests truly expected him to survive.

"Or might that we take yer ugly head now, eh?" Bruenor said. "Queen o' this city . . ."

"Matron Mother," she corrected. "Zeerith Xorlarrin."

"What'er ye might call yerself!" Bruenor snapped at her. "Ye bringed me pain, and now ye're askin' me to just let ye walk away?"

"I only remained to seal the truce, to accept the terms of surrender."

"Terms yerself's namin'!"

"Behold," Zeerith said, and she turned to her left, away from the primordial pit, and waved her hand at the magical webbing. It parted obediently, revealing three forms hanging by filaments, and with swarms of ugly spiders the size of a dwarf's fat hand ready to descend upon them, poison-dripping mandibles clattering eagerly.

Gasps arose from all about. There hung Kenneally and Tuckernuck Harpell, somehow alive. And no jaw fell lower than that of Bruenor Battlehammer, for the third prisoner hanging in that deadly trap was none other than Stokely Silverstream of Icewind Dale.

"Bah!" Bruenor snorted, and it took all of his discipline to not leap out and behead Matron Mother Zeerith Xorlarrin on the spot.

"Their bite is quite poisonous, and quite deadly, even to a dwarf," Zeerith assured them. "And for all the delicate skin they will tear in such numbers, will they even need the poison, I wonder?"

"They die and I'm throwin' ye into the pit," Bruenor promised.

"Spare me your idle threats," Zeerith replied, and she looked to Catti-brie and the Harpells and waggled her finger, warning them from thinking a small fireball might save their friends.

"I have offered the terms," Zeerith said. "Understand that I could already be long gone from this place, and could have left behind three corpses to bring your tears."

"Then why'd ye stay?" Bruenor demanded. This didn't make much sense to him, particularly in light of the fact that this was a powerful drow matron mother standing in front of him. He had heard enough tales from Drizzt, and indeed, had battled these ferocious and fanatical priestesses before.

But Drizzt, who had been pulled from his unconscious state and guided into battle, figured it out then, and he said, "Jarlaxle," without a hint of doubt in his voice.

Zeerith didn't answer. She didn't have to.

Bruenor turned a puzzled expression upon Drizzt, who nodded.

"Agreed, dwarf?" Zeerith asked a moment later.

"Ye come back in a hunnerd years and I'll be here," Bruenor replied. "And don't ye doubt that I'll be throwin' ye into that pit then."

Matron Mother Zeerith turned to the webbing again and waved her hands. The swarm of spiders retreated, and the filaments began to lower the three prisoners to the floor. Catti-brie, the Harpells, and Ambergris rushed over to catch them as they touched down and slouched limply to the floor.

When Zeerith turned back, she focused her stare upon Drizzt, and he noted quite a few swirling emotions when he locked that gaze with his own. Mostly intrigue, which confused him more than a little.

◆ ◆ ◆

FAR FROM THE chambers of Gromph Baenre, in the region of the great Underdark known as the Faerzress, a burst of bright yellow light erupted within the stones of one wall, like the ignition of trapped gasses or the spark of life itself, or something in between.

That fire slid down to the floor and swept out from the stones, speeding in a straight line across the expanses of the Underdark. It did not turn in deference to solid walls, but burned right through, like a heavy stone falling through still water. It shot along the miles, the tens of miles, the hundreds of miles, and moments later entered the cavern of Menzoberranzan, and only the blink of an eye later, delivered its passenger into the room of the archmage.

◆ ◆ ◆

"SHOW ME," JARLAXLE insisted when he found Kimmuriel staring into the crystal necklace of the set he shared with Gromph and Doum'wielle. "Have you found her, then?"

Kimmuriel looked up at him incredulously, an expression that begged the question of why he would bother trying to find Doum'wielle.

He wisely kept that to himself, though. He was spying upon not Doum'wielle, but Gromph, which was a very dangerous,

even reckless thing to do. But Kimmuriel couldn't resist. H
wanted to see the Baenre's face when K'yorl materialized in hi
chamber! Let him try his rudimentary understanding of psioni
power against the assault she would wage!

"Not yet," he answered, for he couldn't let Jarlaxle know hi
target without tacitly admitting that he had been behind thi
brewing catastrophe.

"I see," Jarlaxle replied, unconvinced, and Kimmurie
knew that Jarlaxle had seen right through his pathetic attemp
to dodge. "Well, do inform me when you have located he
I wish to save the poor girl, and expect that she will prov
of value."

Had he spent the few moments to follow the logical con
clusion of the exchange, Kimmuriel would have realized tha
Jarlaxle, when he learned of the disaster about to befall Hous
Baenre and Menzoberranzan, would surely link it to him.

But he was simply too excited to care at that momen
and he dived back into the connecting crystals of the neck
lace, seeking Gromph.

He found the archmage clawing at his own eyes an
screaming, falling away, Gromph's face a mask of sheer horro

And Kimmuriel knew exultation, and swung his view throug
the scrying device, determined to see his mother.

Then Kimmuriel, too, began clawing at his own eyes, fallin
back in abject terror, stumbling right over backward and fallin
to the floor—and that alone saved his sanity when the fall brok
the connection to Gromph's chambers in Sorcere.

◆ ◆ ◆

THRICE THE HEIGHT of a drow, two-headed, with the bright blu
and red horrible faces of a mandrill or a baboon, bipedal an
two-armed—though those arms were waving tentacles, reple
with suckers that could catch and hold and haul prey in to b
devoured—and with a scaled and sinewy saurian body, gre

and powerful, the summoned beast had to squat to fit within the confines of the room.

Until it did not squat and simply crashed through the stone ceiling with hardly an inconvenience, and swept its great tail about, which ended in blades that seemed as if they would be more fitting set upon the claymore of a mountain giant, the mighty weapons easily slicing through the mushroom-wood and stones of the walls, tearing them with hardly a hesitation—despite the powerful enchantments that had been placed to fortify the walls of the tower of the archmage of Menzoberranzan. Dweomers seemed like child's play in the face of this beast.

One baboon head screeched at the other in protest, and the other spat back, the continuing, millennia-old battle between the dueling identities of this one great beast.

That one of the most powerful wizards of the mortal realms shivered and melted, pissed in his own robes, and couldn't find a single word to cry out for help or for mercy, didn't impress the demon.

After all, to the Prince of Demons Gromph Baenre was of no more concern than an insect.

◆ ◆ ◆

JARLAXLE RUSHED BACK into Kimmuriel's chamber to find the psionicist in a near-catatonic state, trembling on the floor.

"What?" Jarlaxle insisted, truly unnerved in seeing Kimmuriel in such a state. Kimmuriel unnerved! Kimmuriel, who had lived in the hive cities of mind flayers!

"Not K'yorl," Kimmuriel began to babble, over and over.

Purely on a hunch, Jarlaxle took off his magical eye patch and set it upon the face of his friend, and indeed, the protective and calming powers of the item did bring some small measure of composure over Kimmuriel. Still, the psionicist stared at Jarlaxle bug-eyed, trembling so badly that Jarlaxle could hear his teeth rattling.

"What is it, my friend?" Jarlaxle implored.

"Not K'yorl," Kimmuriel stuttered. "Gromph . . . summoned . . ."

"Gromph tried to summon your mother?" a truly perplexed Jarlaxle asked, as Kimmuriel continued to stammer and stutter the name of K'yorl.

Finally, Kimmuriel found a moment of clarity, and grabbed Jarlaxle desperately, hoisting himself up to look closely into Jarlaxle's face.

"Gromph," he stammered. "The archmage . . . gate . . ."

"For K'yorl?"

Kimmuriel nodded, but quickly shook his head.

"An Abyssal gate?" Jarlaxle prodded. He knew that what remained of K'yorl Odran, Matron Mother Oblodra, was rumored to be imprisoned in the lower planes in the service of a balor.

Kimmuriel nodded so excitedly that it seemed as if his head might pop off.

"Not K'yorl . . ."

Jarlaxle stared intently as Kimmuriel managed to whisper out the name, "Demogorgon."

Demogorgon, the Prince of Demons, the most powerful creature of the Abyss, a beast even Lolth would not challenge in battle.

Jarlaxle bolted upright, letting go of Kimmuriel, who dropped back to the stone floor. The mercenary glanced all around, as if expecting some terrible catastrophe to fall upon him. He knew of Demogorgon—everyone knew of Demogorgon—and such thoughts were not misplaced.

Perhaps all of Faerûn would soon know misery.

◆ ◆ ◆

It all seemed calm after the initial celebration in learning that the two Harpells and Stokely Silverstream were still alive.

"I will be allowed to leave in peace?" Matron Mother Zeerith asked Drizzt, and again he noted a bit of curiosity in her manner, and it left him off balance.

"I will see to it," Drizzt said, or started to say, as a huge commotion erupted from across the primordial pit, in the small antechamber that held the lever controlling the flow of magic into this area from the under-chambers of the broken Hosttower of the Arcane in distant Luskan.

All of the others jumped to attention, turning back, weapons ready—and that included Zeerith, Drizzt noted, and she, like the rest, gasped in surprise when out of that chamber came a tall drow male dressed in the distinctive robes that even Drizzt recognized to be the garb of the Archmage of Menzoberranzan.

Stumbling, Gromph rushed across the bridge, nearly overbalancing and tumbling to his death into the pit more than once. He steadied himself as he came across, though he kept looking back the way he had come, as if expecting some great monster to come in close pursuit.

"Bah, but what trick's this?" Bruenor demanded, rushing to Matron Mother Zeerith, who stood there shaking her head and seeming at a complete loss.

Drizzt, too, didn't know what to make of this. He recognized the archmage, but why would that one come now, and why would he cross over to their side of the pit? For surely Gromph Baenre could have destroyed them all from across the way.

Drizzt's confusion turned to horror, though, when Catti-brie ran out in front of him to meet the charge of the archmage.

"You cannot be here!" she cried, lifting her enchanted staff at the drow. "Be gone!"

Gromph skidded to a stop, and seemed for all the world as though he only then realized there were others in the room. He looked at the woman opposing him, his amber eyes, bloodshot now and with scratches all around them, flaring dangerously.

But Catti-brie didn't blink and didn't back down.

Swirling mists gathered in Gromph's wake, as if the very floor was awakening to his passage, to his call.

And small fires danced behind Catti-brie as she stalked opposite, keeping herself squared to the dangerous drow.

Drizzt moved up beside Zeerith, but suddenly felt as if this whole thing was quite beyond him. He looked to Zeerith, and could tell that she, too, wanted nothing to do with the battle that simmered on the ledge in front of them all.

"Do not challenge me, foolish woman," Gromph warned. "Not now."

"If you come intending battle, you will face me," Catti-brie said. The fires behind her flared more intensely, and forms appeared in them, alive and begging release.

But Gromph's gray mists, too, took shape, diabolical and dark.

The archmage growled and reached out behind him, turning to face the antechamber across the way. With a growl he let loose a tremendous bolt of lightning that sizzled across the pit, arcing and sparking through the archway to resound sharply within the stones of the small chamber. The bolt was so powerful it left all the air of the large chamber smelling like a battered field after a violent thunderstorm.

"I will be followed," he growled in response to Catti-brie's puzzled look. "That chamber must be sealed!"

"Do it! Oh, do it!" cried another voice, and all turned to see Jarlaxle stumbling into the room. "Shut it! Destroy it! Eliminate it! Oh, quickly!

"You know?" Gromph demanded.

The flames rushed in at Catti-brie, leaping upon her and limning her form. She lifted her staff, which blackened, hot lines of fire veining it.

"Dull the power of the water beasts," Catti-brie demanded, in a voice that seemed different then, hissing and crackling as if infused with the stuff of fire.

Gromph launched into a spell, as did Penelope, Kipper, and Toliver, all rushing over. One spell designed to mute magic after another went into the pit, assailing the swirl of water elementals, driving them from the area immediately below the antechamber.

And all the while, Catti-brie cast her own enchantment, calling to the primordial to rise up. The chamber shook, all the complex of Gauntlgrym rumbled under the power of the godlike beast. Up came a wall of lava carrying great black boulders, targeted by the will of Catti-brie. The eruption leaped above the level of the stunned companions, exploding into the antechamber across the way, the lava stones crashing and bouncing off the walkway bridge in their descent. So violent was the belch of the rumbling primordial that it sent half the onlookers tumbling to the floor.

But not Catti-brie, who held her ground and held fast her concentration, her demands to the fire beast.

It was over as abruptly as it had started, the molten vomit settling back into the pit, the water elementals leaping back into their entrapping spin. Gusts of steam filled the chamber, turning everything ghostlike, but when the mists cleared enough, Drizzt could see that the walkway across the pit was no more, smashed and brought down by falling boulders, and the angry orange glow of the lava filling the antechamber fast darkened to black as it cooled, entombing the lever and the room.

Drizzt looked for Catti-brie and found her, standing opposite Gromph, the two wizards once again staring at each other threateningly.

Drizzt inched forward, ready to leap upon the archmage if he made a move against Catti-brie.

But Gromph Baenre, who had just fled the most feared beast of the lower planes, offered only a respectful bow.

Catti-brie didn't blink, and she threw off her fiery coat, the living flames rushing at her demand to leap upon the thick webbing that covered the back wall of House Xorlarrin's altar room. The webs disintegrated under the touch of the living flames, the spiders shrieked and curled in smoky death, and Matron Mother Zeerith gasped and stumbled back to fall into a sitting position on the altar stone.

Gromph's lips curled in a smile, and to the shock of all in the room, he bowed to Catti-brie yet again.

Then Catti-brie wore a curious expression, and it seemed to Drizzt as if she were listening to something, as if the archmage, perhaps, was silently in her thoughts, speaking to her.

"You need us," Catti-brie said at length. "And I need you."

The mighty Archmage Gromph Baenre looked at the woman curiously.

But he did not disagree.

Epilogue

T HAT SAME BUSY DAY, THE FIFTEENTH OF NIGHTAL IN Dalereckoning 1486, the Year of the Nether Mountain Scrolls, when the boundary of the Faerzress was broken and the dwarves claimed victory in Gauntlgrym and Demogorgon entered the Underdark of Faerûn, Bruenor Battlehammer stood in front of the Throne of the Dwarf Gods in the upper audience hall of Gauntlgrym.

In the seat in front of him rested the body of Connerad Brawnanvil, Twelfth King of Mithral Hall.

"Gairm mi Conneradhe Brawnanvil Ard-Righ a' chiad air Gauntlgrym!" Bruenor said, thus declaring Connerad as the First King of Gauntlgrym, and a great cheer and clanging of tankards together echoed through the great hall.

"Adhlaic Conneradhe comh-glormhor," cried Bruenor. "Bury Connerad in glory!"

No sooner was Connerad taken away than King Emerus Warcrown was helped into the seat by Ragged Dain and Mandarina Dobberbright. The old king rested back comfortably, though his breathing sounded slow and labored.

"Me old friend, ye've earned yer spot here," Bruenor whispered to him, leaning forward and putting his lips very near Emerus's ear. "I thank ye for lettin' me give Connerad the place o' honor as the first."

"Aye," Emerus responded. It seemed like he might want to say more, but clearly, he hadn't the strength.

"And now's yer turn," Bruenor whispered. "Ye'll rule well."

He started to back off, to formerly announce the new King of Gauntlgrym, but with sudden and surprising strength, Emerus grabbed him by the collar and tugged him back.

"No," Emerus whispered in Bruenor's ear. "Moradin's callin' me, me friend. It's time."

Bruenor pulled back and stood straight. He wanted to argue, but saw the light already leaving the gray eyes of old Emerus Warcrown.

"*Gairm mi Emerus Warcrown Ard-Righ an darna air Gauntlgrym!*" Bruenor declared as loudly as he could, for he knew that Emerus, dear Emerus, was already slipping far, far away, and he wanted his dear old friend to hear the proclamation that he might carry it proudly to the table of Moradin.

Soon after, the shouts echoed throughout the reclaimed dwarven homeland, from the entry cavern to the Forge, "All hail Bruenor Battlehammer, Third King of Gauntlgrym!"

◆ ◆ ◆

DEMOGORGON'S PATH OF devastation meandered from Sorcere on Tier Breche to the exit of the cavern housing Menzoberranzan, leaving in its wake great piles of rubble, including large sections of more than one drow manor, and many dead dark elves, and scores more who had been driven mad by the mere sight of the great and terrible beast.

The whole city held its collective breath, for though the march of the Prince of Demons took only a short while, so great echoed the cries, so horrified sounded the calls, that every House huddled down as quietly as possible, not wanting to attract any attention.

Accusations would flow soon enough, and fears expressed, and venomous words issued, from one House to another, and many toward Baenre, but behind every angry word sounded fear, true and not without cause.

How much greater would the consternation and tribulation have been if the drow of Menzoberranzan saw then the walls of the Faerzress, where more flares of brilliant and powerful light sparked as other demon lords sought to pass the broken boundary.

In Errtu's lair in the Abyss, the Spider Queen Lolth purred contentedly. With her rivals soon to be gone, she would find great gains.

◆ ◆ ◆

WHAT HAD AT first seemed garish now resonated as respectful, as the bodies of the two dead kings, both heroically posed, were set on small pedestals behind the Throne of the Dwarf Gods. Connerad and Emerus appeared as they had in life, only now they were entombed in a skin of cooling lava Catti-brie had crafted.

The elemental had told her this was the way the dwarves had done it in the early days of the original Gauntlgrym, preserving their kings in a coat of black stone. Indeed, following the guidance of the elemental beast, the dwarves dug out long-broken hallways and uncovered a most ancient burial ground, and there found the graves of Gauntlgrym's earliest residents. They found no perfect statues, like the ones they had just created for Connerad and Emerus, but the top slabs of the many cairns they did discover were fashioned with a bas-relief of the dwarf entombed within.

And so King Bruenor ordered that the graveyard be fully opened, and demanded proper cairns for every dwarf that had fallen in retaking this ancient Delzoun home.

"He has determined that Thibbledorf Pwent will have a statue as well," Catti-brie informed Drizzt a few days later.

"A statue akin to Connerad and Emerus, and not a simple grave?"

"The first dwarf to fall in the reclamation of Gauntlgrym," Catti-brie replied.

"Your pet primordial will oblige, I expect," Drizzt said with a chuckle.

"My pet . . ." Catti-brie replied with a sigh, for that, she understood very pointedly, was hardly the case. In fact, she was already beginning to understand that the beast was more eagerly seeking release.

"On the wall opposite the throne," Catti-brie explained. "Bruenor wants Pwent where he can see him when holding court. To draw strength."

Drizzt nodded. It seemed reasonable.

"He's asked Penelope and Kipper to retrieve the body from Longsaddle, that it can be properly interred," Catti-brie explained, and Drizzt nodded again.

"I am going with them," the woman added, and there was more in that declaration than her simple round-trip intentions for Bruenor's errand, Drizzt knew. She was telling him, reminding him, that she meant to settle there, in Longsaddle.

Drizzt nodded yet again, and smiled, though it was hard for him to do so. He had been beside Bruenor for so very long—the idea of leaving now was not an easy thing to absorb.

But he would accompany Catti-brie, he knew, if not this time then the next, when she would travel to Longsaddle to make it her home.

"You have time, my love," Catti-brie assured him. "We have so very much work to do. I wish to make the reign of my father the king a long one, but that will not be, unless . . ."

Drizzt looked at her curiously.

"The magic is failing," Catti-brie said. "The fire beast will find its way out of the pit long before King Bruenor is dead of old age."

"You said 'unless.' "

"There may be a way," the woman replied. "I have much to do."

* * *

AMONG THE RECONSTRUCTION, the further securing of the mines and newly discovered chambers, fortifying the lower levels and sealing off the wild Underdark, beside the shouts of gang leaders directing the labor, the first hiss of Gauntlgrym's ovens, the first rings of dwarven smithy hammers, King Bruenor Battlehammer focused his attention on the throne room, to make it his own.

He would put the statue of Thibbledorf Pwent, the encased mummy of his loyal shield dwarf, up on the wall directly in front of his throne. From that he would draw strength.

And so, too, would he draw strength from the grand chair he installed to the right of his throne, the one into which he invited Mallabritches Fellhammer, to great celebration.

Greater celebration found the halls of Gauntlgrym soon after, when a third grand chair was placed, this time to the left of the throne, and there sat Fist, Tannabritches Fellhammer, healed and feisty and ready for battle.

"Two queens, eh?" more than one dwarf snickered and winked whenever the subject of that third chair came up in the gossip of the halls.

"Ah, but suren Bruenor'll lucky-like find that this was the way in the days of old, eh?" one or another would always answer.

Bruenor didn't care about the jokes or winks or any hint of scandal. He was following the whispers of the dwarf gods. He was following the echoes in his heart.

He was Bruenor, Bruenor Battlehammer, Third King of Gauntlgrym.

He wasn't restless, as he had been in the days of his previous life in Mithral Hall. The road did not call to him, not now at least. This was where he belonged. This, he believed, was why he had been allowed back to Faerûn in a living body.

◆ ◆ ◆

"You're mad," Penelope Harpell scoffed when Catti-brie outlined the plan to her, Kipper, and, surprisingly, Jarlaxle— who had shown up in their camp quite unexpectedly—to the Harpells, at least—on the first night back on the surface above Gauntlgrym, on the road to Longsaddle.

"You do not understand the power with which you are dealing," Kipper chimed in, shaking his head doubtfully.

"I understand that the power is safely contained in the pit, and there I mean to keep it," the woman replied.

"I believe he was referring to the other power you mean to involve," Penelope clarified for Kipper. "Few in Faerûn would draw wands against that one!"

"I—" Catti-brie started.

"But I do," Jarlaxle interrupted before she could begin her argument. "There is a way."

Catti-brie nodded and motioned for him to continue.

"Luskan is my city," Jarlaxle explained, and the Harpells seemed a bit taken aback by the bold admission, though of course they had heard the rumors that the drow were behind the dark powers ruling the City of Sails. "And I know the archmage well. He cannot return to the Underdark and Menzoberranzan now, so I expect he will accept my invitation."

"And rebuild the Hosttower?" Kipper asked with great skepticism. "We speak of ancient magic here, lost to the world likely."

"I speak of an ancient archmage, whose bones should long ago have turned to dust," Jarlaxle replied slyly. "And yet here he is. If any wizard short of Elminster himself has a chance, it is Archmage Gromph."

Penelope offered Catti-brie a sympathetic look. "It seems a desperate plan."

"It is," the woman admitted. "But what is the alternative? Am I to allow the fire beast to destroy all that my father has reclaimed?

And in that eruption, the primordial is surely likely to take tens of thousands of people of the Sword Coast into fiery ruin beside King Bruenor."

The Harpells exchanged looks.

"We will do all that we can to help you," Kipper said.

"The libraries of the Ivy Mansion are at your disposal," Penelope added.

"Yours, but not the drow wizard's!" Kipper was quick to say. "Pray keep him far from the borders of Longsaddle."

"If the archmage is in need of any of your tomes, I will come personally for a visit," Jarlaxle assured them with a tip of his great hat and a rather salty wink aimed at Penelope.

"And now I must bid you farewell," the drow mercenary added. "It would seem that I have an archmage to placate, and that is not as easy a task as you might believe."

"You trust him?" Kipper asked when Jarlaxle had gone.

Catti-brie, staring off into the direction where the mercenary had disappeared, nodded. "I do, and so does my husband, who knows Jarlaxle well."

"There are many gears turning where that one is concerned," Penelope warned her. "And not all with your benefit in mind."

"All with Jarlaxle's benefit in mind, though," Kipper agreed.

Catti-brie smiled and turned to face her Harpell friends. "The world is an interesting place," she said. She left it at that, and held on to her smile.

Because she understood the darkness that might be ahead, and if she let the smile go, she was terribly afraid that she'd not soon find it again.

◆ ◆ ◆

IN A CHAMBER below the lowest levels of the reclaimed dwarven homeland, Gromph Baenre awaited the return of Jarlaxle, and he was surprised indeed when his brother entered beside Matron Mother Zeerith Xorlarrin and Kimmuriel Oblodra.

Gromph glared at the psionicist balefully, but Kimmuriel cut him short with a quiet and innocent whisper of, "What did you do?"

Gromph cleared his throat. He didn't much like the vulnerability his error had brought upon him, but he had, after all, summoned Demogorgon to the Prime Material Plane.

"I thought that King Bruenor had changed his mind and would now allow Matron Mother Zeerith to leave at this time," the now-former Archmage of Menzoberranzan asked Jarlaxle, quite eager to change the subject.

"You are correct," Zeerith answered.

"Bruenor professed his desire to speak with Zeerith more completely before she was granted her freedom," Jarlaxle replied. "But I thought differently."

"And so you took her."

Jarlaxle casually shrugged.

"You seem to have many night crawlers wriggling about in twisted plans," said Gromph.

"Oh, indeed I do, my brother!" Jarlaxle was happy to admit. "There is a broken city, my dearest homeland, in need of my careful caress."

"You speak the part of a fool."

"If we wish to discuss foolish actions . . ." Jarlaxle replied, and let the clear reference to Demogorgon hang in the air. Gromph's growl showed that he did not miss the point.

"Pray leave us," Jarlaxle bade Zeerith and Kimmuriel, and when they moved into the next chamber, he turned to Gromph.

"If you or that miserable Oblodran make reference again to the . . . trouble . . . in Sorcere, I will turn you both into frogs and drop you into a pond of hungry carp."

"Be at ease," Jarlaxle bade him. "There may be good consequences for that strange event, if we are clever."

"If we are clever, we will move to the other side of the world."

Jarlaxle scoffed at the notion. "You think this is ended, brother?" he asked. "It is only just begun."

"You intend to go against the matron mothers?" Gromph asked, incredulous.

Jarlaxle didn't answer, but neither did he blink.

"Then you should bring them Drizzt Do'Urden's head to lift your station before you ultimately deceive them."

"Dear brother, I will bring them more than Drizzt's head," Jarlaxle promised. "I will bring them Drizzt."

◆